Hold Tight

Hold Tight

Harlan Coben

THORNDIKE
WINDSOR
PARAGON

This Large Print edition is published by Thorndike Press, Waterville, Maine USA and by BBC Audiobooks Ltd, Bath, England

Thorndike Press, a part of Gale, Cengage Learning.

Thorndike Press® Large Print Core.

The text of this Large Print edition is unabridged.

Other aspects of the book may vary from the original edition.

Set in 16 pt. Plantin.

Printed on permanent paper.

LIBRARY OF CONGRESS CATALOGING-IN-PUBLICATION DATA

Coben, Harlan, 1962-
Hold tight / by Harlan Coben.
p. cm. — (Thorndike Press large print core)
ISBN-13: 978-1-4104-0567-8 (alk. paper)
ISBN-10: 1-4104-0567-2 (alk. paper)
1. Large type books. I. Title.
PS3553.O225H65 2008b
813'.54—dc22

2008005381

BRITISH LIBRARY CATALOGUING-IN-PUBLICATION DATA AVAILABLE

Published in 2008 in the U.S. by arrangement with Dutton, a member of Penguin Group (USA) Inc.

Published in 2008 in the U.K. by arrangement with The Orion Publishing Group Ltd.

U.K. Hardcover: 978 1 405 68730 0 (Windsor Large Print)
U.K. Softcover: 978 1 405 68731 7 (Paragon Large Print)

Printed in the United States of America
1 2 3 4 5 6 7 12 11 10 09 08

In loving memory of my children's
four grandparents:

Carl and Corky Coben
Jack and Nancy Armstrong

We miss all of you very much

AUTHOR'S NOTE

The technology used in this book is all real. Not only that, but all the software and equipment described are readily available to the general public for purchase. The product names have been changed, but really, who is that going to stop?

1

Marianne nursed her third shot of Cuervo, marveling at her endless capacity to destroy any good in her pathetic life, when the man next to her shouted, "Listen up, sweetcakes: Creationism and evolution are totally compatible."

His spittle landed on Marianne's neck. She made a face and shot the man a quick glance. He had a big bushy mustache straight out of a seventies porn flick. He sat on her right. The overbleached blonde with brittle hair of straw he was trying to impress with this stimulating banter was on her left. Marianne was the unlucky luncheon meat in their bad-pickup sandwich.

She tried to ignore them. She peered into her glass as if it were a diamond she was sizing up for an engagement ring. Marianne hoped that it would make the mustache man and straw-haired woman disappear. It didn't.

"You're crazy," Straw Hair said.

"Hear me out."

"Okay, I'll listen. But I think you're crazy."

Marianne said, "Would you like to switch stools, so you can be next to one another?"

Mustache put a hand on her arm. "Just hold on, little lady, I want you to hear this too."

Marianne was going to protest, but it might be easier not to. She turned back to her drink.

"Okay," Mustache said, "you know about Adam and Eve, right?"

"Sure," Straw Hair said.

"You buy that story?"

"The one where he was the first man and she was the first woman?"

"Right."

"Hell, no. You do?"

"Yes, of course." He petted his mustache as if it were a small rodent that needed calming. "The Bible tells us that's what happened. First came Adam, then Eve was formed out of his rib."

Marianne drank. She drank for many reasons. Most of the time it was to party. She had been in too many places like this, looking to hook up and hoping it would come to more. Tonight, though, the idea of leaving with a man held no interest. She was drinking to numb and damn it if it wasn't working. The mindless chatter, once she let go, was distracting. Lessened the pain.

She had messed up.

As usual.

Her entire life had been a sprint away from anything righteous and decent, looking for the next unobtainable fix, a perpetual state of boredom punctuated by pathetic highs. She'd destroyed something good and now that she'd tried to get it back, well, Marianne had screwed that up too.

In the past, she had hurt those closest to her. That was her exclusive club of whom to emotionally maim — those she loved most. But now, thanks to her recent blend of idiocy and selfishness, she could add total strangers to the list of victims of the Marianne Massacre.

For some reason, hurting strangers seemed worse. We all hurt those we love, don't we? But it was bad karma to hurt the innocent.

Marianne had destroyed a life. Maybe more than one.

For what?

To protect her child. That was what she'd thought.

Dumb ass.

"Okay," Mustache said, "Adam begot Eve

or whatever the hell the term was."

"Sexist crap," Straw Hair said.

"But the word of God."

"Which has been proven wrong by science."

"Now just wait, pretty lady. Hear me out." He held up his right hand. "We have Adam" — then he held up his left — "and we have Eve. We have the Garden of Eden, right?"

"Right."

"So Adam and Eve have two sons, Cain and Abel. And then Abel kills Cain."

"Cain kills Abel," Straw Hair corrected.

"You sure?" He frowned, thinking about it. Then he shook it off. "Look, whatever. One of them dies."

"Abel dies. Cain kills him."

"You're sure?"

Straw Hair nodded.

"Okay, that leaves us with Cain. So the question is, who did Cain reproduce with? I mean, the only other available woman is Eve and she's getting on in years. So how did mankind continue to survive?"

Mustache stopped, as if waiting for applause. Marianne rolled her eyes.

"Do you see the dilemma?"

"Maybe Eve had another kid. A girl."

"So he had sex with his sister?" Mustache asked.

"Sure. In those days, everyone did everyone, didn't they? I mean, Adam and Eve were the first. There had to be some early incest."

"No," Mustache said.

"No?"

"The Bible forbids incest. The answer lies in science. That's what I mean. Science and religion can indeed coexist. It's all about Darwin's theory of evolution."

Straw Hair looked genuinely interested. "How?"

"Think about it. According to all those Darwinists, what did we descend from?"

"Primates."

"Right, monkeys or apes or whatever. So anyway Cain is cast out and he's wandering around this glorious planet on his own. You with me?"

Mustache tapped Marianne's arm, making sure she was paying attention. She turned sluglike in his direction. Lose the porn mustache, she thought, and you might have something here.

Marianne shrugged. "With you."

"Great." He smiled and arched an eyebrow. "And Cain is a man, right?"

Straw Hair wanted back in: "Right."

"With normal male urges, right?"

"Right."

"So he's walking around. And he's feeling his oats. His natural urges. And one day, while walking through a forest" — another smile, another pet of the mustache — "Cain stumbles across an attractive monkey. Or gorilla. Or orangutan."

Marianne stared at him. "You're kidding, right?"

"No. Think about it. Cain spots something from the monkey family. They're the closest to human, right? He jumps one of the females, they, well, you know." He brought his hands together in a silent clap in case she didn't know. "And then the primate gets pregnant."

Straw Hair said, "That's gross."

Marianne started to turn back to her drink, but the man tapped her arm again.

"Don't you see how that makes sense? The primate has a baby. Half ape, half man. It's apelike, but slowly, over time, the dominance of mankind comes to the forefront. See? Voilà! Evolution and creationism made one."

He smiled as though waiting for a gold star.

"Let me get this straight," Marianne said. "God is against incest, but He's into bestiality?"

The mustached man gave her a patronizing, there-there pat on the shoulder.

"What I'm doing here is trying to explain that all the smarty-pants with their science degrees who believe that religion is not compatible with science are lacking in imagination. That's the problem. Scientists just look through their microscopes. Religionists just look at the words on the page. Neither is seeing the forest in spite of the trees."

"That forest," Marianne said. "Would that be the same one with the attractive monkey?"

The air shifted then. Or maybe it was Marianne's imagination. Mustache stopped talking. He stared at her for a long moment. Marianne didn't like it. There was something different there. Something off. His eyes were black, lightless glass, like someone had randomly jammed them in, like they held no life in them. He blinked and then moved in closer.

Studying her.

"Whoa, sweetheart. Have you been crying?"

Marianne turned to the straw-haired woman. She stared too.

"I mean, your eyes are red," he went on. "I don't mean to pry or anything. But, I mean, are you okay?"

"Fine," Marianne said. She thought that

maybe there was a slur in her voice. "I just want to drink in peace."

"Sure, I get that." He raised his hands. "Didn't mean to disturb you."

Marianne kept her eyes on the liquor. She waited for movement in her peripheral vision. It didn't happen. The man with the mustache was still standing there.

She took another deep sip. The bartender cleaned a mug with the ease of a man who'd done it for a very long time. She half-expected him to spit in it, like something from an old Western. The lights were low. There was the standard dark mirror behind the bar with the anticosmetic glass, so you could scope out your fellow patrons in a smoky thus flattering light.

Marianne checked the mustache man in the mirror.

He glared at her. She locked on those lightless eyes in the mirror, unable to move.

The glare slowly turned into a smile, and she felt it chill her neck. Marianne watched him turn away and leave, and when he did, she breathed a sigh of relief.

She shook her head. Cain reproducing with an ape — sure, pal.

Her hand reached for her drink. The glass shook. Nice distraction, that idiotic theory, but her mind couldn't stay away from the bad place for long.

She thought about what she had done. Had it really seemed like a good idea at the time? Had she really thought it through — the personal price, the consequences to others, the lives altered forever?

Guess not.

There had been injury. There had been injustice. There had been blind rage. There had been the burning, primitive desire for revenge. And none of this biblical (or heck, evolutionary) "eye for an eye" stuff — what had they used to call what she'd done?

Massive retaliation.

She closed her eyes, rubbed them. Her stomach started gurgling. Stress, she imagined. Her eyes opened. The bar seemed darker now. Her head began to spin.

Too early for that.

How much had she drunk?

She grabbed hold of the bar, the way you do on nights like this, when you lie down after you have too much to drink and the bed starts twirling and you hang on because the centrifugal force will hurl you through the nearest window.

The gurgling in her stomach tightened. Then her eyes opened wide. A thunderbolt of agony ripped through her abdomen. She opened her mouth, but the scream wouldn't come — blind pain squeezed it shut. Marianne doubled over.

"Are you okay?"

Straw Hair's voice. She sounded very far away. The pain was horrible. The worst she had felt, well, since childbirth. Giving birth — God's little test. *Oh, guess what — that little being you are supposed to love and care for more than yourself? When it first comes out, it is going to cause physical pain you can't begin to fathom.*

Nice way to start a relationship, don't you think?

Wonder what Mustache would make of that.

Razor blades — that was what it felt like — clawed at her insides as if fighting to get out. All rational thought fled. The pain consumed her. She even forgot about what she'd done, the damage she had caused, not just now, today, but throughout her life. Her parents had withered and been aged by her teenage recklessness. Her first husband had been destroyed by her constant infidelity, her second husband by the way she treated him, and then there were her kid, the few people who'd befriended her for more than a few weeks, the men she'd used before they used her. . . .

The men. Maybe that was about payback

too. Hurt them before they hurt you.

She was sure that she was going to vomit.

"Bathroom," she managed.

"I got you."

Straw Hair again.

Marianne felt herself falling off the stool. Strong hands slithered underneath her armpits and kept her upright. Someone — Straw Hair — guided her toward the back. She stumbled toward the bathroom. Her throat felt impossibly dry. The pain in her stomach made it impossible to stand upright.

The strong hands held on to her. Marianne kept her eyes on the floor. Dark. She could only see her own feet shuffling, barely lifting. She tried to look up, saw the bathroom door not far ahead, wondered if she'd ever get there. She did.

And kept on going.

Straw Hair still held her under the armpits. She steered Marianne past the bathroom door. Marianne tried to put on the brakes. Her brain wouldn't obey the command. She tried to call out, to tell her savior that they'd passed the door, but her mouth wouldn't work either.

"Out this way," the woman whispered. "It will be better."

Better?

She felt her body push against the metal

rod of an emergency door. The door gave way. Back exit. Made sense, Marianne figured. Why mess up a bathroom? Better to do it in a back alley. And get some fresh air. Fresh air might help. Fresh air might make her feel better.

The door opened all the way, hitting the outside wall with a bang. Marianne stumbled out. The air did indeed feel good. Not great. The pain was still there. But the coolness on her face felt good.

That was when she saw the van.

The van was white with tinted windows. The back doors were open like a mouth waiting to swallow her whole. And standing there, right by those doors, now taking hold of Marianne and pushing her up inside the van, was the man with the bushy mustache.

Marianne tried to pull up, but it was no use.

Mustache tossed her in as if she were a sack of peat moss. She landed on the van's floor with a thud. He crawled in, closed the back doors, and stood over her. Marianne rolled to a fetal position. Her stomach still ached, but fear was taking over now.

The man peeled off his mustache and smiled at her. The van started moving. Straw Hair must be driving.

"Hi, Marianne," he said.

She couldn't move, couldn't breathe. He sat next to her, pulled his fist back, and punched her hard in the stomach.

If the pain had been bad before, it went to another dimension now.

"Where's the tape?" he asked.

And then he began to hurt her for real.

2

"Are you sure you want to do this?"

There are times you run off a cliff. It is like one of those Looney Tunes cartoons, where Wile E. Coyote sprints really hard and he's still running even though he's already gone off the cliff and then he stops and looks down and knows he will plummet and that there is nothing he can do to stop it.

But sometimes, maybe most times, it isn't that clear. It is dark and you are near the edge of the cliff but you're moving slowly, not sure what direction you're heading in. Your steps are tentative but they are still blind in the night. You don't realize how close you are to the edge, how the soft earth could give way, how you could just slip a bit and suddenly plunge into the dark.

This is when Mike knew that he and Tia were on that edge — when this installer, this young yah-dude with the rat-nest hair and the muscleless, overtattooed arms and the dirty, long fingernails, looked back at them and asked that damn question in a voice too ominous for his years.

Are you sure you want to do this . . . ?

None of them belonged in this room. Sure, Mike and Tia Baye (pronounced *bye* as in good-*bye*) were in their own home, a split-level-cum-McMansion in the suburb of Livingston, but this bedroom had become enemy territory to them, strictly forbidden. There were still, Mike noticed, a surprising amount of remnants from the past. The hockey trophies hadn't been put away, but while they used to dominate the room, they now seemed to cower toward the back of the shelf. Posters of Jaromir Jagr and his most recent favorite Ranger hero, Chris Drury, were still up, but they'd been faded by the sun or maybe lack of attention.

Mike drifted back. He remembered how his son, Adam, used to read *Goosebumps* and Mike Lupica's book about kid athletes who overcame impossible odds. He used to study the sports page like a scholar with the Talmud, especially the hockey stats. He wrote to his favorite players for autographs and hung them with Sticky Tack. When they'd go to Madison Square Garden,

Adam would insist they wait by the players' exit on 32nd Street near Eighth Avenue so that he could get pucks autographed.

All of that was gone, if not from this room, then from their son's life.

Adam had outgrown those things. That was normal. He was no longer a child, barely an adolescent, really, moving too hard and too fast into adulthood. But his bedroom seemed reluctant to follow suit. Mike wondered if it was a bond to the past for his son, if Adam still found comfort in his childhood. Maybe a part of Adam still longed to return to those days when he wanted to be a physician, like his dear old dad, when Mike was his son's hero.

But that was wishful thinking.

The Yah-Dude Installer — Mike couldn't remember his name, Brett, something like that — repeated the question: "Are you sure?"

Tia had her arms crossed. Her face was stern — there was no give there. She looked older to Mike, though no less beautiful. There was no doubt in her voice, just a hint of exasperation.

"Yes, we're sure."

Mike said nothing.

Their son's bedroom was fairly dark, just the old gooseneck desk lamp was on. Their voices were a whisper, even though there was no chance that they'd be seen or heard. Their eleven-year-old daughter, Jill, was in school. Adam, their sixteen-year-old, was on his school's junior overnight trip. He hadn't wanted to go, of course — such things were too "lame" for him now — but the school made it mandatory and even the "slackiest" of his slacker friends would be there so they could all bemoan the lameness in unison.

"You understand how this works, right?"

Tia nodded in perfect unison to Mike's shaking his head.

"The software will record every keystroke your son makes," Brett said. "At the end of the day, the information is packaged and a report will be e-mailed to you. It will show you everything — every Web site visited, every e-mail sent or received, every instant message. If Adam does a PowerPoint or creates a Word document, it will show you that too. Everything. You could watch him live-time if you want. You just click this option over here."

He pointed to a small icon with the words LIVE SPY! in a red burst. Mike's eyes moved about the room. The hockey trophies mocked him. Mike was surprised that Adam had not put them away. Mike had played college hockey at Dartmouth. He was drafted by the New York Rangers, played for their Hartford team for a year, even got to play in two NHL games. He had passed on his love of hockey to Adam. Adam had started to skate when he was three. He became a goalie in junior hockey. The rusted goalpost was still outside on the driveway, the net torn from the weather. Mike had spent many a contented hour shooting pucks at his son. Adam had been terrific — a top college prospect for certain — and then six months ago, he quit.

Just like that. Adam laid down the stick and pads and mask and said he was done.

Was that where it began?

Was that the first sign of his decline, his withdrawal? Mike tried to rise above his son's decision, tried not to be like so many pushy parents who seemed to equate athletic skill with life success, but the truth was, the quitting had hit Mike hard.

But it had hit Tia harder.

"We are losing him," she said.

Mike wasn't as sure. Adam had suffered an immense tragedy — the suicide of a friend — and sure, he was working out some adolescent angst. He was moody and quiet. He spent all his time in this room, mostly on this wretched computer, playing fantasy games or instant-messaging or who knew what. But wasn't that true of most teenagers? He barely spoke to them, responding rarely, and when he did, with grunts. But again — was that so abnormal?

It was her idea, this surveillance. Tia was a criminal attorney with Burton and Crimstein in Manhattan. One of the cases she'd worked on involved a money launderer named Pale Haley. Haley had been nailed by the FBI when they'd eavesdropped on his Internet correspondences.

Brett, the installer, was the tech guy at Tia's law firm. Mike stared now at Brett's dirty fingernails. The fingernails were touching Adam's keyboard. That's what Mike kept thinking. This guy with these disgusting nails was in their son's room and he was having his way with Adam's most prized possession.

"Be done in a second," Brett said.

Mike had visited the E-SpyRight Web site and seen the first inducement in big, bold letters:

**ARE YOUR CHILDREN
BEING APPROACHED
BY CHILD MOLESTERS?
ARE YOUR EMPLOYEES
STEALING FROM YOU?**

and then, in even bigger and bolder letters, the argument that sold Tia:

YOU HAVE THE RIGHT TO KNOW!

The site listed testimonials:

"Your product saved my daughter from this parent's worst nightmare — a sexual predator! Thanks, E-SpyRight!"

Bob — Denver, CO

"I found out my most trusted employee was stealing from our office. I couldn't have done it without your software!"

Kevin — Boston, MA

Mike had resisted.

"He's our son," Tia had said.

"I know that. Don't you think I know that?"

"Aren't you concerned?"

"Of course I'm concerned. But."

"But what? We're his parents." And then, as though rereading the ad, she said, "We have the right to know."

"We have the right to invade his privacy?"

"To protect him? Yes. He's our son."

Mike shook his head.

"We not only have the right," Tia said,

stepping closer to him. "We have the responsibility."

"Did your parents know everything you did?"

"No."

"How about everything you thought? Every conversation with a friend?"

"No."

"That's what we're talking about here."

"Think about Spencer Hill's parents," she countered.

That stunned him into silence. They looked at each other.

She said, "If they could do it over again, if Betsy and Ron had Spencer back —"

"You can't do that, Tia."

"No, listen to me. If they had to do it over again, if Spencer was alive, don't you think they'd wish they'd kept a closer eye on him?"

Spencer Hill, a classmate of Adam's, had committed suicide four months ago. It had been devastating, of course, hitting Adam and his classmates hard. Mike reminded Tia of that fact.

"Don't you think that explains Adam's behavior?"

"Spencer's suicide?"

"Of course."

"To a point, yes. But you know he was already changing. That just sped things up."

"So maybe if we give him more room . . ."

"No," Tia said, her tone cutting off any debate. "That tragedy may make Adam's behavior more understandable — but it doesn't make it less dangerous. If anything, it's just the opposite."

Mike thought about that. "We should tell him," he said.

"What?"

"Tell Adam we're monitoring his online behavior."

She made a face. "What's the point in that?"

"So he knows he's being watched."

"This isn't like putting a cop on your tail so you don't speed."

"It's exactly like that."

"He'll just do whatever it is he's doing at a friend's house or use an Internet café or something."

"So? You have to let him know. Adam puts his private thoughts on that computer."

Tia took a step closer to him and put a hand on his chest. Even now, even after all these years, her touch still had an effect on him. "He's in trouble, Mike," she said. "Don't you see that? Your son is in trouble. He might be drinking or doing drugs or who knows what. Stop burying your head in the sand."

"I'm not burying my head anywhere."

Her voice was almost a plea. "You want the easy way out. You're hoping, what, that Adam will just outgrow this?"

"That's not what I'm saying. But think about it. This is new technology. He puts his secret thoughts and emotions down there. Would you have wanted your parents to know all that about you?"

"It's a different world now," Tia said.

"You sure about that?"

"What's the harm? We're his parents. We want what's best for him."

Mike shook his head again. "You don't want to know a person's every thought," he said. "Some things should remain private."

She took her hand off him. "You mean, a secret?"

"Yes."

"Are you saying that a person is entitled to their secrets?"

"Of course they are."

She looked at him then, in a funny way, and he didn't much like it.

"Do you have secrets?" she asked him.

"That's not what I meant."

"Do you have secrets from me?" Tia asked again.

"No. But I don't want you to know my every thought either."

"And I don't want you to know mine."

They both stopped, on that line, before she stepped back.

"But if it's a choice of protecting my son or giving him his privacy," Tia said, "I'm going to protect him."

The discussion — Mike didn't want to classify it as an argument — lasted for a month. Mike tried to coax his son back to them. He invited Adam to the mall, the arcade, concerts even. Adam refused. He stayed out of the house until all hours, curfews be damned. He stopped coming down to eat dinner. His grades slipped. They managed to get him to visit a therapist once. The therapist thought that there might be depression issues. He suggested perhaps medication, but he wanted to see Adam again first. Adam pointedly refused.

When they insisted that he go back to the therapist, Adam ran away for two days. He wouldn't answer his mobile phone. Mike and Tia were frantic. It ended up that he'd just been hiding at a friend's house.

"We're losing him," Tia had argued again.

And Mike said nothing.

"In the end, we're just their caretakers,

Mike. We get them for a little while and then they live their lives. I just want him to stay alive and healthy until we let him go. The rest will be up to him."

Mike nodded. "Okay, then."

"You sure?" she said.

"No."

"Neither am I. But I keep thinking about Spencer Hill."

He nodded again.

"Mike?"

He looked at her. She gave him the crooked smile, the one he'd first seen on a cold autumn day at Dartmouth. That smile had corkscrewed into his heart and stayed there.

"I love you," she said.

"I love you too."

And with that they agreed to spy on their oldest child.

3

There had been no truly damaging or insightful instant message or e-mail at first. But that changed in a big way three weeks later.

The intercom in Tia's cubicle buzzed.

A brash voice said, "My office now."

It was Hester Crimstein, the big boss at her law firm. Hester always buzzed her underlings herself, never had her assistant do it. And she always sounded a little pissed off, as though you should have already known that she wanted to see you and magically materialized without her having to waste time with the intercom.

Six months ago, Tia had gone back to work as an attorney for the law firm of Burton and Crimstein. Burton had died years ago. Crimstein, the famed and much-feared lawyer Hester Crimstein, was very much alive and in charge. She was known internationally as an expert on all things criminal and even hosted her own show on truTV with the clever moniker *Crimstein on Crime*.

Hester Crimstein snapped — her voice was always a snap — through the intercom, "Tia?"

"I'm on my way."

She jammed the E-SpyRight report into her top drawer and started down the row with the glass-enclosed offices on one side, the ones for the senior partners with the bright sunshine, and the airless cubicles on the other. Burton and Crimstein had a total caste system with one ruling entity. There were senior partners, sure, but Hester Crimstein would not allow any of them to add their name to the masthead.

Tia reached the spacious corner office suite. Hester's assistant barely glanced up when she walked by. Hester's door was open. It usually was. Tia stopped and knocked on the wall next to the door.

Hester walked back and forth. She was a small woman, but she didn't look small. She looked compact and powerful and sort of dangerous. She didn't pace, Tia thought, so much as stalk. She gave off heat, a sense of power.

"I need you to take a deposition in Boston on Saturday," she said without preamble.

Tia stepped into the room. Hester's hair

was always frizzy, a sort of bottled off-blond. She somehow gave you the sense that she was harried and yet totally together. Some people command your attention — Hester Crimstein actually seemed to take you by the lapels and shake you and make you stare into her eyes.

"Sure, no problem," Tia said. "Which case?"

"Beck."

Tia knew it.

"Here's the file. Bring that computer expert with you. The guy with the awful posture and the nightmare-inducing tattoos."

"Brett," Tia said.

"Right, him. I want to go through the guy's personal computer."

Hester handed it to her and resumed her pacing.

Tia glanced at it. "This is the witness at the bar, right?"

"Exactly. Fly up tomorrow. Go home and study."

"Okay, no problem."

Hester stopped pacing. "Tia?"

Tia had been paging through the file. She was trying to keep her mind on the case, on Beck and this deposition and the chance to go to Boston. But that damn E-SpyRight report kept barging in. She looked at her boss.

"Something on your mind?" Hester asked.

"Just this deposition."

Hester frowned. "Good. Because this guy is a lying sack of donkey dung. You understand me?"

"Donkey dung," Tia repeated.

"Right. He definitely didn't see what he says he saw. Couldn't have. You got me?"

"And you want me to prove that?"

"No."

"No?"

"Just the opposite, in fact."

Tia frowned. "I'm not following. You don't want me to prove that he's a lying sack of donkey dung?"

"Exactly."

Tia gave a small shrug. "Care to elaborate?"

"I'd be delighted. I want you to sit there and nod sweetly and ask a million questions. I want you to wear something formfitting and maybe even low cut. I want you to smile at him as though you're on a first date and you're finding everything he says fascinating. There is to be no skepticism in your tone. Every word he says is the gospel truth."

Tia nodded. "You want him to talk freely."

"Yes."

"You want it all on the record. His entire story."

"Yes again."

"So you can nail his sorry ass later in court."

Hester arched an eyebrow. "And with the famed Crimstein panache."

"Okay," Tia said. "Got it."

"I'm going to serve up his balls for breakfast. Your job, to keep within this metaphor, is to do the grocery shopping. Can you handle that?"

That report from Adam's computer — how should she handle it? Get in touch with Mike, for one. Sit down, hash through it, figure their next best step. . . .

"Tia?"

"I can handle it, yes."

Hester stopped pacing. She took a step toward Tia. She was at least six inches shorter, but again it didn't feel that way to Tia. "Do you know why I picked you for this task?"

"Because I'm a Columbia Law School grad, a damn fine attorney, and in the six months I've been here, you've barely given me work that would challenge a rhesus monkey?"

"Nope."

"Why, then?"

"Because you're old."

Tia looked at her.

"Not that way. I mean, what are you, mid-forties? I have at least ten years on you. I mean the rest of my junior lawyers are babies. They'll want to look like heroes. They'll think they can prove themselves."

"And I won't?"

Hester shrugged. "You do, you're out."

Nothing to say to that so Tia kept her mouth closed. She lowered her head and looked at the file, but her mind kept wrestling her back to her son, to his damn computer, to that report.

Hester waited a beat. She gave Tia the stare that had made many a witness crack. Tia met it, tried not to feel it. "Why did you choose this firm?" Hester asked.

"Truth?"

"Preferably."

"Because of you," Tia said.

"Should I be flattered?"

Tia shrugged. "You asked for the truth. The truth is, I've always admired your work."

Hester smiled. "Yeah. Yeah, I'm the balls."

Tia waited.

"But why else?"

"That's pretty much it," Tia said.

Hester shook her head. "There's more."

"I'm not following."

Hester sat down at her desk chair. She signaled for Tia to do the same. "You want me to elaborate again?"

"Okay."

"You chose this firm because it is run by a feminist. You figured that I'd understand why you'd take years off to raise your kids."

Tia said nothing.

"That about right?"

"To some degree."

"But see, feminism isn't about helping a fellow sister. It's about an equal playing field. It's about giving women choices, not guarantees."

Tia waited.

"You chose motherhood. That shouldn't punish you. But it shouldn't make you special either. You lost those years in terms of work. You got out of line. You don't just get to cut back in. Equal playing field. So if a guy took off work to raise his kids, he'd be treated the same. You see?"

Tia made a noncommittal gesture.

"You said you admire my work," Hester went on.

"Yes."

"I chose not to have a family. Do you admire that?"

"I don't think it's a question of admiration or not."

"Precisely. And it's the same with your choice. I chose career. I didn't get out of that line. So law-career-wise, I'm in the front now. But at the end of the day, I don't get to go home to the handsome doctor and the picket fence and the two-point-four kids. You understand what I'm saying?"

"I do."

"Wonderful." Hester's nostrils flared as she turned the famed glare up a notch. "So when you're sitting in this office — in *my* office — your thoughts are all about me, how to please and serve me, not what you're going to make for dinner or whether your kid will be late for soccer practice. You follow?"

Tia wanted to protest but the tone didn't leave much room for debate. "I follow."

"Good."

The phone rang. Hester picked it up. "What?" Pause. "That moron. I told him to shut his mouth." Hester spun the chair away. That was Tia's cue. She rose and headed out, wishing like hell she was only worried about something as inane as dinner or soccer practice.

In the corridor she stopped and took out her mobile phone. She stuck the file under her arm, and even after Hester's scolding, her mind went straight back to the e-mail message in the E-SpyRight report.

The reports were often so long — Adam surfed a lot and visited so many sites, so many "friends" on places like MySpace and Facebook — that the printouts were ridiculously voluminous. For the most part she skimmed them now, as though that also made it somehow less an invasion of privacy, when in truth, she couldn't stand knowing so much.

She hurried back to her desk. The requisite family photograph was on her desk. The four of them — Mike, Jill, Tia and, of course, Adam, in one of the few moments he would grant them an audience — out on the front stoop. All of the smiles looked forced, but this picture brought her such comfort.

She pulled out the E-SpyRight report and found the e-mail that had startled her so. She read it again. It hadn't changed. She thought about what to do and realized that it wasn't her decision alone.

Tia took out her cell phone and put in Mike's number. Then she typed out the text and hit SEND.

Mike was still wearing his ice skates when the text came in.

"That Handcuffs?" Mo asked.

Mo had already taken off the skates. The locker room, like all hockey locker rooms, stunk horribly. The problem was that the sweat got into all the pads. A big oscillating fan swayed back and forth. It didn't help much. The hockey players never noticed. A stranger would have entered and nearly passed out from the stench.

Mike looked at his wife's phone number.

"Yup."

"God, you are so whipped."

"Yeah," Mike said. "She texted me. Totally whipped."

Mo made a face. Mike and Mo had been friends since their Dartmouth days. They'd played on the hockey team there — Mike the leading scorer at left wing, Mo the tough goon at defenseman. Nearly a quarter century after graduating — Mike now the transplant surgeon, Mo doing murky work for the Central Intelligence Agency — they still played those roles.

The other guys removed their pads gingerly. They were all getting older and hockey was a young man's game.

"She knows this is your hockey time, right?"

"Right."

"So she should know better."

"It's just a text, Mo."

"You bust your balls at the hospital all week," he said, with that small smile that never let you know for sure if he was kidding or not. "This is hockey time, sacred time. She should know that by now."

Mo had been there on that cold winter day when Mike first saw Tia. Actually, Mo had seen her first. They'd been playing the home opener against Yale. Mike and Mo were both juniors. Tia had been in the stands. During the pregame warm-up — the part where you skate in a circle and stretch — Mo had elbowed him and nodded toward where Tia sat and said, "Nice sweater puppies."

That was how it began.

Mo had a theory that all women would go for either Mike or, well, him. Mo got the ones attracted to the bad boy while Mike took the girls who saw picket fences in his baby blues. So in the third period, with Dartmouth comfortably ahead, Mo picked a fight and beat the hell out of someone on Yale. As he punched the guy out, he turned and winked at Tia and gauged her reaction.

The refs broke up the fight. As Mo skated into the penalty box, he leaned toward

Mike and said, "Yours."

Prophetic words. They met up at a party after the game. Tia had come with a senior, but she had no interest. They talked about their pasts. He told her right away that he wanted to be a doctor and she wanted to know when he first knew.

"Seems like always," he'd answered.

Tia wouldn't accept that answer. She dug harder, which he'd soon learn was always her way. Eventually he surprised himself by telling her how he had been a sickly kid and how doctors became his heroes. She listened in a way no one else ever had or would. They didn't so much start a relationship as plunge into it. They ate together in the cafeteria. They studied together at night. Mike would bring her wine and candles to the library.

"Do you mind if I read her text?" Mike said.

"She's such a pain in the ass."

"Express that then, Mo. Don't hold back."

"If you were in church, would she be texting you?"

"Tia? Probably."

"Fine, read it. Then tell her we're on our way to a really great titty bar."

"Yeah, okay, I'll do that."

Mike clicked and read the message:

Need to talk. Something I found in computer report. Come straight home.

Mo saw the look on his friend's face. "What?"

"Nothing."

"Good. So we're still on for the titty bar tonight."

"We were never on for a titty bar."

"You one of those sissies who prefer to call them 'gentlemen's clubs'?"

"Either way, I can't."

"She making you come home?"

"We got a situation."

"What?"

Mo didn't know from the word "personal."

"Something with Adam," Mike said.

"My godson? What?"

"He's not your godson."

Mo wasn't the godfather because Tia wouldn't allow it. But that didn't stop Mo from thinking he was. When they had the baby-naming, Mo had actually come up to the front and stood next to Tia's brother, the real godfather. Mo just glared at him. And Tia's brother hadn't said a word.

"So what's wrong?"

"Don't know yet."

"Tia is too overprotective. You know that."

Mike put down his cell phone. "Adam quit the hockey team."

Mo made a face as if Mike had suggested that his son had gotten into devil worship or bestiality. "Whoa."

Mike unlaced his skates, slid them off.

"How could you not tell me that?" Mo asked.

Mike reached for his blade protectors. He unsnapped his shoulder pads. More guys walked by, saying good-bye to Doc. Most knew to give Mo, even off the ice, wide berth.

"I drove you here," Mo said.

"So?"

"So you left your car at the hospital. It'll waste time to drive you back there. I'll take you home."

"I don't think that's a good idea."

"Tough. I want to see my godson. And figure out what the hell you're doing wrong."

4

When Mo turned down their street, Mike spotted Susan Loriman, his neighbor, outside. She was pretending to be doing a yard chore — weeding or planting or something like that — but Mike knew better. They pulled into the driveway. Mo looked at the neighbor on her knees.

"Wow, nice ass."

"Her husband probably thinks so."

Susan Loriman rose. Mo watched.

"Yeah, but her husband's an asshole."

"What makes you say that?"

He gestured with his chin. "Those cars."

In the driveway sat her husband's muscle car, a souped-up red Corvette. His other car was a jet-black BMW 550i, while Susan drove a gray Dodge Caravan.

"What about them?"

"They his?"

"Yes."

"I got this friend," Mo said. "Hottest chick

you've ever seen. Hispanic or Latina or some such thing. She used to be a professional wrestler with the moniker Pocahontas, you remember, when they had those sexy numbers on Channel Eleven in the morning?"

"I remember."

"So anyway, this Pocahontas told me something she does. Whenever she sees a guy in a car like that, whenever he kinda pulls up to her in his muscle wheels and revs his engine and gives the eye, you know what she says to him?"

Mike shook his head.

" 'Sorry to hear about your penis.' "

Mike had to smile.

" 'Sorry to hear about your penis.' That's it. Ain't that great?"

"Yeah," Mike admitted. "That's pretty awesome."

"Tough to come back from that line."

"Indeed it is."

"So your neighbor here — her husband, right? — he's got two of them. What do you think that means?"

Susan Loriman looked over at them. Mike had always found her gut-wrenchingly attractive — the hot mom of the neighborhood, what he had heard the teens refer to as a MILF, though he didn't like to think in such coarse acronyms. Not that Mike would ever do anything about it, but if you're breathing, you still notice things like that. Susan had long so-black-it's-blue hair and in the summer she always wore it in a ponytail down her spine with cut-off shorts and fashionable sunglasses and a mischievous smile on her knowing red lips.

When their kids were younger, Mike would see her on the playground by Maple Park. It didn't mean a thing but he liked to look at her. He knew one father who intentionally picked her son to be on his Little League team just so Susan Loriman would show up at their games.

Today there were no sunglasses. Her smile was tight.

"She looks sad as hell," Mo said.

"Yeah. Look, give me a moment, okay?"

Mo was going to crack wise, but he saw something on the woman's face. "Yeah," he said. "Sure."

Mike approached. Susan tried to hold the smile, but the fault lines were starting to give way.

"Hey," he said.

"Hi, Mike."

He knew why she was outside pretending to garden. He didn't make her wait.

"We won't have Lucas's tissue typing results until the morning."

She swallowed, nodded too fast. "Okay."

Mike wanted to reach out and touch her. In an office setting he might have. Doctors do that. It just wouldn't play here. Instead he went with a canned line: "Dr. Goldfarb and I will do everything we can."

"I know, Mike."

Her ten-year-old son, Lucas, had focal segmental glomerulosclerosis — FSGS for short — and was in pretty desperate need of a kidney transplant. Mike was one of the leading kidney transplant surgeons in the country, but he had passed this case to his partner, Ilene Goldfarb. Ilene was the head of transplant surgery at New York-Presbyterian and the best surgeon he knew.

He and Ilene dealt with people like Susan every day. He could give the usual spiel about separating but the deaths still ate at him. The dead stayed with him. They poked him at night. They pointed fingers. They pissed him off. Death was never welcome, never accepted. Death was his enemy — a constant outrage — and he'd be damned if he'd lose this kid to that son of a bitch.

In the case of Lucas Loriman, it was, of course, extra personal. That was the main reason he took second chair to Ilene. Mike knew Lucas. Lucas was something of a nerdy kid, too sweet for his own good, complete with glasses that always seemed to be sliding too far down his nose and hair that required a shotgun to keep down. Lucas loved sports and couldn't play them a lick. When Mike would take practice shots at Adam in the driveway, Lucas would wander over and watch. Mike would offer him a stick, but Lucas didn't want that. Realizing too early in life that playing was not his destiny, Lucas liked to broadcast: "Dr. Baye has the puck, he fakes left, shoots for the five-hole . . . brilliant save by Adam Baye!"

Mike thought about that, about that sweet kid pushing his glasses up and thought again, I'll be damned if I'm going to let him die.

"Are you sleeping?" Mike asked.

Susan Loriman shrugged.

"You want me to prescribe something?"

"Dante doesn't believe in that stuff."

Dante Loriman was her husband. Mike didn't want to admit it in front of Mo, but his assessment had been spot-on — Dante was an asshole. He was nice enough on the outside, but you saw the narrowing of the eyes. There were rumors he was mobbed up, but that could have been based more on looks. He had the slicked-back hair, the wifebeater tees, the too-much cologne and the too-glitzy jewelry. Tia got a kick out of him — "nice change from this sea of clean-cuts" — but Mike always felt as though there was something wrong, the machismo of a guy who wanted to measure up but somehow knew he never did.

"Do you want me to talk to him?" Mike asked.

She shook her head.

"You guys use the Drug Aid on Maple Avenue, right?"

"Yes."

"I'll call in a prescription. You can pick it up if you want."

"Thanks, Mike."

"I'll see you in the morning."

Mike came back toward the car. Mo was waiting with his arms folded across his chest. He wore sunglasses and was aiming for the epitome of cool.

"A patient?"

Mike walked past him. He didn't talk about patients. Mo knew that.

Mike stopped in front of his house and just looked at it for a moment. Why, he wondered, did a house seem as fragile as his patients? When you looked left and right, the street was lined with them, houses like this, filled with couples who had driven out from wherever and stood on the lawn and looked at the structure and thought, "Yes, this is where I'm going to live my life and raise my kids and protect all our hopes and dreams. Right here. In this bubble of a structure."

He opened the door. "Hello?"

"Daddy! Uncle Mo!"

It was Jill, his eleven-year-old princess, tearing around the corner, that smile plastered on her face. Mike felt his heart warm — the reaction was instantaneous and universal. When a daughter smiles at her father like that, the father, no matter what his station in life, is suddenly king.

"Hey, sweetheart."

Jill hugged Mike and then Mo, flowing smoothly between them. She moved with the ease of a politician working a crowd. Behind her, almost cowering, was her friend Yasmin.

"Hi, Yasmin," Mike said.

Yasmin's hair hung straight down in front of her face, like a veil. Her voice was barely audible. "Hi, Dr. Baye."

"You guys have dance class today?" Mike asked.

Jill shot a warning look across Mike's bow in a way no eleven-year-old should be able to do. "Dad," she whispered.

And he remembered. Yasmin had stopped dance. Yasmin had pretty much stopped all activity. There had been an incident in school a few months back. Their teacher, Mr.

Lewiston, normally a good guy who liked to go a step too far to keep the kids interested, had made an inappropriate comment about Yasmin having facial hair. Mike was fuzzy on the details. Lewiston immediately apologized, but the pre-adolescent damage was done. Classmates started calling Yasmin "XY" as in the chromosome — or just "Y," which they could claim was short for Yasmin but really was just a new way of picking on her.

Kids, as we know, can be cruel.

Jill stuck by her friend, worked harder to keep her in the mix. Mike and Tia were proud of her for it. Yasmin quit, but Jill still loved dance class. Jill loved, it seemed, almost everything she did, approaching every activity with an energy and enthusiasm that couldn't help but jazz everyone around her. Talk about nature and nurture. Two kids — Adam and Jill — raised by the same parents but with polar opposite personalities.

Nature every time.

Jill reached behind her and grabbed Yasmin's hand. "Come on," she said.

Yasmin followed.

"Later, Daddy. Bye, Uncle Mo."

"Bye, sweetheart," Mo said.

"Where are you two going?" Mike asked.

"Mom told us to go outside. We're going to ride bikes."

"Don't forget the helmets."

Jill rolled her eyes but in a good-natured way.

A minute later, Tia came out from the kitchen and frowned in Mo's direction. "What is he doing here?"

Mo said, "I heard you're spying on your son. Nice."

Tia gave Mike a look that singed his skin. Mike just shrugged. This was something of a nonstop dance between Mo and Tia — outward hostility but they'd kill for each other in a foxhole.

"I think it's a good idea actually," Mo said.

That surprised them. They both looked at him.

"What? I got something on my face?"

Mike said, "I thought you said we were overprotecting him."

"No, Mike, I said *Tia* overprotects him."

Tia gave Mike another glare. He suddenly remembered where Jill had learned how to silence her father with a look. Jill was the pupil — Tia the master.

"But in this case," Mo continued, "much as it pains me to admit it, she's right. You're his parents. You're supposed to know all."

"You don't think he has a right to his privacy?"

"Right to . . . ?" Mo frowned. "He's a dumb kid. Look, all parents spy on their kids in some ways, don't they? That's your job. Only you see their report cards, right? You talk to his teacher about what he's up to in school. You decide what he eats, where he lives, whatever. So this is just the next step."

Tia was nodding.

"You're supposed to raise them, not coddle them. Every parent decides how much independence they give a kid. You're in control. You should know it all. This isn't a republic. It's a family. You don't have to micromanage, but you should have the ability to step in. Knowledge is power. A government can abuse it because they don't have your best interest at heart. You do. And you're both smart. So what's the harm?"

Mike just looked at him.

Tia said, "Mo?"

"Yep?"

"Are we having a moment?"

"God, I hope not." Mo slid onto the stool by the kitchen island. "So what did you find?"

"Don't take this the wrong way," Tia said, "but I think you should go home."

"He's my godson. I have his best interest at heart too."

"He's not your godson. And based on what you just argued, there is no one who has a greater interest than his parents. And as much as you might care about him, you don't fit that category."

He just stared at her.

"What?"

"I hate it when you're right."

"How do you think I feel?" Tia said. "I was sure spying on him was the way to go until you agreed."

Mike watched. Tia kept plucking her lower lip. He knew that she only did that when she was panicking. The joking was a cover.

Mike said, "Mo."

"Yeah, yeah, I can take a hint. I'm out of here. One thing though."

"What?"

"Can I see your cell phone?"

Mike made a face. "Why? Doesn't yours work?"

"Let me just see it, okay?"

Mike shrugged. He handed it to Mo.

"Who's your carrier?" Mo asked.

Mike told him.

"And all of you have the same phone? Adam included?"

"Yes."

Mo stared at the cell phone some more. Mike looked at Tia. She shrugged. Mo turned the phone over and then handed it back.

"What was that all about?"

"I'll tell you later," Mo said. "Right now you better take care of your kid."

5

"So what did you see on Adam's computer?" Mike asked.

They sat at the kitchen table. Tia had already made coffee. She was drinking a decaf Breakfast Blend. Mike was going with pure black espresso. One of his patients worked for a company that made coffee machines with pods rather than filters. He gave Mike one as a gift after a successful transplant. The machine was simple: You take your pod, you put it in, it makes the coffee.

"Two things," Tia said.

"Okay."

"First off, he's invited to a party tomorrow night at the Huffs," Tia said.

"And?"

"And the Huffs are away for the weekend. According to the e-mail, they will all spend the night getting high."

"Booze, drugs, what?"

"The e-mail isn't clear. They plan on coming up with some excuse to sleep over so they can get — and I quote — 'totally wasted.' "

The Huffs. Daniel Huff, the father, was the captain of the town police force. His son — everyone called him DJ — was probably the biggest troublemaker in the grade.

"What?" she said.

"I'm just processing."

Tia swallowed. "Who are we raising, Mike?"

He said nothing.

"I know you don't want to look at these computer reports, but . . ." Her eyes closed.

"What?"

"Adam watches online porn," she said. "Did you know that?"

He said nothing.

"Mike?"

"So what do you want to do about that?" he asked.

"You don't think it's wrong?"

"When I was sixteen, I sneaked *Playboy*."

"That's different."

"Is it? That's what we had then. We didn't have the Internet. If we did, sure, I probably would have gone in that direction — anything to see a naked woman. It's society today. You can't turn anything on without getting an eye- or earful. If a sixteen-year-old boy wasn't interested in seeing naked women, that would be bizarre."

"So you approve?"

"No, of course not. I just don't know what to do about it."

"Talk to him," she said.

"I have," Mike said. "I've explained the birds-n-bees. I've explained that sex is best when blended with love. I've tried to teach him to respect women, not objectify them."

"That last one," Tia said. "He's not getting that last one."

"No male teenager gets that last one. Hell, I'm not even sure any male adult gets that one."

Tia sipped from her mug. She let the unasked question hang in the air.

He could see the crow's-feet in her eyes. She stared at them in the mirror a lot. All women have body-image issues, but Tia had always had a great deal of confidence in her looks. Lately, though, he could see that she was no longer looking at her reflection and feeling okay. She had started coloring her gray. She was seeing the lines, the sags, the normal aging stuff, and it was bothering her.

"It's different with a grown man," she said.

He was going to try to say something comforting but decided to quit while ahead.

Tia said, "We've opened a Pandora's box."

He hoped that she was still talking about Adam. "We have indeed."

"I want to know. And I hate knowing."

He reached out and took her hand. "What do we do about this party?"

"What do you think?"

"We can't let him go," he said.

"So we keep him in the house?"

"I guess."

"He told me that he and Clark were going to Olivia Burchell's to hang out. If we just forbid him to go, he'll know something is up."

Mike shrugged. "Too bad. We're parents. We're allowed to be irrational."

"Okay. So we tell him we want him home tomorrow night?"

"Yep."

She bit her lower lip. "He's been good all week, did all his homework. We normally let him go out on Friday nights."

It would be a battle. They both knew that. Mike was ready for a battle, but did he want one here? You have to choose your spots. And forbidding him from going to Olivia Burchell's house — it would make Adam suspicious.

"How about if we give him a curfew?" he asked.

"And what do we do when he breaks it?

Show up at the Huffs?"

She was right.

"Hester called me in her office," Tia said. "She wants me to go to Boston tomorrow for a deposition."

Mike knew how much that meant to her. Since going back to work, most of her assignments had been scut work. "That's great."

"Yeah. But that means I won't be home."

"No problem, I can handle it," Mike said.

"Jill is having a sleepover at Yasmin's. So she won't be around."

"Okay."

"So any idea how to keep Adam from going to this party?"

"Let me think about it," Mike said. "I may have an idea."

"Okay."

He saw something cross her face. Then he remembered. "You said two things were bothering you."

She nodded and something happened to her face. Not much. If you were playing poker, you might call it a tell. That was the thing when you are married a long time. You can read the tells so easily — or maybe your partner doesn't care to hide them anymore. Whatever, Mike knew that this was not going to be good news.

"An instant-message exchange," Tia said.

"From two days ago."

She reached into her purse and pulled it out. Instant-messaging. Kids talked via typing in live time to one another. The results came out with the name and a colon like some awful screenplay. Parents, most of whom had spent many an adolescent hour doing the same thing on plain old phones, bemoaned this development. Mike didn't really see the problem. We had phones, they have IM and texting. Same thing. It reminded Mike of those old people who curse out the younger generation's video games while hopping on a bus to Atlantic City to play video slots. Hypocrisy, right?

"Take a look."

Mike slipped on his reading glasses. He had just started using them a few months back and had quickly grown to detest the inconvenience. Adam's screen name was still HockeyAdam1117. He had picked that out years ago. The number was Mark Messier's, his favorite hockey player, and Mike's own number seventeen from his Dartmouth days, combined. Funny that Adam hadn't changed it. Or maybe again that made perfect sense. Or maybe, most likely, it meant nothing.

CeeJay8115: U ok?
HockeyAdam1117: I still think we

should say something.
CeeJay8115: It's long over. Just stay quiet and all safe.

According to the timer, there was no typing for a full minute.

CeeJay8115: U there?
HockeyAdam1117: Yes
CeeJay8115: All ok?
HockeyAdam1117: All ok.
CeeJay8115: Good. C U Fri.

That was the end.

"'Stay quiet and all safe,'" Mike repeated.

"Yes."

"What do you think it means?" he asked.

"No idea."

"Could be something with school. Like maybe they saw someone cheat on a test or something."

"Could be."

"Or it could be nothing. Could be like part of one of those online adventure games."

"Could be," Tia said again, clearly not buying.

"Who is CeeJay8115?" Mike asked.

She shook her head. "It's the first time I've seen Adam IM with him."

"Or her."
"Right, or her."
"'See you Friday.' So CeeJay8115 will be at the Huff party. Does that help us?"
"I don't see how."
"So do we ask him about it?"
Tia shook her head. "It's too vague, don't you think?"
"I do," Mike agreed. "And it would mean letting him know we're spying on him."
They both stood there. Mike read it again. The words didn't change.
"Mike?"
"Yeah."
"What would Adam need to stay quiet about in order to be safe?"

Nash, the bushy mustache in his pocket, sat in the van's passenger seat. Pietra, the straw-haired wig off, drove.
In his right hand, Nash held Marianne's mobile device. It was a BlackBerry Pearl. You could e-mail, take pictures, watch videos, text, synch your calendar and address book with your home computer, and even make phone calls.
Nash touched the button. The screen lit up. A photograph of Marianne's daughter popped up. He stared at it for a moment. Pitiful, he thought. He hit the icon to get to

her e-mail, found the e-mail addresses he wanted, began to compose:

> *Hi! I'm going to Los Angeles for a few weeks. I will be in touch when I get back.*

He signed it "Marianne," did the copy feature, and pasted the same message into two other e-mails. Then he hit SEND. Those who knew Marianne wouldn't search too hard. This, from what Nash could figure, was her modus operandi — disappearing and then popping back up.

But this time . . . well, disappearing, yes.

Pietra had drugged Marianne's drink while Nash kept her occupied with the Cain-ape theory. When they had her in the van, Nash had beaten her. He had beaten her badly and for a long time. He had beaten her at first to elicit pain. He wanted her to talk. When he was sure she had told him everything, he then beat her to death. He was patient. There are fourteen stationary bones in the face. He wanted to snap and cave in as many as possible.

Nash had punched Marianne's face with almost surgical precision. Some shots were designed to neutralize an opponent — take the fight out of them. Some shots were designed to cause horrible pain. Some were designed to cause physical destruction. Nash knew them all. He knew how to keep his knuckles and hands protected while using maximum force, how to make the proper fist so you don't hurt yourself, how to use the palm strike effectively.

Right before Marianne died, when the breathing was raspy from the blood lodged in her throat, Nash did what he always did in those situations. He stopped and made sure that she was still conscious. Then he had her look up at him, locked his gaze on hers, saw the terror in her eyes:

"Marianne?"

He wanted her attention. He got it. And then he whispered the last words she would ever hear:

"Please tell Cassandra I miss her."

And then, finally, he allowed her to die.

The van was stolen. The license plates had been changed to confuse the issue. Nash slipped into the backseat. He jammed a bandana into Marianne's hand and tightened her fingers around it. He used a razor to cut off Marianne's clothing. When she was naked, he took fresh clothes out of a shopping bag. He struggled but he managed to get them on her. The pink top was too snug but that was the point. The leather skirt was ridiculously short.

Pietra had picked them out.

They had started off with Marianne in a bar in Teaneck, New Jersey. Now they were in Newark, the slums of the Fifth Ward, known for its streetwalkers and murders. That was what she'd be mistaken for — another beaten whore. Newark had a per capita murder rate three times nearby New York City's. So Nash had beaten her good and knocked out most of her teeth. Not all of them. Removing all her teeth would make it too obvious he wanted to hide her identity.

So he left some intact. But a dental match — assuming they found enough evidence to warrant looking for a match — would be hard and take a long time.

Nash slipped the mustache back on and Pietra put on the wig. It was an unnecessary precaution. No one was around. They unloaded the body in a Dumpster. Nash looked down at Marianne's corpse.

He thought of Cassandra. His heart felt heavy, but it gave him strength too.

"Nash?" Pietra said.

He gave her a small smile and got back into the van. Pietra put the van in drive and they were gone.

Mike stood by Adam's door, braced himself,

opened it.

Adam, dressed in black goth, swung around quickly. "Ever hear of knocking?"

"This is my house."

"And this is my room."

"Really? You paid for it?"

He hated the words as soon as they came out. Classic parental justification. Kids scoff and tune it out. He would have when he was young. Why do we do that? Why — when we swear we won't repeat the wrongs of the previous generation — do we always do exactly that?

Adam had already clicked on a button that blackened his screen. He didn't want Dad knowing where he'd been surfing. If he only knew . . .

"I got good news," Mike said.

Adam turned to him. He folded his arms across his chest and tried to look surly, but it wasn't happening. The kid was big — bigger than his father already — and Mike knew that he could be tough. He'd been fearless in goal. He didn't wait for his defensemen to protect him. If someone had gone into his crease, Adam had taken them out.

"What?" Adam said.

"Mo got us box seats to the Rangers against the Flyers."

His expression didn't change. "For

when?"

"Tomorrow night. Mom's going to Boston to take a deposition. Mo's going to pick us up at six."

"Take Jill."

"She's having a sleepover at Yasmin's."

"You're letting her overnight at XY's?"

"Don't call her that. It's mean."

Adam shrugged. "Whatever."

Whatever — always a great teenage comeback.

"So come home after school and I'll pick you up."

"I can't go."

Mike took in the room. It looked somehow different from when he'd sneaked in with the tattooed Brett, he of the dirty fingernails. That thought got to him again. Brett's dirty fingernails had been on the keyboard. It was wrong. Spying was wrong. But then again, if they hadn't, Adam would be heading to a party with drinking and maybe drugs. So spying had been a good thing. Then again Mike had gone to a party or two like that when he was underage. He had survived. Was he any worse for wear?

"What do you mean you can't go?"

"I'm going to Olivia's."

"Your mother told me. You go to Olivia's all the time. This is Rangers-Flyers."

"I don't want to go."

"Mo bought the tickets already."

"Tell him to take someone else."

"No."

"No?"

"Yeah, no. I'm your father. You're going to the game."

"But —"

"No buts."

Mike turned and left the room before Adam could say another word.

Wow, Mike thought. Did I really say *No buts?*

6

The house was dead.

That was how Betsy Hill would describe it. Dead. It wasn't merely quiet or still. The house was hollow, gone, deceased — its heart had stopped beating, the blood had stopped flowing, the innards had begun to decay.

Dead. Dead as a doornail, whatever the hell that meant.

Dead as her son, Spencer.

Betsy wanted to move out of this dead house, anywhere really. She did not want to stay in this rotting corpse. Ron, her husband, thought it was too soon. He was probably right. But Betsy hated it here now. She floated through the house as if she, not Spencer, were the ghost.

The twins were downstairs watching a DVD. She stopped and looked out the window. The lights were on at all the neighboring houses. Their houses were still alive. They had troubles too. A daughter on drugs, a wife with a wandering eye and hands to match, a husband who'd been out of work too long, a son with autism — every house had its share of tragedy. Every house and every family had its secrets.

But their houses were still alive. They still breathed.

The Hill house was dead.

She looked down the block and thought that every one of them, every neighbor, had come to Spencer's funeral. They'd been quietly supportive, offering shoulders and comfort, trying to hide the accusation in their eyes. But Betsy saw it. Always. They didn't want to voice it, but they so very much wanted to blame her and Ron — because that way something like this could never happen to them.

They were all gone now, her neighbors and friends. Life never really changes, if you're not the family. For friends, even close ones, it is like watching a sad movie — it genuinely moves you and you hurt and then it reaches a point where you don't want to feel that sadness anymore and so you let the movie end and you go home.

Only the family is forced to endure.

Betsy moved back into the kitchen. She made the twins dinner — hot dogs and macaroni and cheese. The twins had just turned seven. Ron liked to barbecue the hot dogs, rain or shine, winter or summer, but the twins would complain when the hot dog got even a little "black." She microwaved them. The twins were happier.

"Dinner," she called out.

The twins ignored her. They always did. So had Spencer. The first call had become just that — a first call. They'd grown accustomed to ignoring it. Was that part of the problem? Had she been too weak a mother? Had she been too lenient? Ron would get on her about that, how she let too much slide. Had that been it? If she'd been tougher on Spencer . . .

Lots of ifs.

The so-called experts say that teenage suicide is not the fault of the parents. It is a disease, like cancer or something. But even they, the experts, looked at her with something approaching suspicion. Why had he not been seeing a therapist steadily? Why had she, his mom, ignored the changes in Spencer, written them off as just typical teenage mood swings?

He'd grow out of it, she'd thought. That's what teenagers do.

She moved into the den. The lights were out, the TV illuminating the twins. They looked nothing alike. In vitro had gotten her pregnant with them. Spencer had been an only child for nine years. Was that part of the reason too? She had thought that having a sibling would be good for him, but really, doesn't any child just want his parents' unending and undivided attention?

The TV flickered off their faces. Children look so brain-dead when they're watching TV. Their jaws slackened, their eyes too wide — it was pretty horrible.

"Now," she said.

Still no movement.

Tick, tick, tick — and then Betsy exploded: "NOW!"

The scream startled them. She moved over and clicked the TV off.

"I said, dinner now! How many times am I supposed to call you?"

The twins scattered silently toward the kitchen. Betsy closed her eyes and tried to take a deep breath. That was how she was. Calm followed by the blowup. Talk about mood swings. Perhaps it was hereditary. Perhaps Spencer was doomed from the womb.

They sat at the table. Betsy came over and summoned up a plastic smile. Yep, all good now. She served them and tried to engage them. One twin chatted, the other wouldn't. That was how it had been since Spencer. One twin handled it by totally ignoring it. The other sulked.

Ron wasn't home. Again. Some nights he would come home and park the car in the garage and just sit there and cry. Betsy sometimes feared that he'd keep the engine on, close the garage door, and do like his only son. End the pain. There was such perverse irony in this whole thing. Her son had taken his own life, and the most obvious way to end the ensuing pain was to do likewise.

Ron never talked about Spencer. Two days after Spencer's death, Ron picked up his son's dinner chair and put it in the basement. The three kids each had lockers with their names on it. Ron had taken Spencer's off, started filling it with nonsense. Out of sight, she guessed.

Betsy handled it differently. There were times she tried to throw herself into her other projects, but grief made everything feel heavy, as if she were in one of those dreams where you're running through deep snow, where every movement feels as though you're swimming through a pool of syrup. Then there were times, like now, when she wanted to bathe in the grief. She wanted to let it all crash in and destroy her anew, with an almost masochistic glee.

She cleaned up dinner, got the twins ready for bed. Ron still wasn't home. That was okay. They didn't fight, she and Ron. Not once since Spencer's death. They hadn't made love either. Not once. They lived in the same house, still made conversation, still loved each other, but they'd separated as if any tenderness would be too much to bear.

The computer was on, Internet Explorer already up on its home page. Betsy sat down and typed in the address. She thought about her friends and neighbors, their reaction to the death of her son. Suicide truly was different. It was somehow less tragic, gave it more distance. Spencer, the thinking went, had clearly been an unhappy soul, and thus the boy was already somewhat broken. Better someone broken gets tossed away than someone whole. And the worst part of that, for Betsy at least, was that it actually made some sense, this awful rationale. You hear about a child who was already starving, dying in some African jungle, and it isn't nearly as tragic as the pretty little girl who lives down the street getting cancer.

It all seems relative and that's pretty damn horrible.

She typed in the MySpace address — www.myspace.com/Spencerhillmemorial. Spencer's classmates had created this page for him a few days after his death. There were pictures and collages and comments.

In the spot where one usually placed the default picture, there was a graphic of a flickering candle.

The song "Broken Radio" by Jesse Malin with some help from Bruce Springsteen, one of Spencer's favorites, played. The quote next to the candle was from that song: "The angels love you more than you know."

Betsy listened to it for a while.

In the days after Spencer's death, this was where Betsy spent most nights — going through this Internet site. She read the comments from kids she never knew. She looked at the many pictures of her son throughout the years. But after a while, it turned sour. The pretty high school girls who'd set it up, who also bathed in the now-deceased Spencer, had barely given him the time of day in life. Too little too late. All claimed to miss him, but so few seemed to have known him.

The comments read less like epitaphs than some arbitrary scribbling in a dead boy's yearbook:

"I'll always remember gym class with Mr. Myers. . . ."

That had been seventh grade. Three years ago.

"Those touch football games, when Mr. V would want to quarterback . . ."

Fifth grade.

"We all chilled at that Green Day concert. . . ."

Eighth grade.

So little recent. So little truly heartfelt. The mourning seemed more for show than anything else — public displays of grief for those who really didn't mourn all that much, her son's death a speed bump on the way to college and a good job, a tragedy, sure, but closer to a résumé-enhancing life requisite like joining Key Club or running for student council treasurer.

There was so little from his real friends — Clark and Adam and Olivia. But maybe that was how it was. Those who really grieve don't do it in public — it truly hurts, so you keep it to yourself.

She hadn't checked the site in three weeks. There had been little activity. That was how it was, of course, especially with the young. They were on to other things. She watched the slide show. It took all of the photographs and kind of made them look like they were being tossed on a big pile. The images would rotate into view, stop, and then the next one would come circling down on top of it.

Betsy watched and felt the tears come.

There were many old photographs from Hillside Elementary School. There was Mrs.

Roberts's first-grade class. And Mrs. Rohrback's third grade. Mr. Hunt for fourth grade. There was a picture of his intramural homeroom basketball team — Spencer had been so excited by that victory. He'd hurt his wrist the game before — nothing serious, just a little sprain — and Betsy had wrapped it for him. She remembered buying the ACE bandage. In the photograph, Spencer was holding up that hand in victory.

Spencer hadn't been much of an athlete but in that game, he had hit the winning basket with six seconds left. Seventh grade. She wondered if she'd ever seen him happier.

A local policeman had found Spencer's body on the roof of the high school.

On the computer monitor the pictures continued to swirl by. Betsy's eyes grew wet. Her vision blurred.

The school roof. Her beautiful son. Scattered amongst the debris and broken bottles.

By then everyone had gotten Spencer's good-bye text. Text. That was how their son told them what he was about to do. The first text had gone to Ron, who'd been in Philadelphia on a sales call. Betsy's cell phone had received the second, but she was at Chuck E. Cheese's, the arcade-pizzeria where parental migraines are born, and didn't hear the text come in. It wasn't until an hour later, after Ron left six messages on her phone, each more frantic than the last, that she found the text sitting on her phone, the final message from her boy:

I'm sorry, I love you all, but this is too hard. Good-bye.

It took the police two days to find him on the roof of the high school.

What was too hard, Spencer?

She would never know.

He had sent that text to a few other people too. Close friends. That was where Spencer had told her he was going. To hang out with Clark and Adam and Olivia. But none of them had seen him. Spencer had not shown up. He had gone out on his own. He had pills with him — stolen from home — and swallowed too many of them because something was too hard and he wanted to end his life.

He had died alone on that roof.

Daniel Huff, the town cop who had a son Spencer's age, a kid named DJ who Spencer hung out with a little, had come to the door. She remembered opening it, seeing his face and simply collapsing.

Betsy blinked away the tears. She tried to focus again on the slide show, on the images of her son alive.

And then, just like that, a picture rotated into view that changed everything.

Betsy's heart stopped.

The picture was gone as fast as it had come. More pictures piled over it. She put her hand to her chest, tried to clear her mind. The picture. How could she get to that picture again?

She blinked again. Tried to think.

Okay, first off. It was part of an online slide show. The show would repeat. She could simply wait. But how long until it would start up again? And then what? It would fly by again, staying in view only a few seconds. She needed a closer look.

Could she freeze the screen when it came back on?

There had to be a way.

She watched the other photographs swirl by, but they weren't what she wanted. She wanted that other picture back.

The one with the sprained wrist.

She thought again back to that intramural game from seventh grade because she remembered something a little odd. Hadn't she just been thinking about that moment? When Spencer wore the ACE bandage? Yes, of course. That had been the catalyst, really.

Because the day before Spencer's suicide, something similar had happened.

He had fallen and hurt his wrist. She had offered to wrap it again, as she had back when he was in seventh grade. But instead, Spencer had wanted her to buy a wrist sleeve. She had. He had worn it the day he died.

For the first and — obviously — last time.

She clicked on the slide show. It brought her to a site, slide.com, and asked her for her password. Damn. It had probably been created by one of the kids. She thought about that. Security wouldn't be great on something like this, would it? You were just setting it up and letting your fellow students use it to put whatever photographs they wanted into the rotation.

So the password had to be something simple.

She typed in: SPENCER.

Then she hit OK.

It worked.

The pictures were laid out. According to the heading, there were 127 photographs in here. She quickly scanned through the thumbnails until she found the one she wanted. Her hand was shaking so badly she could barely get the mouse on the image. She did and then she clicked the left button.

The photograph came up full size.

She just stopped and stared.

Spencer was smiling in the picture, but it was the saddest smile she had ever seen. He was sweating; his face had the sheen of someone high. He looked drunk and defeated. He wore the black T-shirt, the same one he wore on that last night. His eyes were red — maybe from drink or drugs but certainly from the flash. Spencer had beautiful light blue eyes. The flash always made him look like the devil. He was standing outdoors, so it had to have been taken at night.

That night.

Spencer had a drink in his hand, and there, on that same hand, was the wrist sleeve.

She froze. There was only one explanation.

This picture had been taken the night Spencer died.

And as she looked around, into the background of the photograph, and saw people milling about, she realized something else.

Spencer hadn't been alone, after all.

7

As he had nearly every weekday for the past decade, Mike woke up at five in the morning. He worked out for exactly one hour. He drove into New York City over the George Washington Bridge and arrived at NewYork-Presbyterian's transplant center by seven A.M.

He threw on the white coat and rounded on patients. There were times when this threatened to become routine. It didn't vary much, but Mike liked to remind himself of how important this was to that person lying in the bed. You are in a hospital. That alone made you feel vulnerable and scared. You are ill. You may very well be dying and it seems to you that the person who stands in the way between you and greater suffering, between you and death, is your doctor.

How does your doctor not develop a bit of a God complex?

More than that, sometimes Mike thought it was healthy to have that complex, albeit benevolently. You mean a lot to your patient. You should act like it.

There were doctors who rushed through it. There were times Mike wanted to do that too. But the truth is, if you give your all, it only takes an extra minute or two per patient. So he listened and held a hand if that was required or stayed a little aloof — depending on the patient and how he read them.

He was at his desk by nine A.M. The first patient had already arrived. Lucille, his RN, would be working them up. That gave him maybe ten minutes to review the charts and overnight test results. He remembered his neighbor and quickly searched for the Loriman results in the computer.

Nothing posted yet.

That was odd.

A strip of pink drew Mike's eye. Someone had stuck a Post-it note onto his phone.

See me
— Ilene

Ilene Goldfarb was his practice partner and head of transplant surgery at NewYork-Presbyterian. They had met during their residency in transplant surgery and now lived in the same town. He and Ilene were friends, Mike guessed, but not close ones, which made the partnership work well. They lived maybe two miles apart, had kids who attended the same schools, but other than that, they had few mutual interests, didn't need to socialize, and totally trusted and respected the other's work.

Do you want to test your doctor friend on his medical recommendation? Ask him this: If your kid was sick, what doctor would you send him to?

Mike's answer was Ilene Goldfarb. And that told you everything you needed to know about her competence as a physician.

He headed down the corridor. His feet padded silently on the industrial-gray wall-to-wall. The prints lining the off-white hallway were gentle on the eyes, simple and with about as much personality as the artwork you'd find in a mid-scale motel chain. He and Ilene had wanted the entire office to whisper, "This is about the patient and the patient only." In the offices, they displayed only professional diplomas and citations because that seemed to comfort. They did not keep anything personal — no pencil holder made by a child, no family photographs, nothing like that.

Your child often came here to die. You

don't want to see the image of someone else's smiling, healthy children. You just don't.

"Hey, Doc Mike."

He turned. It was Hal Goldfarb, Ilene's son. He was a high school senior, two years older than Adam. He'd made Princeton early decision and planned to go in premed. He'd managed to get school credit to spend three mornings a week interning for them.

"Hey, Hal. How's school?"

He gave Mike a big smile. "Coasting."

"Senior year after you've already been admitted to college — the dictionary definition of coasting."

"You got it."

Hal was dressed in khakis and a blue dress shirt and Mike couldn't help but notice the contrast with Adam's goth black and feel a pang of envy. As if reading his mind, Hal said, "How's Adam?"

"Okay."

"I haven't seen him in a while."

"Maybe you should give him a call," Mike said.

"Yeah, I should. It'd be great to hang out."

Silence.

"Mom in her office?" Mike asked.

"Yes. Go right in."

Ilene sat behind her desk. She was a

slight woman, small-boned except for her talonlike fingers. She wore her brown hair pulled back in a severe ponytail and had horn-rimmed glasses that nicely straddled the border between looking bookish and in vogue.

"Hey," Mike said.

"Hey."

Mike held up the pink Post-it note. "What's up?"

Ilene let loose a long breath. "We got a big problem."

Mike sat. "With?"

"Your neighbor."

"Loriman?"

Ilene nodded.

"Bad tissue test result?"

"Weird test result," she said. "But it had to happen sooner or later. I'm surprised this is our first."

"Do you want to clue me in?"

Ilene Goldfarb took off the glasses. She put one of the earpieces in her mouth and chewed on it. "How well do you know the family?"

"They live next door."

"You close?"

"No. Why, what's that got to do with anything?"

"We may have," Ilene said, "something of

an ethical dilemma."

"How so?"

"Dilemma might be the wrong word." Ilene looked off, talking more to herself than Mike right now. "More like a blurry ethical line."

"Ilene?"

"Hmm."

"What are you talking about?"

"Lucas Loriman's mother will be here in half an hour," she said.

"I saw her yesterday."

"Where?"

"In her yard. She's doing a lot of pretend gardening."

"I bet."

"Why do you say that?"

"Do you know her husband?"

"Dante? Yes."

"And?"

Mike shrugged. "What's going on, Ilene?"

"It's about Dante," she said.

"What about him?"

"He's not the boy's biological father."

Just like that. Mike sat there for a moment.

"You're kidding me."

"Yeah, that's what I'm doing. You know me — Dr. Kidder. Good one, right?"

Mike let it sink in. He didn't ask if she

was sure or wanted to take more tests. She would have thought of all those angles. Ilene was right too — the bigger surprise was that they hadn't run into this before. Two floors below them were the geneticists. One of them told Mike that in random population tests, more than ten percent of men were raising children that, unbeknownst to them, weren't biologically theirs.

"Any reaction to this news?" Ilene said.

"Wow?"

Ilene nodded. "I wanted you to be my medical partner," she said, "because I love your way with words."

"Dante Loriman is not a nice man, Ilene."

"That was my vibe."

"This is bad," Mike said.

"So is his son's condition."

They sat there and let that sit in the room, heavy.

The intercom buzzed. "Dr. Goldfarb?"

"Yes."

"Susan Loriman is here. She's early."

"Is she here with her son?"

"No," the nurse said. "Oh, but her husband is with her."

"What the hell are you doing here?"

County Chief Investigator Loren Muse ignored him and headed over to the corpse.

"Sweet Lord," one of the uniforms said in a hushed voice, "look what he did to her face."

The four of them stood now in silence. Two were first-on-the-scene uniforms. The third was the homicide detective who'd technically be in charge of the case, a lazy lifer with a potbelly and world-weary manner named Frank Tremont. Loren Muse, the lead investigator for Essex County and the lone woman, was the shortest of the group by nearly a foot.

"DH," Tremont pronounced. "And I'm not talking baseball terminology."

Muse looked a question at him.

"DH, as in Dead Hooker."

She frowned at his chuckle. Flies buzzed about the pulpy mess that at one time had been a human face. There was no nose or eye sockets or even much of a mouth anymore.

One of the uniforms said, "It's like someone shoved her face into a meat grinder."

Loren Muse looked down at the body. She let the two uniforms jabber. Some people jabber to ward off the nerves. Muse wasn't one of them. They ignored her. So did Tremont. She was his immediate superior, all their superiors really, and she could feel the resentment coming off them like humidity from the sidewalk.

"Yo, Muse."

It was Tremont. She looked at him in that brown suit with the belly from too many nights of beer and too many days of doughnuts. He was trouble. There had been complaints leaked to the media since she'd been promoted to chief investigator of Essex County. Most came from a reporter named Tom Gaughan, who just so happened to be married to Tremont's sister.

"What is it, Frank?"

"Like I asked you before — what the hell are you doing here?"

"I need to explain myself to you?"

"I caught this one."

"So you did."

"And I don't need you looking over my shoulder."

Frank Tremont was an incompetent ass but because of his personal connections and years of "service," fairly untouchable. Muse ignored him. She bent down, still staring at the raw meat that had once been a face.

"You get an ID yet?" she asked.

"No. No wallet, no purse."

"Probably stolen," one of the uniforms volunteered.

Lots of male head-nodding.

"Gang got her," Tremont said. "Look at that."

He pointed to a green bandana still clutched in her hand.

"Could be that new gang, bunch of black guys who call themselves Al Qaeda," one of the uniforms said. "They wear green."

Muse stood and started circling the corpse. The ME van arrived. Someone had police-taped the scene. A dozen hookers, maybe more, stood behind the line, each stretching her neck for a better view.

"Have the uniforms start talking to the working girls," Muse said. "Get a street name at least."

"Gee, really?" Frank Tremont sighed dramatically. "You don't think I already thought of that?"

Loren Muse said nothing.

"Hey, Muse."

"What, Frank?"

"I don't like you being here."

"And I don't like that brown belt with black shoes. But we both have to live with it."

"This isn't right."

Muse knew that he had a point. The truth is, she loved her prestigious new position as chief investigator. Muse, still in her thirties, was the first female to hold that title. She was proud. But she missed the actual work.

She missed homicide. So she got involved when she could, especially when a seasoned jackass like Frank Tremont was on the job.

The medical examiner, Tara O'Neill, came over and shooed the uniforms away.

"Holy crap," O'Neill whispered.

"Nice reaction, Doc," Tremont said. "I need prints right away so I can run her through the system."

The ME nodded.

"I'm going to help question the hookers, round up some of the leading gang scumbags," Tremont said. "If that's okay with you, boss."

Muse didn't respond.

"Dead hooker, Muse. There isn't really enough of a headline for you here. Hardly a priority."

"Why isn't she a priority?"

"Huh?"

"You said not a headline for me here. I get that. And then you added, 'hardly a priority.' Why not?"

Tremont smirked. "Oh, right, my bad. A dead hooker is priority number one. We treat her like the governor's wife was just whacked."

"That attitude, Frank. It's why I'm here."

"Right, sure, that's why. Let me tell you how people look at dead hookers."

"Don't tell me — like they're asking for it?"

"No. But listen and you might learn: If you don't want to end up dead by a Dumpster, don't turn tricks in the Fifth Ward."

"You ought to make that your epitaph," Muse said.

"Don't get me wrong. I will get this sicko. But let's not play games about priorities and headlines." Tremont moved a little closer, so that his belly was almost pressing against her. Muse did not back up. "This is my case. Go back to your desk and leave the work to the grown-ups."

"Or?"

Tremont smiled. "You don't want that kind of trouble, little lady. Believe me."

He stormed off. Muse turned back around. The ME was concentrating very hard on opening her work case, pretending not to have heard.

Muse shook it off and studied the body. She tried to be the clinical investigator. The facts: The victim was a Caucasian female. Judging by the skin and general frame she looked to be about forty, but the streets had a way of aging you. No visible tattoos.

No face.

Muse had only seen something this destructive once before. When she was twenty-three, she spent six weeks with state troopers on the New Jersey Turnpike. A truck crossed a divider and smashed head-on into a Toyota Celica. The Toyota driver had been a nineteen-year-old girl coming home from college break.

The destruction had been mind-blowing.

When they finally pried the metal off, that nineteen-year-old girl had no face either. Like this.

"Cause of death?" Muse asked.

"Not sure yet. But man, this perp is one sick son of a bitch. The bones aren't just broken. It's almost like they were ground into small chunks."

"How long ago?"

"I would guess ten, twelve hours. She wasn't killed here. Not enough blood."

Muse already knew that. She examined the hooker's clothes — her pink bra top, her tight leather skirt, the stiletto heels.

She shook her head.

"What?"

"This is all wrong," Muse said.

"How's that?"

Her phone vibrated. She checked the caller ID. It was her boss, County Prosecutor Paul Copeland. She looked over at Frank Tremont. He gave her a five-finger wave and grinned.

She answered. "Hey, Cope."
"What are you doing?"
"Working a crime scene."
"And pissing off a colleague."
"A subordinate."
"A pain-in-the-ass subordinate."
"But I'm in charge of him, right?"
"Frank Tremont is going to make a lot of noise. Get that media on us, rile up his fellow investigators. Do we really need the aggravation?"
"I think we do, Cope."
"What makes you say that?"
"Because he has this case all wrong."

8

Dante Loriman came into Ilene Goldfarb's office first. He gave Mike a little too firm a handshake. Susan came in behind him. Ilene Goldfarb stood and waited behind her desk. She had the glasses back on now. She reached across and gave them both quick handshakes. Then she sat down and opened the manila folder in front of her.

Dante sat next. He never looked at his wife. Susan took the chair next to him. Mike stayed in the back of the room, out of sight. He folded his arms and leaned against the wall. Dante Loriman began carefully to roll up his sleeves. First the right sleeve, then the left. He placed his elbows on his thighs and seemed to beckon Ilene Goldfarb to hit him with the worst.

"So?" Dante said.

Mike watched Susan Loriman. Her head was up. She sat hold-your-breath still. Too still. As if feeling his gaze, Susan turned her lovely face toward him. Mike aimed for neutral. This was Ilene's show. He was just a spectator.

Ilene continued to read the file, though that seemed more for show. When she was done, she folded her hands on the desk and looked somewhere between the two parents.

"We ran the necessary tissue typing tests," she began.

Dante interrupted. "I want to be the one."

"Excuse me?"

"I want to give Lucas a kidney."

"You're not a match, Mr. Loriman."

Just like that.

Mike kept his eyes on Susan Loriman. Now it was her turn to play neutral.

"Oh," Dante said. "I thought the father . . ."

"It varies," Ilene said. "There are many factors, as I think I explained to Mrs. Loriman during her previous visit. Ideally we want the HLA typing to have a six antigen match. Based on the HLA typing, you wouldn't be a good candidate, Mr. Loriman."

"How about me?" Susan asked.

"You're better. You're not perfect. But you're a better match. Normally your best chance is a sibling. Each child inherits half his antigens from each parent and there are four combinations of inherited antigens possible. Put simply, a sibling has a twenty-five percent chance of being an identical match, a fifty percent chance of being a half match — a three antigen — and a twenty-five percent chance of not being a match at all."

"And which is Tom?"

Tom was Lucas's younger brother.

"Unfortunately, the news is bad there. Your wife is the best match we have so far. We will also put your son on the cadaver kidney transplant bank, see if we can find a better candidate, but I would call that unlikely. Mrs. Loriman might be considered good enough, but frankly she is not an ideal donor."

"Why not?"

"Her match is a two. The closer we are to a six, the more likely your son's body will not reject the new kidney. You see, the better the antigen match, the less likely he will have to spend his life taking medications and doing constant dialysis."

Dante ran his hand through his hair. "So what do we do now?"

"We have a little time maybe. Like I said, we can put his name on the list. We search and keep working with dialysis. If nothing better comes along, we use Mrs. Loriman."

"But you'd like to find better," Dante said.

"Yes."

"We have some other relatives who said they'd donate to Lucas if they could," Dante said. "Maybe you could test them."

Ilene nodded. "Make up a list — names, addresses, and exactly how they are blood related."

Silence.

"How sick is he, Doc?" Dante spun around and looked behind. "Mike? Be straight with us. How bad is this?"

Mike looked at Ilene. Ilene gave a little go-ahead nod.

"Bad," Mike said.

He looked at Susan Loriman when he said it. Susan looked away.

They discussed options for another ten minutes or so and then the Lorimans left. When Mike and Ilene were alone, Mike took the chair Dante had been in and raised his palms to the sky. Ilene pretended to be busy putting files away.

"What gives?" Mike said.

"You thought I should tell them?"

Mike didn't reply.

"My job is to treat their son. He is my patient. The father isn't."

"So the father has no rights here?"

"I didn't say that."

"You took medical tests. You learned something from them that you kept from a patient."

"Not my patient," Ilene countered. "My patient is Lucas Loriman, the son."

"So we bury what we know?"

"Let me ask you this. Suppose I found out from some test that Mrs. Loriman was cheating on Mr. Loriman, would I be obligated to tell him?"

"No."

"How about if I found out that she was dealing drugs or stealing money?"

"You're reaching, Ilene."

"Am I?"

"This isn't about drugs or money."

"I know, but in both cases it is irrelevant to the health of my patient."

Mike thought about that. "Suppose you found a medical problem in Dante Loriman's test. Suppose you found out that he had a lymphoma. Would you tell him?"

"Of course."

"But why? As you just pointed out, he's not your patient. He's not your concern."

"Come on, Mike. That's different. My job is to help my patient — Lucas Loriman — get better. Mental health is part of that. Before we do a transplant, we make our patients go through psychiatric counseling, right? Why? Because we worry about their mental health in these situations. Causing tremendous upheaval in the Loriman household will not benefit my patient's health. Period, end of story."

They both took a second.

"It's not that easy," Mike said.

"I know."

"This secret will weigh heavy on us."

"That's why I shared it with you." Ilene spread her arms and smiled. "Why should I be the only one with sleepless nights?"

"You're a great partner."

"Mike?"

"Yes?"

"If it was you, if I ran a test like this and found out that Adam wasn't your biological son, would you want to know?"

"Adam not my son? Have you seen the size of his ears?"

She smiled. "I'm trying to make a point. Would you want to know?"

"Yes."

"Just like that?"

"I'm a control freak. You know that. I need to know everything."

Mike stopped.

"What?" she said.

He sat back, crossed his legs. "Are we

going to keep avoiding the elephant in the room?"

"That was my plan, yes."

Mike waited.

Ilene Goldfarb sighed. "Go ahead, say it."

"If our first credo is indeed 'First do no harm' . . ."

She closed her eyes. "Yeah, yeah."

"We don't have a good donor for Lucas Loriman," Mike said. "We're still trying to find one."

"I know." Ilene closed her eyes and said, "And the most obvious candidate would be the biological father."

"Right. He's our best chance now for a solid match."

"We need to test him. That's priority one."

"We can't bury it," Mike said. "Even if we want to."

They took that in.

"So now what do we do?" Ilene asked.

"I'm not sure we have much of a choice."

Betsy Hill waited to confront Adam in the high school parking lot.

She looked behind her at "Mom Row," the curb along Maple Avenue where the moms — yes, there was the occasional dad but that was more the exception that proved the rule

— sat in idling cars or gathered to chat with other moms, waiting for school to let out so they could shepherd their offspring to the violin lesson or the orthodontist appointment or the karate class.

Betsy Hill used to be one of those mothers.

She had started as one of those mothers at the kindergarten drop-off at Hillside Elementary and then middle school at Mount Pleasant and finally here, just twenty yards from where she now stood. She remembered waiting for her beautiful Spencer, hearing the bell, peering out the windshield, watching the kids erupt-exit like ants scattering after a human boot toes their hill. She'd smile when she first laid eyes on him and most of the time, especially in the early days, Spencer would smile back.

She missed being that young mother, the naïveté you are granted with your firstborn. It was different now, with the twins, even before Spencer's death. She looked back at those mothers, at the way they did it without a care or thought or fear, and she wanted to hate them.

The bell sounded. The doors opened. The students made their way out in giant waves.

And Betsy almost started looking for Spencer.

It was one of those brief moments when your brain just can't go there anymore, and you forget how horrible everything is now, and you think, for just a brief second, that it was all a bad dream. Spencer would walk out, his backpack on one shoulder, his posture in teenage stoop, and Betsy would see him and think that he needed a haircut and looked pale.

People talk about the stages of grief — denial, anger, bargaining, depression, acceptance — but those stages tend to blend more in tragedy. You never stop denying. Part of you is always angry. And the whole idea of "acceptance" is obscene. Some shrinks prefer the word "resolution." Semantically the notion was better, but it still made her want to scream.

What exactly was she doing here?

Her son was dead. Confronting one of his friends would not change that.

But for some reason it felt like it might.

So maybe Spencer hadn't been alone that whole night. What did that change? Cliché, yes, but it wouldn't bring him back. What was she hoping to find here?

Resolution?

And then she spotted Adam.

He was walking alone, the backpack weighing him down — weighing them all down, when she thought about it. Betsy kept her eyes on Adam and moved right so that she would be in his path. Like most kids, Adam walked with his eyes down. She waited, adjusting her stance a little left or right, making sure that she stayed in front of him.

Finally, when he got close enough, she said, "Hi, Adam."

He stopped and looked up. He was a nice-looking boy, she thought. They all were at this age. But Adam too had changed. They had all crossed some adolescent line. He was big now, tall with muscles, much more a man than a boy. She could still see the child in his face, but she could also see something like a challenge too.

"Oh," he said. "Hi, Mrs. Hill."

Adam started to walk away, now veering toward his left.

"Can I talk to you a moment?" Betsy called out.

He glided to a stop. "Uh, sure. Of course."

Adam jogged toward her with athletic ease. Adam had always been a good athlete. Not Spencer. Had that been part of it? Life is so much easier in towns like this when you're a good athlete.

He stopped maybe six feet in front of her. He couldn't meet her eye, but few high school boys could. For a few seconds she did not say anything. She just looked at him.

"You wanted to talk to me?" Adam said.

"Yes."

More silence. More staring. He squirmed.

"I'm really sorry," he said.

"About?"

That answer surprised him.

"About Spencer."

"Why?"

He didn't reply, his eyes everywhere but on her.

"Adam, look at me."

She was still the adult; he was still the kid. He obeyed.

"What happened that night?"

He swallowed and said, "Happened?"

"You were with Spencer."

He shook his head. His face drained of color.

"What happened, Adam?"

"I wasn't there."

She held up the picture from the MySpace page, but his eyes were back on the ground.

"Adam."

He looked up. She thrust the picture toward his face.

"That's you, isn't it?"

"I don't know, it might be."

"This was taken the night he died."

He shook his head.

"Adam?"

"I don't know what you're talking about, Mrs. Hill. I didn't see Spencer that night."

"Look again —"

"I have to go."

"Adam, please —"

"I'm sorry, Mrs. Hill."

He ran away then. He ran back toward the brick edifice and around the back and out of sight.

9

Chief Investigator Loren Muse checked her watch. Meeting time.

"You got my goodies?" she asked.

Her assistant was a young woman named Chamique Johnson. Muse had met Chamique during a somewhat famous rape trial. After a rough start in the office, Chamique had made herself fairly indispensable.

"Right here," Chamique said.

"This is big."

"I know."

Muse grabbed the envelope. "Everything in here?"

Chamique frowned. "Oh, no, you did not just ask me that."

Muse apologized and headed across the hall to the office of the Essex County prosecutor — more specifically, the office of her boss, Paul Copeland.

The receptionist — someone new and Muse was terrible with names — greeted her with a smile. "They're all waiting for you."

"Who's waiting for me?"

"Prosecutor Copeland."

"You said, 'they're all.' "

"Pardon?"

"You said, 'they're all' waiting for me. 'They're all' suggests more than one. Probably more than two."

The receptionist looked confused. "Oh, right. There must be four or five of them."

"With Prosecutor Copeland?"

"Yes."

"Who?"

She shrugged. "Other investigators, I think."

Muse was not sure what to make of this. She had asked for a private meeting to discuss the politically sensitive situation with Frank Tremont. She had no idea why there would be other investigators in his office.

She heard the laughter even before she got into the room. There were indeed six of them, including her boss, Paul Copeland. All men. Frank Tremont was there. So were three more of her investigators. The last man looked vaguely familiar. He held a notebook and pen and there was a tape recorder on the table in front of him.

Cope — that's what everyone called Paul Copeland — was behind his desk and laughing hard at something Tremont had just whispered to him.

Muse felt her cheeks burn.

"Hey, Muse," he called out.

"Cope," she said, nodding toward the others.

"Come in and close the door."

She entered. She stood there and felt all eyes turn toward her. More cheek burn. She felt set up and tried to glare at Cope. He was having none of it. Cope just smiled like the handsome dope he could be. She tried to signal with her eyes that she wanted to talk to him alone first — that this felt a bit like an ambush — but again he would have none of it.

"Let's get started, shall we?"

Loren Muse said, "Okay."

"Wait, do you know everyone here?"

Cope had caused office ripples when he first took over as county prosecutor and stunned all by promoting Muse to be his county chief investigator. The job was usually given to a gruff old-timer, always male, who was supposed to show the political appointee through the system. Loren Muse was one of the youngest investigators in the department when he selected her. When asked by the media what criteria he had used to select a young female over more seasoned male veterans, he answered in one word: "Merit."

Now here she was, in a room with four of those same passed-by old-timers.

"I don't know this gentleman," Muse said, nodding toward the man with the pad and pen.

"Oh, I'm sorry." Cope put out his hand like a game show host and slapped on the TV-ready smile. "This is Tom Gaughan, a reporter for *The Star-Ledger.*"

Muse said nothing. Tremont's hack of a brother-in-law. This was getting better and better.

"Mind if we start now?" he asked her.

"Suit yourself, Cope."

"Good. Now Frank here has a complaint. Frank, go ahead, the floor is yours."

Paul Copeland was closing in on forty years old. His wife had died of cancer right after the birth of their now-seven-year-old daughter, Cara. He had raised her alone. Until now anyway. There were no longer any pictures of Cara on his desk. There used to be. Muse remembered that when he first started, Cope had kept one on the bookshelf right behind his chair. Then one day, after they'd grilled a child molester, Cope had taken it down. She never asked him about it, but she figured that there had been a connection.

There was no picture of his fiancée either, but on Cope's coatrack, Muse could see a tuxedo wrapped in plastic. The wedding was next Saturday. Muse would be there. She was, in fact, one of the bridesmaids.

Cope sat behind his desk, giving Tremont the floor. There were no other chairs available, so Muse was left standing. She felt exposed and pissed off. A subordinate was about to start in on her — and Cope, her supposed champion, was going to let it happen. She tried hard not to shout sexism at every turn, but if she'd been male, there would have been no way she'd have to take Tremont's nonsense. She'd have the power to fire his ass, political and media repercussions notwithstanding.

She stood and seethed.

Frank Tremont hitched up his belt, even though he remained seated. "Look, no disrespect to Ms. Muse here —"

"Chief Investigator Muse," Loren said.

"Excuse me?"

"I'm not Ms. Muse. I have a title. I'm chief investigator. Your boss."

Tremont smiled. He slowly turned toward his fellow investigators and then toward his brother-in-law. His amused expression seemed to say, *See what I mean?*

"Kinda sensitive, aren't you" — then switching into full-tilt sarcasm — "Chief Investigator Muse?"

Muse glanced at Cope. Cope stayed still. His face offered no solace. He simply said, "Sorry about the interruption, Frank, go on."

Muse felt her hands tighten into fists.

"Right, anyway, I have twenty-eight years of law enforcement experience. I caught this hooker case down in the Fifth Ward. Now it's one thing for her to show up uninvited. I don't like it. It isn't protocol. But okay, if Muse here wants to pretend she can be helpful, fine. But she starts giving orders. Starts taking over, undermining my authority in front of the uniforms."

He spread his arms. "That ain't right."

Cope nodded. "You did indeed catch this case."

"Right."

"Tell me about it."

"Huh?"

"Tell me about the case."

"We don't know much yet. Hooker found dead. Someone bashed in her face good. ME thinks she was beaten to death. No ID yet. We asked some of the other hookers, but no one knows who she is."

"Do the other hookers not know her

name," Cope asked, "or they don't know her at all?"

"They ain't talking much, but you know how it is. No one sees nothing. We'll work them."

"Anything else?"

"We found a green bandana. It ain't an exact match but it's the colors of a new gang. I'm having some of the known members picked up. We'll grill them, see if we can get one to give up the mutt. We're also working the computers, see if we can get someone with a similar MO working prostitutes in the area."

"And?"

"And so far, nothing. I mean, we got plenty of dead hookers. I don't have to tell you that, boss. This is the seventh this year."

"Fingerprints?"

"We ran them through local. No hits. We'll go NCIC, but that'll take some time."

Cope nodded. "Okay, so your complaint about Muse is . . . ?"

"Look, I don't want to step on any toes, but let's face it: She shouldn't have this job anyway. You picked her because she's a woman. I get that. That's the reality today. A guy puts in his years, works hard, it don't mean nothing if someone has black skin or no dick. I get that. But this is discrimination too. I mean, just because I'm a guy and she's a gal doesn't mean it should fly, right? If I was her boss and I questioned everything she did, well, she'd probably scream rape or harassment or something and I'd get my ass sued off."

Cope nodded again. "That makes sense." He turned toward Loren. "Muse?"

"What?"

"Any comment?"

"For one, I'm not sure I'm the only one in the room with no dick."

She looked at Tremont.

Cope said, "Anything else?"

"I feel sandbagged."

"Not at all," Cope said. "You are his superior, but that doesn't mean you should be babysitting him, right? I'm your superior, do I babysit you?"

Muse fumed.

"Investigator Tremont has been here a long time. He has friends and respect. That's why I'm giving him this opportunity. He wants to go to the press with this in a big way. Make a formal complaint. I asked him to have this meeting. Be reasonable. Let him invite Mr. Gaughan, so he can see how we work in an open and nonhostile fashion."

They all looked at her.

"Now I will ask again," Cope said to her.

His eyes met hers. "Do you have any comments on what Investigator Tremont just said?"

Cope had a smile on his face now. Not a big one. Just the corners of his mouth twitching. And she suddenly understood.

"I do," Muse said.

"The floor is yours."

Cope sat back now and put his hands behind his head.

"Let's start with the fact that I don't think the victim was a prostitute."

Cope raised his eyebrows as though this were the most stunning sentence anyone had ever uttered. "You don't?"

"No."

"But I saw her clothes," Cope said. "I heard Frank's report just now. And the location of the body — everyone knows that's where hookers hang out."

"Including the killer," Muse said. "That's why he dumped her there."

Frank Tremont burst out laughing. "Muse, you're full of crap. You need evidence, sweetie, not just intuition."

"You want evidence, Frank?"

"Sure, let's hear it. You got nothing."

"How about her skin color."

"Meaning?"

"Meaning she is Caucasian."

"Oh, this is precious," Tremont said, holding up both palms. "Oh, I love this." He looked at Gaughan. "You getting this down, Tom, because this is simply priceless. I suggest that maybe, just maybe, a prostitute isn't priority one and I'm a bigoted Neanderthal. But when she claims that our victim can't possibly be a whore because she's white, well, that's solid police work."

He wagged a finger in her direction. "Muse, you need a little more time on the streets."

"You said that there were six other murdered prostitutes."

"Yeah, so?"

"Do you know that all six were African American?"

"That don't mean squat. Maybe the other six were — I don't know — tall. And this one was short. That mean she wasn't a hooker?"

Muse walked over to the bulletin board on Cope's wall. She pulled a photograph from her envelope and tacked it up. "This was taken at the crime scene."

They all looked.

"It's the crowd behind the police tape," Tremont said.

"Very good, Frank. But next time raise your hand and wait until I call on you."

Tremont crossed his arms. "What are we supposed to be looking at?"

"What do you see here?" she asked.

"Hookers," Tremont said.

"Exactly. How many?"

"I don't know. You want me to count?"

"Just an estimate."

"Maybe twenty."

"Twenty-three. That's good, Frank."

"And your point?"

"Please count how many of them are white."

No one had to look long to see the answer: zero.

"Are you now trying to tell me, Muse, that there are no white hookers?"

"There are. But very few in that area. I went back three months. According to the arrest files, no Caucasian has been arrested for solicitation within a three-block radius during that entire time period. And as you pointed out, her fingerprints aren't on file. How many local prostitutes can you say that about?"

"Plenty," Tremont said. "They come in from out of state, stay a while, die or move on to Atlantic City." Tremont spread his hands. "Wow, Muse, you're great. I might as well quit now."

He chuckled. Muse did not.

Muse pulled out more photographs and put them up. "Take a look at the victim's arms."

"Right, so?"

"No needle marks, not one. Prelim tox shows no illegal drugs in her system. So again, Frank, you tell me: How many white hookers in the Fifth Ward aren't junkies?"

That slowed him down.

"She's well nourished," Muse went on, "which means a little but not much today. Plenty of hookers are well nourished. No major bruises or breaks prior to this incident, also unusual for a hooker working this area. We can't tell much about her dental work because most of her teeth were knocked out — those that are left were well taken care of. But take a look at this."

She put up another huge photograph on the bulletin board.

"Shoes?" Tremont said.

"Gold star, Frank."

Cope's glance told her to tone down the sarcasm.

"And hooker shoes," Tremont continued. "Stiletto heel, do-me pumps. Look at those ugly puppies you're wearing, Muse. You ever wear heels like those?"

"No, I don't, Frank. How about you?"

That got a chuckle from the room. Cope

shook his head.

"So what's your point?" Tremont asked. "They're straight out of the hooker catalog."

"Look at the bottom of the soles."

She used a pencil to point.

"What am I supposed to see?"

"Nothing. That's the point. No scuff marks. Not one."

"So they're new."

"Too new. I had the photo enlarged." She put up another photograph. "Not one single scratch. No one has walked in them. Not even once."

The room went quiet.

"So?"

"Good comeback, Frank."

"Up yours, Muse, this doesn't mean —"

"By the way, she had no semen in her."

"So? Maybe this was her first trick of the night."

"Maybe. She also has a tan that you need to examine."

"A what?"

"A tan."

He tried to look incredulous, but he was losing his support. "There's a reason, Muse, why these girls are called street hookers. Streets, you see, are outside. These girls work outside. A lot."

"Forgetting the fact that we really haven't had much sun lately, the tan lines are wrong. They cut up over here" — she pointed to the shoulders — "and there's no tan near the abdomen — the area is totally pale. In short, this woman wore shirts, not bikini tops. And then there's that bandana found clutched in her hand."

"Grabbed off the perp during the attack."

"No, not grabbed off. It's an obvious plant. The body was moved, Frank. So we're supposed to believe that she clutched it off his head while she struggled — and they just left it there when they dumped her body? Does that sound credible?"

"Could be the gang was sending a message."

"Could be. But then there's the beating itself."

"What about it?"

"It's overdone. No one beats up someone with that much precision."

"You have a theory?"

"An obvious one. Someone didn't want us to recognize her. And something else. Look where she was dumped."

"At a well-known spot for whores."

"Exactly. We know she wasn't murdered there. She was dumped there. Why that spot? If she was a hooker, why would you want us to know that? Why dump a hooker in a well-known hooker locale? I will tell you why. Because if she's mistaken early for a hooker and some lazy fat-assed investigator takes the case and sees the easiest route —"

"Who you calling fat-assed?"

Frank Tremont stood. And Cope quietly said, "Sit down, Frank."

"Are you going to let her — ?"

"Shh," Cope said. "Hear that sound?"

Everyone stopped.

"What?"

Cope cupped his hand to his ear. "Listen, Frank. Hear it?" His voice was a whisper. "That's the sound of your incompetence being made obvious to the masses. Not just your incompetence, but your suicidal stupidity at going after your superior when the facts do not back you up."

"I don't have to take this —"

"Shh, listen. Just listen."

Muse was trying hard not to laugh.

"Were you listening, Mr. Gaughan?" Cope asked.

Gaughan cleared his throat. "I heard what I had to."

"Good, because so did I. And since you asked to record this meeting, well, I felt obliged to do so too." Cope produced a small tape recorder from behind a book on his desk. “Just in case, you know, your boss wanted to hear exactly what happened in here and your recorder malfunctioned or something. We wouldn’t want anyone to think you’d slant the story in favor of your brother-in-law, would we?”

Cope smiled at them. They did not smile back.

“Gentlemen, any other comments? No, good. Back to work, then. Frank, you take the rest of the day off. I want you to think about your options and maybe check out some of the great retirement packages we offer.”

10

When Mike got home, he looked at the Lorimans' house. No movement. He knew that he'd have to take the next step.

First, do no harm. That was the credo.

And second?

That was a little trickier.

He threw his keys and wallet on the little tray Tia had set up because Mike was always losing his keys and wallet. It actually worked. Tia had called when she landed in Boston. She was doing some prep work now and deposing the witness in the afternoon. It could go a while but she'd grab the first shuttle she could. No rush, he told her.

"Hi, Daddy!"

Jill rounded the corner. When Mike saw her smile, the Lorimans and everything else just slid off him in a pure, easy groove.

"Hi, honey. Is Adam in his room?"

"No," Jill said.

So much for the easy groove.

"Where is he?"

"I don't know. I thought he was down here."

They started to call for him. No answer.

"Your brother was supposed to babysit," Mike said.

"He was here ten minutes ago," she said.

"And now?"

Jill frowned. When she frowned, her entire body seemed to get into it. "I thought you were going to the hockey game tonight."

"We are."

Jill seemed agitated.

"Honey, what's wrong?"

"Nothing."

"When did you see your brother last?"

"I don't know. A few minutes ago." She started biting a nail. "Shouldn't he be with you?"

"I'm sure he'll be right back," Mike said.

Jill looked uncertain. Mike felt the same.

"Are you still dropping me off at Yasmin's?" she asked.

"Of course."

"Let me get my bag, okay?"

"Sure."

Jill headed up the stairs. Mike checked his watch. He and Adam had made a plan — they were supposed to leave here in a half hour, drop Jill at her friend's, head into

Manhattan for the Rangers game.

Adam should be home. He should be watching his sister.

Mike took a deep breath. Okay, let's not panic yet. He decided to give Adam another ten minutes. He sorted through the mail and thought again about the Lorimans. No use stalling. He and Ilene had made a decision. Time to act on it.

He hit the computer, brought up their phone book, clicked on the Lorimans' contact information. Susan Loriman's cell phone was in the list. He and Tia had never called it, but that was how it was with neighbors — you had all the numbers in case there was ever an emergency.

This qualified.

He dialed the number. Susan answered on the second ring.

"Hello?"

She had a warm, soft voice, almost sounding a little hushed. Mike cleared his throat.

"It's Mike Baye," he said.

"Is everything okay?"

"Yes. I mean, nothing new. Are you alone right now?"

Silence.

Susan said, "We returned that DVD."

He heard another voice — sounded like Dante's — ask, "Who is that?"

"Blockbuster," she said.

Okay, Mike thought, not alone. "You have my number?"

"Very soon. Thanks."

Click.

Mike rubbed his face with both hands. Great. Just great.

"Jill!"

She came to the top of the stairs. "What?"

"Did Adam say anything when he got home?"

"He just said, 'Hi, squirt.' "

She smiled when she said that.

Mike could hear his son's voice. Adam loved his sister, and she loved him. Most siblings fight, but they rarely did. Maybe their differences worked in that way. No matter how cold or surly Adam got, he never took it out on his little sister.

"Any idea where he went?"

Jill shook her head. "Is he okay?"

"He's fine, don't worry. I'll take you to Yasmin's in a few minutes, okay?"

Mike took the stairs two at a time. He felt a small pang in his knee, an old injury from his hockey days. He'd had it operated on a few months ago by his friend, an orthopedic surgeon named David Gold. He told David that he didn't want to give up hockey and asked him if playing had caused the long-term damage. David gave him a prescription for Percocet and replied: "I don't get a lot of ex–chess players here — you tell me."

He opened Adam's door. The room was empty. Mike looked for clues as to where his son had gone. There were none.

"Oh, he wouldn't . . . ," Mike said out loud.

He checked his watch. Adam should definitely be home by now — should have been home the whole time. How could he leave his sister alone? He knew better than that. Mike took out his cell phone and pushed the speed dial. He heard it ring and then Adam's voice came on and asked him to leave a message.

"Where are you? We need to leave soon for the Rangers. And you just left your sister alone? Call me immediately."

He pressed the END button.

Ten more minutes passed. Nothing from Adam. Mike called again. Left another message through gritted teeth.

Jill said, "Dad?"

"Yes, sweetheart."

"Where's Adam?"

"I'm sure he'll be home soon. Look, I'll drop you off at Yasmin's and come back for your brother, okay?"

Mike called, left a third message on Adam's cell explaining that he'd be back soon. He flashed back to last time he had done this — leaving repeated messages on the voice mails — when Adam had run away and they didn't hear from him for two days. Mike and Tia had gone nuts trying to find him, and in the end it had been nothing.

He better not be playing that game again, Mike thought. And then, at the very same moment, he thought: God, I hope he's playing that game again.

Mike took out a sheet of paper, jotted down a note, left it on the kitchen table:

ADAM,
I'M DROPPING JILL OFF, BE READY WHEN I GET BACK.

Jill's backpack had a New York Rangers insignia on the back. She didn't care much for hockey, but it had been her older brother's. Jill cherished Adam's hand-me-downs. She had taken lately to wearing a much-too-large-for-her green windbreaker from when Adam played Pee Wee hockey. Adam's name was stenciled in threaded script on the right chest.

"Dad?"

"What, sweetheart?"

"I'm worried about Adam."

She did not say it like a little girl playing grown-up. She said it like a kid too wise for her years.

"Why do you say that?"

She shrugged.

"Has he said anything to you?"

"No."

Mike pulled onto Yasmin's street, hoping that Jill would say more. She didn't.

In the old days — way back when Mike was a kid — you just dropped kids off and drove away or maybe waited in the car for the front door to open. Now you walked your offspring all the way to the door. Normally this bothered Mike somewhat, but when there was a sleepover, especially at this relatively young age, Mike liked to check in. He knocked on the door and Guy Novak, Yasmin's father, answered.

"Hey, Mike."

"Hey, Guy."

Guy still wore his suit from work, though the tie was undone. He wore too-fashionable framed tortoiseshell glasses and his hair looked strategically mussed. Guy was yet another father in town who worked on Wall Street, and for the life of him, Mike could never figure out what any of them did. Hedge funds or trust accounts or credit services or

IPOs or working on the floor or trading securities or selling bonds, whatever — it all became one big blurry mass of finance to Mike.

Guy had been divorced for years and, according to the scuttlebutt Mike got from his eleven-year-old daughter, dated a lot.

"His girlfriends always kiss up to Yasmin," Jill had told him. "It's kind of funny."

Jill pushed passed them. "Bye, Dad."

"Bye, pumpkin."

Mike waited a second, watched her disappear, then he turned to Guy Novak. Sexist, yes, but he preferred to leave his child with a single mom. Something about his prepubescent daughter spending a night in the same house with only an adult male — it shouldn't matter. Mike took care of the girls sometimes without Tia. But still.

They both stood there. Mike broke the silence.

"So," Mike said, "what do you have planned for the night?"

"Might take them to the movies," Guy said. "Ice cream at Cold Stone Creamery. I, uh, hope you don't mind. I have a girlfriend coming out tonight. She'll go with us."

"No problem," Mike said, thinking: Even better.

Guy glanced behind him. When he saw

both girls were out of sight, he turned back to Mike. "You got a second?" he asked.

"Sure, what's up?"

Guy stepped outside onto the stoop. He let the door close behind him. He looked into the street and put his hands deep in his pockets. Mike watched him in profile.

"Everything all right?" Mike asked.

"Jill has been great," Guy said.

Mike was not sure how to react to that so he stayed silent.

"I'm not sure what to do here. I mean, as a parent, you do all you can, right? You try your best to raise them, feed them, educate them. Yasmin already had to deal with a divorce at a very young age. But she adjusted to that. She was happy and outgoing and popular. And then, well, something like this happens."

"You mean with Mr. Lewiston?"

Guy nodded. He bit down and his jaw began to quake. "You've seen the changes in Yasmin, haven't you?"

Mike opted for the truth. "She seems more withdrawn."

"Do you know what Lewiston said to her?"

"Not really, no."

He closed his eyes, took a deep breath, opened them again. "I guess Yasmin was acting up in class, not paying attention, whatever, I don't know. When I confronted Lewiston, he said he gave her two warnings. The thing is, Yasmin has a little facial hair. Not much, but you know, a bit of a mustache. Not something a father would notice, and her mother, well, she's not around, so I never thought about electrolysis or whatever. So anyway he's explaining chromosomes and she's whispering in the back of the room and Lewiston finally snaps. He says, 'Some women display male traits like facial hair — Yasmin, are you listening?' Something like that."

Mike said, "Awful."

"Inexcusable, right? He doesn't apologize right away because, he says, he didn't want to draw more attention to what he said. Meanwhile every kid in the class starts cracking up. Yasmin is beyond mortified. They start calling her the Bearded Lady and XY — for the male chromosome. He apologizes the next day, implores the kids to stop, I go in, shout at the principal, but now it's like unringing a bell, you know what I mean?"

"I do."

"Kids."

"Yeah."

"Jill has stuck by Yasmin — the only one.

Amazing for an eleven-year-old to do that. I know she's probably taking some ribbing for that."

"She can handle it," Mike said.

"She's a good kid."

"So is Yasmin."

"You should be proud. That's all I'm saying.

"Thanks," Mike said. "It'll pass, Guy. Give it some time."

Guy looked off. "When I was in third grade, there was this boy named Eric Hellinger. Eric always had a huge smile on his face. He dressed like such a dork, but he seemed oblivious, you know? Just always smiling. One day he vomited in the middle of class. It was nasty. The smell was so bad we had to leave the classroom. Anyway, the kids start picking on him after that. Called him Smellinger. It never ended. Eric's life changed. The smile fled, and to tell you the truth, even when I saw him alone in the halls in high school years later, it was like the smile never came back."

Mike said nothing, but he knew a story like this. Every childhood has one, their own Eric Hellinger or Yasmin Novak.

"It's not getting better, Mike. So I'm putting the house on the market. I don't want to move. But I don't know what else to do."

"If there is any way Tia or I can help . . . ," Mike began.

"I appreciate that. And I appreciate you letting Jill sleep over tonight. It means the world to Yasmin. And to me. So thank you."

"No problem."

"Jill said you're taking Adam to a hockey game tonight."

"That's the plan."

"Then I won't keep you any longer. Thanks for listening."

"You're welcome. You have my cell number?"

Guy nodded. Mike patted the man's shoulder and headed back to the car.

That was how life was — a teacher loses his cool for ten seconds and it changes everything for one little girl. Nuts when you think about it. It also made Mike wonder about Adam.

Had something similar happened to his son? Had one incident, maybe something small even, changed Adam's path?

Mike thought about those time-travel movies, the ones where you go back and change one thing and then everything else changes, a ripple effect. If Guy could go back in time and keep Yasmin out of school for that day, would everything be as it was? Would Yasmin be happier — or by forcing her to move and maybe learning a lesson about how cruel people can be, will she end up ultimately better off?

Who the heck knew?

The house was still empty when Mike got home. No sign of Adam. No message from him either.

Still thinking about Yasmin, Mike headed into the kitchen. The note he left still sat on the kitchen table, untouched. There were dozens of photographs on the refrigerator, all neatly aligned in magnet sleeve-frames. Mike found one of Adam and himself from last year when they went to Six Flags Great Adventure. Mike was normally terrified of big rides, but his son had somehow persuaded him to go on something aptly called The Chiller. Mike loved it.

When they got off, father and son posed for a dumb picture with a guy dressed like Batman. They both had their hair messed from the ride, arms around Batman's shoulders, goofy grins on their faces.

That had been just last summer.

Mike remembered now sitting in the coaster, waiting for that ride to start, heart pumping. He turned to Adam, who gave him a crooked smile and said, "Hold tight," and then, right then, he flashed back more than a decade, when Adam was four and they were at this same park and there was a crush of people entering the stuntman show, a total crush, and Mike held his son's hand and told him to "hold tight," and he could feel the little hand dig into his but the crush got bigger and the little hand slipped from his and Mike felt that horrible panic, as if a wave hit them at the beach and it was washing his baby out with the tide. The separation lasted only a few seconds, ten at the most, but Mike would never forget the spike in his blood and the terror of those brief few moments.

Mike stared for a solid minute. Then he picked up his phone and called Adam's cell phone again.

"Please call home, son. I'm worried about you. I'm on your side, always, no matter what. I love you. So call me, okay?"

He hung up and waited.

Adam listened to the last message from his father and almost started to cry.

He thought about calling him back. He thought about dialing his dad's number and telling him to come get him and then they could go to that Rangers game with Uncle Mo and maybe Adam would tell them everything. He held his cell phone. His father's number was speed-dial one. His finger hovered by the digit. All he had to do was press down.

From behind him a voice said, “Adam?”

He moved his finger away.

“Let’s go.”

11

Betsy Hill watched her husband, Ron, pull his Audi into the garage. He was still such a handsome man. His salt-and-pepper hair had gone pretty much to salt, but his blue eyes, so like his dead son's, still shone and his face remained smooth. Unlike most of his colleagues he'd kept the gut off, worked out just enough, watched what he ate.

The picture she'd printed off the MySpace page sat on the table in front of her. For the past hour she had sat here wondering what to do. The twins were with her sister. She didn't want them home for this.

She heard the door from the garage open and then Ron called out, "Bets?"

"In the kitchen, honey."

Ron bounded into the room with a smile on his face. It had been a long time since she had seen him smile and as soon as she did, she slid the picture under a magazine and out of view. She wanted, even for a few minutes anyway, to protect that smile.

"Hi," he said.

"Hi, how was work?"

"Fine, good." He still smiled. "I have a surprise."

"Oh?"

Ron came over, bent down and kissed her cheek, tossed the brochure on the kitchen table. Betsy reached for it.

"A one-week cruise," he said. "Look at the itinerary, Bets. I bookmarked the page with a Post-it note."

She turned to the page and looked down. The cruise left Miami Beach and hit the Bahamas, St. Thomas and some private island owned by the ship.

"Same itinerary," Ron said. "Exact same itinerary as on our honeymoon. The ship is different, of course. That old vessel isn't running anymore. This one is brand-new. I got the top deck too — a cabin with a balcony. I even got someone to watch Bobby and Kari."

"We can't just leave the twins for a week."

"Sure we can."

"They're still too vulnerable, Ron."

The smile started fading. "They'll be fine."

He wants this gone, she thought. Not

wrong, of course. Life goes on. This was his way of coping. He wanted it gone. And eventually, she knew, he will want her gone too. He might hang on for the twins, but all the good memories — that first kiss outside the library, the overnight at the shore, the spectacular sun-drenched honeymoon cruise, scraping that horrid wallpaper off at their starter home, that time at the farmers' market when they started laughing so hard, tears ran down their faces — all of that was gone now.

When Ron sees her, he sees his dead son.

"Bets?"

She nodded. "Maybe you're right."

He sat down next to her and held her hand. "I talked to Sy today. They need a manager at the new Atlanta office. It would be a wonderful opportunity."

He wants to run, she thought again. For now he wants her with him, but she will always bring him pain. "I love you, Ron."

"I love you too, honey."

She wanted him happy. She wanted to let him go because Ron did have that ability. He needed to run away. He couldn't face it. He couldn't run with her. She would always remind him of Spencer, of that terrible night on the roof of the school. But she loved him, needed him. Selfish or not, she was terrified of losing him.

"What do you think about Atlanta?" he asked.

"I don't know."

"You'll love it."

She had thought about moving but Atlanta was a long way to go. She had lived her whole life in New Jersey.

"It's a lot to take in," he said. "Let's take one step at a time. First the cruise, okay?"

"Okay."

He wants to be anywhere but here. He wants to go back. She would try, but it won't work. You can't go back. Not ever. Especially not when you have the twins.

"I'm going to go get changed," Ron said.

He kissed her cheek again. His lips felt cold. Like he was already gone. She would lose him. Might take another three months or two years, but the only man she had ever loved would eventually leave. She could feel him pulling away even as he kissed her.

"Ron?"

He stopped with one hand on the stair's railing. When he looked back, it was as though he'd been caught, as though he'd just missed a chance to make a clean escape. His shoulders sunk.

"I need to show you something," Betsy said.

■ ■ ■ ■

Tia sat in a Boston Four Seasons's conference room while Brett, the office computer guru, toyed with the laptop. She checked the caller ID and saw it was Mike.

"On your way to the game?"

"No," he said.

"What happened?"

"Adam's not here."

"He didn't come home at all?"

"He came home, he hung out in his room a little and then he took off."

"He left Jill alone?"

"Yes."

"That's not like him."

"I know."

"I mean, he's been irresponsible and all, but leaving his sister without supervision . . ."

"I know."

Tia thought a moment. "Did you try his cell phone?"

"Of course I tried his cell phone. How stupid do you think I am?"

"Hey, don't take this out on me," Tia said.

"Then don't ask me questions like I'm a moron. Of course I called him. I called him several times. I even left — gasp — messages for him to call me back."

Tia watched Brett pretend not to listen in. She moved away from him.

"I'm sorry," she said. "I didn't mean —"

"Me neither. We're both on edge."

"So what should we do?"

"What can we do?" Mike said. "I'll wait here."

"And if he doesn't come home?"

There was a pause.

"I don't want him at the party," Mike said.

"I agree."

"But if I go over and stop him . . ."

"That would be weird too."

"What do you think?" he asked.

"I think you should go over and stop him anyway. You can try to be subtle about it."

"How would that work?"

"I don't know. The party won't start for a couple of hours probably. We can think about it."

"Yeah, okay. Maybe I'll get lucky and find him before that."

"Did you try calling his friends' houses? Clark or Olivia's?"

"Tia."

"Right, of course you did. Should I come home?"

"And do what?"

"I don't know."

"Nothing you can do here. I got it under control. I shouldn't have even called."

"Yes, you should have. Don't try to protect me from stuff like this. I want to be kept in the loop."

"I will, don't worry."

"Call me when you hear from him."

"Okay."

She hung up.

Brett looked up from the computer. "Problem?"

"You were listening?"

Brett shrugged. "Why don't you check his E-SpyRight report?"

"Maybe I'll tell Mike to do that later."

"You can do it from here."

"I thought I could only get it off my own computer."

"Nah. You can access it anywhere you have an Internet connection."

Tia frowned. "That doesn't sound secure."

"You still need your ID and password. You just go to the E-SpyRight page and sign in. Maybe your kid got an e-mail or something."

Tia thought about it.

Brett moved to his laptop and typed something in. He spun it toward her. The E-SpyRight home page was up. "I'm going to, like, grab a soda downstairs," he said. "You want something?"

She shook her head.

"All yours," Brett said.

He headed for the door. Tia slid into the chair and began typing. She brought up the report and asked for anything that came in today. There was almost nothing, just a quick instant-message conversation with the mysterious CeeJay8115.

CeeJay8115: What's wrong?
HockeyAdam1117: His mother approached me after school.
CeeJay8115: What did she say?
HockeyAdam1117: She knows something.
CeeJay8115: What did you tell her?
HockeyAdam1117: Nothing. I ran.
CeeJay8115: We will discuss tonight.

Tia read it again. Then she took out her cell phone and hit the speed dial. "Mike?"

"What?"

"Find him. Find him no matter what."

Ron held the photograph.

He stared at it, but Betsy could tell he had stopped seeing it. His body language was beyond troubling. He twitched and stiffened. He put the picture on the table and crossed his arms over his chest. He picked it up again.

"What does this change?" he asked.

He started blinking rapidly, the way a stutterer might when he's trying to get out a particularly difficult word. The sight terrified Betsy. Ron hadn't done that rapid blink in years. Her mother-in-law had explained that Ron had gotten beaten up a lot when he was in second grade and hid it from her. That was when the blink started. It had gotten better as he'd gotten older. It barely surfaced now. Even after they heard about Spencer, Betsy hadn't seen the blink.

She wished that she could take the picture back. Ron had come home and tried to reach out and she'd slapped his hand away.

"He wasn't alone that night," she said.

"So?"

"Didn't you hear what I said?"

"Maybe he went out with his friends first. So what?"

"Why didn't they say anything?"

"Who knows? They were scared, maybe Spencer told them not to, or maybe, probably, you got the date wrong. Maybe he saw them briefly and then went out. Maybe this picture was taken earlier in the day."

"No. I confronted Adam Baye at school —"

"You what?"

"I waited until school ended. I showed him the photograph."

Ron just shook his head.

"He ran away from me. There was definitely something there."

"Like what?"

"I don't know. But remember Spencer had a bruise by his eye when the police found him."

"They explained that. He probably passed out and fell on his face."

"Or maybe someone hit him."

Ron's voice grew soft. "No one hit him, Bets."

Betsy said nothing. The blinking got worse. Tears started spilling down Ron's cheeks. She reached for him but he pulled away.

"Spencer mixed pills and alcohol. Do you understand that, Betsy?"

She said nothing.

"Nobody forced him to steal that bottle of vodka from our cabinet. Nobody forced him to take those pills from my medicine chest. Where I left them. Just in view. We know that, right? That was my prescription bottle that, yes, I just left out. The ones I kept asking for renewals when, really, I should have been over the pain and moved on, right?"

"Ron, it's not . . ."

"Not what? You don't think I see it?"

"See what?" she asked. But she knew. "I don't blame you, I swear."

"Yeah, you do."

She shook her head. But he never saw it. Ron was up and out the door.

12

Nash was ready to strike.

He waited in the lot at the Palisades Mall in Nyack. The mall was pure Americana ginormous. Yes, the Mall of America outside Minneapolis was bigger, but this mall was newer, crammed with huge megastores in a megamall, none of those cute little eighties-trendy boutiques. They had warehouse price clubs, expansive chain bookstores, an IMAX theater, an AMC with fifteen screens, a Best Buy, a Staples, a full-size Ferris wheel. The corridors were wide. Everything was big.

Reba Cordova had gone into Target.

She had parked her Aberdeen green Acura MDX far away from the entrance. That would help, but this would still be risky. They parked the van next to her Acura, on the driver's side. Nash had come up with the plan. Pietra was currently inside following Reba Cordova. Nash had also gone into Target briefly — to make a quick purchase.

Now he waited for Pietra's text.

He had considered the mustache, but no, that would not do here. Nash needed to look open and trusting. Mustaches did not do that. Mustaches, especially the bushy one he had used with Marianne, dominate a face. If you ask for a description, few witnesses go beyond the mustache. So it often worked.

But not for this.

Nash stayed in the car and prepared. He fixed his hair in the rearview mirror and ran the electric razor over his face.

Cassandra had liked it when he was clean-shaven. Nash's beard had a tendency to get heavy and could scratch her by five o'clock.

"Please shave for me, handsome," Cassandra would tell him with that sideways glance that made his toes curl. "Then I will cover your face with kisses."

He thought about that now. He thought about her voice. His heart still ached. He had long ago accepted that it would always hurt. You live with pain. The hole would always be there.

He sat in the driver's seat and watched the people walk back and forth in the mall parking lot. They were all alive and breathing while his Cassandra was dead. Her beauty had no doubt rotted away by now. It was hard to imagine.

His cell phone buzzed. A text from Pietra:

At checkout. Leaving now.

He gave his eyes a quick swipe with his forefinger and thumb and climbed out of the car. He opened the back door of the van. His purchase, a Cosco Scenera 5-Point Convertible Car Seat, the cheapest in the store at forty bucks, was out of the box.

Nash glanced behind him.

Reba Cordova wheeled a red shopping cart with several plastic bags in it. She looked harried and happy, like so many of the suburban sheep. He wondered about that, about their happiness, if it was real or self-inflicted. They had everything they wanted. The nice house, two cars, financial security, children. He wondered if that was all women needed. He wondered about the men at the office who provided this life for them and if they felt likewise.

Behind Reba Cordova, he could see Pietra. She was keeping her distance. Nash took in the surroundings. An overweight man with hippie hair, a rat-nest beard, and a tie-dyed shirt hoisted up his plumber-butt jeans and started toward the entrance. Disgusting. Nash had seen him circle around in his beat-up Chevy Caprice, spending minutes searching for a closer space that would save him from walking ten seconds. America the Fat.

Nash had positioned the van's side door to be near the Acura's driver's side. He leaned in and started fiddling with the car seat. The driver's side mirror was positioned so he could see her approach. Reba clicked her remote control and the back hatch opened. He waited till she was close.

"Darn!" he said. He said it loud enough for Reba to hear but in a voice that seemed more amused than annoyed. He stood upright and scratched his head as if confused. He looked at Reba Cordova and smiled in the most nonthreatening manner possible.

"Car seat," he said to her.

Reba Cordova was a pretty woman with small doll-like features. She looked up and gave him a nod of sympathy.

"Who wrote these installation instructions," he continued, "NASA engineers?"

Reba smiled now, commiserating. "It's ridiculous, isn't it?"

"Totally. The other day I was setting up Roger's Pack 'n Play — Roger's my two-year-old. Do you have one of those? A Pack 'n Play, I mean."

"Sure."

"It was supposed to be easy to fold up and put away, but, well, Cassandra — that's my wife — she says I'm just hopeless."

"So is my husband."

He laughed. She laughed. She had, Nash thought, a very nice laugh. He wondered if Reba's husband appreciated it, if he was a funny man and liked to make his wife with the doll-like features laugh and if he still stopped and marveled at the sound.

"I hate to bother you," he said, still being Mr. Friendly, hands down and spread, "but I have to pick up Roger at Little Gym and, well, Cassandra and I are both sticklers for safety."

"Oh, so am I."

"So I wouldn't dream of picking him up without a car seat and I forgot to switch our other into this car and so I stopped here to buy one . . . well, you know how it is."

"I do."

Nash held up the manual and just shook his head. "Do you think maybe you could take a quick look?"

Reba hesitated. He could see it. A primal reaction — more a reflex. He was, after all, a stranger. We are trained by both biology and society to fear the stranger. But evolution has given us societal niceties too. They were in a public parking lot and he seemed like a nice man, a dad and all, and he had a car seat and, well, it would be rude to say no, wouldn't it?

These calculations all took mere seconds, no more than two or three, and in the end, politeness beat out survival.

It often did.

"Sure."

She put her bundles in the back of the car and started over. Nash leaned into his own van. "I think it's just this one strap over here. . . ."

Reba moved closer. Nash stood up to give her room. He glanced around. The fat guy with the Jerry Garcia beard and tie-dyed tee was still waddling toward the entrance, but he wouldn't notice anything that did not involve a doughnut. And sometimes, it is indeed best to hide in plain sight. Don't panic, don't rush, don't make a fuss.

Reba Cordova leaned in and that spelled her doom.

Nash watched the exposed back of her neck. It took seconds. He reached in and pushed the spot behind her earlobe with one hand, while covering her mouth with the other. The move effectively shut off the blood to her brain.

Her legs kicked out feebly, but only for a few seconds. He dug in harder and Reba

Cordova went still. He slid her in, hopped in behind her, closed the door. Pietra followed up. She shut Reba's car door. Nash took her keys from Reba's hand. He used the remote to lock her car. Pietra moved to the driver's seat of their van.

She started it up.

"Wait," Nash said.

Pietra turned. "Shouldn't we hurry?"

"Stay calm."

He thought a moment.

"What is it?"

"I will drive the van," he said. "I want you to take her vehicle."

"What? Why?"

"Because if we leave it here, they will realize that this is where she was grabbed. If we move her car, we may be able to confuse them."

He tossed her the keys. Then he used the plastic cuffs to tie Reba down. He jammed a cloth in her mouth. She started to struggle.

He cupped her delicate, pretty face in both hands, almost as though he were about to kiss her.

"If you escape," he said, staring into those doll-like eyes, "I will grab Jamie instead. And it will be bad. Do you understand?"

The sound of her child's name froze Reba.

Nash moved to the front seat. To Pietra he said, "Just follow me. Drive normally."

And they started on their way.

Mike tried to relax with his iPod. Aside from hockey, he had no other outlet. Nothing truly relaxed him. He liked family, he liked work, he liked hockey. Hockey would only last so much longer. The years were catching up. Hard thing to admit. A lot of his job was standing in an operating room for hours at a stretch. In the past, hockey had helped keep him in shape. It probably was still good for the cardio, but his body was taking a beating. His joints ached. The muscle pulls and minor sprains came in greater frequency and extended their stays.

For the first time Mike felt on the downside of life's roller coaster — the back nine of life, as his golfer friends put it. You know it, of course. When you hit thirty-five or forty, you know on one level that you are no longer the physical specimen you once were. But denial is a pretty powerful thing. Now, at the tender of age of forty-six, he knew that no matter what he did, the slide would not only continue but accelerate.

Cheerful thought.

The minutes passed slowly. He did not bother calling Adam's phone anymore. He would get the messages or not. On his iPod, Mat Kearney was asking the appropriate musical question, "Where we gonna go from here?" He tried to close his eyes, vanish in the music, but it wouldn't happen. He started pacing. That didn't do it. He considered driving around the block on a search, but that seemed stupid. He eyed his hockey stick. Maybe shooting on the goal outside would help.

His cell phone rang. He grabbed it without checking the caller ID. "Hello?"

"Any word?"

It was Mo.

"No."

"I'll come over."

"Go to the game."

"Nah."

"Mo —"

"I'll give the tickets to another friend."

"You don't have another friend."

"Well, that's true," Mo said.

"Look, let's give him another half hour. Leave the tickets at Will Call."

Mo didn't reply.

"Mo?"

"How badly do you want to find him?"

"What do you mean?"

"Remember when I asked to look at your cell phone?"

"Yes."

"Your model comes with a GPS."

"I'm not sure I follow."

"GPS. It stands for Global Positioning System."

"I know what it stands for, Mo. What are you talking about with my cell phone?"

"A lot of the new phones come with GPS chips built in."

"Like when they do that triangulation on TV with cell towers?"

"No. That's TV. That's also old technology. It started a few years ago with something called a SIDSA Personal Locator. It was mostly used for Alzheimer's patients. You put it in the guy's pocket and it was maybe the size of a pack of playing cards and if he wandered off, you could find him. Then uFindKid started doing the same thing with kids' cell phones. Now it's built into almost every phone by every phone company."

"There's a GPS in Adam's phone?"

"Yours too, yes. I can give you the Web address. You go on, you pay the fee with a credit card. You click on and you'll see a map like on any GPS locator — like on MapQuest — with street names and everything. It will tell you exactly where the phone is."

Mike said nothing.

"Did you hear what I said?"

"Yes."

"And?"

"And I'm on it."

Mike hung up. He hopped online and pulled up the Web address for his cell carrier. He put in the phone number, provided a password. He found the GPS program, clicked the hyperlink and a bunch of options popped up. You could get a month of GPS service for $49.99, six months for $129.99, or a full year for $199.99. Mike was actually dumb enough to start considering the alternatives, automatically calculating what would be the best deal, and then he shook his head and clicked monthly. He didn't want to think about still doing this a year from now, even if it was a much better value.

It took a few more minutes for the approval to go through and then there was another list of options. Mike clicked on the map. The entire USA appeared with a dot in his home state of New Jersey. Gee, that was helpful. He clicked the ZOOM icon, a magnifying glass, and slowly and almost dramatically, the map started to move in, first to the region, then the state, then the city and finally, right down to the street.

The GPS locator placed a big red dot right on a street not far from where Mike now sat. There was a box that read CLOSEST AD-

DRESS. Mike clicked it, but he really didn't need to. He knew the address already.

Adam was at the Huffs' house.

13

Nine P.M. Darkness had fallen over the Huff house.

Mike pulled up to the curb across the street. There were lights on inside. Two cars were in the driveway. He thought about how to play this. He stayed in the car and once again tried Adam's phone. No answer. The Huffs' phone number was unlisted, probably because Daniel Huff was a cop. Mike didn't have the son, DJ's, cell phone.

There was really no choice.

He tried to think about how he could explain his being here without tipping his hand. He couldn't really think of one.

So now what?

He considered heading home. The boy was underage. Drinking was dangerous, yes, but hadn't Mike done likewise when he was a kid? There had been beers in the woods. There had been shot parties at Pepe Feldman's house. He and his friends weren't heavily into the dope scene, but he had hung out at his buddy Weed's house — clue for parents: If your kid is nicknamed "Weed," it probably has little to do with legitimate gardening — when his folks were out of town.

Mike had found his way back. Would he have grown up better adjusted if his parents just barged in like this?

Mike looked at the door. Maybe he should just wait. Maybe he should let him drink, party, whatever, and stay out here and then when he came out, Mike could watch him, make sure he was okay. That way he wouldn't embarrass him or lose his son's trust.

What trust?

Adam had left his sister alone. Adam refused to return his calls. And worse — on Mike's end — he was already spying like mad. He and Tia watched his computer. They eavesdropped in the most invasive way possible.

He remembered the Ben Folds song. "If you can't trust, you can't be trusted."

He was still debating how to play it when the Huffs' front door opened. Mike started to slide down in his seat, which truly felt foolish. But it wasn't any of the kids he saw leaving the house. It was Captain Daniel Huff of the Livingston police force.

The father who was supposed to be away.

Mike was not sure how to handle this. But it really didn't matter much. Daniel Huff paced with purpose. He paced on a straight line toward Mike. There was no hesitation. Huff had a destination in mind.

Mike's car.

Mike sat up. Daniel Huff met his eye. He did not wave or smile; he didn't frown or look apprehensive either. It might have been Mike's knowledge of Huff's occupation, but he looked to Mike very much like a cop who'd pulled him over and was keeping his face neutral so that maybe you'd just admit you'd been speeding or had a stash of drugs in the trunk.

When Huff got close enough, Mike rolled down his window and managed a smile.

"Hey, Dan," Mike said.

"Mike."

"Was I speeding, Officer?"

Huff smiled tightly at the poor joke. He came right up to the car. "License and registration, please."

They both chuckled, neither finding the joke particularly humorous. Huff put his hands on his hips. Mike tried to say something. He knew that Huff was waiting for an explanation. Mike just wasn't sure that he wanted to give him one.

After the forced chuckles died out and a few

uncomfortable seconds had passed, Daniel Huff got to it. "I saw you parked out here, Mike."

He stopped. Mike said, "Uh-huh."

"Everything okay?"

"Sure."

Mike tried not to be annoyed. You're a cop, big deal. Who approaches friends on the street like this except some superior know-it-all? Then again, maybe it did seem weird to see a guy you know doing what looked like surveillance in front of your domicile.

"Would you like to come in?"

"I'm looking for Adam."

"That's why you're parked out here?"

"Yes."

"So why didn't you just knock on the door?"

Like he was Columbo.

"I wanted to make a call first."

"I didn't see you talking on your cell phone."

"How long were you watching me, Dan?"

"A few minutes."

"The car has a speaker phone. You know. Hands-free. That's the law, isn't it?"

"Not when you're parked. You can just put the phone to your ear when you're parked."

Mike was getting tired of this dance. "Is Adam here with DJ?"

"No."
"You're sure?"
Huff frowned. Mike dived into the silence.
"I thought the boys were meeting up here tonight," Mike said.
"What made you think that?"
"I thought that was the message I got. That you and Marge were going to be away and that they were going to meet up here."
Huff frowned again. "That I was going away?"
"For the weekend. Something like that."
"And you thought I'd allow teenage boys to spend that kind of time in this house unsupervised?"
This was not going well.
"Why don't you just call Adam?"
"I did. His phone doesn't seem to be working. He forgets to charge it a lot."
"So you drove over?"
"Right."
"And sat in the car and didn't knock on the door?"
"Hey, Dan, I know you're a cop and all, but give me a break, will you? I'm just looking for my son."
"He's not here."
"How about DJ? Maybe he knows where Adam is."

"He's not here either."

He waited for Huff to offer to call his son. He didn't. Mike did not want to press it. This had gone far enough. If there had been a drink-n-drug fest planned for the Huff residence, it was off now. He didn't want to follow up anymore with this man until he knew more. Huff had never been his favorite and even less so now.

Then again, how do you explain the GPS locator?

"Good talking to you, Dan."

"Same to you, Mike."

"If you hear from Adam . . ."

"I'll be sure to have him call you. Have a great night. And drive safely."

" 'Whiskers on kittens,' " Nash said.

Pietra was back in the driver's seat. Nash had her follow him for approximately forty-five minutes. They parked the minivan at a lot near a Ramada in East Hanover. When it was found, the first assumption would be Reba had vanished there. The police would wonder why a married woman was visiting a hotel lot so close to her home. They would think maybe she had a liaison with a boyfriend. Her husband would insist that it was impossible.

Eventually, like with Marianne, it might

be straightened out. But it would take time.

They took the articles Reba had bought from Target with them. Leaving them in the back might give the police a clue. Nash went through the bag. She had bought underwear and books and even some old family-friendly movies on DVD.

"Did you hear what I said, Reba?" He held up the DVD case. " 'Whiskers on kittens.' "

Reba was hog-tied. Her doll-like features still looked so dainty, like porcelain. Nash had taken the gag out. She looked up and groaned.

"Don't struggle," he said. "It will only make it hurt more. And you'll be doing enough suffering later."

Reba swallowed. "What . . . what do you want?"

"I'm asking you about this movie you bought." Nash held up the DVD case. "*The Sound of Music.* A classic."

"Who are you?"

"If you ask me one more question, I will start hurting you immediately. That means you will suffer more and die sooner. And if you annoy me enough, I will grab Jamie and do the same to her. Do you understand?"

The little eyes blinked as though he had reached out and slapped her. Tears sprang to them. "Please —"

"Do you remember *The Sound of Music*, yes or no?"

She tried to stop crying, tried to swallow the tears away.

"Reba?"

"Yes."

"Yes what?"

"Yes," she managed. "I remember."

Nash smiled at her. "And the line 'whiskers on kittens.' Do you remember it?"

"Yes."

"Which song was it from?"

"What?"

"The song. Do you remember the name of the song?"

"I don't know."

"Sure you do, Reba. Stop and think."

She tried, but fear, he knew, could have a paralyzing effect.

"You're confused," Nash said. "That's okay. It's from the song 'My Favorite Things.' Remember it now?"

She nodded. Then remembering: "Yes."

Nash smiled, pleased. "'Doorbells,'" he said.

She looked totally lost.

"Do you remember that part too? Julie Andrews is sitting with all these children and they had nightmares or were scared of the thunder or something and she's trying to comfort them so she tells them to start thinking about their favorite things. To take their mind off the fear. You remember, right?"

Reba started crying again, but she managed a nod.

"And they sing, 'Doorbells.' Doorbells, for crying out loud. Think about that. I could probably ask a million people to list their top five favorite things in the world and not one — *not one!* — would say doorbells. I mean, imagine: *'My favorite thing? Well, obviously doorbells. Yes, siree, that's my very favorite. A friggin' doorbell. Yep, when I really want to get happy, when I want to get turned on, I ring a doorbell. Man, that's the ticket. You know what gets me hot? One of those doorbells that make a chiming sound. Oh, yeah, that does it for me.'* "

Nash stopped, chuckled, shook his head. "You can almost see it on *Family Feud,* right? Top ten answers up on the board — your favorite things — and you say, 'Doorbell,' and Richard Dawson points behind him and goes, 'Survey says . . .' "

Nash made a buzzing noise and formed an X with his arms.

He laughed. Pietra laughed too.

"Please," Reba said. "Please tell me what you want."

"We'll get to that, Reba. We will. But I will

give you a hint."

She waited.

"Does the name Marianne mean anything to you?"

"What?"

"Marianne."

"What about her?"

"She sent you something."

The look of terror multiplied.

"Please don't hurt me."

"I'm sorry, Reba. I'm going to. I'm going to hurt you very badly."

And then he crawled into the back of the van and proved good to his word.

14

When Mike got home, he slammed the door and started for the computer. He wanted to bring up the GPS computer Web site and see exactly where Adam was. He wondered about that. The GPS was approximate, not exact. Could Adam have been in the vicinity? A block away maybe? In the woods nearby or the Huffs' backyard?

He was about to call up the Web site when he heard a knock on the front door. He sighed, rose, looked out the window. It was Susan Loriman.

He opened the door. She had her hair down now and no makeup and he once again hated himself for thinking that she was a very attractive woman. Some women just have it. You can't quite pinpoint why or how. Their faces and figures are nice, sometimes great, but there is that intangible, the one that makes a man a little weak in the knees. Mike would never act upon it, but if you didn't recognize it for what it was and realize that it was there, it could be even more dangerous.

"Hi," she said.

"Hi."

She didn't come in. That would set tongues wagging if any of the neighbors were watching and in a neighborhood like this there was bound to be one. Susan stood on the stoop, arms folded, a neighbor asking for a cup of sugar.

"Do you know why I called you?" he asked.

She shook her head.

He wondered how to handle this. "As you know, we need to test your son's closest biological relatives."

"Okay."

He thought about Daniel Huff's dismissal of him, the computer upstairs, the GPS in his son's phone. Mike wanted to break this to her slowly, but now was not the time for subtlety.

"That means," he said, "we need to test Lucas's biological father."

Susan blinked as though he smacked her.

"I didn't mean to just blurt —"

"You did test his father. You said he wasn't a good match."

Mike looked at her. "*Biological* father," he said.

She blinked and took a step back.

"Susan?"

"It's not Dante?"

"No. It's not Dante."

Susan Loriman closed her eyes.

"Oh, God," she said. "This can't be."

"It is."

"Are you sure?"

"Yes. You didn't know?"

She said nothing.

"Susan?"

"Are you going to tell Dante?"

Mike wondered how to answer that. "I don't think so."

"Think?"

"We are still sorting through all the ethical and legal implications here —"

"You can't tell him. He'll go crazy."

Mike stopped, waited.

"He loves that boy. You can't take that away from him."

"Our main concern is Lucas's well-being."

"And you think telling Dante he's not his real father will help him?"

"No, but listen to me, Susan. Our main concern is Lucas's health. That's priority one, two and three. That trumps every other concern. Right now that means finding the best possible donor for the transplant. So I'm not raising this with you to be nosy or to break up a family. I'm raising this as a concerned physician. We need to get the biological father tested."

She lowered her head. Her eyes were wet. She bit down on her lower lip.

"Susan?"

"I need to think," she said.

He normally would press this, but there was no reason to right now. Nothing would happen tonight and he had his own concerns. "We will need to test the father."

"Just let me think this through, okay?"

"Okay."

She looked at him with sad eyes. "Don't tell Dante. Please, Mike."

She didn't wait for him to respond. She turned and left. Mike closed the door and headed back upstairs. Nice couple of weeks for her. *"Susan Loriman, your son may have a fatal illness and needs a transplant. Oh, and your husband is about to find out the kid isn't his! What's next? We're going to Disneyland!"*

The house was so silent. Mike wasn't used to it. He tried to remember the last time he'd been here alone — no kids, no Tia — but the answer eluded him. He liked downtime by himself. Tia was the opposite. She wanted people around her all the time.

She came from a big family and hated to be alone. Mike normally reveled in it.

He got back to the computer and clicked the icon. He'd bookmarked the GPS site. A cookie had saved the sign-on name, but he needed to enter the password. He did. There was a voice in his head that screamed for him to let it go. Adam has to lead his own life. He has to make and learn from his own mistakes.

Was he being overprotective to make up for his own childhood?

Mike's father had never been there. Not his fault, of course. He had been an immigrant from Hungary, running away right before Budapest fell in 1956. His father, Antal Baye — it was pronounced *bye* not *bay* and had a French origin though no one could trace the tree back that far — hadn't spoken a word of English when he arrived at Ellis Island. He started off as a dishwasher, scraped together enough to open a small luncheonette off McCarter Highway in Newark, worked his ass off seven days a week, made a life for himself and his family.

The luncheonette served three meals, sold comic books and baseball cards, newspapers and magazines, cigars and cigarettes. Lottery tickets were a big item, though Antal never really liked to sell them. He felt that it was doing the community a disservice, encouraging his hardworking clientele to throw away money on false dreams. He had no problem selling cigarettes — that was your choice and you knew what you were getting. But something about selling the false dream of easy money bothered the man.

His father never had time for Mike's Pee-Wee hockey games. That was just a given. Men like him just didn't do that. He was interested in everything about his son, asked constantly about it, wanted to know every detail, but his work hours did not allow time for a leisure activity of any sort, certainly not sitting and watching. The one time he had come, when Mike was nine years old and playing a game outdoors, his father, so exhausted from work, had fallen asleep against a tree. Even that day, Antal wore his work apron, the grease stains from that morning's bacon sandwiches dotting the white.

That was how Mike always saw his father, with that white apron on, behind the counter, selling the kids candy, looking out for shoplifters, quick-cooking breakfast sandwiches and burgers.

When Mike was twelve years old, his father tried to stop a local hood from shoplifting. The hood shot his father and killed him. Just like that.

The luncheonette went into foreclosure. Mom went into the bottle and didn't get out until early Alzheimer's ate away enough to not make a difference. She now lived in a nursing home in Caldwell. Mike visited once a month. His mother had no idea who he was. Sometimes she called him Antal and asked him if he wanted her to prepare potato salad for the lunch rush.

That was life. Make difficult choices, leave home and all you love, give up everything you have, travel halfway around the world to a strange land, build a life for yourself — and some worthless pile of scum ends it all with a trigger pull.

That early rage turned to focus for young Mike. You channel it out or you internalize it. He became a better hockey player. He became a better student. He studied and worked hard and kept busy because when you're busy you don't think of what should have been.

The map came up on the computer. This time the red dot was blinking. That meant, Mike knew from the little tutorial, that the person was on the move, probably in a car. The Web site had explained that GPS locators eat up battery life. To conserve energy, rather than sending out a continuous signal, they give off a hit every three minutes. If the person stopped moving for more than five minutes, the GPS would turn itself off, starting again when it sensed motion.

His son was crossing the George Washington Bridge.

Why would Adam be doing that?

Mike waited. Adam was clearly traveling by car. Whose? Mike watched the red dot blink across the Cross Bronx Expressway, down the Major Deegan, into the Bronx. Where was he going? This made no sense. Twenty minutes later, the red dot seemed to stop moving on Tower Street. Mike didn't know the area at all.

Now what?

Stay here and watch the red dot? That didn't make much sense. But if he drove in and tried to track Adam down, he might move again.

Mike stared at the red dot.

He clicked the icon that would tell him the address. It gave him 128 Tower Street. He clicked for the address link. It was a residence. He asked for a satellite view — this was where the map turned into exactly what it sounded like: a photo from a satellite above the street. It showed him very little, the top of buildings in the middle of a city street.

He moved down the block and clicked for address links. Nothing much popped up.

So who or what was he visiting?

He asked for a telephone number to 128 Tower Street. It was an apartment building so it didn't have one. He needed an apartment number.

Now what?

He hit MapQuest. The START or default address was called "home." Such a simple word yet suddenly it seemed too warm and personal. The printout told him it would take forty-nine minutes to get there.

He decided to drive in and see what was what.

Mike grabbed his laptop with the built-in wireless. His plan, as it were, was that if Adam was no longer there, he would drive until he could piggyback on someone else's wireless network and look up Adam's location on the GPS again.

Two minutes later, Mike got into his car and started on his way.

15

As he pulled onto Tower Street, not far from where the GPS had told him Adam was, Mike scanned the block for his son or a familiar face or vehicle. Did any of them drive yet? Olivia Burchell, he thought. Had she turned seventeen? He wasn't sure. He wanted to check the GPS, see if Adam was still in the right area. He pulled to the side and turned on his laptop. No wireless network detected.

The crowd outside his car window was young and dressed in black with pale faces and black lipstick and eye mascara. They wore chains and had strange facial (and probably corporeal) piercings and, of course, the requisite tattoo, the best way to show that you're independent and shocking by fitting in and doing what all your friends do. Nobody is comfortable in his own skin. The poor kids want to look rich, what with the expensive sneakers and the bling and what have you. The rich want to look poor, gangsta tough, apologizing for their softness and what they see as their parents' excess, which, without doubt, they will emulate someday soon. Or was something less dramatic at play here? Was the grass simply greener on the other side? Mike wasn't sure.

Either way he was glad Adam had only taken to the black clothes. So far, no piercing, tattoos or makeup. So far.

The emos — they were no longer called goths, according to Jill, though her friend Yasmin had insisted that they were two separate entities and this led to much debate — dominated this particular stretch. They grazed about with open mouths and vacant eyes and slacker bad posture. Some people lined up at a nightclub on one corner, others frequented a bar on another. There was a place advertising "nonstop 24-hour Go-Go" and Mike couldn't help but wonder if that was true, if there was really a go-go dancer there every day, even at four A.M. or two in the afternoon. How about on Christmas morning or July Fourth? And who were the sad people who both worked and frequented such a place at such an hour?

Could Adam be inside?

There was no way to know. Dozens of such places lined the streets. Big bouncers with earplugs you usually associate with either the Secret Service or Old Navy employees stood guard. It used to be only some clubs had bouncers. Now, it seemed, all had at least two beefy guys — always with a tight black T-shirt that exposed bloated biceps, always with a shaved head as if hair were a sign of weakness — working the door.

Adam was sixteen. These places weren't supposed to let anyone in under the age of twenty-one. Unlikely Adam, even with a fake ID, could pass. But who knows? Maybe there was a club in this area that was known for looking the other way. That would explain why Adam and his friends would drive so far to go here. Satin Dolls, the famed gentlemen's club that was used as Bada Bing! on *The Sopranos,* was just a few miles from their house. But Adam wouldn't be able to get in.

That had to be why he came all the way here.

Mike drove down the street with the laptop in the passenger seat next to him. He stopped at the corner and hit VIEW WIRELESS NETWORKS. Two popped up but both had security features. He couldn't get on. Mike moved another hundred yards, tried again. On his third time, he hit pay dirt. "Netgear" network came up with no security features at all. Mike quickly hit the CONNECT button and he was on the Internet.

He had already bookmarked the GPS home page and told it to save his screen name. Now he brought it up and typed in his simple password — ADAM — and waited.

The map came up. The red dot hadn't moved. According to the disclaimer, the GPS only gave you markings to within forty feet. So it was hard to pinpoint exactly where Adam was, but he was definitely close by. Mike shut down the computer.

Okay, now what?

He found a spot up ahead and pulled in. The area would be kindly described as seedy. There were more windows boarded up than containing anything resembling the glass family. The brick all seemed to be a muddy brown and in various stage of either disintegration or collapse. The stench of sweat and something harder to define clogged the air. Storefronts had their graffiti-splattered metal hoods pulled down in protection. Mike's breath felt hot in his throat. Everyone seemed to be perspiring.

The women wore spaghetti straps and small shorts, and at the risk of seeming hopelessly old-fashioned and politically incorrect, he wasn't sure if these were just teenage partyers or working girls.

He stepped out of his car. A tall black

woman approached and said, "Hey, Joe, want to party with Latisha?"

Her voice was deep. Her hands were big. And now Mike wasn't sure "her" would be accurate.

"No, thanks."

"You sure? It would open up new worlds."

"I'm sure it would, but my worlds are open enough as it is."

Posters of bands you never heard of with names like Pap Smear and Gonorrhea Pus plastered any free space. On one stoop, a mother propped her baby on her hip, sweat glistening off her face, a bare lightbulb swinging behind her. Mike spotted a makeshift parking lot in an abandoned alleyway. The sign said ALL NIGHT, $10. A Latino man wearing a wifebeater tee and cut-off shorts stood by the drive, counting money. He eyed Mike and said, "What you want, bro?"

"Nothing."

Mike moved on. He found the address that the GPS showed him. It was a walk-up residence jammed between two loud clubs. He looked inside and saw about a dozen buzzers to ring. No names on the buzzers — just numbers and letters to indicate each.

So now what?

He didn't have a clue.

He could wait out here for Adam. But what good would that do? It was ten o'clock at night. The places were just starting to fill up. If his son was here partying and had directly disobeyed him, it could be hours before he came out. And then what? Would Mike pop out in front of Adam and his friends and say, "Aha, got ya!" Would that somehow be helpful? How would Mike explain how he ended up here?

What did Mike and Tia want out of this anyway?

This was yet another problem with spying. Forget the obvious violation of privacy for the moment. There was the issue of enforcement. What do you do when you find something going on? Wouldn't interfering and thus losing your child's trust do as much or more damage as a night of underage drinking?

Depends.

Mike wanted to make sure his boy was safe. That was all. He remembered what Tia had said, something about our job being to escort them safely to adulthood. It was true in part. The teen years were so angst-filled, so hormone-fueled, so much emotion packed in and then raised to the tenth power — and it all passed so quickly. You couldn't tell a teen that. If you could hand down one piece of wisdom to a teenager, it would be simple: This too shall pass — and it would pass quickly. They wouldn't listen, of course, because that's the beauty and waste of youth.

He thought about Adam's instant-messaging with CeeJay8115. He thought about Tia's reaction and his own gut instinct. He was not a religious man and didn't believe in psychic powers or anything like that, but he didn't like to go against what he would describe as certain vibes in both his personal and professional life. There were times things simply felt wrong. It could be in a medical diagnosis or in what route to take on a long car trip. It was just something in the air, a crackle, a hush, but Mike had learned to ignore it at his own peril.

Right now every vibe was screaming that his son was in serious trouble.

So find him.

How?

He had no idea. He started back up the street. Several hookers propositioned him. Most seemed male. One guy in a business suit claimed to be "representing" a variety pack of "steaming hot" ladies and all Mike had to do was give him a laundry list of physical attributes and desires and said representative would procure him the proper mate or mates. Mike actually listened to the sales pitch before turning it down.

He kept his eyes moving. Some of the young girls frowned when they felt his gaze. Mike looked around and realized that he was probably the oldest person on this crowded street by something like twenty years. He noticed that every club made the clientele wait for at least a few minutes. One had a pitiful velvet rope, maybe a yard long, and the guy would make whoever wanted to come in stand behind it for maybe ten seconds before opening the door.

Mike was turning to the right when something caught his eye.

A varsity jacket.

He spun quickly and spotted the Huff kid walking the other way.

Or at least it looked like DJ Huff. That varsity jacket the kid always wore was on his back. So maybe that was him. Probably.

No, Mike thought, he was sure. It was DJ Huff.

He had disappeared down a side street. Mike quickly picked up his pace and followed him. When he lost sight of the kid, he started to jog.

"Whoa! Slow down, gramps!"

He had bumped into some kid with a shaved head and a chain hanging from his lower lip. His buddies laughed at the gramps line. Mike frowned and slid past him. The street was packed now, the crowd seeming to grow with each step. As he hit the next block, the black goths — oops, emos — seemed to thin out in favor of a more Latino crowd. Mike heard Spanish being spoken. The baby-powder white skin had been exchanged for shades of olive. The men wore dress shirts unbuttoned all the way so as to show the bright white, ribbed tee underneath. The women were salsa sexy and called the men *"coños"* and wore outfits that were so sheer they seemed more like sausage casing than clothing.

Up ahead Mike saw DJ Huff bear right down another street. It looked like he had a cell phone pressed against his ear. Mike hurried to catch up to him . . . but then what would he do? Again. Grab him and say, "Aha!" Maybe. Maybe he would just follow him, see where he was going. Mike didn't know what was going on here, but he didn't like it. Fear started nibbling at the base of his brain.

He veered right.

And the Huff boy was gone.

Mike pulled up. He tried to gauge the speed, how much time had elapsed. There was one club about a quarter of the way down the block. That was the only visible door. DJ Huff had to have gone in there. The line outside the place was long — the longest Mike had seen. Had to be a hundred kids. The crowd was a mix — the emos, Latinos, African Americans, even a few of what they used to call yuppies.

Wouldn't Huff have had to wait on line?

Maybe not. There was a super-huge bodyguard behind a velvet rope. A stretch limousine pulled up. Two leggy girls stepped out. A man nearly a foot shorter than the leggy girls took his seemingly rightful place between them. The super-huge bouncer opened the velvet rope — this rope being about ten feet long — and let them right in.

Mike sprinted toward the entrance. The bouncer — a big black guy with arms the relative thickness of your average hundred-year-old redwood — gave Mike a bored look, as if Mike were an inanimate object. A chair maybe. A disposable razor.

"I need to get in," Mike said.

"Name."

"I'm not on any list."

The bouncer just looked at him some more.

"I think my son might be inside. He's underage."

The bouncer said nothing.

"Look," Mike said, "I don't want any trouble —"

"Then get to the end of the line. Though I don't think you'll get in anyway."

"This is something of an emergency. His friend just came in two seconds ago. His name is DJ Huff."

The bouncer took a step closer. First his chest, big enough to use as a squash court, then the rest of him. "I'm going to have to ask you to move now."

"My son is underage."

"I heard you."

"I need to get him out or it could mean big trouble."

The bouncer ran his catcher-mitt hand across his cleanly shaven black dome. "Big trouble, you say?"

"Yes."

"My, my, now I'm really worried."

Mike reached into his wallet, peeled off a bill.

"Don't bother," the bouncer said. "You're not getting in."

"You don't understand."

The bouncer took another step. His chest was almost against Mike's face now. Mike closed his eyes, but he didn't step back. Hockey training — you don't back down. He opened his eyes and stared at the big man.

"Back up," Mike said.

"You're going to be leaving us now."

"I said, back up."

"I'm not going anywhere."

"I'm here to find my son."

"There is no one underage in here."

"I want to go in."

"Then get on the end of the line."

Mike kept his eyes locked on the big man's. Neither moved. They looked like prizefighters, albeit in different weight classes, being given instructions at center ring. Mike could feel a crackle in the air. He felt a tingle in his limbs. He knew how to fight. You don't get that far in hockey without knowing how to use your fists. He wondered if this guy was for real or just show muscle.

"I'm going inside," Mike said.

"You serious?"

"I have friends with the police department," Mike said, a total bluff. "They'll raid the place. If you have underage kids in here, you'll go down."

"My, my. I'm scared again."

"Get out of my way."

Mike stepped to the right. The big bodyguard followed him, blocking his path.

"You realize," the big bouncer said, "that this is about to get physical."

Mike knew the cardinal rule: Never, ever

show fear. "Yup."

"A tough guy, eh."

"You ready to go?"

The bouncer smiled. He had terrific teeth, pearly white against his black skin. "No. Do you want to know why? Because even if you are tougher than I think, which I doubt, I got Reggie and Tyrone right there." He pointed with this thumb to two other big guys dressed in black. "We aren't here to prove our manhood by taking on some dumb ass, so we don't need to fight fair. If you and I 'go' " — he said it in a way that mocked Mike's voice — "they'll join in. Reggie has got a police Taser. You understand?"

The bouncer folded his arms across his chest, and that was when Mike spotted the tattoo.

It was a green letter D on his forearm.

"What's your name?" Mike asked.

"What?"

"Your name," Mike said to the bouncer. "What is it?"

"Anthony."

"And your last name?"

"What's it to you?"

Mike pointed to his arm. "The D tattoo."

"That has nothing to do with my name."

"Dartmouth?"

Anthony the bouncer stared at him. Then

he nodded slowly. "You?"

"Vox clamantis in deserto," Mike said, reciting the school's motto.

Anthony handled the translation: "A voice crying in the wilderness." He smiled. "Never quite got that."

"Me neither," Mike said. "You play ball?"

"Football. All-Ivy. You?"

"Hockey."

"All-Ivy?"

"And All-American," Mike said.

Anthony arched an eyebrow, impressed.

"You have any children, Anthony?"

"I have a three-year-old son."

"And if you thought your kid was in trouble, would you, Reggie and Tyrone be able to stop you from getting inside?"

Anthony let loose a long breath. "What makes you so sure your kid is inside?"

Mike told him about seeing DJ Huff in the varsity jacket.

"That kid?" Anthony shook his head. "He didn't come in here. You think I'd let some chicken-ass in a high school varsity jacket in? He ran down that alley."

He pointed about ten more yards up the street.

"Any idea where it goes?" Mike asked.

"Dead-ends, I think. I don't go back there. No reason to. It's for junkies and the like.

Now I need a favor from you."
Mike waited.
"Everyone is watching us going at it here. I just let you go, I lose cred — and out here I live on cred. You know what I'm saying?"
"I do."
"So I'm going to cock my fist and you're going to run off like a scared little girl. You can run down the alley if you want. Do you understand me?"
"Can I ask one thing first?"
"What?"
Mike reached into his wallet.
"I already told you," Anthony said. "I don't want —"
Mike showed him a picture of Adam.
"Have you seen this kid?"
Anthony swallowed hard.
"This is my son. Have you seen him?"
"He's not in here."
"That's not what I asked."
"Never seen him. And now?"
Anthony grabbed Mike by the lapel and cocked his fist. Mike cowered and screamed, "Please don't, okay, I'm sorry, I'm going!" He pulled back. Anthony let him go. Mike started to run. Behind him he heard Anthony say, "Yeah, boy, you better run. . . ."
Some of the patrons applauded. Mike sprinted down the block and turned into

the alley. He almost tripped over a row of dented trash cans. Broken glass crunched beneath his feet. He stopped short, looked ahead, and saw yet another hooker. Or at least he figured that she was a hooker. She leaned against a brown Dumpster as if it were a part of her, another limb, and if it was gone she would fall and never get up. Her wig was a purplish hue and looked like something stolen from David Bowie's closet in 1974. Or maybe Bowie's dented trash can. It looked like bugs were crawling in it.

The woman smiled toothlessly at him.

"Hey, baby."

"Did you see a boy run through here?"

"Lots of boys run through here, sugar."

If her voice had picked up a notch, it may have registered as languid. She was skinny and pale and though the word "junkie" wasn't tattooed on her forehead, it might as well have been.

Mike looked for a way out. There was none. There was no exit, no doors. He spotted several fire escapes, but they looked pretty rusty. So if Huff had indeed gone here, how had he gotten out? Where had he gone to — or had he sneaked out while he argued with Anthony? Or had Anthony been lying to him, trying to get rid of him?

"You looking for that high school boy, sugar?"

Mike stopped and turned back to the junkie.

"The high school boy. All young and handsome and everything? Ooo, baby, it excites me just to talk about him."

Mike took a tentative step toward her, almost afraid that a big step might cause too much vibration and make her fall apart and vanish into the rubble already at her feet. "Yes."

"Well, come here, sugar, and I'll tell you where he is."

Another step.

"Closer, sugar. I don't bite. Unless you into that kind of thing."

Her laugh was a nightmarish cackle. Her front bridge dropped down when she opened her mouth. She chewed bubble gum — Mike could smell it — but it didn't cover up the decay from some sort of dead tooth.

"Where is he?"

"You got some money?"

"Plenty if you tell me where he is."

"Let me see some."

Mike didn't like it, but he didn't know what else to do. He pulled out a twenty-dollar bill. She reached out a bony hand. The hand reminded Mike of his old *Tales from the Crypt* comic books, the skeleton reaching out of the coffin.

"Tell me first," he said.

"You don't trust me?"

Mike didn't have time. He ripped the bill and gave her half. She took it, sighed.

"I'll give you the other half when you talk," Mike said. "Where is he?"

"Why, sugar," she said, "he's right behind you."

Mike started to turn when someone punched him in the liver.

A good liver shot will take out all the fight and temporarily paralyze you. Mike knew that. This one didn't do that, but it came damn close. The pain was staggering. Mike's mouth opened, but no sound came out. He dropped to one knee. A second blow came from the side and hit him in the ear. Something hard ricocheted across his head. Mike tried to process, tried to swim through the onslaught, but another blow, a kick this time, got him underneath the ribs. He flopped onto his back.

Instinct took over.

Move, he thought.

Mike rolled and felt something sharp dig into his arm. Broken glass probably. He tried to scramble away. But another blow hit him in the head. He could almost feel his brain jar to the left. A hand grabbed his ankle.

Mike kicked out. His heel connected with something soft and pliable. A voice yelled, "Damn!"

Someone jumped on him. Mike had been in scrapes before, though always on ice. Still he'd learned a few things. For example, you don't throw punches if you don't have to. Punches break hands. At a distance, yes, you might do that. But this was in close. He bent his arm and swung blindly. His forearm connected. There was a cracking, squelching noise and blood spurted.

Mike realized that he'd hit a nose.

He took another blow, tried to roll with it. He kicked out wildly. It was dark, the night filling with grunts of exertion. He reared his head back, tried to head-butt.

"Help!" Mike shouted. "Help! Police!"

He somehow scrambled to his feet. He couldn't see faces. But there was more than one of them. More than two, he guessed. They all jumped him at the same time. He crashed against the Dumpsters. Bodies, including his, tumbled to the ground. Mike fought hard, but they were all over him now. He managed to scratch a face with his fingernails. His shirt got torn.

And then Mike saw a blade.

That froze him. For how long, he couldn't

say. But long enough. He saw the blade and he froze and then he felt a dull thud on the side of his head. He dropped back, his skull smacking the pavement. Someone pinned down his arms. Someone else got his legs. He felt a thud on his chest. Then the blows seemed to come from everywhere. Mike tried to move, tried to cover up, but his arms and legs wouldn't obey.

He could feel himself slipping away. Surrendering.

The blows stopped. Mike felt the weight on his chest lessen. Someone had gotten up or been knocked off him. His legs were free.

Mike opened his eyes, but there were only shadows. A final kick, a toe shot, landed squarely on the side of his head. All became darkness until finally there was nothing at all.

16

At three in the morning, Tia tried Mike's phone yet again.

No answer.

The Boston Four Seasons was beautiful and she loved her room. Tia loved staying in fancy hotels — who didn't? She loved the sheets and the room service and flipping the television by herself. She had worked hard until midnight, burying herself in preparation for tomorrow's deposition. The cell phone sat in her pocket, set on vibrate. When it wouldn't go off, Tia would pull it out and check the bars and make sure that she hadn't maybe missed the vibration.

But no calls came in.

Where the hell was Mike?

She called him, of course. She called the house. She called Adam's cell phone. Panic played at her fringes; she tried hard not to let it all the way in. Adam was one thing. Mike another. Mike was a grown man. He was ridiculously competent. That was one of the things that first attracted her to him. Antifeminist as that might sound, Mike Baye made her feel safe and warm and fully protected. He was a rock.

Tia wondered what to do.

She could get in the car and drive home. It would take about four hours, maybe five. She could be home by morning. But what exactly would she do when she arrived? Should she call the police — but would they listen so soon and really what would they do at this hour?

Three A.M. Only one person she could think to call.

His number was on her BlackBerry, though she had never actually used it. She and Mike shared a Microsoft Outlook program that contained one address and phone book, plus a calendar, for both of them. They synchronized their BlackBerrys with each other and in this way, the theory went, they would know each other's appointments. It also meant that they would have all the other's personal and business contact information.

And in that way, it showed they had no secrets, didn't it?

She thought about that — about secrets and inner thoughts, about our need for them, and as a mother and wife, her fear of them. But there was no time now. She found the number and hit the SEND button.

If Mo had been asleep, he didn't sound like it.

"Hello?"

"It's Tia."

"What's wrong?"

She could hear the fear in his voice. The man had no wife, no kids. In many ways, he only had Mike. "Have you heard from Mike?"

"Not since about eight thirty." Then he repeated: "What's wrong?"

"He was trying to find Adam."

"I know."

"We spoke about that around nine, I guess. Haven't heard a word since."

"Did you call his cell?"

Tia now knew how Mike had felt when she'd asked him something equally idiotic. "Of course."

"I'm getting dressed as we speak," Mo said. "I'll drive over and check the house. Do you still hide the key in that fake rock by that fence post?"

"Yes."

"Okay, I'm on my way."

"Do you think I should call the police?"

"Might as well wait until I get there.

Twenty, thirty minutes tops. He might have just fallen asleep in front of the TV or something."

"You believe that, Mo?"

"No. I'll call you when I get there."

He hung up. Tia swung her legs out of the bed. Suddenly the room had lost all appeal. She hated sleeping alone, even in deluxe hotels with high-thread-count sheets. She needed her husband next to her. Always. It was rare they spent nights apart and she missed him more than she wanted to say. Mike wasn't necessarily a big man, but he was substantial. She liked the warmth of his body next to hers, the way he kissed her forehead whenever he got up, the way he'd rest his strong hand on her sleeping back.

She remembered one night when Mike was a little out of breath. After much prodding, he had admitted to feeling a tightness in his chest. Tia, who wanted to be strong for her man, nearly collapsed when she heard that. It had ended up being bad indigestion, but she had openly wept at just the thought. She pictured her husband clutching his chest and falling to the floor. And she knew. She knew then and there that someday it could very well happen, maybe not for thirty or forty or fifty years, but it would happen, that or something equally horrible, because that was what happens to every couple, happy or not, and that she simply would not survive if it happened to him. Sometimes, late at night, Tia would watch him sleep and whisper to both Mike and the powers that be: "Promise me I'll go first. Promise me."

Call the police.

But what would they do? Nothing yet. On TV the FBI rushes out. Tia knew from a recent update on criminal law that an adult over eighteen could not even be declared missing this close in, unless she had serious evidence that he'd been kidnapped or was in physical danger.

She had nothing.

Besides, if she called now, the best-case scenario was that they'd have an officer stop by the house. Mo might be there. There could be some sort of misunderstanding.

So wait the twenty or thirty minutes.

Tia wanted to call Guy Novak's house and talk to Jill, just to hear her voice. Something to reassure. Damn. Tia had been so happy about this trip and getting into this luxurious room and throwing on the big terry cloth robe and ordering room service and now all she wanted was the familiar. This room had no life, no warmth. The loneliness made her shiver. Tia got up and lowered the air-conditioning.

It was all so damn fragile, that was the thing. Obvious, sure, but for the most part we block — we refuse to think about how easily our lives could be torn asunder, because when we recognize it, we lose our minds. The ones who are fearful all the time, who need to medicate to function? It is because they understand the reality, how thin the line is. It isn't that they can't accept the truth — it's that they can't block it.

Tia could be that way. She knew it and fought hard to keep it at bay. She suddenly envied her boss, Hester Crimstein, for not having anybody. Maybe that was better. Sure, on a larger scale, it was healthy to have people out there you cared about more than yourself. She knew that. But then there was the abject fear you would lose it. They say possessions own you. Not so. Loved ones own you. You are forever held hostage once you care so much.

The clock wouldn't move.

Tia waited. She flicked on the television. Infomercials dominated the late-night landscape. Commercials for training and jobs and schools — the only people who watch TV at this crazy hour, she guessed, had none of those things.

The cell phone finally buzzed at nearly four in the morning. Tia snatched it up, saw

Mo's number on the caller ID, answered it.

"Hello?"

"No sign of Mike," Mo said. "No sign of Adam either."

Loren Muse's door read ESSEX COUNTY CHIEF INVESTIGATOR. She stopped and silently read it every time she opened the door. Her office was in the right-hand corner. Her detectives had desks on the same floor. Loren's office was windowed and she never closed her door. She wanted to feel one with them and yet above them. When she needed privacy, which was rare, she used one of the interrogation rooms that also lined the station.

Only two other detectives were in when she arrived at six thirty A.M. and both were about to head out when the shift changed at seven. Loren checked the blackboard to make sure that there were no new homicides. There were none. She hoped to get the results from the NCIC on the fingerprints of her Jane Doe, the not-a-whore in the morgue. She checked the computer. Nothing yet.

The Newark police had located a working surveillance camera not far from the Jane Doe murder scene. If the body had been transported to that spot in a car — and there was no reason to think someone carried it — then the vehicle could very well be on the tape. Of course, figuring out which one would be a hell of a task. Probably hundreds of vehicles would be on it and she doubted one would have a sign on the back reading BODY IN TRUNK.

She checked her computer and yep, the stream had been downloaded. The office was quiet, so she figured, well, why not? She was about to hit the PLAY button when someone rapped lightly on her door.

"Got a second, Chief?"

Clarence Morrow stood outside her doorway and leaned his head in. He was nearing sixty, a black man with a coarse gray-white mustache and a face where everything looked a little swollen, as if he'd just gotten into a fight. There was gentleness to him and unlike every other guy in this division, he never swore or drank.

"Sure, Clarence, what's up?"

"I almost called you at home last night."

"Oh?"

"I thought I figured out the name of your Jane Doe."

That made Loren sit up. "But?"

"We got a call from the Livingston PD about a Mr. Neil Cordova. He lives in town and owns a chain of barbershops. Married, two kids, no record. Anyway, he said his wife, Reba, was missing and, well, she roughly matched your Jane Doe's description."

"But?" Muse said again.

"But she disappeared yesterday — after we found the body."

"You're sure?"

"Positive. The husband said he saw her that morning before he went to work."

"He could be lying."

"I don't think so."

"Did anyone look into it?"

"Not at first. But here's the funny thing. Cordova knew someone on the police force in town. You know how it is out there. Everyone knows someone. They found her car. It was parked at the Ramada in East Hanover."

"Ah," Muse said. "A hotel."

"Right."

"So Mrs. Cordova wasn't really missing?"

"Well," Clarence said, stroking his chin, "that's the funny thing."

"What is?"

"Naturally the Livingston cop felt like you did. Mrs. Cordova hooked up with some lover and was late getting home or something. That's when he called me — the Livingston cop, that is. He didn't want to be the one to tell his friend, the husband, this news. So he calls me to do it. As a favor."

"Go on."

"So what do I know — I call Cordova. I explain that we found his wife's car in a local hotel lot. He tells me that's impossible. I tell him it's there right now, if he wants to go see it." He stopped. "Damn."

"What?"

"Should I have told him that? I mean, thinking back on it. Might have been an invasion of her privacy to tell him. And suppose he showed up there with a gun or something? Man, I didn't think that through." Clarence frowned under his coarse mustache. "Should I have kept quiet about the car, Chief?"

"Don't worry about it."

"Okay, whatever. Anyway, this Cordova refuses to believe what I'm suggesting."

"Like most men."

"Right, sure, but then he says something interesting. He says he first started to panic when she didn't pick up their nine-year-old daughter from some special ice-skating class in Airmont. That wouldn't be like her. He said she'd planned to spend some time at the Palisades Mall in Nyack — he said she likes to buy the kids basics at Target — and then head over to pick up the girl."

"And the mother never showed?"

"Right. The ice rink called the father's cell phone when they couldn't reach the mother. Cordova drove up and picked the kid up. He figured that maybe his wife got stuck in traffic or something. There was an accident on 287 earlier in the day and she was bad about keeping her cell phone charged, so he was concerned but didn't go into full panic when he didn't reach her. As it got later and later, he got more and more worried."

Muse thought about it. "If Mrs. Cordova met up with a boyfriend at a hotel, she might have just forgotten to pick up the kid."

"I agree, except for one thing. Cordova already went online and checked his wife's credit card records. She had been up at the Palisades Mall that afternoon. She did indeed buy stuff at Target. Spent forty-seven dollars and eighteen cents."

"Hmm." Muse signaled for Clarence to take a seat. He did so. "So she goes way up to the Palisades Mall and then comes all the way back down to meet the lover, forgetting her kid who is getting skating lessons right near the mall." She looked at him. "Does sound weird."

"You had to hear his voice, Chief. The husband's, I mean. He was so distraught."

"I guess you could check with the Ramada, see if anybody recognizes her."

"I did. I had the husband scan a photo and e-mail it over. No one remembers seeing her."

"That doesn't mean much. New people are probably on duty and she could have sneaked in after, I don't know, her lover checked in. But her car is still there?"

"Yep. And that's weird, isn't it? For the car to still be there? You have your affair, you get back in your car, you drive home, or whatever. So even if it was an affair, wouldn't you think by now it's an affair gone wrong? Like he grabbed her or there was some violence —"

"— or she ran away with him."

"Right, that could be it too. But it's a nice car. Acura MDX, four months old. Wouldn't you take that?"

Muse thought about it, shrugged.

Clarence said, "I want to look into it, okay?"

"Go for it." She thought about it some more. "Do me a favor. Check and see if any other women have been reported missing in Livingston or that area. Even if just for a short while. Even if the cops didn't take it too seriously."

"Already did it."

"And?"

"None. Oh, but some woman called to

report her husband and son were missing." He checked his pad. "Her name is Tia Baye. Husband is Mike, son is Adam."

"The locals looking into it?"

"I guess, I don't really know."

"If it wasn't for the missing kid too," Muse said, "maybe this Baye guy ran off with Mrs. Cordova."

"You want me to look for a connection?"

"If you want. If that's the case, it's not a criminal matter anyway. Two consenting adults are allowed to disappear together for a little while."

"Yeah, okay. But, Chief?"

Muse loved that he called her that. Chief. "What?"

"I got a feeling there's something more here."

"Go with that then, Clarence. Keep me in the loop."

17

In a dream there is a beeping sound and then the words: *"I'm so sorry, Dad. . . ."*

In reality Mike heard someone speaking Spanish in the dark.

He spoke enough of it — you can't work at a hospital on 168th Street and not speak at least medical Spanish — and so he recognized that the woman was praying furiously. Mike tried to turn his head, but it wouldn't move. Didn't matter. All was black. His head thudded at the temples as the woman in the dark repeated her prayer over and over.

Meanwhile, Mike had his own mantra going on:

Adam. Where is Adam?

Mike slowly realized that his eyes were closed. He tried to open them. That wouldn't happen right away. He listened some more and tried to focus on his eyelids, on the simple act of lifting them up. It took a little while but eventually they began to blink. The thudding in his temples grew into hammer pounds. He reached a hand up and pushed at the side of his head, as if he could contain the pain that way.

He squinted at the fluorescent light on the white ceiling. The Spanish praying continued. The familiar smell filled the air, that combination of harsh cleaners, bodily functions, wilting fauna and absolutely no natural air circulation. Mike's head dropped to the left. He saw the back of a woman hunched over a bed. Her fingers moved over the prayer beads. Her head seemed to be resting on a man's chest. She alternated between sobs and prayers — and a blend of the two.

He tried to reach his hand out and say something comforting to her. Ever the doctor. But there was an IV in his arm and it slowly dawned on him that he too was a patient. He tried to remember what had happened, how he could possibly have ended up here. It took a while. His brain was cloudy. He fought through it.

There had been a terrible unease in him when he woke up. He had tried to push that away but for the sake of his memory he let it back in now. And as soon as he did, that mantra came back to him, this time just the one word:

Adam.

The rest flooded in. He had gone to look for Adam. He had talked to that bouncer, Anthony. He had gone down that alley. There had been that scary woman with the horrible wig. . . .

There had been a knife.

Had he been stabbed?

He didn't think so. He turned the other way. Another patient. A black man with his eyes closed. Mike looked for his family, but there was no one here for him. That shouldn't surprise him — he might have only been out for a short time. They would have to contact Tia. She was in Boston. It would take time for her to arrive. Jill was at the Novaks' house. And Adam . . . ?

In the movies, when a patient wakes up like this, it's in a private room and the doctor and nurse are already there, as though they'd been waiting all night, smiling down with lots of answers. There was no health professional in sight. Mike knew the routine. He searched for his call button, found it wrapped around the bed railings, and pressed for the nurse.

It took some time. Hard to say how much. Time crawled by. The praying woman's voice faded into silence. She stood up and wiped her eyes. Mike could see the man in the bed now. Considerably younger than the woman. Mother-son, he figured. He wondered what brought them here.

He looked out the windows behind her. The shades were open and there was sunlight.

Daytime.

He had lost consciousness at night. Hours ago. Or maybe days. Who knew? He started pressing the call button even though he knew that it did no good. Panic began to take hold. The pain in his head steadily grew — someone was taking a jackhammer to his right temple.

"Well, well."

He turned toward the doorway. The nurse, a heavy woman with reading glasses perched upon her huge bosom, strolled in. Her name tag read BERTHA BONDY. She looked down at him and frowned.

"Welcome to the free world, sleepyhead. How are you feeling?"

It took Mike a second or two to find his voice. "Like I kissed a Mack truck."

"Probably be more sanitary than what you were doing. Are you thirsty?"

"Parched."

Bertha nodded, picked up a cup of ice. She tilted it to his lips. The ice tasted medicinal, but man it felt good in his mouth.

"You're at Bronx-Lebanon Hospital," Bertha said. "Do you remember what happened?"

"Someone jumped me. Bunch of guys, I guess."

"Hmm hmm. What's your name?"

"Mike Baye."

"Can you spell the last name for me?"

He did, figuring this was a cognitive test, so he volunteered some information. "I'm a physician," he said. "I do transplant surgery out of NewYork-Presbyterian."

She frowned some more, as though he'd given her the wrong answer. "For real?"

"Yes."

More frowning.

"Do I pass?" he asked.

"Pass?"

"The cognitive test."

"I'm not the doctor. He'll be by in a little while. I asked your name because we don't know who you are. You came in with no wallet, no cell phone, no keys, nothing. Whoever rolled you took it all."

Mike was about to say something else but a stab of pain ripped across his skull. He rode it out, bit down, counted in his head to ten. When it passed, he spoke again.

"How long have I been out?"

"All night. Six, seven hours."

"What time is it?"

"Eight in the morning."

"So no one notified my family?"

"I just told you. We didn't know who you were."

"I need a phone. I need to call my wife."

"Your wife? You sure?"

Mike's head felt fuzzy. He was probably on some kind of medication, so maybe that was why he couldn't figure out why she'd asked something so asinine.

"Of course I'm sure."

Bertha shrugged. "The phone's next to your bed, but I'll have to ask them to hook it up. You'll probably need help dialing, right?"

"I guess."

"Oh, do you have medical insurance? We have some forms that need to be filled out."

Mike wanted to smile. First things first. "I do."

"I'll send someone from admissions up to get your information. Your doctor should be by soon to talk about your injuries."

"How bad are they?"

"You took a pretty solid beating and since you were out that long, there was obviously a concussion and head trauma. But I'd rather let the doctor give you the details, if that's okay. I'll see if I can hurry him along."

He understood. Floor nurses should not

be giving him the diagnosis.

"How's the pain?" Bertha asked.

"Medium."

"You're on some pain meds now, so it'll be getting worse before it gets better. I'll hook up a morphine pump for you."

"Thanks."

"Back soon."

She started for the door. Mike thought of something else. "Nurse?"

She turned back toward him.

"Isn't there a police officer who wants to talk to me or something?"

"Excuse me?"

"I was assaulted and, from what you're saying, robbed. Wouldn't a cop be interested?"

She folded her arms across her chest. "And you think, what, they'd just sit here and wait for you to wake up?"

She had a point — like the doctor waiting on TV.

Then Bertha added: "Most people don't bother to report this kind of thing anyway."

"What kind of thing?"

She frowned again. "You want me to call the police for you too?"

"I better call my wife first."

"Yeah," she said. "Yeah, I think that's probably best."

He reached for the bed's control button.

Pain tore across his rib cage. His lungs stopped. He fumbled for the control and pushed the top button. His body curled up with the bed. He tried to squiggle more upright. He slowly reached now for the phone. He got it to his ear. It wasn't hooked up yet.

Tia must be in a panic.

Was Adam home by now?

Who the hell had jumped him?

"Mr. Baye?"

It was Nurse Bertha reappearing at the door.

"Dr. Baye," he corrected.

"Oh, silly me, I forgot."

He hadn't said it to be obnoxious, but letting a hospital know that you were a fellow physician had to be a good idea. If a cop is pulled over for speeding, he always lets the other cop know what he does for a living. File it under "Can't Hurt."

"I found an officer here for another matter," she said. "Do you want to talk to him?"

"Yes, thanks, but could you also hook up the phone?"

"Should be ready for you any minute now."

The uniformed officer entered the room. He was a small man, Latino with a thin mustache. Mike placed him in his mid-thirties.

He introduced himself as Officer Guttierez.

"Do you really want to file a report?" he asked.

"Of course."

He frowned too.

"What?"

"I'm the officer who brought you in."

"Thank you."

"You're welcome. Do you know where we found you?"

Mike thought a second. "Probably in that alley by that club. I forget the street."

"Exactly."

He looked at Mike and waited. And Mike finally saw it.

"It's not what you think," Mike said.

"What do I think?"

"That I was rolled by a hooker."

"Rolled?"

Mike tried to shrug. "I watch a lot of TV."

"Well, I'm not big on jumping to conclusions, but here's what I do know: You were found in an alley frequented by prostitutes. You're a solid twenty or thirty years older than the average club goer in that area. You're married. You got jumped and robbed and beaten in a way I've seen before, when a john gets" — he made quote marks with his fingers — " 'rolled by a hooker or her pimp.' "

"I wasn't there to solicit," Mike said.

"Uh-huh, no, no, I'm sure you were in that alley for the view. It's pretty special. And don't get me started on the delights of the aroma. Man, you don't have to explain to me. I totally get the allure."

"I was looking for my son."

"In that alley?"

"Yes. I saw a friend of his. . . ." The pain returned. He could see how this would go. It would take some time to explain. And then what? What would this cop find anyway?

He needed to reach Tia.

"I'm in a lot of pain right now," Mike said.

Guttierez nodded. "I understand. Look, here's my card. Call if you want to talk some more or fill out a complaint, okay?"

Guttierez put his card on the night table and left the room. Mike ignored it. He fought through the pain, reached for the phone, and dialed Tia's cell phone.

18

Loren Muse watched the street surveillance tape from near where her Jane Doe's body was dumped. Nothing jumped out at her, but then again, what had she expected? Several dozen vehicles drove past that lot at that hour. You couldn't really eliminate any. The body could be in the trunk of even the smallest car.

Still she kept watching and hoping and when the tape rolled to the end, she had gotten a big fat goose egg for her trouble.

Clarence knocked and stuck his head in again. "You're not going to believe this, Chief."

"I'm listening."

"First off, forget that missing man. The Baye guy. Guess where he was?"

"Where?"

"A Bronx hospital. His wife goes away on business and he goes out and gets mugged by a hooker."

Muse made a face. "A Livingston guy going for a hooker in that area?"

"What can I tell you — some people like slumming. But that's not the big news." Clarence sat down without being asked, which was out of character. His shirtsleeves were rolled up, and there was a hint of a smile breaking through the fleshy face.

"The Cordovas' Acura MDX is still in the hotel lot," he said. "The local cops knocked on some doors. She's not there. So I went backward."

"Backward?"

"The last place we knew where she was. The Palisades Mall. It's a huge mall and they got a pretty extensive security setup. So I called them."

"The security office?"

"Right, and here's the thing: Yesterday, around five P.M., some guy came in to say he saw a woman in a green Acura MDX walk to her car, load some stuff in, and then walk to a man's white van parked next to her. He says she gets in the van, not forced or anything, but then the door closes. The guy figures, no big deal except another woman comes along and gets in the woman's Acura. Then both cars drove out together."

Muse sat back. "The van and the Acura?"

"Right."

"And another woman is driving the Acura?"

"Right. So anyway, this guy reports it to the security office and the guards are like, uh, so? They don't pay any attention — I mean, what are they going to do? So they just file it. But when I call, they remember and pull the report. First off, this all took place right outside the Target. The guy came in to make the report at five fifteen P.M. We know that Reba Cordova made her purchase at Target at four fifty-two P.M. The receipt is date-stamped."

Bells started clanging, but Muse wasn't sure where they were coming from.

"Call Target," she said. "I bet they have surveillance cameras."

"We're coordinating with Target's home office as we speak. Probably take a couple of hours, no more. Something else. Maybe important, maybe not. We were able to figure out what she bought at Target. Some kid DVDs, some kid underwear, clothes — all stuff for kids."

"Not what you buy if you plan on running away with a paramour."

"Exactly, unless you're taking the kids, which she didn't. And more than that, we opened her Acura in the hotel lot, and there is no Target bag inside. The husband checked the house, in case she stopped home. No Target stuff there either."

A cold shiver started up near the base of Muse's neck.

"What?" he asked.

"I want that report from the security office. Get the guy's phone number — the one who reported seeing her get in a van. See what else he remembers — vehicles, descriptions of the passengers, anything. I'm sure the security guard didn't go over all that with him. I want to know everything."

"Okay."

They talked another minute or two, but her mind whirred and her pulse raced. When Clarence left, Muse picked up her phone and hit the cell phone for her boss, Paul Copeland.

"Hello?"

"Where are you?" Muse asked.

"I just dropped Cara off."

"I need to bounce something off you, Cope."

"When?"

"Soon as possible."

"I'm supposed to meet my bride-to-be at some restaurant to finalize the seating chart."

"The seating chart?"

"Yeah, Muse. The seating chart. It's this thing that tells people where to sit."

"And you care about this?"

"Not even a little."

"Let Lucy do it, then."

"Right, like she doesn't already. She drags me to all these things, but I'm not allowed to speak. She says I'm just eye candy."

"You are, Cope."

"Yes, true, but I have a brain too."

"That's the part of you I need," she said.

"Why, what's up?"

"I'm having one of my crazier hunches, and I need you to tell me if I'm on to something or going off the deep end."

"Is it more important than who sits at the same table as Aunt Carol and Uncle Jerry?"

"No, this is just a homicide."

"I'll make the sacrifice. On my way."

The sound of the phone woke Jill up.

She was in Yasmin's bedroom. Yasmin was trying too hard to fit in with the other girls by pretending to be extra boy-crazy. There was a poster of Zac Efron, the hottie from the *High School Musical* movies on one wall, and another of the Sprouse twins from *The Suite Life*. There was one of Miley Cyrus from *Hannah Montana* — okay, a girl, not a hottie, but still. It all seemed so desperate.

Yasmin's bed was near the door while Jill slept by the window. Both beds were blanketed with stuffed animals. Yasmin once told Jill that the best part about divorce was the competitive spoiling — both parents go out of their way with the gifts. Yasmin only saw her mom maybe four, five times a year, but she sent stuff constantly. There were at least two dozen Build-A-Bears, including one dressed like a cheerleader and another, perched next to Jill's pillow, that was done up like a pop star with rhinestone shorts, a halter top, and a wire microphone wrapped around her furry face. A ton of Webkinz animals, including three hippos alone, spilled onto the floor. Back issues of *J-14* and *Teen People* and *Popstar!* magazines littered the nightstand. The carpet was deep shag, something her parents told her had gone out in the 1970s but seemed to be making an odd comeback in teen bedrooms. There was a brand-new iMac on the desk.

Yasmin was good with computers. So was Jill.

Jill sat up. Yasmin blinked and looked over at her. In the distance, Jill could hear a rumbling voice on the phone. Mr. Novak. There was a Homer Simpson clock on the nightstand between them. It read seven fifteen A.M.

Early for a call, Jill knew, especially on a weekend.

The girls had stayed up late last night. First they went out for dinner and ice cream with Mr. Novak and his annoying new girlfriend, Beth. Beth was probably forty years old and laughed at everything Mr. Novak said like, well, like the annoying boy-crazy girls at their school did to make a boy like them. Jill thought you outgrew that at some stage. Maybe not.

Yasmin had a plasma TV in her room. Her father let them watch as many movies as they wanted. "It's the weekend," Guy Novak said with a big smile. "Have at it." So they microwaved some popcorn and watched PG-13 and even one R-rated film that would probably have freaked out Jill's parents.

Jill got out of bed. She had to pee, but right now she wondered about last night, what had happened, if her father had tracked Adam down. She was worried. She had called Adam's phone herself. If he was keeping away from Mom and Dad, okay, that made sense. But she had never considered the possibility that he wouldn't respond to calls and texts from his little sister. Adam always responded to her.

But not this time.

And that made Jill worry even more.

She checked her cell phone.

"What are you doing?" Yasmin asked.

"Checking to see if Adam called me back."

"Did he?"

"No. Nothing."

Yasmin fell silent.

There was a light rap on the door and then it opened. Mr. Novak popped his head in and whispered, "Hey, why are you guys awake?"

"The phone woke us," Yasmin said.

"Who was it?" Jill asked.

Mr. Novak looked at her. "That was your mommy."

Jill's body stiffened. "What's wrong?"

"Nothing's wrong, sweetheart," Mr. Novak said, and Jill could see it was a great big lie. "She just asked if we could keep you today. I figured we'd go to the mall later or maybe a movie. How does that sound?"

"Why does she want me to stay?" Jill asked.

"I don't know, honey. She just said something's come up and asked the favor. But she said to tell you that she loves you and everything is fine."

Jill said nothing. He was lying. She knew it. Yasmin knew it. She looked over at Yasmin. It wouldn't do to press the issue. He wouldn't tell them. He was protecting them because their eleven-year-old minds couldn't handle the truth or whatever nonsense adults use to excuse lying.

"I'm going to run out for a while," Mr. Novak said.

"Where?" Yasmin asked.

"The office. I need to pick up some stuff. But Beth just stopped by. She's downstairs watching TV, if you need anything."

Yasmin smirked. "Just stopped by?"

"Yes."

"Like she didn't sleep here? Right, Dad. How old do you think we are?"

He frowned. "That's enough, young lady."

"Whatever."

He closed the door. Jill sat on the bed. Yasmin moved closer to her.

"What do you think happened?" Yasmin asked.

Jill didn't reply, but she didn't like where her thoughts were taking her.

Cope came into Muse's office. He was, Muse thought, looking rather natty in his new blue suit.

"Press conference today?" Muse asked.

"How did you guess?"

"Your suit is natty."

"Do people still say natty?"

"They should."

"Agreed. I am the picture of nattiness. I am nattatious. The Natt Man. The Nattster."

Loren Muse held up a sheet of paper. "Look what just came in to my office."

"Tell me."

"Frank Tremont's letter of resignation. He is putting in for retirement."

"Quite a loss."

"Yes."

Muse looked at him.

"What?"

"Your stunt yesterday with that reporter."

"What about it?"

"It was a tad patronizing," Muse said. "I don't need you rescuing me."

"I wasn't rescuing you. If anything, I was setting you up."

"How's that?"

"You either had the goods to blow Tremont out of the water or you didn't. One of you was going to look like an ass."

"Him or me, was that it?"

"Exactly. Truth is, Tremont is a snitch and a terrible distraction in this office. I wanted him gone for selfish reasons."

"Suppose I didn't have the goods."

Cope shrugged. "Then you might be the one handing in your resignation."

"You were willing to take that risk?"

"What risk? Tremont is a lazy moron. If he could outthink you, you don't deserve to be the chief."

"Touché."

"Enough. You didn't call me to talk about Frank Tremont. So what's up?"

She told him all about the disappearance of Reba Cordova — the witness at Target, the van, the parking lot at the Ramada in East Hanover. Cope sat in the chair and looked at her with gray eyes. He had great eyes, the kind that change color in different light. Loren Muse had something of a crush on Paul Copeland, but then again, she'd also had something of a crush on his predecessor, who was considerably older and couldn't have looked more different. Maybe she had a thing for authority figures.

The crush was harmless, more an appreciation than any kind of real-life longing. He didn't keep her up at night or make her hurt or intrude on any of her fantasies, sexual or otherwise. She loved Paul Copeland's attractiveness without coveting it. She wanted those qualities in whatever man she dated, though Lord knows she had never found it.

Muse knew about her boss's past, about the horror he'd gone through, the hell of recent revelations. She had even helped see him through it. Like so many other men she knew, Paul Copeland was damaged, but damaged worked for him. Lots of guys in politics — and that's what this job was, a political appointment — are ambitious but haven't known suffering. Cope had. As a prosecutor it made him both more sympathetic and less likely to accept defense excuses.

Muse gave him all the facts on the Reba Cordova disappearance without her theories. He watched her face and nodded slowly.

"Let me guess," Cope said. "You think that this Reba Cordova is somehow connected to your Jane Doe."

"Yes."

"Are you thinking, what, a serial killer?"

"It could be, though serial killers normally work alone. There was a woman involved in this one."

"Okay, let's hear why you think they're linked."

"First the MO."

"Two white women about the same age," Cope said. "One is found dressed like a hooker in Newark. The other, well, we don't know where she is."

"That's part of it, but here is the big thing that drew my eye. The use of deception and diversion."

"I'm not following."

"We have two well-to-do white women in their forties vanishing within, what, twenty-four hours of each other. That's a strange similarity right there. But more than that, in the first case, with our Jane Doe, we know the killer went through elaborate staging to fool us, right?"

"Right."

"Well, he did the same with Reba Cordova."

"By parking the car at a motel?"

She nodded. "In both cases, he worked hard to throw us off the track with false clues. In the case of Jane Doe, he set it up so we would think she was a hooker. In the case of Reba Cordova, he made it look like she was a woman cheating on her husband who ran off with her lover."

"Eh." Cope made a face. "That's pretty weak."

"Yes. But it is something. Not to be racist, but how often does a nice-looking family woman from a suburb like Livingston just run off with a lover?"

"It happens."

"Maybe, but she would plan better, wouldn't she? She wouldn't drive up to a shopping mall near where her daughter takes ice-skating lessons and buy some kid underwear and then, what, throw them away and run to her lover? And then we have the witness, a guy named Stephen Errico, who saw her go into a van at the Target. And he saw another woman drive away."

"If that's what really happened."

"It did."

"Okay, but even so. How else are you tying Reba Cordova with our Jane Doe?"

Muse arched an eyebrow. "I'm saving the best for last."

"Thank God."

"Let's go back to Stephen Errico."

"The witness at the mall?"

"Right. Errico makes his report. On its own, sure, I don't blame the security guys at the Palisades. It sounds like nothing. But I looked him up on the Web. He's got his own blog page with his photograph — a big, heavy guy with a bushy beard and Grateful Dead shirt — and when I talked to him, he is clearly something of a conspiracy nut. Errico also likes to insinuate himself into the story. You know, the kind of guy who goes to the mall and hopes to see a shop-lifter?"

"Right."

"But that also makes him damn specific. Errico said he saw a woman matching Reba Cordova's description get into a white Chevy van. But more than that, he actually took down the van's license plate."

"And?"

"I ran the plate. It belongs to a woman named Helen Kasner of Scarsdale, New York."

"Does she own a white van?"

"She does, and she was at the Palisades Mall yesterday."

Cope nodded, seeing where she was going. "So you figure someone switched plates on Ms. Kasner?"

"Exactly. Oldest trick in the book but still effective — you steal a car to commit a crime, then you switch plates in case someone sees it. More deception. But a lot of criminals don't realize that the most effective method is to switch plates with a vehicle that's the same make as yours. It confuses even more."

"So you're figuring the van in the Target lot was stolen."

"You don't agree?"

"I guess I do," Cope said. "It certainly adds weight to Mr. Errico's story. I get why we should worry about Reba Cordova. But I still don't see how she ties in with our Jane Doe."

"Take a look at this."

She swiveled her computer monitor in his

direction. Cope turned his attention to the screen.

"What is this?"

"A security tape from a building near the Jane Doe murder scene. I was watching it this morning, thinking it was total waste of time. But now . . ." Muse had the tape all lined up. She pressed the PLAY button. A white van appeared. She hit PAUSE and the image froze.

Cope moved closer. "A white van."

"A white Chevy van, yup."

"Must be a zillion white Chevy vans registered in New York and New Jersey," Cope said. "Could you get the license plate?"

"Yes."

"And can I assume it's a match with the one that belongs to the Kasner woman?"

"No."

Cope's eyes narrowed. "No?"

"No. Totally different number."

"Then what's the big deal?"

She pointed at the screen. "This license plate — JYL-419 — belongs to a Mr. David Pulkingham of Armonk, New York."

"Does Mr. Pulkingham own a white van too?"

"Yes."

"Could he be our guy?"

"He's seventy-three and has no record."

"So you figure another plate switch?"

"Yep."

Clarence Morrow leaned his head in the office. "Chief?"

"Yes."

He saw Paul Copeland and straightened as though ready to salute. "Good morning, Mr. Prosecutor."

"Hey, Clarence."

Clarence waited.

"It's okay," Muse said. "What have you got?"

"I just got off the phone with Helen Kasner."

"And?"

"I had her check her van's plate. You were right. The license plate was switched and she never noticed."

"Anything else?"

"Yep, the kicker. The license plate on the car now?" Clarence pointed to the white van on the computer screen. "It belongs to Mr. David Pulkingham."

Muse looked at Cope, smiled, raised her palms to the sky. "That enough of a link?"

"Yeah," Cope said. "That'll do."

19

Yasmin whispered, "Let's go."

Jill looked at her friend. The little mustache on her face, the one that had caused all the trouble, was gone, but for some reason Jill could still see it. Yasmin's mother had visited from wherever she lived now — somewhere down south, Florida maybe — and had taken her to some fancy doctor's office and gotten her electrolysis. It helped her appearance but it hadn't helped make school one bit less horrible.

They were sitting at the kitchen table. Beth, the "girlfriend du week" as Yasmin called her, had tried to impress them with a fancy omelette breakfast complete with sausage links and Beth's "legendary hotcakes," but the girls had passed, to Beth's crestfallen disappointment, in favor of frozen Eggos with chocolate chips.

"Okay, girls, you enjoy," Beth said through clenched teeth. "I'm going to sit in the yard and get some sun."

As soon as Beth was out the door, Yasmin got up from the table and sneaked over to the bay window. Beth was not in view. Yasmin looked left, then right, then she smiled.

"What is it?" Jill asked.

"Check this out," Yasmin said.

Jill rose and joined her friend.

"Look. In the corner behind the big tree."

"I don't see anything."

"Look closer," Yasmin said.

It took a moment or two and then Jill saw something gray and wispy and she realized what Yasmin meant. "Beth's smoking?"

"Yup. She's hiding behind a tree and lighting up."

"Why hide?"

"Maybe she's worried about smoking in front of impressionable youth," Yasmin said with a wry grin. "Or maybe Beth doesn't want my dad to know. He hates smokers."

"Are you going to rat her out?"

Yasmin smiled, shrugged. "Who knows? We rat out everybody else, don't we?" She started rifling through a purse. Jill gave a little gasp.

"Is that Beth's?"

"Yes."

"We shouldn't do that."

Yasmin just made a face and continued her rummaging.

Jill moved closer and peered in. "Anything interesting?"

"No." Yasmin put it down. "Come on, I want to show you something."

She dropped the purse on the counter and headed up the stairs. Jill followed. There was a window in the bathroom at the landing. Yasmin took a quick peak. So did Jill. Beth was indeed behind the tree — they could see her clearly now — and she was puffing on that cigarette as if she were underwater and had finally found a lifeline. She took deep hard puffs and closed her eyes and the lines on her face smoothed out.

Yasmin moved away without a word. She beckoned Jill to follow. They entered her father's room. Yasmin headed straight to his night table and opened the drawer.

Jill was hardly shocked. This, in truth, was one of the things they had in common. They both liked to explore. All kids do to some extent, Jill guessed, but in her house, her dad called her "Harriet the Spy." She was always sneaking into places she didn't belong. When Jill was eight, she found old pictures in her mom's drawer. They were hidden in the back, under a bunch of old postcards and pillboxes she'd bought on a trip to Florence during a summer break in college.

In one picture was a boy who looked to be about her age at the time — eight or maybe nine. He stood next to a girl maybe a year or two younger. The girl, Jill immediately knew, was her mother. She turned the picture over. Someone had written in delicate script, "Tia and Davey" and the year.

She had never heard of a Davey. But she learned. Her snooping had taught her a valuable lesson. Parents like to keep things secret too.

"Look here," Yasmin said.

Jill looked into the drawer. Mr. Novak had a roll of condoms on the top. "Eeuw, gross."

"Do you think he used them with Beth?"

"I don't want to think about it."

"How do you think I feel? He's my father." Jill closed the drawer and opened the one below it. Her voice suddenly became a whisper.

"Jill?"

"What?"

"Take a look at this."

Yasmin dug her hand past old sweaters, a metal box of some kind, rolls of socks, and then it stopped. She pulled something into a view and smiled.

Jill jumped back. "What the . . . ?"

"It's a gun."

"I know it's a gun!"

"And it's loaded."

"Put it away. I can't believe your dad has a loaded gun."

"So do lots of dads. Want me to show you how to take off the safety?"

"No."

But Yasmin did it anyway. They both stared at the weapon in awe. Yasmin handed it to Jill. At first Jill put up her hand refusing, but then something about its shape and color drew her. She let it rest in her palm. She marveled at the weight, at the coolness, at the simplicity.

"Can I tell you something?" Yasmin asked.

"Sure."

"You promise you won't tell."

"Of course I won't tell."

"When I first found it, I fantasized about using it on Mr. Lewiston."

Jill carefully set the weapon down.

"I could almost see it, you know? I would go into class. I would keep it in my backpack. Sometimes I think about waiting until after class, shooting him when no one is around, wiping my fingerprints off the gun, making a clean getaway. Or I would go to his house — I know where he lives, it's in West

Orange — and I would kill him there and no one would suspect me. And then other times I think about doing it right in the classroom, with everyone still there, and all the other kids would see, and maybe I would even turn the gun that way, but then I quickly thought, no, that would be too Columbine and I'm not like some goth outcast."

"Yasmin?"

"Yeah?"

"You're kind of scaring me."

Yasmin smiled. "It was just, like, a random thought, you know. Harmless. I'm not going to do it or anything."

Silence.

"He will pay," Jill said. "You know that, right? Mr. Lewiston?"

"I do know," Yasmin said.

They heard a car pull into the driveway. Mr. Novak was home. Yasmin calmly picked up the gun, put it in the bottom of the drawer, arranged everything just so. She took her time, no rush, even when the door opened and they heard her father call out, "Yasmin? Girls?"

Yasmin closed the drawer, smiled, moved toward the door.

"We're coming, Dad!"

Tia didn't bother to pack.

As soon as she hung up with Mike, she ran down to the lobby. Brett was still rubbing sleep from his eyes, and his hair had the disheveled look of the great untouched. He'd volunteered to drive her to the Bronx. Brett's van was loaded with computer equipment and smelled like a bong, but he kept his foot pressed on the pedal. Tia sat next to him and made some phone calls. She woke up Guy Novak and briefly explained that Mike had been in an accident and could he watch Jill for a few extra hours? He had been properly sympathetic and quickly agreed.

"What should I tell Jill?" Guy Novak asked her.

"Just tell her something's come up. I don't want her worrying."

"Sure thing."

"Thanks, Guy."

Tia sat up and stared at the road as though that might make the trip shorter. She tried to piece together what happened. Mike said he had used a cell phone GPS. He tracked down Adam in some strange location in the Bronx. He drove there, maybe saw the Huff kid, and then he got assaulted.

Adam was still missing — or maybe, like last time, he had merely decided to drop out of sight for a day or two.

She called Clark's house. She spoke to

Olivia too. Neither had seen Adam. She called the Huff household, but there was no answer. For most of the night and even this morning, preparing for the deposition had kept the terror partially occupied — at least until Mike had called from the hospital. No more. Raw fear rose up and took hold. She started shifting in her seat.

"Ya okay?" Brett asked.

"Fine."

But she wasn't fine. She kept flashing to the night Spencer Hill had vanished and committed suicide. She remembered getting the call from Betsy. . . .

"Has Adam seen Spencer . . . ?"

The panic in Betsy's voice. The pure fear. No anxiety in the end. She had been worried and, in the end, she had earned every second of it.

Tia closed her eyes. It was suddenly hard to breathe. She felt her chest hitch. She gulped down breaths.

"You want me to open a window?" Brett asked.

"I'm fine."

She collected herself and called the hospital. She managed to reach the doctor, but she learned nothing she didn't already know. Mike had been beaten and robbed. From what she could make of it, a group of men had jumped her husband in an alley. He had suffered a severe concussion and had been unconscious for several hours, but he was resting comfortably and would be fine.

She reached Hester Crimstein at home. Her boss expressed moderate concern for Tia's husband and son — and maximum concern for her case.

"Your son has run away before, right?" Hester asked.

"Once."

"So that's probably what's going on with him, don't you think?"

"It might be something more."

"Like what?" Hester asked. "Look, what time is the deposition again?"

"Three P.M."

"I'll ask for a continuance. If it's not granted, you have to go back up."

"You're joking, right?"

"From the sound of it, there is nothing you can do from there. You can have phone access throughout. I'll get you the private jet so you can leave from Teterboro."

"This is my family we're talking about."

"Right, and I'm talking about missing a few hours from them. You're not going to do anything to make them feel better, just yourself. In the meantime, I'm dealing with an innocent man who may end up serving a twenty-five-year prison term if we screw this up."

Tia wanted to quit right on the spot, but something took hold and calmed her enough to say, "Let's see about the continuance."

"I'll call you back."

Tia hung up the phone, looked at it in her hand as if it were some strange new growth. Did that really happen?

When she reached Mike's room, Mo was already there. He stormed across the room, two fists at his side. "He's fine," Mo said, as soon as she entered. "He just fell back asleep."

Tia crossed the room. There were two other beds in the room, both with patients. Neither of them had visitors right now. When Tia looked down and saw Mike's face, it felt as though a cement block had landed on her stomach.

"Oh dear God . . ."

Mo came up behind her and put his hands on her shoulders. "It looks worse than it is."

She hoped so. She had not known what to expect, but this? His right eye was swollen shut. There was a cut like something from a straight razor across one cheek while a bruise welled up on the other one. His lip was split. One arm was under the blanket, but she could see two huge bruises on the other forearm.

"What did they do to him?" she whispered.

"They're dead men," Mo said. "You hear me? I'm going to track them down and I'm not going to beat them. I'm going to kill them."

Tia put her hand on her husband's forearm. Her husband. Her beautiful, handsome, strong husband. She had fallen in love with this man at Dartmouth. She had shared her bed with him, had children, chosen him to be her companion for life. It was not something that you think about often, but there it was. You actually choose one fellow human being to share a life with — it was the most frightening thing when you think about it. How had she let them drift apart, even a little? How had she let the routine become routine and not done everything every second of their life together to make it even better, even more passionate?

"I love you so much," she whispered.

His eyes blinked open. She could see fear in his eyes too — and maybe that was the worst thing of all. In all the time she had known Mike, she had never seen fear in him. She had never seen him cry either. He did, she guessed, but he was the sort that did not show it. He wanted to be the strong shoulder, and old-fashioned as it might sound, she wanted that too.

He looked straight up in the air, eyes wide now, as if seeing some imaginary attacker.

"Mike," Tia said. "I'm right here."

His eyes moved toward hers, met hers, but the fear did not let go. If seeing her was a comfort, he wasn't showing that either. Tia took his hand.

"You're going to be fine," she said.

His eyes stayed on hers and now she could see it. She knew what he'd say even before the words came out of his mouth.

"What about Adam? Where is he?"

20

Dolly Lewiston saw the car drive past her house again.

It slowed. Like the last time. And the time before.

"It's him again," she said.

Her husband, a fifth-grade teacher named Joe Lewiston, did not look up. He was correcting papers with a little too much focus.

"Joe?"

"I heard you, Dolly," he snapped. "What do you want me to do about it?"

"He has no right." She watched him drive off, the car seeming to dissolve in the distance. "Maybe we should call the police."

"And say what?"

"That he's stalking us."

"He drives down our road. It's not against the law."

"He slows down."

"That's not against the law either."

"You can tell them what happened."

He made a snorting noise, kept his eye on his papers. "I'm sure the police will be very sympathetic."

"We have a child too."

She had, in fact, been watching little Allie, their three-year-old, on the computer. The K-Little Gym Web site lets you watch your child via a webcam in the room — snack time, building blocks, reading, independent work, singing, whatever — so you could always check in on them. This was why Dolly chose K-Little.

Both she and Joe worked as elementary schoolteachers. Joe worked at Hillside school teaching fifth grade. She taught second graders in Paramus. Dolly Lewiston wanted to quit her job, but they needed both salaries. Her husband still loved teaching, but somewhere along the way the love had faded away for Dolly. Some might note that she'd lost her passion for teaching right around the same time Allie was born, but she thought it was more than that. Still, she did her job and fended off complaining parents, but all she really wanted to do was watch the K-Little Web site and make sure her baby was safe.

Guy Novak, the man in the car who drove by their house, had not been able to watch his daughter or make sure she was safe. So on one level, Dolly totally got where he was coming from and even sympathized with his frustration. But that didn't mean she was about to let him hurt her family. The world was often simply a case of us or them, and she'd be damned if it would be her family.

She turned to look at Joe. His eyes were closed, his head down.

She came up behind him and put her hand on his shoulders. He winced at her touch. The wince lasted a second, no more, but she felt it ripple through her whole body. He had been so tense the last few weeks. She kept her hands there, didn't pull them away, and he relaxed. She started rubbing his shoulders. He used to love that. It took a few minutes but his shoulders started to soften.

"It's okay," she said.

"I just lost my cool."

"I know."

"I went out to the edge, like I always do, and then . . ."

"I know."

She did. It was what made Joe Lewiston a good teacher. He had passion. He kept his students listening, told them jokes, sometimes crossed the line into inappropriateness but the kids loved that about him. It made them pay attention and learn more. Parents had gotten mildly upset by Joe's antics before, but he had enough defenders to protect himself. The large majority of parents fought for their kid to get Mr. Lewiston. They liked the fact that their children enjoyed school and had a teacher who showed genuine enthusiasm and didn't just go through the motions. Unlike Dolly.

"I really hurt that girl," he said.

"You didn't mean to. All the kids and parents still love you."

He said nothing.

"She'll get over it. This is all going to pass, Joe. It'll be fine."

His lower lip started quaking. He was falling apart. Much as she loved him, much as she knew that he was a far better teacher and person than she would ever be, Dolly also knew that her husband was not the strongest man. People thought he was. He came from a big family, growing up the youngest of six siblings, but his father had been too domineering. He'd belittled his youngest, gentlest son, and in turn, Joe found an escape in being funny and entertaining. Joe Lewiston was the finest man she had ever known, but he was also weak.

That was okay with her. It was Dolly's job to be the strong one. It fell to her to hold her husband and her family together.

"I'm sorry I snapped," Joe said.

"That's okay."

"You're right. This will pass."

"Exactly." She kissed his neck and then the spot behind the earlobe. His favorite. She used her tongue and gently swirled. She waited for the small moan. It never came. Dolly whispered, "Maybe you should stop correcting papers for a little while, hmm?"

He pulled away, just a little. "I, uh, really need to finish these."

Dolly stood and took a step back. Joe Lewiston saw what he'd done, tried to recover.

"Can I take a rain check?" he asked.

That was what *she* used to say when not in the mood. That was, in fact, the "wife" line in general, wasn't it? He had always been the aggressor that way — no weakness there — but the last few months, since the slip of the tongue, pardon the wording, he had been different even in that.

"Sure," she said.

Dolly turned away.

"Where are you going?" he asked.

"I'll be back," Dolly said. "I just need to run to the store and then I'll pick up Allie. You finish correcting your papers."

Dolly Lewiston dashed upstairs, logged online, looked up Guy Novak's address, got directions. She also checked her school e-mail address — there was always a complaining parent — but it hadn't been working for the past two days. Still nothing.

"My e-mail is still on the fritz," she called down.

"I'll check on it," he said.

Dolly printed out the directions to Guy Novak's house, folded the paper into quarters, and jammed it into her pocket. On the way out, she kissed her husband on the top of his head. He told her that he loved her. She told him that she loved him too.

She grabbed her keys and started after Guy Novak.

Tia could see it in their faces: The police weren't buying Adam's disappearance.

"I thought you could do an Amber Alert or something," Tia said.

There were two cops who looked almost comical together. One was a tiny Latino in uniform named Guttierez. The other was a tall black woman who introduced herself as Detective Clare Schlich.

Schlich was the one who replied to her question: "Your son doesn't meet the Amber Alert criteria."

"Why not?"

"There has to be some evidence he was abducted."

"But he's sixteen years old and he's missing."

"Yes."

"So what kind of evidence do you need?"

Schlich shrugged. "A witness might be nice."

"Not every abduction has a witness."

"That's correct, ma'am. But you need some evidence of an abduction or threat of physical harm. Do you have any?"

Tia wouldn't call them rude; "patronizing" would be the better word. They dutifully took down the information. They did not dismiss their concerns, but they weren't about to drop everything and put all their manpower on this one. Clare Schlich made her position clear with questions and follow-ups on what Mike and Tia told her:

"You monitored your son's computer?"

"You activated the GPS on his cell?"

"You were concerned enough about his behavior to follow him into the Bronx?"

"He's run away before?"

Like that. On one level, Tia didn't blame the two cops, but all she could see was that Adam was missing.

Guttierez had already talked to Mike earlier. He added, "You said you saw Daniel Huff Junior — DJ Huff — on the street?

That he might have been out with your son?"

"Yes."

"I just spoke to his father. He's a cop, did you know that?"

"I do."

"He said his son was home all night."

Tia looked at Mike. She saw something explode behind his eyes. His pupils became pinpricks. She had seen that look before. She put a hand on his arm, but there was no calming him.

"He's lying," Mike said.

The cop shrugged his shoulders. Tia watched Mike's swollen face darken. He looked up at her, then at Mo, and said, "We're out of here. Now."

The doctor wanted Mike to stay another day, but that wasn't going to happen. Tia knew better than to play the concerned wife. She knew that Mike would get over his physical injuries. He was so damn tough. This was his third concussion — the first two he'd suffered in a hockey rink. Mike had lost teeth and had stitches in his face more times than a man should and had broken his nose twice and his jaw once and never, not once, missed a game — in most cases, he had even finished playing in the games where he'd been hurt.

Tia also knew there would be no arguing this point with her husband — and she didn't want to. She wanted him out of bed and looking for their son. Doing nothing, she knew, would hurt far more.

Mo helped Mike sit up. Tia helped him get on his clothes. There were bloodstains on them. Mike didn't care. He rose. They were almost out the door when Tia felt her cell phone vibrate. She prayed that it was Adam. It wasn't.

Hester Crimstein did not bother with hello.

"Any word on your son?"

"Nothing. The police are dismissing him as a runaway."

"Isn't he?"

That stopped Tia.

"I don't think so."

"Brett told me you spy on him," Hester said.

Brett and his big mouth, she thought. Wonderful. "I monitor his online activity."

"You say tomato, I say tomahto."

"Adam wouldn't run away like this."

"Gee, no parent has ever said that before."

"I know my son."

"Or that," Hester added. "Bad news: We didn't get the continuance."

"Hester —"

"Before you say you won't go back to Boston, hear me out. I've already arranged for a limo to come pick you up. It's outside the hospital right now."

"I can't —"

"Just listen, Tia. You owe me that much. The driver will take you to Teterboro Airport, which isn't far from your house. I have my private plane. You have a cell phone. If any word comes in at all, the driver can take you there. There is a phone on the plane. If you hear something while in the air, my pilot can have you there in record time. Maybe Adam will be found in, I don't know, Philadelphia. It will pay to have a private plane at your disposal."

Mike looked a question at Tia. Tia shook her head and signaled for them to keep moving. They did.

"When you get up to Boston," Hester went on, "you do the deposition. If anything happens during the deposition, you stop immediately and go home on the private plane. It is a forty-minute flight from Boston to Teterboro. Chances are, your kid is just going to walk through the door with some teenage excuse because he was out drinking with friends. Either way, you will be home in a matter of hours."

Tia pinched the bridge of her nose.

Hester said, "I'm making sense, right?"

"You are."

"Good."

"But I can't."

"Why not?"

"I wouldn't be able to concentrate."

"Oh, that's crap. You know what I want with this deposition."

"You want flirty. My husband is in the hospital —"

"He's already being released. I know all, Tia."

"Fine, my husband has been assaulted and my son is still missing. Do you really think I will be up for a flirtatious deposition?"

"Up for it? Who the hell cares if you're up for it? You just need to do it. There is a man's freedom at stake here, Tia."

"You need to find somebody else."

Silence.

"Is that your final answer?" Hester said.

"Final answer," Tia said. "Is this going to cost me my job?"

"Not today," Hester said. "But soon enough. Because now I know that I can't depend on you."

"I'll work hard to get your trust back."

"You won't get it back. I'm not big on second chances. I got too many lawyers working for me who will never need one. So I'll put you back on crap detail until you quit. Too bad. I think you had potential."

Hester Crimstein hung up the phone.

They found their way outside. Mike was still watching his wife. "Tia?"

"I don't want to talk about it."

Mo drove them home.

Tia asked, "What do we do?"

Mike popped down a pain pill. "Maybe you should pick up Jill."

"Okay. Where are you going?"

"For starters," Mike said, "I want to have a little chat with Captain Daniel Huff about why he lied."

21

Mo said, "This Huff guy's a cop, right?"

"Right."

"So he won't intimidate easily."

They had already parked outside the Huff house, almost exactly where Mike had been last night before it all exploded around him. He didn't listen to Mo. He stormed toward the door. Mo followed. Mike knocked and waited. He hit the doorbell and waited some more.

No one answered.

Mike circled around back. He banged on that door too. No answer. He cupped his hands around his eyes and the window and peered in. No movement. He actually checked the knob. The door was locked.

"Mike?"

"He's lying, Mo."

They walked back to the car.

"Where to?" Mo asked.

"Let me drive."

"No. Where to?"

"The police station. Where Huff works."

It was a short ride, less than a mile. Mike thought about this route, the short one that Daniel Huff took pretty much every day to work. How lucky to have such a quick commute. Mike thought of the wasted hours sitting in traffic at the bridge and then he wondered why he was thinking about something so inane and realized that he was breathing funny and that Mo was watching him out of the corner of his eye.

"Mike?"

"What?"

"You got to keep your cool here."

Mike frowned. "This coming from you."

"Yep, this coming from me. You can either rejoice in the rich irony of my appealing for common sense or you can realize that if I'm advocating for prudence, there must be a pretty good reason for it. You can't go into a police station to confront an officer half-cocked."

Mike said nothing. The police station was a converted old library up on a hill with horrible parking. Mo started circling for a space.

"Did you hear me?"

"Yeah, Mo, I heard you."

There were no spots in front.

"Let me circle down on the south lot."

Mike said, "No time. I'll take care of this myself."

"No way."

Mike turned to him.

"Sheesh, Mike, you look horrible."

"If you want to be my driver, fine. But you're not my babysitter, Mo. So just drop me off. I need to talk to Huff alone anyway. You'll make him suspicious. Alone I can go at him father to father."

Mo pulled to the side. "Remember what you just said."

"What about it?"

"Father to father. He's a father too."

"Meaning?"

"Think about it."

Mike felt the pain rip across his ribs when he stood. Physical pain was an odd thing. He had a high threshold, he knew that. Sometimes he even found it comforting. He liked feeling the hurt after a hard workout. He liked making his muscles sore. On the ice, guys would try to intimidate with hard hits, but it had the opposite effect on him. There was an almost bring-it-on quality that came out when he took a good hit.

He expected the station to be sleepy. He had only been here once before, to request keeping his car on the street overnight. The town had an ordinance making it illegal to park on the street after two A.M., but their driveway was being repaved and so he stopped by to get permission to keep the cars out for the week. There had been one cop at the desk and all the desks behind him had been empty.

Today there had to be at least fifteen cops, all in action.

"May I help you?"

The uniformed officer looked too young to be working the desk. Maybe this was another example of how TV shaped us, but Mike always expected a grizzled veteran to be working the desk, like that guy who told everyone "Let's be careful out there" on *Hill Street Blues*. This kid looked about twelve. He was also staring at Mike with undisguised surprise and pointing at his face.

"Are you here about those bruises?"

"No," Mike said. The other officers started moving faster. They handed off papers and called one another and cradled receivers under their necks.

"I'm here to see Officer Huff."

"Do you mean Captain Huff?"

"Yes."

"May I ask what this is regarding?"

"Tell him it's Mike Baye."

"As you can see, we are pretty busy right now."

"I do see," Mike said. "Something big going on?"

The young cop gave him a look, clearly suggesting that it was none of his concern. Mike caught snippets about a car parked in a Ramada hotel lot, but that was about it.

"Do you mind sitting over there while I try to reach Captain Huff?"

"Sure."

Mike moved toward a bench and sat down. There was a man next to him in a suit, filling out paperwork. One of the cops called out, "We've checked with the entire staff now. No one reports seeing her." Mike idly wondered what that was about, but only to try to keep his blood down.

Huff had lied.

Mike kept his eyes on the young officer. When the kid hung up, he looked up and Mike knew this was not going to be good news.

"Mr. Baye?"

"Dr. Baye," Mike corrected. This time maybe it would come across as arrogant, but sometimes people treated a doctor differently. Not often. But sometimes.

"Dr. Baye. I'm afraid that we are having a very busy morning. Captain Huff has asked me to assure you that he will call you when he can."

"That's not going to do it," Mike said.

"Excuse me?"

The station was pretty much open space. There was a divider that was maybe three feet high — why do all stations have that? Who is that going to stop? — with a little gate you could swing open. Toward the back, Mike could see a door that clearly said CAPTAIN on it. He moved fast, causing all kinds of new pains to sparkle across his ribs and face. He stepped past the front desk.

"Sir?"

"Don't worry, I know the way."

He opened the latch and started hurrying toward the captain's office.

"Stop right now!"

Mike didn't think the kid would shoot, so he kept moving. He was at the door before anyone could catch up to him. He grabbed the knob and turned. Unlocked. He flung it open.

Huff was at his desk on the phone.

"What the hell . . . ?"

The kid officer at the front desk followed quickly, ready to tackle, but Huff waved him off.

"It's okay."

"I'm sorry, Captain. He just ran back here."

"Don't worry about it. Close the door, okay?"

The kid didn't look happy about it, but he obeyed. One of the walls was windowed. He stood there and looked through it. Mike gave him a quick glare and then turned his attention to Huff.

"You lied," he said.

"I'm busy here, Mike."

"I saw your son before I got jumped."

"No, you didn't. He was home."

"That's crap."

Huff did not stand. He didn't invite Mike to sit. He put his hands behind his head and leaned back. "I really don't have time for this."

"My son was at your house. Then he drove to the Bronx."

"How do you know that, Mike?"

"I have a GPS on my son's phone."

Huff raised his eyebrows. "Wow."

He must have already known this. His New York colleagues would have told him. "Why are you lying about this, Huff?"

"How exact is that GPS?"

"What?"

"Maybe he wasn't with DJ at all. Maybe he was at a neighbor's house. The Lubetkin boy lives two houses down. Or maybe, heck, he was at my house before I got home. Or maybe he just hung out nearby and thought about going in but changed his mind."

"Are you serious?"

There was a knock on the door. Another cop leaned his head in. "Mr. Cordova is here."

"Put him in room A," Huff said. "I'll be there in a second."

The cop nodded and let the door close. Huff rose. He was a tall man, hair slicked back. He normally had the cop-calm thing going on, like when they'd met up in front of his house the night before. He still had it, but the effort seemed to drain him now. He met Mike's eyes. Mike did not look away.

"My son was home all night."

"That's a lie."

"I have to go now. I'm not talking about this with you anymore."

He started walking to the door. Mike stepped into his path.

"I need to talk to your son."

"Get out of my way, Mike."

"No."

"Your face."

"What about it?"

"Looks like you've already taken enough of a beating," Huff said.

"You want to try me?"

Huff said nothing.

"Come on, Huff. I'm already injured. You want to try again?"

"Again?"

"Maybe you were there."

"What?"

"Your son was. I know that. So let's do this. But this time we go face-to-face. One-on-one. No group of guys jumping me when I'm not looking. So come on. Put away your gun and lock your office door. Tell your buddies out there to leave us alone. Let's see just how tough you are."

Huff gave a half smile. "You think that will help you find your son?"

And that was when Mike saw it — what Mo had been saying. He had been talking about face-to-face and one-on-one, but what he really should have been saying was what Mo said: father to father. Not that reminding him of that would appeal to Huff. Just the opposite. Mike was trying to save his kid — and Huff was doing the same. Mike didn't give a damn about DJ Huff — and Huff didn't give a damn about Adam Baye.

They were both out to protect their sons. Huff would fight to do so. Win or lose, Huff wouldn't give up his child. The same with the other parents — Clark's or Olivia's or whoever's — that was Mike's mistake. He and Tia were talking to the adults who'd jump on a grenade to protect their offspring. What they needed to do was circumvent the parental sentinels.

"Adam is missing," Mike said.

"I understand that."

"I spoke to the New York police about it. But who do I talk to here about helping me find my son?"

"Tell Cassandra I miss her," Nash whispered.

And then, finally, at long last, it was over for Reba Cordova.

Nash drove to the U-Store-It on Route 15 in Sussex County.

He backed the truck into the dock of his garagelike storage unit. Darkness had fallen. No one else was around or looking. He had placed the body in a trash can on the very outside chance someone could see. Storage units were great for this sort of thing. He remembered reading about an abduction where the kidnappers kept the victim in one of these units. The victim died of accidental suffocation. But Nash knew other stories too — ones that would make your lungs collapse. You see the posters of the missing, you wonder about the missing, those kids on milk cartons, the women who just innocently left home one day, and sometimes, more often than you want to know, they are kept tied and gagged and even alive in places like this.

Cops, Nash knew, believed that criminals followed a certain specific pattern. That may be so — most criminals are morons — but Nash did the opposite. He had beaten Marianne beyond recognition, but this time he had not touched Reba's face. Part of that was just logistics. He knew that he could hide Marianne's true identity. Not so with Reba. By now her husband had probably reported her missing. If a fresh corpse was found, even one bloodied and battered, the police would realize that the odds it belonged to Reba Cordova were strong.

So change the MO: Don't let the body be found at all.

That was the key. Nash had left Marianne's body where they could find it, but Reba would simply vanish. Nash had left her car in the hotel lot. The police would think that she had gone there for an illicit tryst. They would focus on that, work that avenue, investigate her background to see if she had a boyfriend. Maybe Nash would get extra lucky. Maybe Reba did have someone on the side. The police would zero in on him for certain. Either way, if no body was found, they would have nothing to go on and probably assume that she had been a runaway. There would be no tie between Reba and Marianne.

So he would keep her here. For a while at least.

Pietra had the dead back in her eyes. Years ago, she had been a gorgeous young actress in what used to be called Yugoslavia. There had been ethnic cleansing. Her husband and son were killed before her eyes in ways too gruesome to imagine. Pietra was not so lucky — she survived. Nash had worked as a military mercenary back then. He had rescued her. Or what was left of her. Since then Pietra only came to life when she had to act, like back in the bar when they grabbed Marianne. The rest of the time there was nothing there. It had all been scooped out by those Serbian soldiers.

"I promised Cassandra," he said to her. "You understand that, don't you?"

Pietra looked off. He studied her profile.

"You feel bad about this one, don't you?"

Pietra said nothing. They put Reba's body in a mixture of wood chips and manure. It would keep for a while. Nash did not want to risk stealing another license plate. He took out the black electrical tape and changed the F to an E — that might be enough. In the corner of the shed, he had a pile of other "disguises" for his van. A magnetic sign advertising Tremesis Paints. Another that read CAMBRIDGE INSTITUTE. He chose instead to put on a bumper sticker he'd bought at a religious conference entitled The Lord's Love last October. The sticker read:

GOD DOESN'T BELIEVE IN ATHEISTS

Nash smiled. Such a kind, pious sentiment. But the key was, you noticed it. He put it on with two-sided tape so he could easily peel it off if he so desired. People would read the bumper sticker and be offended or impressed. Either way, they'd notice. And when you notice things like that, you don't notice the license plate number.

They got back in the car.

Until he met Pietra, Nash had never bought that the eyes were the window to the soul. But here, in her case, it was obvious. Her eyes were beautiful, blue with yellow sparkles, and yet you could see that there was nothing behind them, that something had blown out the candles and that they would never be relit.

"It had to be done, Pietra. You understand that."

She finally spoke. "You enjoyed it."

There was no judgment. She knew Nash long enough for him not to lie.

"So?"

She looked off.

"What is it, Pietra?"

"I knew what happened to my family," she said.

Nash said nothing.

"I watched my son and my husband suffer in horrible ways. And they watched me suffer too. That was the last sight they saw before dying — me suffering with them."

"I know this," Nash said. "And you say I enjoyed this. But normally, so do you, right?"

She answered without hesitation. "Yes."

Most people assumed that it would be the opposite — that the victim of such horrific violence would naturally be repulsed by any future bloodshed. But the truth was, the world does not work that way. Violence breeds violence — but not just in the obvious, retaliatory way. The molested child grows up to become the adult molester. The son traumatized by his father abusing his mother is far more likely to one day beat his own wife.

Why?

Why do we humans never really learn the

lessons we are supposed to? What is in our makeup, in fact, that draws us to that which should sicken us?

After Nash saved her, Pietra had craved vengeance. It was all she thought about during her recuperation. Three weeks after she was discharged from the hospital, Nash and Pietra tracked down one of the soldiers who'd tortured her family. They managed to get him alone. Nash tied and gagged him. He gave Pietra the pruning shears and left her alone with him. It took three days for the soldier to die. By the end of the first, the soldier was begging Pietra to kill him. But she didn't.

She loved every moment.

In the end, most people find revenge to be a wasted emotion. They feel empty after doing something so horrible to another human being, even one who maybe deserved it. Not Pietra. The experience just made her thirst for more. And that was a big part of why she was with him today.

"So what's different this time?" he asked.

Nash waited. She took her time, but eventually she got to it.

"The not knowing," Pietra said in a hushed tone. "*Never* knowing. Inflicting physical pain . . . we do that, no problem." She looked back at the storage unit. "But to make a man go through the rest of his life wondering what happened to the woman he loved." She shook her head. "I think that is worse."

Nash put a hand on her shoulder. "It can't be helped right now. You understand that, right?"

She nodded, looked straight ahead. "But someday?"

"Yes, Pietra. Someday. When we finish this up, we will let him know the truth."

22

When Guy Novak pulled back into his driveway, his hands were at two and ten. His grip on the wheel turned his knuckles white. He just sat there, foot on the brake, wanting so much to feel anything but this tremendous impotence.

He glanced at his reflection in the rearview mirror. His hair was thinning. He was starting to let the part in his hair drift toward his ear. It wasn't a noticeable comb-over, not yet, but isn't that what everyone thinks? The part moves so slowly south you don't notice it on a day-to-day or even week-to-week basis and the next thing you know, people are snickering at you behind your back.

Guy stared at the man in the mirror and couldn't believe it was him. The part, however, would continue to drift. He knew that. Better the wisps of hair than that shiny chrome up top.

He took one hand off the wheel, shifted

into park, turned the ignition key. He took another glance at the man in the rearview mirror.

Pathetic.

Not a man at all. Driving by a house and slowing down. Wow, what a tough guy. Show some balls, Guy — or are you too afraid to do anything to the scumbag who destroyed your child?

What kind of father is that? What kind of man?

A pathetic one.

Oh, sure, Guy had complained to the principal like some tattletale baby. The principal made all the right sympathetic sounds and did nothing. Lewiston still taught. Lewiston still went home at night and kissed his pretty wife and probably lifted his little girl in the air and listened to her giggle. Guy's wife, Yasmin's mother, had left when Yasmin was less than two. Most people blamed his ex for abandoning her family, but in truth, Guy hadn't been man enough. So his ex started sleeping around and after a while, she didn't really care if he found out or not.

That had been his wife. Not strong enough to hold on to her. Okay, that was one thing.

But now we were talking about his child.

Yasmin. His lovely daughter. The only manly thing he had accomplished in his entire life. Fathering a child. Raising her. Being her primary caretaker.

Wasn't his first job to protect her?

Good job, Guy.

And now he was not even man enough to fight for her. What would Guy's father have said about that? He'd sneer and give him that look that made Guy feel so worthless. He'd call him a sissy because if someone had done something like that to anyone in his old man's inner circle, George Novak would have punched out his lights.

That was what Guy so badly wanted to do.

He stepped out of the car and started up the walk. He had lived here twelve years now. He remembered holding his ex's hand as they approached it for the first time, the way she smiled at him. Had she already been screwing around behind his back then? Probably. For years after she left him, Guy would wonder if Yasmin was really his. He would try to block it, try to claim it wouldn't matter, try to ignore that doubt eating away at him. But after a while he couldn't take it anymore. Two years ago, Guy surreptitiously arranged a paternity test. It took three painful weeks to get the results, but in the end, it was worth it.

Yasmin was his.

This might again sound pathetic, but knowing the truth made him a better father. He made sure that she was happy. He put her needs ahead of his. He loved Yasmin and cared for her and never belittled her like his father had done to him.

But he hadn't protected her.

He stopped and looked at the house now. If he was going to put it on the market, it could probably use a fresh coat of paint. The shrubs would need to be trimmed too.

"Hey!"

The female voice was unfamiliar. Guy turned and squinted into the sunlight. He was stunned to see Lewiston's wife getting out of her car. Her face was twisted in rage. She started toward him.

Guy stood without moving.

"What do you think you're doing," she said, "driving past my house?"

Guy, never good with fast retorts, replied, "It's a free country."

Dolly Lewiston did not stop. She came at him so fast he feared that she might strike him. He actually put his hands up and took a step back. Pathetic weakling yet again. Afraid not only to stick up for his child but of her tormentor's wife too.

She stopped and put a finger in his face.

"You stay away from my family, you hear me?"

It took him a moment to gather his thoughts. "Do you know what your husband did to my daughter?"

"He made a mistake."

"He made fun of an eleven-year-old girl."

"I know what he did. It was dumb. He is very sorry. You have no idea."

"He made my daughter's life a living hell."

"And so, what, you want to do the same to us?"

"Your husband should quit," Guy said.

"For one slip of the tongue?"

"He took away her childhood."

"You're being melodramatic."

"Do you really not remember what it was like back then — being the kid who got picked on every day? My daughter was a happy kid. Not perfect, no. But happy. And now . . ."

"Look, I'm sorry. I really am. But I want you to stay away from my family."

"If he hit her — I mean, like slapped her or something — he'd be gone, right? What he did to Yasmin was even worse."

Dolly Lewiston made a face. "Are you for real?"

"I'm not letting this go."

She took a step toward him. This time he did not back up. Their faces were maybe a foot apart, no more. Her voice became a whisper. "Do you really think being called a name is the worst that can happen to her?"

He opened his mouth but nothing came out.

"You're going after my family, Mr. Novak. My family. The people I love. My husband made a mistake. He apologized. But you still want to attack us. And if that's the case, we will defend ourselves."

"If you're talking about a lawsuit —"

She chuckled. "Oh, no," she said, still in that whisper. "I'm not talking about courts."

"Then what?"

Dolly Lewiston tilted her head to the right. "Have you ever been physically assaulted, Mr. Novak?"

"Is that a threat?"

"It's a question. You said that what my husband did was worse than a physical assault. Let me assure you, Mr. Novak. It is not. I know people. I give them the word — I just hint that someone is trying to hurt me — they'll come by here one night when you're sleeping. When your daughter is sleeping."

Guy's mouth felt dry. He tried to stop his knees from turning to rubber.

"That definitely sounds like a threat, Mrs. Lewiston."

"It isn't. It's a fact. If you want to go after us, we aren't going to sit on our hands and let you. I will go after you with everything I have. Do you understand?"

He didn't reply.

"Do yourself a favor, Mr. Novak. Worry about taking care of your daughter, not my husband. Let it go."

"I won't."

"Then the suffering has just begun."

Dolly Lewiston turned around and left without another word. Guy Novak felt the quake in his legs. He stayed and watched her get in her car and drive away. She did not look back but he could see a smile on her face.

She's nuts, Guy thought.

But did that mean he should back down? Hadn't he backed down his whole damn life? Wasn't that the problem from the get-go here — that he was a man you walked all over?

He opened the front door and headed inside.

"Everything okay?"

It was Beth, his latest girlfriend. She tried too hard to please. They all did. There was such a shortage of men in this age group and so they all tried so hard to both please and not appear desperate and none of them could quite pull it off. Desperation was like that. You could try to mask it, but the smell permeates all covers.

Guy wished that he could get past that. He wished that the women could get past it too, so that they would see him. But that was how it was and so all these relationships stayed on a superficial level. The women would want more. They would try not to pressure and that just felt like pressure. Women were nesters. They wanted to get closer. He wouldn't. But they would stay anyway until he broke it off with them.

"Everything is fine," Guy said to her. "Sorry if I took too long."

"Not at all."

"The girls okay?"

"Yes. Jill's mom came by and picked her up. Yasmin is up in her room."

"Okay, great."

"Are you hungry, Guy? Would you like me to fix you something to eat?"

"Only if you'll join me."

Beth beamed a little, and for some reason that made him feel guilty. The women he dated made him feel both worthless and superior at the same time. Feelings of self-loathing consumed him once again.

She came over and kissed his cheek. "You go relax and I'll start making lunch."

"Great, I'm just going to quickly check my e-mail."

But when Guy checked his computer, there was only one new e-mail. It came from an anonymous Hotmail account and the short message chilled Guy's blood.

Please listen to me. You need to hide your gun better.

Tia almost wished that she'd taken up Hester Crimstein's offer. She sat in her house and wondered if she had ever felt more useless in her entire life. She called Adam's friends, but no one knew anything. Fear built in her head. Jill, no dummy when it came to her parents' moods, knew something was seriously off.

"Where's Adam, Mommy?"

"We don't know, honey."

"I called his cell," Jill said. "He didn't answer."

"I know. We're trying to find him."

She looked at her daughter's face. So adult. The second kid grows up so much differently from the first. You so overprotect your first. You watch his every step. You think his every breath is somehow God's divine plan.

The earth, moon, stars, sun — they all revolve around a firstborn.

Tia thought about secrets, about inner thoughts and fears, and how she'd been trying to find her son's. She wondered if this disappearance confirmed that she'd been right to do it or wrong. We all have our problems, she knew. Tia had anxiety issues. She religiously made the kids wear headgear when playing any sort of sport — eyewear too when it was called for. She stayed at the bus stop until they got in, even now, even when Adam was far too old for such treatment and would never stand it, so she hid and watched. She didn't like them crossing busy streets or heading to the center of town on their bikes. She didn't like carpooling because that other mother might not be as careful a driver. She listened to every story about every child tragedy — every car accident, every pool drowning, every abduction, every plane crash, anything. She listened and then she came home and looked it up online and read every article on it and while Mike would sigh and try to calm her down by talking about the long-shot odds, prove to her that her anxiety was unfounded, it would do no good.

Long odds still happened to someone. And now it was happening to her.

Had these been anxiety issues — or had Tia been right all along?

Once again Tia's cell jangled and once again she grabbed it fast, hoping with everything she had that it was Adam. It wasn't. The number was blocked.

"Hello?"

"Mrs. Baye? This is Detective Schlich."

The tall woman cop from the hospital. The fear struck yet again. You think that you can't keep feeling fresh waves, but the stabs never make you numb. "Yes?"

"Your son's phone was found in a trash can not far from where your husband got jumped."

"So he was there?"

"Well, yes, we assumed that already."

"And someone must have stolen his phone."

"That's another question. The most likely reason for tossing the phone was that someone — probably your son — saw your husband there and realized how he'd been tracked down."

"But you don't know that."

"No, Mrs. Baye, I don't know that."

"Will this development make you take the case more seriously?"

"We were always taking it seriously," Schlich said.

"You know what I meant."

"I do. Look, we call this street Vampire Row because there is no one here during the day. No one. So tonight, when the clubs and bars open again, yes, we will go out and ask questions."

Hours yet. Nightfall.

"If anything else develops, I will let you know."

"Thank you."

Tia was hanging up the phone when she saw the car pull into her driveway. She moved toward the window and watched as Betsy Hill, Spencer's mother, stepped out of the vehicle and started toward her door.

Ilene Goldfarb woke up early in the morning and flicked on the coffee maker. She slipped into her robe and slippers and padded down her driveway to grab the paper. Her husband, Herschel, was still in bed. Her son, Hal, had been out late last night, as befits a teenager in his last year of high school. Hal had already been accepted at Princeton, her alma mater. He had worked hard to get there. Now he blew off steam, and she was fine with that.

The morning sun warmed the kitchen. Ilene sat in her favorite chair and curled her legs under her. She pushed away the medical journals. There were a lot of them. Not only was she a renowned transplant surgeon but her husband was considered the top cardiac man in northern New Jersey, practicing out of Valley Hospital in Ridgewood.

Ilene sipped the coffee. She read the paper. She thought about the simple pleasures of life and how rarely she indulged them. She thought about Herschel, upstairs, how handsome he was when they met in medical school, how they had survived the insane hours and rigors of medical school, of internship, of residency, of surgical fellowships, of work. She thought about her feelings for him, how they had mellowed over the years into something she found comforting, how Herschel had recently sat her down and suggested a "trial separation" now that Hal was about to leave the nest.

"What's left?" Herschel had asked her, spreading his hands. "When you really think about us as a couple, what's left, Ilene?"

Sitting alone in the kitchen, scant feet from where her husband of twenty-four years had asked that question, she could still hear his words echo.

Ilene had pushed herself and worked so hard, gone for it all, and she had gotten it: the incredible career, the wonderful family, the big house, respect of peers and friends.

Now her husband wondered what was left. What indeed. The mellow had been such a slow slide, so gradual, that she had never really seen it. Or cared to see it. Or wanted more. Who the hell knew?

She looked toward the stairs. She was tempted to go back up right this very moment and crawl into bed with Herschel and make love to him for hours, like they used to too many years ago, boink those "what's left" doubts right out of his head. But she couldn't make herself get up. She just couldn't. So she read the paper and sipped her coffee and wiped her eyes.

"Hey, Mom."

Hal opened the refrigerator and drank straight from the container of orange juice. There was a time she'd correct him on this — she'd tried for years — but really, Hal was the only one who drank orange juice and too many hours get wasted on stuff like that. He was going off to college now. Their time together was running out. Why fill it with nonsense like that?

"Hey, sweetheart. Out late?"

He drank some more, shrugged. He wore shorts and a gray T-shirt. There was a basketball cropped under his arm.

"Are you playing at the high school gym?" she asked.

"No, Heritage." Then he took one more swig and said to her, "You okay?"

"Me? Of course. Why wouldn't I be?"

"Your eyes look red."

"I'm fine."

"And I saw those guys come by."

He meant the FBI agents. They had come and asked questions about her practice, about Mike, about stuff that simply made no sense to her. Normally she would have talked to Herschel about it, but he seemed more concerned with preparing for the rest of his life without her.

"I thought you'd gone out," she said.

"I stopped to pick up Ricky and doubled back down the street. They looked like cops or something."

Ilene Goldfarb said nothing.

"Were they?"

"It's not important. Don't worry about it."

He let it go, bounced the ball and himself out the door. Twenty minutes later, the phone rang. She glanced at the clock. Eight A.M. At this hour it had to be the service, though she wasn't on call. The operators often made mistakes and routed the messages to the wrong doctor.

She checked the caller ID and saw the name LORIMAN.

Ilene picked up and said hello.

"It's Susan Loriman," the voice said.

"Yes, good morning."

"I don't want to talk to Mike about this" — Susan Loriman stopped as if searching for the right word — "this situation. About finding Lucas a donor."

"I understand," she said. "I have office hours on Tuesday, if you want —"

"Could you meet me today?"

Ilene was about to protest. The last thing right now she wanted to do was protect or even help a woman who had gotten herself into this kind of trouble. But this wasn't about Susan Loriman, she reminded herself. It was about her son and Ilene's patient, Lucas.

"I guess so, yes."

23

Tia opened the door before Betsy Hill had a chance to knock and asked without preamble: "Do you know where Adam is?"

The question startled Betsy Hill. Her eyes widened and she stopped. She saw Tia's face and quickly shook her head. "No," she said, "I have no idea."

"Then why are you here?"

Betsy Hill shook her head. "Adam is missing?"

"Yes."

Betsy's face lost color. Tia could only imagine what horrible memory this was conjuring up. Hadn't Tia thought before about how similar this whole thing was to what happened to Spencer?

"Tia?"

"Yes."

"Did you check the high school roof?"

Where Spencer was found.

There was no argument, no more discussion. Tia called out to Jill that she'd be right back — Jill would soon be old enough to leave alone for brief spells and it couldn't be helped — and then both women ran toward Betsy Hill's car.

Betsy drove. Tia sat frozen in the front passenger seat. They had driven two blocks when Betsy said, "I talked to Adam yesterday."

Tia heard the words, but they didn't fully reach her. "What?"

"Do you know about the memorial they did for Spencer on MySpace?"

Tia tried to swim through the haze, pay attention. The memorial site on MySpace. She remembered hearing about it a few months ago.

"Yes."

"There was a new picture on it."

"I don't understand."

"It was taken right before Spencer died."

"I thought he was alone the night he died," Tia said.

"So did I."

"I'm still not following."

"I think," Betsy Hill said, "that Adam was with Spencer that night."

Tia turned to face her. Betsy Hill had her eyes on the road. "And you talked to him about this yesterday?"

"Yes."
"Where?"
"In the lot after school."
Tia remembered the instant messages with CeeJay8115:
What's wrong?
His mother approached me after school.
Tia asked, "Why didn't you come to me?"
"Because I didn't want to hear your explanation, Tia," Betsy said. There was an edge in her voice now. "I wanted to hear Adam's."
The high school, a sprawling edifice of numbing brick, loomed in the distance. Betsy had barely come to a stop when Tia was already out the door and sprinting toward the brick building. Spencer's body, she remembered, had been found on one of the lower roofs, a well-known smoking hangout from way back when. There was a ledge by a window. The kids would hop up there and scale a gutter.
"Wait," Betsy Hill called out.
But Tia was almost there. It was Saturday, but there were still plenty of cars in the lots. All SUVs and minivans. There were kids' baseball games and soccer clinics. Parents stood on the sidelines clutching Starbucks cups, gabbing on cell phones, snapping

photos with long-range lenses, fiddling with BlackBerrys. Tia had never liked going to Adam's sporting events because as much as she didn't want to, she ended up caring too much. She loathed those pushy parents who lived and breathed their child's athletic prowess — found them both petty and pitiful — and wanted to be nothing like them. But when she watched her own son compete, she felt so much, worried so about Adam's happiness, that his highs and lows wore her down.

Tia blinked away the tears and kept running. When she reached the ledge, she stopped short.

The ledge was gone.

"They destroyed it after Spencer was found," Betsy said, coming up behind her. "They wanted to make sure that the kids couldn't get up there anymore. I'm sorry. I forgot about that."

Tia looked up. "Kids can always find a new way," she said.

"I know."

Tia and Betsy quickly searched for a new approach, couldn't find any. They sprinted around to the front entrance. The door was locked, so they banged on it until a custodian with KARL stenciled onto his uniform appeared.

"We're closed," Karl said through the door's glass window.

"We need to get to the roof," Tia shouted.

"The roof?" He frowned. "What on earth for?"

"Please," Tia said. "You have to let us in."

The custodian's gaze slid to the right and when he spotted Betsy Hill, a jolt tore through him. No doubt. He had recognized her. Without another word, he grabbed his keys and threw open the doors.

"This way," he said.

They all ran. Tia's heart pounded so hard that she was sure it would burst through her rib cage. Tears were still filling her eyes. Karl opened a door and pointed to the corner. There was a ladder attached to a wall, the kind of thing you normally associate with a submarine. Tia did not hesitate. She sprinted for it and began to climb. Betsy Hill was right behind her.

They reached the roof, but they were on the opposite side from where they needed to be. Tia sprinted over the tar and gravel with Betsy right behind her. The roofs were uneven. One time they had to jump down almost a full story. They both did it without hesitation.

"Around this corner," Betsy called out.

They made the turn onto the right roof and pulled up.

There was no body.

That was the key thing. Adam was not up here. But someone had been.

There were broken beer bottles. There were cigarette butts and what looked like the remains of pot. What had they called those butts? Roaches. But that wasn't what made Tia stay very still.

There were candles.

Dozens of them. Most were burnt down to a waxy mess. Tia went over and touched them. The residue had hardened on most, but one or two were still malleable, as if they had just been burnt down recently.

Tia turned. Betsy Hill stood there. She didn't move. She didn't cry. She just stood there and stared at the candles.

"Betsy?"

"That's where they found Spencer's body," she said.

Tia squatted down, looked at the candles, knew that they looked familiar.

"Right where those candles are. That exact spot. I came up here before they moved Spencer. I insisted. They wanted to take him down, but I said no. I wanted to see him first. I wanted to see where my boy died."

Betsy took a step closer. Tia did not move.

"I used the ledge, the one they knocked off. One of the police officers tried to give me a boost. I told him to leave me the hell alone. I made them all move back. Ron thought I was crazy. He tried to talk me out of it. But I climbed up. And Spencer was right there. Right where you are now. He lay on his side. His legs were curled up in a fetal position. That was how he slept too. In a fetal position. Until he was ten he still sucked his thumb when he slept. Do you ever watch your children sleep, Tia?"

Tia nodded. "I think all parents do."

"Why do you think that is?"

"Because they look so innocent."

"Maybe." Betsy smiled. "But I think it's because we can just stare at them and marvel at them and not feel weird about it. If you stare at them like that during the day, they'll think you're nuts. But when they're sleeping . . ."

Her voice drifted off. She started to look around and said, "This roof is pretty big."

Tia was confused by the change of subjects. "I guess."

"The roof," Betsy said again. "It's big. There are broken bottles all over the place."

She looked at Tia. Not sure how to respond, Tia said, "Okay."

"Whoever burnt those candles," Betsy went on. "They picked the exact spot where Spencer was found. It was never in the papers. So how did they know? If Spencer was alone that night, how did they know to burn the candles exactly where he died?"

Mike knocked on the door.

He stood on the stoop and waited. Mo stayed in the car. They were less than a mile from where Mike had gotten jumped last night. He wanted to go back to that alley, see what he could remember or dig up or, well, whatever. He really didn't have a clue. He was flailing and poking and hoping something would lead him closer to his son.

This stop, he knew, was probably his best chance.

He had called Tia and told her about having no luck with Huff. Tia had told him about her visit with Betsy Hill to the school. Betsy was still at the house.

Tia said, "Adam has been a lot more withdrawn since the suicide."

"I know."

"So maybe there's more to what happened that night."

"Like what?"

Silence.

"Betsy and I still need to talk," Tia said.
"Be careful, okay?"
"What do you mean?"
Mike did not reply, but both of them knew. The truth was, horrible as it might seem, that their interests and the Hills' interests might no longer be in harmony. Neither one of them wanted to say it. But they both knew.
"Let's just find him first," Tia said.
"That's what I'm trying to do. You work your end, I'll work mine."
"I love you, Mike."
"I love you too."
Mike knocked again. There was no answer at the door. He lifted his hand to knock a third time when the door opened. Anthony the bouncer filled the doorway. He folded his massive arms and said, "You look like hell."
"Thanks, I appreciate that."
"How did you find me?"
"I went online and looked up recent photographs of the Dartmouth football team. You only graduated last year. Your address is registered in the alumni site."
"Smart," Anthony said with a small smile. "We Dartmouth men are very smart."
"I got jumped in that alley."
"Yeah, I know. Who do you think called the police?"

"You?"

He shrugged. "Come on. Let's take a walk."

Anthony closed the door behind him. He was dressed in workout clothes. He wore shorts and one of those tight sleeveless tees that were suddenly the rage not just with guys like Anthony, who could pull it off, but guys Mike's age who simply couldn't.

"It's just a summer gig," Anthony said. "Working at the club. But I like it. I'm going to law school at Columbia in the fall."

"My wife is a lawyer."

"Yeah, I know. And you're a doctor."

"How do you know that?"

He grinned. "You're not the only one who can use college connections."

"You looked me up online?"

"Nah. I called the current hockey coach — a guy named Ken Karl, also worked as the defensive line coach on the football team. Described what you looked liked, told him you claimed to be an All-American. He said 'Mike Baye' right away. Says you were one of the best hockey players the school ever had. You still hold some scoring record."

"So does this mean we have a bond, Anthony?"

The big man didn't reply.

They headed down the stoop. Anthony

turned right. A man approaching in the other direction called out, "Yo, Ant!" and the two men did a complicated handshake before moving on.

Mike said, "Tell me what happened last night."

"Three, maybe four guys kicked the crap out of you. I heard the commotion. When I got there, they were running away. One of the guys had a knife. I thought you were a goner."

"You scared them off?"

Anthony shrugged.

"Thanks."

Another shrug.

"You get a look at them?"

"Not their faces. But they were white guys. Lots of tattoos. Dressed in black. Skanky and skinny and stoned out of their freakin' minds, I bet. Lots of anger. One was cupping his nose and cursing." Anthony smiled again. "I do believe you broke it."

"And you're the one who called the cops?"

"Yup. Can't believe you're out of bed already. I figured you'd be out of commission for at least a week."

They kept walking.

"Last night, the kid with the varsity jacket," Mike said. "Had you seen him before?"

Anthony said nothing.

"You recognized my son's picture too."

Anthony stopped. He plucked sunglasses out of his collar and put them on. They covered his eyes. Mike waited.

"Our Big Green connection only goes so far, Mike."

"You said you're amazed I'm out of bed already."

"That I did."

"You want to know why?"

He shrugged.

"My son is still missing. His name is Adam. He's sixteen years old, and I think he's in a lot of danger."

Anthony kept walking. "Sorry to hear about that."

"I need some information."

"I look like the Yellow Pages to you? I live out there. I don't talk about what I see."

"Don't hand me that 'code of the street' crap."

"And don't hand me that 'Dartmouth men stick together' crap."

Mike put his hand on the big man's arm. "I need your help."

Anthony pulled away, started walking faster. Mike caught up to him.

"I'm not leaving, Anthony."

"Didn't think you would," he said. He

stopped. "Did you like it up there?"

"Where?"

"Dartmouth."

"Yeah," Mike said. "I liked it a lot."

"Me too. It was like a different world. You know what I'm saying?"

"I do."

"No one in this neighborhood knew about that school."

"How did you end up there?"

He smiled, adjusted the sunglasses. "You mean a big black brother from the streets going to lily-white Dartmouth?"

"Yeah," Mike said. "That's exactly what I mean."

"I was a good football player, maybe even great. I got recruited Division 1A. Could have gone Big Ten."

"But?"

"But I also knew my limitations. I wasn't good enough to go pro. So what would be the point? No education, joke diploma. So I went to Dartmouth. Got a full ride and liberal arts degree. No matter what else, I will always be an Ivy League graduate."

"And now you're going to Columbia Law."

"Yup."

"And then? I mean, after you graduate."

"I'm staying in the neighborhood. I didn't

do this to get out. I like it here. I just want to make it better."

"Good to be a stand-up guy."

"Right, but bad to be a snitch."

"You can't walk away from this, Anthony."

"Yeah, I know."

"Under different circumstances, I'd love to keep chatting about our alma mater," Mike said.

"But you got a kid to save."

"Right."

"I've seen your son before, I think. I mean, they all look alike to me, what with the black clothes and the sullen faces, like the world gave them everything and that pisses them off. I got trouble sympathizing. Out here, you get stoned to escape. What the hell do these kids have to escape from — a nice house, parents who love them?"

"It's not that simple," Mike said.

"I guess."

"I came from nothing too. Sometimes I think it's easier. Ambition is natural when you don't have anything. You know what you're driving for."

Anthony said nothing.

"My son is a good kid. He's going through something right now. It's my job to protect him until he finds his way back out."

"Your job. Not mine."

"Did you see him last night, Anthony?"

"Might have. I don't know much. I really don't."

Mike just looked at him.

"There's a club for underage kids. Supposedly it's a safe place for teens to hang out. They got counselors and therapy and stuff like that, but that's supposed to be just a front to party."

"Where is it?"

"Two, three blocks down from my club."

"And when you say, 'just a front to party,' what do you mean exactly?"

"What do you think I mean? Drugs, underage drinking, stuff like that. There are rumors of mind control and crap like that. I don't believe them. One thing though. People who don't belong stay clear."

"Meaning?"

"Meaning they got a rep as very dangerous too. Maybe mobbed up, I don't know. But people don't give them trouble. That's all I mean."

"And you think my son went there?"

"If he was in that area and he was sixteen years old, yeah. Yeah, I think he probably went there."

"Does the place have a name?"

"Club Jaguar, I think. I have an address."

He gave it to him. Mike handed him his business card.

"This has all my phone numbers," Mike said.

"Uh-huh."

"If you see my son . . ."

"I'm not a babysitter, Mike."

"That's okay. My son isn't a baby."

Tia was holding the photograph of Spencer Hill.

"I don't see how you can be sure it's Adam."

"I wasn't," Betsy Hill said. "But then I confronted him."

"He might have just freaked out because he was seeing a picture of his dead friend."

"Could be," Betsy agreed in a way that clearly meant, *Not a chance.*

"And you're sure this picture was taken the night he died?"

"Yes."

Tia nodded. The silence fell on them. They were back at the Baye house. Jill was upstairs watching TV. The sounds of *Hannah Montana* wafted down. Tia sat there. So did Betsy Hill.

"So what do you think this means, Betsy?"

"Everyone said they didn't see Spencer

that night. That he was alone."

"And you think this means that they did?"

"Yes."

Tia pressed a little. "And if he wasn't alone, what would that mean?"

Betsy thought about it. "I don't know."

"You did get a suicide note, right?"

"By text. Anyone can send a text."

Tia saw it again. In a sense the two mothers were at odds. If what Betsy Hill said about the photograph was true, then Adam had lied. And if Adam had lied, then who really knew what happened that night?

So Tia didn't tell her about the instant messages with CeeJay8115, the ones about the mother who approached Adam. Not yet. Not until she knew more.

"I missed some signs," Betsy said.

"Like?"

Betsy Hill closed her eyes.

"Betsy?"

"I spied on him once. Not really spied but . . . Spencer was on the computer and when he left the room, I just sneaked in. To see what he was looking at. You know? I shouldn't have. It was wrong — invading his privacy like that."

Tia said nothing.

"But anyway I hit that back arrow, you

know, at the top of the browser?"

Tia nodded.

"And . . . and he'd been visiting some suicide sites. There were stories about kids who had killed themselves, I guess. Stuff like that. I didn't look too long. And I never did anything about it. I just blocked."

Tia looked at Spencer in the photograph. She looked for signs that the boy would be dead within hours, as if that would somehow show on his face. There was nothing, but what did that mean?

"Did you show this picture to Ron?" she asked.

"Yes."

"What did he make of it?"

"He wonders what difference it makes. Our son committed suicide, he said, so what are you trying to figure out, Betsy? He thinks I'm doing this to get closure."

"Aren't you?"

"Closure," Betsy repeated, nearly spitting the word out as though it tasted bad in her mouth. "What does that even mean? Like somewhere up ahead there's a door and I'll walk through it and then close it and Spencer stays on the other side? I don't want that, Tia. Can you imagine anything more obscene than having closure?"

They went quiet again, the annoying laugh

track from Jill's show the only sound.

"The police think your son ran away," Betsy said. "They think mine committed suicide."

Tia nodded.

"But suppose they're wrong. Suppose they're wrong about both of our boys."

24

Nash sat in the van and tried to figure his next move.

Nash's upbringing had been normal. He knew that psychiatric types would want to examine that statement, searching for some kind of sexual abuse or excess or streak of religious conservatism. Nash thought that they would find nothing. His were good parents and siblings. Maybe too good. They had covered for him the way families do for one another. In hindsight some might view that as a mistake, but it takes a lot for family to accept the truth.

Nash was intelligent and thus he knew early on that he was what some might call "damaged." There is the old catch-22 line that a mentally unstable person can't know, as per their illness, that they are unstable. But that was wrong. You can and do have the insight to see your own crazy. Nash knew that all his wires weren't connected or that there might be some bug in the system. He knew that he was different, that he was not of the norm. That didn't necessarily make him feel inferior — or superior. He knew that his mind went to very dark places and liked it there. He did not feel things the way others did, did not sympathize with people's pain the way others pretended they did.

The key word: "pretended."

Pietra sat in the seat next to him.

"Why does man make himself out to be so special?" he asked her.

She said nothing.

"Forget the fact that this planet — nay, this solar system — is so insignificantly small that we can't even comprehend it. Try this. Imagine you're on a huge beach. Imagine you pick up one tiny grain of sand. Just one. Then you look up and down this long beach that stretches in both directions as far as the eye can see. Do you think our entire solar system is as small as that grain of sand is to that beach in comparison to the universe?"

"I don't know."

"Well, if you did, you'd be wrong. It is much, much smaller. Try this: Imagine you're still holding that tiny grain of sand. Now not just the beach you are on, but all the beaches all over the planet, all of them, all down the coast of California and the East

Coast from Maine down to Florida and on the Indian Ocean and off the coasts of Africa. Imagine all that sand, all those beaches everywhere in the world and now look at that grain of sand you're holding and still, *still,* our entire solar system — forget our planet — is smaller than that compared to the rest of the universe. Can you even comprehend how insignificant we are?"

Pietra said nothing.

"But forget that for a moment," Nash went on, "because man is even insignificant here on this very planet. Let's take this whole argument down to just earth for a moment, okay?"

She nodded.

"Do you realize that dinosaurs walked this planet longer than man?"

"Yes."

"But that's not all. That would be one thing that would show that man is not special — the fact that even on this infinitesimally small planet we haven't even been kings the majority of the time. But take it a step farther — do you realize how much longer the dinosaurs ruled the earth than us? Two times? Five times? Ten times?"

She looked at him. "I don't know."

"Forty-four thousand times longer." He was gesturing wildly now, lost in the bliss of his argument. "Think about that. Forty-four thousand times longer. That's more than one hundred and twenty years for every single day. Can you even comprehend it? Do you think we will survive forty-four thousand times longer than we already have?"

"No," she said.

Nash sat back. "We are nothing. Man. Nothing. Yet we feel as though we are special. We think we matter or that God considers us his favorites. What a laugh."

In college, Nash studied John Locke's state of nature — the idea that the best government is the least government because, put simply, it is closest to the state of nature, or what God intended. But in that state, we are animals. It is nonsense to think we are anything more. How silly to believe that man is above that and that love and friendship are anything but the ravings of a more intelligent mind, a mind that can see the futility and thus must invent ways to comfort and distract itself from it.

Was Nash the sane one for seeing the darkness — or were most people just self-delusional? And yet.

And yet for many years Nash had longed for normalcy.

He saw the carefree and craved it. He realized that he was way above average in intelligence. He was a straight-A student with nearly perfect SAT scores. He matriculated at Williams College, where he majored in philosophy — all the while trying to keep the crazy away. But the crazy wanted out.

So why not let it out?

There was in him some primitive instinct to protect his parents and siblings, but the rest of the world's inhabitants did not matter to him. They were background scenery, props, nothing more. The truth was — a truth he understood early — he derived intense pleasure from harming others. He always had. He didn't know why. Some people derive pleasure from a soft breeze or a warm hug or a victory shot in a basketball game. Nash derived it from ridding the planet of another inhabitant. He didn't ask this for himself, but he saw it and sometimes he could fight it and sometimes he could not.

Then he met Cassandra.

It was like one of those science experiments that start with a clear liquid and then someone adds a small drop — a catalyst — to it and it changes everything. The color changes and the complexion changes and the texture changes. Corny as it sounds, Cassandra was that catalyst.

He saw her and she touched him and it transformed him.

He suddenly got it. He got love. He got hope and dreams and the idea of wanting to wake up and spend your life with another person. They met during their sophomore year at Williams. Cassandra was beautiful, but there was something more there. Every guy had a crush on her, though not really the fantasy-sexual kind you usually associate with college. With her awkward gait and knowing smile, Cassandra was the one you wanted to bring home. She was the one who made you think about buying a house and cutting your lawn and building a barbecue and wiping her brow when she gave birth to your child. You were wowed by her beauty, yes, but you were more wowed by her innate goodness. She was special and could do no harm and you instinctively knew it.

He'd seen a little of that in Reba Cordova, just a little, and there had been a pang when he had killed her, not much of one, but a pang. He thought about her husband, what he would have to go through now, because while he didn't really care, Nash knew something about it.

Cassandra.

She had five brothers and they all adored her and her parents adored her and whenever you walked past her and she smiled at you, even if you were a stranger, you felt the pluck deep in your heart. Her family called her Cassie. Nash did not like that. She was Cassandra to him and he loved her and on the day he married her, he understood what people meant when they said you were "blessed."

They came back to Williams for homecoming and reunions and they always stayed in North Adams at the Porches Inn. He could see her there, at that inn in the gray house, her head resting on his stomach as a recent song reminded him, her eyes on the ceiling, him stroking her hair as they talked about nothing and everything and that was how he saw her when he looked back now, how he pictured her — before she felt sick and they said it was cancer and they cut up his beautiful Cassandra and she died, just like every other insignificant organism on this tiny nothing of a planet.

Yes, Cassandra died and that was when he knew for certain that it was all a crock and a joke and once she was gone, Nash didn't have the strength to worry about stopping the crazy anymore. There was no need. So he let the crazy out, all out, with a sudden flooding rush. And once it was out, there was no putting it back.

Her family tried to console him. They had "faith" and explained again that he had been "blessed" to have her at all and that she would be waiting for him in some beautiful place for all eternity. They needed it, he guessed. The family had already picked up after another tragedy — her oldest brother, Curtis, had been killed three years before in some sort of robbery gone bad — but at least, in that case, Curtis had lived a life of trouble. Cassandra had been crushed when her brother died, had cried for days until Nash wanted to let the crazy out just to find a way to ease her pain, but in the end, those who had faith could rationalize Curtis's death. Faith let them explain it as part of some grand scheme.

But how do you explain losing someone as loving and warm as Cassandra?

You can't. So her parents talked about the hereafter, but they didn't really believe that. No one else did. Why cry at death if you believe that you will spend eternity in bliss? Why mourn the loss of someone when that person was now in a better place? Wasn't that horribly selfish of you — keeping a loved one from someplace better? And if you did believe that you spent eternity in paradise with the loved one, there would never be anything to fear — life is not even one breath next to eternity.

You cry and mourn, Nash knew, because

deep inside, you knew it was a crock.

Cassandra wasn't with her brother Curtis, bathing in white light. What was left of her, what hadn't been taken by the cancer and the chemo, was rotting away in the ground.

At the funeral, her family talked about fate and plans and all that nonsense too. That this had been his beloved's fate — to live briefly, touch everyone who saw her, raise him to a wonderful height, let him drop to the ground with a splat. This has been his fate too. He wondered about that. Even when he was with her, there had been moments where containing his true nature — his honest, most godlike state of nature — had been difficult. Would he have been able to maintain the peace inside? Or had he been hardwired from day one to go back to the dark place and cause destruction, even if Cassandra had survived?

It was impossible to know. But either way this was his fate.

Pietra said, "She would have never said anything."

He knew that she was talking about Reba. "We don't know that."

Pietra looked out the side window.

"Eventually the police will get an ID on Marianne," he said. "Or someone will realize that she's missing. The police will look into it. They'll talk to her friends. Reba would have told them then for certain."

"You are sacrificing many lives."

"Two so far."

"And the survivors. Their lives are altered."

"Yes."

"Why?"

"You know why."

"Are you going to claim Marianne started it?"

"Started is not the right word. She changed the dynamics."

"So she dies?"

"She made a decision that altered and could potentially destroy lives."

"So she dies?" Pietra repeated.

"All our decisions carry weight, Pietra. We all play God every day. When a woman buys a new pair of expensive shoes, she could have spent that same money feeding someone who was starving. In a sense, those shoes mean more to her than a life. We all kill to make our lives more comfortable. We don't put it in those terms. But we do."

She didn't argue.

"What's going on, Pietra?"

"Nothing. Forget it."

"I promised Cassandra."

"Yes. So you said."

"We need to keep this contained, Pietra."

"Do you think we can?"

"I do."

"So how many more will we kill?"

He was puzzled by the question. "Do you really care? Have you had enough?"

"I'm just asking about now. Today. With this. How many more will we kill?"

Nash thought about it. He realized now that perhaps Marianne had told him the truth in the beginning. In that case, he needed to go back to square one and snuff out the problem at its source.

"With a little luck," he said, "only one."

"Wow," Loren Muse said. "Could this woman be more boring?"

Clarence smiled. They were going through the credit card receipts for Reba Cordova. There were absolutely no surprises. She bought groceries and school supplies and kid clothes. She bought a vacuum at Sears and returned it. She bought a microwave at P.C. Richard. Her credit card was on file at a Chinese restaurant called Baumgarts, where she ordered takeout every Tuesday night.

Her e-mails were equally dull. She wrote to other parents about playdates. She kept in touch with one daughter's dance instructor and the other's soccer coach. She received the Willard School e-mail. She kept up with her tennis group about scheduling and filling in when one of them couldn't make it. She was on the Williams-Sonoma, Pottery Barn and PetSmart newsletter lists. She wrote to her sister asking her for the name of a reading specialist because one of her daughters, Sarah, was having trouble.

"I didn't know people like this really existed," Muse said.

But she did. She saw them at Starbucks, the harried, doe-eyed women who thought a coffee shop was the perfect place for Mommy and Me hour, what with Brittany and Madison and Kyle in tow, all running around while the mommies — college graduates, former intellectuals — gabbed incessantly about their offspring as if no other child had ever existed. They gabbed about their poopies — yes, for real, their bowel movements! — and their first word and their social skills and their Montessori schools and their gymnastics and their Baby Einstein DVDs and they all had this brain-gone smile, like some alien had sucked their head dry, and Muse despised them on one level, pitied them on another and tried so damn hard not to be envious.

Loren Muse swore, of course, that she would never be like those mommies if she ever did have children. But who knew? Blanket declarations like that reminded her of the people who said that when they were old they'd rather be dead than end up in a nursing home or be a burden to their grown children — and now almost everyone she knew had parents who were either in a nursing home or a burden and none of those old people wanted to die.

If you look at anything from the outside, it is easy to make sweeping ungenerous judgments.

"How is the husband's alibi?" she asked.

"The Livingston police questioned Cordova. It seems pretty solid."

Muse motioned at the paperwork with her jaw. "And is the husband as boring as the wife?"

"I'm still going through all his e-mails, phone records, and credit card stuff, but yeah, so far."

"What else?"

"Well, assuming that the same killer or killers took Reba Cordova and Jane Doe, we have patrolmen checking the spots known for prostitution, seeing if another body gets dumped."

Loren Muse didn't think that was going to happen but it was worth looking into. One of the possible scenarios here was that some serial killer, with the willing or unwilling help of a female accomplice, grabbed suburban women, killed them, and wanted them to appear to be prostitutes. They were going through the computers now, seeing if any other victims in nearby cities fit that description. So far, goose egg.

Muse didn't buy this particular theory anyway. Psychologists and profilers would have a quasi-orgasm at the idea of a serial killer working suburban moms and making them up to be prostitutes. They would pontificate on the obvious mom-whore linkage, but Muse didn't really buy it. There was one question that didn't fit with this scenario, a question that had been bugging her from the moment she'd realized that Jane Doe was not a street hooker: Why hadn't anyone reported Jane Doe missing?

There were two possible reasons she could see. One, nobody knew that she was missing. Jane Doe was on vacation or supposed to be on a business trip or something like that. Or two, someone who knew her had killed her. And that someone didn't want to report her missing.

"Where is the husband now?"

"Cordova? He's still with the Livingston cops. They're going to canvass the neighborhood and see if anyone saw a white van, you know, the usual."

Muse picked up a pencil. She put the eraser end in her mouth and chewed.

There was a knock on her door. She looked up and saw the soon-to-be-retired Frank Tremont filling her doorway.

Third day in a row with the same brown suit, Muse thought. Impressive.

He looked at her and waited. She didn't have time for this, but it was probably better to get it over with.

"Clarence, you mind leaving us alone?"

"Yeah, Chief, sure thing."

Clarence gave Frank Tremont a little nod as he left. Tremont did not return it. When Clarence was out of sight, he shook his head and said, "Did he call you chief?"

"I'm kind of pressed for time, Frank."

"You got my letter?"

His resignation letter. "I did."

Silence.

"I have something for you," Tremont said.

"Excuse me?"

"I'm not out until the end of next month," he said. "So I still need to do work, right?"

"Right."

"So I got something."

She leaned back, hoping he would make it a quick.

"I start looking into that white van. The one at both scenes."

"Okay."

"I don't think it was stolen, unless it was out of the area. There is really nothing reported that matches it. So I started searching rent-a-car companies, seeing if anyone rented a van like the one we described."

"And?"

"There are some, but most I was able to trace down fast and find out they're legit."

"So it's a dead end."

Frank Tremont smiled. "Mind if I sit down a second?"

She waved at the chair.

"I tried one more thing," he said. "See, this guy has been pretty clever. Like you said. Setting up the first to look like a hooker. Parking the second vic's car in a hotel lot. Changing the license plates and all. He doesn't do it in the typical way. So I started wondering. What would be better and less traceable than stealing or renting a car?"

"I'm listening."

"Buying a used one online. Have you seen those sites?"

"Not really, no."

"They sell a zillion cars. I bought one there last year, on autoused.com. You can find real bargains — and since it is person to person, the paperwork is iffy. I mean, we might check dealers, but who is going to track down a car via an online purchase?"

"So?"

"So I called the two major online companies. I asked them to backdate and find me any white Chevy vans sold in this area for the past month. I found six. I called all of them. Four were paid for with checks so we got addresses. Two paid in cash."

Muse sat back. The pencil eraser was still in her mouth. "Pretty clever. You buy the used car. You pay with cash. You give a phony name if any name at all. You get the title, but you never register it or buy insurance. You steal a license plate from a similar make and you're on your way."

"Yep." Tremont smiled. "Except for one thing."

"What?"

"The guy who sold them the car —"

"Them?"

"Yep. Man and a woman. He says mid-thirties. I'm going for a full description, but we may have something better. The guy who sold it, Scott Parsons from Kasselton, works in Best Buy. They have a pretty good security system. All digital. So they save everything. He thinks they may have a time-delay film of them. He's having a tech guy check now. I sent a car to go bring him in, let him look at some mug shots, get the best ID I can."

"We have a sketch artist he can work with?"

Tremont nodded. "Taken care of."

It was a legit lead — the best they'd gotten. Muse wasn't sure what to say.

"What else we got going on?" Tremont asked.

She filled him in on the nothingness of the credit card records, the phone records, the e-mails. Tremont sat back and rested his hands on his paunch.

"When I came in," Tremont said, "you were chewing hard on that pencil. What were you thinking about?"

"The assumption now is that this might be a serial killer."

"You're not buying that," he said.

"I'm not."

"Neither am I," Tremont said. "So let's review what we got."

Muse rose and started pacing. "Two victims. So far, that's it — at least in this area. We have people checking but let's assume that we don't find any more. Let's say this is it. Let's say it is just Reba Cordova — who might be alive for all we know — and Jane Doe."

Tremont said, "Okay."

"And let's take it one step further. Let's say that there is a reason why these two women were the victims."

"Like what?"

"I don't know yet, but just follow me here. If there is a reason . . . forget that. Even if there is no reason and we assume that this is not the work of a serial killer, there has to be a connection between our two victims."

Tremont nodded, seeing where she was going with this. "And if there's a connection between them," he said, "they might very well know each other."

Muse froze. "Exactly."

"And if Reba Cordova knew Jane Doe . . ." Tremont smiled up at her.

"Then Neil Cordova might know Jane Doe too. Call the Livingston Police Department. Tell them to bring Cordova in. Maybe he can identify her for us."

"On it."

"Frank?"

He turned back at her.

"Good work," she said.

"I'm a good cop," he said.

She didn't reply to that.

He pointed at her. "You're a good cop too, Muse. Maybe even a great one. But you're not a good chief. See, a good chief would have gotten the most out of her good cops. You didn't. You need to learn how to manage other people."

Muse shook her head. "Yeah, Frank, that's it. My managerial skills made you screw up and think Jane Doe was a hooker. My bad."

He smiled. "I caught this case," he said.

"And messed it up."

"I may have gotten it wrong to start, but I'm still here. Doesn't matter what I think of you. Doesn't matter what you think of me. All that matters is that we find justice for my victim."

25

Mo drove them to the Bronx. He parked in front of the address Anthony had given him.

"You're not going to believe this," Mo said.

"What?"

"We're being followed."

Mike knew better than to turn around and be obvious about it. So he sat and waited.

"Blue four-door Chevy double-parked down at the end of the block. Two guys, both wearing Yankee caps and sunglasses."

Last night this street had been teeming with people. Now there was practically nobody. Those who were there either slept on a stoop or moved with amazing lethargy, legs congealed together, arms melted against their sides. Mike half expected a patch of tumbleweed to blow through the middle of the street.

"You go in," Mo said. "I got a friend. I'll

give him the license plate and see what he comes up with."

Mike nodded. He got out of the car, trying to be subtle about checking out the car. He barely saw it, but he didn't want to take the chance of looking again. He headed toward the door. There was an industrial-gray metal door with the words CLUB JAGUAR on it. Mike pressed the button. The front door buzzed and he pushed it open.

The walls were done up in a bright yellow usually associated with McDonald's or the children's ward at a trying-too-hard hospital. There was a bulletin board on the right blanketed with sign-up sheets for counseling, for music lessons, for book discussion groups, for therapy groups for drug addicts, alcoholics, the physically and mentally abused. Several flyers were looking for someone to share an apartment and you could tear off the phone number at the bottom. Someone was selling a couch for a hundred bucks. Another person was trying to unload guitar amps.

He moved past the board to the front desk. A young woman with a nose ring looked up and said, "Can I help you?"

He had the photograph of Adam in his hand. "Have you seen this boy?" He put the picture down in front of her.

"I'm just the receptionist," she said.

"Receptionists have eyes. I asked if you've seen him."

"I can't talk about our clients."

"I'm not asking you to talk about them. I'm asking you if you've seen him."

Her lips went thin. He could see now that she also had piercings in the vicinity of her mouth. She stayed still and looked up at him. This, he realized, was going nowhere.

"Can I speak to whoever's in charge?"

"That would be Rosemary."

"Great. Can I speak to her?"

The well-pierced receptionist picked up a phone. She covered the mouthpiece and mumbled into it. Ten seconds later she smiled at him and said, "Miss McDevitt will see you now. Third door on the right."

Mike wasn't sure what he expected, but Rosemary McDevitt was a surprise. She was young, petite and had that sort of raw sensuality that made you think of a puma. She had a purple streak in her dark hair and a tattoo that sneaked up her shoulder and onto her neck. Her top was just a black leather vest, no sleeves. Her arms were toned and she had what looked like leather bands around her biceps.

She stood and smiled and stuck out her hand. "Welcome."

He shook the hand.

"How can I help you?

"My name is Mike Baye."

"Hi, Mike."

"Uh, hi. I'm looking for my son."

He stood close to her. Mike was five ten and he had a little over half a foot on this woman. Rosemary McDevitt looked at Adam's photograph. Her expression gave away nothing.

"Do you know him?" Mike asked.

"You know I can't answer that."

She tried to hand the picture back to him, but Mike didn't take it. Aggressive tactics hadn't gotten him much, so he bit down, took a breath.

"I'm not asking you to betray confidences —"

"Well, yeah, Mike, you are." She smiled sweetly. "That's exactly what you're asking me to do."

"I'm just trying to find my son. That's all."

She spread her arms. "Does this look like a lost and found?"

"He's missing."

"This place is a sanctuary, Mike, you know what I'm saying? Kids come here to escape their parents."

"I'm worried he might be in danger. He

went out without telling anyone. He came here last night —"

"Whoa." She held up a hand to signal for him to stop.

"What?"

"He came here last night. That's what you said, Mike, right?"

"Right."

Her eyes narrowed. "How do you know that, Mike?"

The constant use of his name was grating.

"Pardon me?"

"How do you know your son came here?"

"That's really not important."

She smiled and stepped back. "Sure it is."

He needed a subject change. His eyes took in the room. "What is this place anyway?"

"We're a bit of a hybrid." Rosemary gave him one more look to let him know that she knew what he was trying to do with the question. "Think teen center but with a modern twist."

"In what way?

"Do you remember those midnight basketball programs?"

"In the nineties, right. Trying to keep the kids off the streets."

"Exactly. I won't go into if they worked or not, but the thing is, the programs were geared toward poor, inner-city kids — and to some, there was clearly a racist overtone. I mean, basketball in the middle of the city?"

"And you guys are different?"

"First off, we don't cater strictly to the poor. This may sound somewhat right wing, but I'm not sure we're the best source to help the African American or inner-city teens. They need to do that within their own community. And in the long run, I'm not sure you can stop the temptations with something like this. They need to see that their way out isn't with a gun or drugs, and I doubt a game of basketball will do that."

A group of boys-cum-men shuffled by her office, all duded out in goth black accessorized with a variety of items in the chain-n-stud family. The pants had huge cuffs and you couldn't see their shoes.

"Hey, Rosemary."

"Hey, guys."

They kept walking. Rosemary turned back to Mike. "Where do you live?"

"New Jersey."

"The suburbs, right?"

"Right."

"Teens from your town. How do they get in trouble?"

"I don't know. Drugs, drinking."

"Right. They want to party. They think

they're bored — maybe they are, who knows? — and they want to go out and get high and go to clubs and flirt and all that stuff. They don't want to play basketball. So that's what we do here."

"You get them high?"

"Not like you think. Come on, I'll show you."

She started down the bright yellow corridor. He stayed by her side. She walked with her shoulders back and head high. The key was in her hand. She unlocked a door and started down the stairs. Mike followed.

It was a nightclub or disco or whatever you call them nowadays. It had the cushioned benches and round tables that lit up and the low stools. There was a DJ booth and a wooden floor, no mirrored ball but a bunch of colored lights that swirled in patterns. The words CLUB JAGUAR were spray-painted graffiti style against a back wall.

"This is what teens want," Rosemary McDevitt said. "A place to blow off steam. To party and hang with friends. We don't serve alcohol, but we serve virgin drinks that look like alcohol. We have good-looking bartenders and waitresses. We do what the best clubs do. But the key is, we keep them safe. Do you understand? Kids like your son drive in and try to get fake IDs. They want to buy drugs or find a way to get alcohol even though they are underage. We are trying to prevent that by channeling it in a healthier way."

"With this place?"

"In part. We also offer counseling, if they need that. We offer book clubs and therapy groups and we have a room with Xbox and Playstation 3 and all the rest of what you often associate with a teen center. But this place is the key. This place is what makes us, pardon the teenage vernacular, cool."

"Rumor has it that you serve."

"Rumor is wrong. Most of the rumors are started by the other clubs because they're losing business to us."

Mike said nothing.

"Look, let's say your son came into the city to party. He could go down Third Avenue over there and buy cocaine from one alley. The guy in the stoop fifty yards away from here sells heroin. You name it, the kids buy it. Or they sneak into a club where they'll get wasted or worse. We protect them here. They can get their release in safety."

"Do you take in street kids too?"

"We wouldn't turn them away, but there are other organizations better equipped for that. We aren't trying to change lives in that way because frankly I don't think that works. A kid gone bad or from a wrecked home needs more than what we offer. Our goal is to help keep the basically good kids from slipping up. It is almost the opposite problem — parents are too involved nowadays. They are on their kids twenty-four/seven. The teens today have no room to rebel."

The argument was one he had made to Tia many times over the years. We are too all over them. Mike used to walk the streets by himself. On Saturdays he would play in Branch Brook Park all day and not come back until late. Now his own kids couldn't cross the street without him or Tia watching carefully, afraid of . . . of what exactly?

"So you give them that room?"

"Right."

He nodded. "Who runs this place?

"I do. I started it three years ago after my brother died of a drug overdose. Greg was a good kid. He was sixteen. He didn't play sports so he wasn't popular or anything. Our parents and society in general were too controlling. It was only maybe the second time he had done drugs."

"I'm sorry."

She shrugged, started for the stairs. He followed her up in silence.

"Ms. McDevitt?"

"Rosemary," she said.

"Rosemary. I don't want my son to become another statistic. He came here last night. Now I don't know where he is."

"I can't help you."

"Have you seen him before?"

Her back was still to him. "I have a bigger mission here, Mike."

"So my son is expendable?"

"That's not what I said. But we don't talk to parents. Not ever. This is a place for teens. If it gets out —"

"I won't tell anyone."

"It is part of our mission statement."

"And what if Adam is in danger?"

"Then I would help if I could. But that's not the case here."

Mike was about to argue, but he spotted a bunch of the goths down the corridor.

"Those some of your clients?" he asked, entering her office.

"Clients and facilitators."

"Facilitators?"

"They sort of do everything. They help keep the place clean. They party at night. And they watch the club."

"Like bouncers?"

She tilted her head back and forth. "That's probably too strong a term. They help the newbies fit in. They help maintain control. They keep an eye on the place, make sure no one lights up or does drugs in the bathroom, that kind of thing."

Mike made a face. "The inmates controlling the prison."

"They're good kids."

Mike looked at them. Then back at Rosemary. He studied her for a second. She was fairly spectacular to look at. She had a model's face, the kind with cheekbones that could double as letter openers. He glanced back at the goths. There were four, maybe five of them, all a haze of black and silver. They were trying to look tough and failing miserably.

"Rosemary?"

"Yes?"

"Something about your rap isn't working with me," Mike said.

"My rap?"

"Your sales pitch for this place. On one level it all makes sense."

"And on another?"

He turned and looked at her straight on. "I think you're full of crap. Where is my son?"

"You should leave now."

"If you're hiding him, I'm going to tear this place down brick by brick."

"You're now trespassing, Dr. Baye." She looked down the corridor at the group of goths and gave a small nod. They shuffled toward Mike, surrounding him. "Please leave now."

"Are you going to have your" — he made quote marks with his fingers — " 'facilitators' toss me out?"

The tallest goth smirked and said, "Looks like you've already been tossed around, old man."

The other goths giggled. There was a soft blend of black and pale and mascara and metal. They wanted so to be tough and they weren't and maybe that made them that much scarier. That desperation. That want to be something that you are not.

Mike debated his next move. The tall goth was probably in his early twenties, lanky, big Adam's apple. Part of Mike wanted to go for the sucker punch — just deck the son of a bitch, take out the leader, show them he meant business. Part of him wanted to go with a forearm blow to that bobbing throat, leave the goth with sore vocal chords for the next two weeks. But then the others would probably jump in. He might be able to take on two or three, but maybe not this many.

He was still mulling over his next move when something caught his eye. The heavy metal door buzzed open. Another goth entered. It wasn't the black clothes that made

Mike pull up this time.

It was the black eyes.

The new goth also had a strip of tape across his nose.

His recently broken nose, Mike thought.

Some of the goths came over to the broken-nose guy and offered up lazy high fives. They moved as though swimming through pancake syrup. Their voices too were slow, lethargic, nearly Prozac induced. "Yo, Carson," one managed to utter. "Carson, my man," croaked another. They lifted their hands to slap his back as if this took great effort. Carson accepted the attention as though he was used to it and it was his due.

"Rosemary?" Mike said.

"Yes."

"You not only know my son, you know me."

"How's that?"

"You called me Dr. Baye." He kept his eyes on the goth with the broken nose. "How did you know I was a doctor?"

He didn't wait for the answer. There was no point. He hurried toward the door, bumping the tall goth as he did. The one with the broken nose — Carson — saw him coming. The black eyes widened. Carson stepped back outside. Mike moved faster now, grabbing the metal door before it closed all the way, heading outside.

Carson with the broken nose was maybe ten feet in front of him.

"Hey!" Mike called out.

The punk turned around. His jet-black hair dangled over one eye like a dark curtain.

"What happened to your nose?"

Carson tried to sneer through it. "What happened to your face?"

Mike hurried over to him. The other goths were out the door. It was six against one. In his peripheral vision he saw Mo get out of the car and come toward them. Six against two — but Mo was one of the two. Mike might just take those odds.

He moved up close, getting right into Carson's broken nose and said, "A bunch of limp-dick cowards jumped me when I wasn't looking. That's what happened to my face."

Carson tried to keep the bravado in his voice. "That's too bad."

"Well, thanks, but here's the kicker. Can you imagine being a big enough loser to be one of the cowards who jumped me and ended up with a broken nose?"

Carson shrugged. "Anyone could get in a lucky shot."

"That's true. So maybe the limp-dick loser would like another chance. Man-to-man.

Face-to-face."

The goth leader looked around now, making sure that he had his supporters in place. The other goths nodded back, adjusted metal bracelets, flexed their fingers, and made too much of an effort to look ready.

Mo walked over to the tall goth and grabbed him by the throat before anyone could move. The goth tried to spit out a noise, but Mo's grip kept any sound from coming out.

"If anyone steps forward," Mo said to him, "I hurt you. Not the guy who steps forward. Not the guy who interferes. You. I hurt you very badly, do you understand?"

The tall goth tried to nod.

Mike looked back at Carson. "You ready to go?"

"Hey, I don't got no beef with you."

"I have one with you."

Mike pushed him, school yard style. Taunting. The other goths looked confused, unsure of their next move. Mike pushed Carson again.

"Hey!"

"What did you guys do to my son?"

"Huh? Who?"

"My son, Adam Baye. Where is he?"

"You think I know?"

"You jumped me last night, didn't you?

Unless you want the beating of a lifetime, you better talk."

And then another voice said, "Everybody freeze! FBI!"

Mike looked up. It was the two men with baseball caps, the ones following them before. They held guns in one hand, badges in the other.

One of the officers said, "Michael Baye?"

"Yes?"

"Darryl LeCrue, FBI. We're going to need you to come with us."

26

After saying good-bye to Betsy Hill, Tia closed the front door and headed upstairs. She crept down the corridor, past Jill's room and into her son's. She opened Adam's desk drawer and started rifling through it. Putting that spy software on his computer had felt so right — so why didn't this? Self-loathing rose up in her. It all felt wrong now, this whole invasion of privacy.

But she didn't stop looking.

Adam was a kid. Still. The drawer hadn't been cleaned out in forever, and there were remnants from past "Adam eras," like something unearthed in an archeological dig. Baseball cards, Pokémon cards, Yu-Gi-Oh!, Yamaguchi with a long-dead battery, Crazy Bones — all the "in" items that kids collected and then dispensed with. Adam had been better than most about the must-have items. He didn't beg for more or immediately toss them aside.

She shook her head. They were still in his drawer.

There were pens and pencils and his old orthodontia retainer case (Tia had constantly nagged him about not wearing it), collector pins from a trip to Disney World four years ago, old ticket stubs from a dozen Rangers games. She picked up the stubs and remembered the blend of joy and concentration on his face when he watched hockey. She remembered the way he and his father would celebrate when the Rangers scored, standing and high-fiving and singing the dumb goal-scoring song, which basically consisted of going "oh, oh, oh" and clapping.

She started to cry.

Pull it together, Tia.

She turned to the computer. That was Adam's world now. A kid's room was about his computer. On that screen, Adam played the latest version of Halo online. He talked to both strangers and friends in chat rooms. He conversed with real and cyber buddies via Facebook and MySpace. He played a little online poker but got bored with it, which pleased Mike and Tia. There were funny briefs on YouTube and movie trailers and music videos and, yes, racy material. There were other adventure games or reality simulators or whatever you'd call them where a person could vanish in the same way Tia could vanish into a book, and it was so hard to know if it was a good thing or a bad thing.

The whole sex thing nowadays too — it drove her mad. You want to make it right and control the flow of information for your kids, but that was impossible. Flip on any morning radio and the jocks riffed on boobs and infidelity and orgasms. You open up any magazine or turn on any television show, well, to complain about the nonstop eyeful is passé. So how do you handle it? Do you tell your child it's wrong? And what's wrong exactly?

No wonder people found comfort in black-and-white answers like abstinence but come on, that doesn't work and you don't want to send the message that sex is somehow wrong or evil or even taboo — and yet, you don't want them doing it. You want to tell them it is something good and healthy — but shouldn't be done. So how exactly is a parent supposed to work that balance? Weirdly enough, we all want our children to have our outlook too, as if somehow ours, despite our parents' screwups, is best and healthiest. But why? Were we raised exactly right or did we somehow find this balance on our own? Will they?

"Hey, Mom."

Jill had come to the door. She gave her mother a puzzled look, surprised, Tia guessed, to see her in Adam's room. There was a hush now. It lasted a second, no more, but Tia felt a cold gust across her chest.

"Hey, sweetheart."

Jill was holding Tia's BlackBerry. "Can I play BrickBreaker?"

She loved to play the games on her mom's BlackBerry. Normally this was the time when Tia would gently scold for not asking before taking her phone. Like most kids, Jill did it all the time. She would use the BlackBerry or borrow Tia's iPod or use the bedroom computer because hers wasn't as powerful or leave the portable phone in her room and then Tia couldn't find it.

Now, however, did not seem the time for the standard responsibility lecture.

"Sure. But if anything buzzes, please give it to me right away."

"Okay." Jill took in the whole room. "What are you doing in here?"

"I'm looking around."

"For what?"

"I don't know. A clue to where your brother is, maybe."

"He'll be okay, right?"

"Of course, please don't worry." Then remembering that life does not stop and craving some form of normalcy, Tia asked, "Do you have any homework?"

"It's done."

"Good. Everything else okay?"

Jill shrugged.

"Anything you want to talk about?"

"No, I'm fine. I'm just worried about Adam."

"I know, sweetheart. How are things at school?"

Another shrug. Dumb question. Tia had asked both her children that question several thousand times over the years and never, not once, had she gotten an answer beyond a shrug or "fine" or "okay" or "school is school."

Tia left her son's room then. There was nothing to find here. The printout from the E-SpyRight report was waiting for her. She closed her door and checked the pages. Adam's friends Clark and Olivia had e-mailed him this morning, though the messages were rather cryptic. Both wanted to know where he was and mentioned that his parents had been calling around looking for him.

There was no e-mail from DJ Huff.

Hmm. DJ and Adam conversed a lot. Suddenly no e-mail — as if maybe he knew that Adam wouldn't be around to reply.

There was a gentle knock on her door. "Mom?"

"You can open it."

Jill turned the knob. "I forgot to tell you. Dr. Forte's office called. I have a dentist appointment for Tuesday."

"Right, thanks."

"Why do I have to go to Dr. Forte's anyway? I just had a cleaning."

The mundane. Again Tia welcomed it. "You may need braces soon."

"Already?"

"Yes. Adam was your . . ." She stopped.

"My what?"

She turned back to the E-SpyRight report on her bed, the current one, but it wouldn't help. She needed the one with the original e-mail, the one about the party at the Huffs' house.

"Mom? What's going on?"

Tia and Mike had been good about getting rid of old reports via the shredder, but she had saved that e-mail to show Mike. Where was it? She looked next to her bed. Piles of paper. She started going through them.

"Can I help with something?" Jill asked.

"No, it's fine, sweetheart."

Not there. She stood up. No matter.

Tia quickly jumped back online. The E-SpyRight site was bookmarked in her favorites area. She signed on and clicked the archives button. She found the right date and asked for the old report.

No need to print it out. When it came up on the screen, Tia scanned down until she reached the Huff-party e-mail. She didn't bother with the message itself — about the Huffs being away, about the party and getting high — but now that she thought about it, what had happened to that? Mike had gone by and not only had there been no party, but Daniel Huff was home.

Had the Huffs changed plans?

But that wasn't the point right now. Tia moved the cursor over to check out what most would think would be the least relevant.

The time and date columns.

The E-SpyRight told you not only the time and date the e-mail was sent, but the time and date Adam opened it.

"Mom, what's going on?"

"Just give me a second, sweetie."

Tia picked up the phone and called Dr. Forte's phone. It was Saturday, but she knew that with all the after-school kid activities, the area dentists often had weekend hours. She checked her watch and listened to the third ring, then the fourth. Her heart sank on the fifth ring before salvation:

"Dr. Forte's office."

"Hi, good morning, this is Tia Baye, Adam and Jill's mom?"

"Yes, Mrs. Baye, what can I do for you?"

Tia tried to place the name of Forte's receptionist. She had been there for years, knew everyone, ran the place really. She was the gatekeeper. It came to her. "Is this Caroline?"

"Yes, it is."

"Hi, Caroline. Listen, this may sound like an odd request, but I desperately need a favor from you."

"Well, I'll try. We're pretty jammed up next week."

"No, it's not that. Adam had an after-school appointment on the eighteenth at three forty-five P.M."

No reply.

"I need to know if he was there."

"You mean if he was a no-show?"

"Yes."

"Oh, no, I would have called you. Adam was definitely here."

"Do you know if he was on time?"

"I can give you the exact time, if that would help. It's on the sign-in sheet."

"Yes, that would be great."

More delay. Tia heard the sound of fingers

tapping on a computer. Papers were being shuffled.

"Adam got here early, Mrs. Baye — he signed in at three twenty P.M."

That would make sense, Tia thought. He normally walked directly from school.

"And we saw him on time — at exactly three forty-five P.M. Is that what you needed to know?"

The phone nearly dropped from Tia's hand. Something was so very wrong. Tia checked the screen again — the time and date columns.

The Huff-party e-mail had been sent at 3:32 P.M. It had been read at 3:37 P.M.

Adam hadn't been home then.

This made no sense unless . . .

"Thank you, Caroline." She quickly called Brett, her computer expert. He answered his phone: "Yo."

Tia decided to put him on the defensive. "Thanks for selling me out to Hester."

"Tia? Oh, look, I'm sorry about that."

"Yeah, I bet."

"No, seriously, Hester knows everything around here. Do you realize that she monitors every computer in the place? Sometimes she just reads the personal e-mails for fun. She figures if you're on her property —"

"I wasn't on her property."

"I know, I'm sorry."

Time to move on. "According to the E-SpyRight report, my son read an e-mail at three thirty-seven P.M."

"So?"

"So he wasn't home at that time. Could he have read it elsewhere?"

"You're getting this from E-SpyRight?"

"Yes."

"Then the answer is no. The E-SpyRight is just monitoring his computer activities on that computer only. So if he signed in and read the e-mail elsewhere, it wouldn't be in the report."

"So how could this be?"

"Hmm. Well, first off, are you sure he wasn't home?"

"Positive."

"Well, somebody was. And that somebody was on his computer."

Tia looked again. "It says it was deleted at three thirty-eight P.M."

"So someone went on your son's computer, read the e-mail, and then deleted it."

"Then Adam would have never seen it, right?"

"Probably not."

She quickly dismissed the most obvious suspects: She and Mike were at work that day, and Jill had walked with Yasmin to the

Novaks' house for a playdate.

None of them were home.

How could someone else have gotten it without leaving any signs of a break-in? She thought about that key, the one they hid in the fake rock outside by the fence post.

The caller ID buzzed in. She saw that it was Mo.

"Brett, I'll have to call you back." She clicked over. "Mo?"

"You're not going to believe this," he said, "but the FBI just picked up Mike."

Sitting in the makeshift interrogation room, Loren Muse took a good long look at Neil Cordova.

He was on the short side, small-boned, compact, and handsome in an almost too unblemished way. He looked a little like his wife when you put them side by side. Muse knew this because Cordova had brought photographs of them together, lots of them — on cruises, on beaches, at formals, at parties, in the backyard. Neil and Reba Cordova were photogenic and healthy and liked to pose cheek to cheek. They looked happy in every single photograph.

"Please find her," Neil Cordova said for the third time since entering the room.

She had already said, "We're doing all we

can," twice, so she saved it.

He added, "I want to cooperate in any way I can."

Neil Cordova had close-cropped hair and was dressed in a blazer and tie, as though that was expected of him, as if the outfit itself could help hold him together. There was a nice shine to his shoes. Muse thought about that. Her own father had been big on shined shoes. "Judge a man by the shine on his shoes," he would tell his young daughter. Nice to know. When a fourteen-year-old Loren Muse had found her father's body in the garage — he'd gone in there and blown his brains out — there had indeed been a nice shine to his shoes.

Good advice, Dad. Thanks for the suicide protocol.

"I know how it is," Cordova went on. "The husband is always a suspect, right?"

Muse did not reply.

"And you think Reba had an affair because her car was parked at that motel — but I swear to you, it's not like that. You have to believe me."

Muse made her face stone. "We aren't ruling anything in or out."

"I'll take a polygraph, no lawyer, whatever you need. I just don't want you to waste time looking down the wrong avenue. Reba didn't run away, I know that. And I had nothing to do with what happened to her."

You never believe anybody, Muse thought. That was the rule. She had questioned suspects whose acting skills could put De Niro on unemployment. But the evidence so far backed him, and everything inside her told her that Neil Cordova was telling the truth. Besides, for right now, it didn't matter.

Muse had brought Cordova down to identify the body of her Jane Doe. Foe or ally, that was what she needed desperately. His cooperation. So she said, "Mr. Cordova, I don't think you harmed your wife."

The relief came in immediately but vanished just as fast. This wasn't about him, she saw. He was just worried about the beautiful woman in those beautiful photographs.

"Has anything been bothering your wife lately?"

"Not really, no. Sarah — that's our eight-year-old" — he caught himself, put his knuckle in his mouth, closed his eyes and bit down — "Sarah is having some trouble reading. I told the Livingston police when they asked the same thing. Reba has been worried about that."

That wasn't going to help, but at least he was talking.

"Let me ask you something that may sound

a little strange," Muse said.

He nodded, leaned forward, waiting desperately to assist.

"Has Reba talked to you about any of her friends having trouble?"

"I'm not sure what you mean by having trouble."

"Let me start with this. I assume no one you know is missing."

"You mean, like my wife?"

"I mean like anything. Take it a step further. Are any of your friends away, even on vacation?"

"The Friedmans are in Buenos Aires for the week. She and Reba are very close."

"Good, good." She knew that Clarence was writing this down. He would check and make sure Mrs. Friedman was where she belonged. "Anyone else?"

Neil worked the question, chewing the inside of his mouth.

"I'm trying to think," he said.

"Relax, it's okay. Anything weird with friends, any sort of trouble, anything."

"Reba told me that the Colders were having marital issues."

"That's good. Anything else?"

"Tonya Eastman recently got a bad result on a mammogram, but she hasn't told her husband yet. She's worried he'll leave her.

That's what Reba said. Is this what you want?"

"Yes. Keep going."

He rattled off a few more. Clarence took notes. When Neil Cordova seemed out of steam, Muse got to the heart of the matter.

"Mr. Cordova?"

She met his eye and held it.

"I need you to do me a favor. I really don't want to go into long explanations on why or what it might mean —"

He interrupted her. "Inspector Muse?"

"Yes?"

"Don't waste time holding my hand. What do you want?"

"We have a body here. It is definitely *not* your wife. Do you understand? *Not* your wife. This woman was found dead the night before. We don't know who she is."

"And you think I might?"

"I want you to take a look and see."

His hands lay folded in his lap, and he sat up a little too straight. "Okay," he said. "Let's go."

Muse had considered using photographs for this part and sparing him the horror of viewing the actual corpse. Pictures don't work though. If she had a clear one of the face, sure, maybe, but in this case, it was as if the face had spent too much time under a lawn mower. There was nothing but bone fragments and frayed sinew. Muse could have shown him photos of the torso with the height and weight listed, but experience showed that it was hard to get a real feel that way.

Neil Cordova hadn't wondered about the venue for this interrogation, but that was understandable. They were on Norfolk Street in Newark — the county morgue. Muse had already set it up so they wouldn't have to waste time driving over. She opened the door. Cordova tried to keep his head high. His gait was steady, but the shoulders told more; Muse could see the bunching through the blazer.

The body was ready. Tara O'Neill, the medical examiner, had wrapped gauze around the face. That was the first thing Neil Cordova noticed — the bandages like something out of a mummy movie. He asked why they were there.

"Her face suffered extensive damage," Muse said.

"How am I supposed to recognize her?"

"We were hoping by body type, maybe height, anything."

"I think it would help if I could see the face."

"It won't help, Mr. Cordova."

He took a deep swallow, took another look.

"What happened to her?"

"She was beaten badly."

He turned to Muse. "Do you think something like this happened to my wife?"

"I don't know."

Cordova closed his eyes for a moment, gathered himself, opened them, nodded. "Okay." He nodded some more. "Okay, I understand."

"I know this isn't easy."

"I'm fine." She could see the wet in his eyes. He took one swipe with his sleeve. He looked so much like a little boy when he did that Muse nearly hugged him. She watched him turn back to the body.

"Do you know her?"

"I don't think so."

"Take your time."

"The thing is, she's naked." His eyes were still on the bandaged face, as if trying to maintain modesty. "I mean, if she's someone I know, I would have never seen her that way, you know what I mean?"

"I do. Would it help if we clothed her somehow?"

"No, that's okay. It's just . . ." He frowned.

"What?"

Neil Cordova's eyes had been on the victim's neck area. Now they traveled south to her legs. "Can you turn her over?"

"Onto her stomach?"

"Yes. I need to see the back of the leg mostly. But yes."

Muse glanced at Tara O'Neill, who immediately brought an orderly over. They carefully turned Jane Doe facedown. Cordova took a step forward. Muse did not move, not wanting to disturb his concentration. Tara O'Neill and the orderly stepped away. Neil Cordova's eyes continued down the legs. They stopped at the back of her right ankle.

There was a birthmark.

Seconds passed. Muse finally said, "Mr. Cordova?"

"I know who this is."

Muse waited. He started shaking. His hand fluttered to his mouth. His eyes closed.

"Mr. Cordova?"

"It's Marianne," he said. "Dear God, it's Marianne."

27

Dr. Ilene Goldfarb slid into the diner booth across from Susan Loriman.

"Thank you for seeing me," Susan said.

They had discussed going out of town, but in the end Ilene had nixed that idea. Anyone who saw them would simply assume that they were two ladies at lunch, an activity Ilene had never had the time nor desire to indulge in because she worked too many hours at the hospital and feared becoming, well, one of the ladies who lunched.

Even when her children were young, traditional motherhood never called to her. There had never been a yearning to give up her medical career to stay at home and play a more traditional role in her children's lives. Just the opposite — she couldn't wait until maternity leave was over and she could respectably go back to work. Her kids seemed no worse for it. She hadn't always been there, but in her mind that had helped make her children that much more independent with a healthier life attitude.

At least that was what she'd told herself.

But last year, there had been a party held at the hospital in her honor. Many of her former residents and interns came to pay respects to their favorite teacher. Ilene overheard one of her best students raving to Kelci about what a dedicated teacher Ilene had been and how proud she must be to have Ilene Goldfarb for a mother. Kelci, with a drink or two in her, responded, "She spent so much time here I never got to see any of that."

Yep. Career, motherhood, happy marriage — she had juggled all three with shocking ease, hadn't she?

Except now the balls were dropping to the floor with a splat. Even her career was in jeopardy, if what those agents had told her was true.

"Is there anything new from the donor banks?" Susan Loriman asked.

"No."

"Dante and I are working on something. A major donor drive. I went to Lucas's elementary school. Mike's daughter, Jill, goes to the same one. I spoke to a few of the teachers. They love the idea. We're going to hold it next Saturday, get everyone to sign up for the donor bank."

Ilene nodded. "That might be helpful."

"And you're still looking, right? I mean, it's not hopeless?"

Ilene was simply not in the mood. "It's not hopeful either."

Susan Loriman bit down on her lower lip. She had that effortless beauty it was hard not to envy. Men got funny around that kind of beauty, Ilene knew. Even Mike spoke with a weird vibe in his voice when Susan Loriman was in the room.

The diner waitress came over with a pot of coffee. Ilene nodded for her to pour, but Susan asked what herbal teas they carried. The waitress looked at her as if she'd asked for an enema. Susan said any tea would do. The waitress came back with a Lipton tea bag and poured hot water into the mug.

Susan Loriman stared down at the drink as if it held some divine secret.

"Lucas was a difficult birth. The week before he was born I caught pneumonia and I started coughing so hard I actually cracked a rib. I was hospitalized. The pain was unreal. Dante stayed with me the whole time. He wouldn't leave my side."

Susan slowly brought the tea to her lips, using both hands as though cradling an injured bird.

"When we found out Lucas was sick, we

held a family meeting. Dante put on this whole brave act and talked about how we'd beat it as a family — 'We are Lorimans,' he kept saying — and then that night he walked outside and cried so hard I thought he would hurt himself."

"Mrs. Loriman?"

"Please call me Susan."

"Susan, I get the picture. He's a Hallmark-card father. He bathed him when he was young. He changed his diapers and coached his soccer team, and he'd be crushed to learn that he isn't the boy's father. Does that about sum it up?"

Susan Loriman took another sip of tea. Ilene thought about Herschel, about having nothing left. She wondered if Herschel was having an affair, maybe with that cute new divorced receptionist who laughed at all his jokes, and figured that the answer was probably yes.

"What's left, Ilene . . . ?"

A man who asks that has long since checked out of the marriage. Ilene was just late in realizing that he was already gone.

Susan Loriman said, "You don't understand."

"I'm not sure I need to. You don't want him to know. I get that. I get that Dante would be hurt. I get that your family might suffer. So please save it. I really don't have time. I could lecture you on how maybe all of this should have crossed your mind nine months before Lucas was born, but it's the weekend, my time, and I have my own problems. I also, to speak candidly, don't care about your moral failures, Mrs. Loriman. I care about your son's health. Period, end of story. If hurting your marriage helps cure him, I'll sign your divorce papers. Am I making myself clear?"

"You are."

Susan cast her eyes down. Demure — it was a word that Ilene had heard before but never quite gotten. But that was what she was seeing right now. How many men would weaken — *had* weakened — at such a move?

It was wrong to make this personal. Ilene took a breath, tried to push past her own situations — her repulsion to adultery, her fears about her future without the man she'd chosen to spend her life with, her worries about her practice and the questions those federal agents had asked.

"But I really don't see why he has to know," Ilene said.

Now Susan looked up and something akin to hope entered her face.

"We could approach the biological father

discreetly," Ilene said. "Ask him to take a blood test."

The hope fled. "You can't do that."

"Why not?"

"You just can't."

"Well, Susan, that's your best bet." Her tone was sharp now. "I'm trying to help you, but either way, I'm not here to listen to you tell me about the wonder of Dante the cuckold husband. I care about your family dynamics but only to a point. I'm your son's doctor, not your shrink or pastor. If you're looking for understanding or salvation, I'm not your girl. Who's the father?"

Susan closed her eyes. "You don't understand."

"If you don't give me a name, I will tell your husband."

Ilene had not planned on saying that, but the anger rose up and took control.

"You're putting your indiscretion ahead of your child's health. That's pathetic. And I won't let it happen."

"Please."

"Who's the father, Susan?"

Susan Loriman looked off, gnawed the lower lip.

"Who's the father?"

And finally she answered: "I don't know."

Ilene Goldfarb blinked. The answer just

sat there, between them, a gulf Ilene wasn't sure how to cross. "I see."

"No, you don't."

"You had more than one lover. I know that's embarrassing or whatever. But we just bring each one in."

"I didn't have more than one lover. I didn't have any lover."

Ilene waited, not sure where this was headed.

"I was raped."

28

Mike sat in the interrogation room and tried to remain calm. On the wall in front of him, there was a large rectangular mirror that he assumed was one-way glass. The other walls were done up in school-lavatory green. The floor was gray linoleum.

Two men were in the room with him. One sat in the corner, almost like a scolded child. He had a pen and clipboard with him and kept his head down. The other guy — the officer who had held up the badge and gun in front of Club Jaguar — was black with a diamond stud in his left ear. He paced and carried an unlit cigarette in his hand.

"I'm Special Agent Darryl LeCrue," the pacer said. "This here is Scott Duncan — the liaison between the DEA and the U.S. Attorney's Office. You've been read your rights?"

"I have."

LeCrue nodded. "And you're willing to speak with us?"

"I am."

"Please sign the waiver on the table."

Mike did. Under normal circumstances he wouldn't. He knew better. Mo would call Tia. She would get here, be his lawyer or get him one. He should shut up until then. But he didn't really care about any of that right now.

LeCrue continued to pace. "Do you know what this is about?" he asked.

"No," Mike said.

"No idea at all?"

"None."

"What were you doing at Club Jaguar today?"

"Why were you guys following me?"

"Dr. Baye?"

"Yes."

"I smoke. Do you know that?"

The question puzzled Mike. "I see the cigarette."

"Is it lit?"

"No."

"Do you think that pleases me?"

"I wouldn't know."

"My point exactly. I used to smoke right in this very room. Not because I wanted to intimidate the suspects or blow smoke in their faces, though I did that sometimes. No, the reason I smoked is because I liked it. It relaxed me. Now that they've passed all these new laws, I'm not allowed to light up. You hear what I'm saying?"

"I guess so."

"In other words, the law won't let a man relax. That bothers me. I need my smokes. So when I'm in here, I'm grumpy. I carry this cigarette with me and long to light it up. But I can't. It's like leading the horse to water but not letting him drink. Now I don't want your sympathy, but I need you to understand how it is because you are already pissing me off." He slammed his hand against the table but kept his tone even. "I'm not going to answer your questions. You're going to answer mine. We on the same page?"

Mike said, "Maybe I should wait for my lawyer."

"Cool." He turned to Duncan in the corner. "Scott, do we have enough to arrest him?"

"Yes."

"Groovy. Let's do that. Put him in the system on a weekend. When do you think his bail hearing will be?"

Duncan shrugged. "Hours from now. Might even have to wait until the morning."

Mike tried to keep the panic off his face. "What's the charge?"

LeCrue shrugged. "We can come up with something, can't we, Scott?"

"Sure."

"So it's up to you, Dr. Baye. You seemed in a rush to get out before. So let's start this again and see how it plays. What were you doing at Club Jaguar?"

He could argue some more, but it felt like the wrong move. So did waiting for Tia. He wanted out. He needed to find Adam.

"I was looking for my son."

He expected LeCrue to follow up on that, but he simply nodded and said, "You were about to get into a fight, weren't you?"

"Yes."

"Was that going to help you find your son?"

"I was hoping it might."

"You want to explain."

"I was in that neighborhood last night," he began.

"Yes, we know."

Mike stopped. "Were you following me then too?"

LeCrue smiled, held out the cigarette as a reminder, and arched an eyebrow.

"Tell us about your son," LeCrue said.

Warning flags shot up. Mike didn't like this.

He didn't like the threats or being followed or any of it, but he especially didn't like the way LeCrue asked him about his son. But again, what were his options?

"He's missing. I thought he might be at Club Jaguar."

"And that's why you went there last night?"

"Yes."

"You figured that he might be there?"

"Yes."

Mike filled them in on pretty much everything. There was no reason not to — he had told the police the same story at the hospital and at the police station.

"Why were you so worried about him?"

"We were supposed to go to a Rangers game last night."

"The hockey team?"

"Yes."

"They lost, you know."

"I didn't."

"Good game though. Lots of fights." LeCrue smiled again. "I'm one of the few brothers who follows hockey. I used to love basketball but the NBA bores me now. Too many fouls, you know what I mean?"

Mike figured that this was some disruption technique. He said, "Uh-huh."

"So when your son didn't show up, you

looked for him in the Bronx?"

"Yes."

"And you got jumped."

"Yes." Then: "If you guys were watching me, how come you didn't help?"

He shrugged. "Who said we were watching?"

Then Scott Duncan looked up and added, "Who said we didn't help?"

Silence.

"Have you ever been to that place before?"

"Club Jaguar? No."

"Never?"

"Never."

"Just to be clear: You're telling me that before last night, you'd never been to Club Jaguar?"

"Not even last night."

"Excuse me?"

"I never made it there last night. I got jumped before I got there."

"How did you end up in that alley anyway?"

"I was following someone."

"Who?"

"His name is DJ Huff. He's a classmate of my son's."

"So then, what you're telling us is that you were never inside Club Jaguar before today?"

Mike tried to keep the exasperation from his voice. "That's right. Look, Agent LeCrue, is there any way we can rush this? My son is missing. I'm worried about him."

"Of course you are. So let's move right along, shall we? What about Rosemary McDevitt, the president and founder of Club Jaguar?"

"What about her?"

"When was the first time you two met?"

"Today."

LeCrue turned to Duncan. "You buy that, Scott?"

Scott Duncan lifted his hand, palm down, tilted it back and forth.

"I'm having trouble with that one too."

"Please listen to me," Mike said, trying to keep the pleading out of his voice. "I need to get out of here and find my son."

"You don't trust law enforcement?"

"I trust them. I just don't think they see my son as a priority."

"Fair enough. Let me ask you this. Do you know what a pharm party is? The pharm is spelled with a p-h, not an f."

Mike thought about it. "The term is not completely unfamiliar, but I can't place it."

"Maybe I can help, Dr. Baye. You're a medical doctor, isn't that correct?"

"It is."

"So calling you doctor is cool. I hate calling every dumb ass with a diploma 'doctor' — Ph.D.s or chiropractors or the guy who helps me get my contact lenses at Pearle Express. You know what I mean?"

Mike tried to get him back on track. "You asked me about pharm parties?"

"Yeah, that's right. And you're in a rush and all and I'm just blathering away. So let me get to it. You're a medical doctor so you understand about the ridiculous costs of pharmaceuticals, right?"

"I do."

"So let me tell you what a pharm party is. Put simply, teens go into their parents' medicine cabinet and steal their drugs. Nowadays every family has some prescriptions lying about — Vicodin, Adderall, Ritalin, Xanax, Prozac, OxyContin, Percocet, Demerol, Valium, you get the point. So what the teens do is, they steal them and get together and put them in a bowl or make a trail mix or whatever. That's the candy dish. Then they get high."

LeCrue stopped. For the first time he grabbed a chair, turned it backward, and sat with his legs straddling the back. He looked hard at Mike. Mike did not blink.

After some time passed, Mike said, "So now I know what a pharm party is."

"Now you do. So anyway, that's how it starts. A bunch of kids get together and figure, hey, these drugs are legal — not like dope or cocaine. Maybe little brother takes the Ritalin because he's overactive. Dad takes OxyContin to relieve the pain from his knee operation. Whatever. They gotta be pretty safe."

"I get it."

"Do you?"

"Yes."

"Do you see how easy it would be? Do you have any prescription drugs lying around at home?"

Mike thought about his own knee, the prescription for Percocet, how he worked hard so he didn't take too many of them. They were indeed in his medicine chest. Would he even notice if a few went missing? And how about parents who didn't know anything about the drugs? Would they be wary of a few missing pills?

"Like you said, all households have them."

"Right, so stay with me a minute. You know the value of the pills. You know these parties are going on. So let's say you're something of an entrepreneur. What do you do? You take it to the next level. You try to turn a profit. Let's say you're the house and getting a cut of the profits. Maybe you encourage the kids to steal more of the drugs from their medicine cabinets. You can even get replacement pills."

"Replacement pills?"

"Sure. If the pills are white, well, you just put in some generic aspirin. Who is going to notice? You can get sugar pills that basically do nothing other than look like other pills. You see? Who'd notice? There's a huge black market for prescribed medications. You can make a mint. But again, think like an entrepreneur. You don't want some small-ass party with eight kids. You want big. You want to attract hundreds if not thousands. Like you might in, say, a nightclub."

Mike was getting it now. "You think that's what Club Jaguar is doing."

Mike suddenly remembered that Spencer Hill had committed suicide using medications from his home. That was the rumor anyway. He stole drugs from his parent's medicine cabinet to overdose.

LeCrue nodded, continued, "You could — if you were really entrepreneurial — take it to another level. All drugs have value on the black market. Maybe there's that old Amoxicillin that you never finished up. Or your grandpa has some extra Viagra in the house. No one keeps track, do they, Doc?"

"Rarely."

"Right, and if some are missing or whatever, well, you chalk it up to the pharmacy ripping you off or you forgot the date or maybe you took an extra one. There is almost no way you trace it back to your teenager stealing them. Do you see how brilliant it is?"

Mike wanted to ask what this had to do with him or Adam, but he knew better.

LeCrue leaned in closer and whispered, "Hey, Doc?"

Mike waited.

"Do you know what the next step up that entrepreneurial ladder would be?"

"LeCrue?" It was Duncan.

LeCrue looked behind him. "What's up, Scott?"

"You like that word. Entrepreneurial."

"I do at that." He turned back to Mike. "You like that word, Doc?"

"It's great."

LeCrue chuckled as if they were old friends. "Anyway, a smart *entrepreneurial* kid can figure out ways of getting even more drugs from his house. How? He calls in the refills early maybe. If both parents work and you got a delivery service, you are home from school before them. And if the parent tries to refill and gets stopped, well, again, they figure it's an error or they lost count. See, once you start down this road, there are just so many ways you can make a beautiful dollar. It is almost foolproof."

The obvious question echoed in Mike's head: Could Adam have done something like that?

"Who would we bust anyway? Think about it. You have a bunch of rich, underage kids — all of whom can afford the best lawyers — who have done what exactly? Taken legally prescribed drugs from their family homes. Who cares? Do you see again how easy this money is?"

"I guess."

"You *guess,* Dr. Baye? Come on, let's not play games here. You don't guess. You know. It is nearly flawless. Now normally you know how we'd operate. We don't want to bust a bunch of dumb teens getting high. We want the big fish. But if the big fish here was smart, she — let's make her a she, so we aren't accused of sexism, okay? — she would let the underage kids handle the drugs for her. Dumb goth kids who'd have to move up a step on the food chain to be called losers, maybe. They'd feel important and if she was a grade-A-felony hottie, she could probably get them to do whatever she wanted, you know what I'm saying?"

"Sure," Mike said. "You think this is what Rosemary McDevitt is doing at Club Jaguar. She has this nightclub and all these underage kids go to it legally. It makes sense, on one level."

"And on another level?"

"A woman whose own brother died of a drug overdose pushing pills?"

LeCrue smiled at that one. "She told you that little sob story, did she? About her brother who didn't have an outlet so he partied too hard and died?"

"It's not true?"

"Total fiction, far as we can tell. She claims that she's from a place called Breman, Indiana, but we've checked the books. No case like the one she describes happened anywhere near there."

Mike said nothing.

Scott Duncan looked up from his note taking. "She's smoking hot though."

"Oh, no doubt," LeCrue agreed. "A fine first-class honey."

"A man can get stupid with a woman who looks like that."

"Sure can, Scott. That's her MO too. Gets a sexual hold on a guy. Not that I'd mind being that guy for a little while, you know what I'm saying, Doc?"

"I'm sorry, I don't."

"You gay?"

Mike tried not to roll his eyes. "Yes, fine, I'm gay. Can we move on with this?"

"She uses men, Doc. Not just the dumb kids. Smarter men. Older men."

He stopped and waited. Mike looked at Duncan and then back at LeCrue. "Is this the part where I gasp and suddenly realize that you're talking about me?"

"Now why would we think something like that?"

"I assume you're about to say."

"I mean, after all" — LeCrue spread his hands like a first-year drama major — "you just said you never even met her until today. Isn't that right?"

"That's right."

"And we totally believe you. So let me ask you something else. How's work? I mean, at the hospital."

Mike sighed. "Let's pretend I'm thrown by your sudden change in subjects. Look, I don't know what you think I've done. I assume it has something to do with this Club Jaguar, not because I did something but because you'd have to be a moron to not realize it. Normally, again, I would wait for my lawyer or at least my wife, the lawyer, to show up. But as I've repeated several times, my son is missing. So let's cut the nonsense.

Tell me what you need to know so I can get back to finding him."

LeCrue arched an eyebrow. "It turns me on when a suspect talks all manly like that. It turn you on, Scott?"

"My nipples," Scott said with a nod. "They're hardening as we speak."

"Now before we get too gooey, I just have a few more questions and then we can end this. Do you have a patient named William Brannum?"

Again Mike wondered what to do and again sided for cooperation.

"Not that I can recall."

"You don't remember the name of every patient?"

"That name doesn't ring any bells, but he might be seen by my practice partner or something."

"That would be Ilene Goldfarb?"

They knew their stuff, Mike thought. "Yes, that's correct."

"We asked her. She doesn't remember him."

Mike didn't blurt out the obvious, *What, you talked to her?* He tried to keep still. They had talked to Ilene already. What the hell was going on here?

The grin was back on LeCrue's face. "Ready to take it to the next entrepreneurial level, Dr. Baye?"

"Sure."

"Good. Let me show you something."

He turned back to Duncan. Duncan handed him a manila folder. LeCrue put the unlit cigarette in his mouth, reached in with tobacco-stained fingernails. He plucked out a sheet of paper and slid it across the table toward Mike.

"Does this look familiar?"

Mike looked down at the sheet of paper. It was a photocopy of a prescription. On the top were printed out his name and Ilene's. It had their address up at NewYork-Presbyterian and their license number. A prescription for OxyContin had been written out to William Brannum.

It had been signed by Dr. Michael Baye.

"Does it look familiar to you?"

Mike made himself stay silent.

"Because Dr. Goldfarb says it isn't hers and she doesn't know the patient."

He slid another piece of paper. Another prescription. This time for Xanax. Also signed by Dr. Michael Baye. Then another.

"Any of these names ringing a bell?"

Mike did not speak.

"Oh, this one is interesting. You want to know why?"

Mike looked up at him.

"Because it is made out to Carson Bledsoe. Do you know who that is?"

Mike thought that maybe he did, but he still said, "Should I?"

"That's the name of the kid with the broken nose you were jawing at when we picked you up."

The next entrepreneurial step, Mike thought. Get your hooks into a doctor's kid. Steal prescription pads and write them yourself.

"Now at best — I mean, if everything breaks your way and the gods are smiling in your direction — you will only lose your medical license and never practice again. That's best-case scenario. You stop being an M.D."

Now Mike knew to shut up.

"See, we've been working this case for a long time. We've been watching Club Jaguar. We know what's going on. We could arrest a bunch of rich kids, but again if you don't cut off the head, what's the point? Last night we got tipped off about some big meeting. That's the problem with this particular entrepreneurial step: You need middlemen. Organized crime is making serious inroads into this market. They can make as much from OxyContin as cocaine, maybe more. So anyway, we're watching. Then last night things started going wrong over there. You, the doctor of record, show up. You get assaulted. And then today you pop up again and wreak havoc. So our fear — the DEA's and U.S. Attorney's Office — is that the whole Club Jaguar enterprise will fold its tent and we'll be left with nothing. So we need to crack down now."

"I have nothing to say."

"Sure you do."

"I'm waiting for my attorney."

"You don't want to play it that way because we don't think you wrote those. See, we also got some legitimate prescriptions you've written. We tried to match the handwriting. It isn't yours. So that means you either gave your prescription pads to someone else — a big-time felony — or someone stole them from you."

"I got nothing to say."

"You can't protect him, Doc. You all think you can. Parents try all the time. But not this way. Every doctor I know keeps pads at home. Just in case he needs to write a prescription from there. It is easy to steal drugs from the medicine cabinet. It is probably even easier to steal prescription pads."

Mike stood. "I'm leaving now."

"Like hell you are. Your son is one of those rich kids we talked about, but this graduates him to the big time. He can be charged with conspiracy and distribution of a schedule two narcotic for starters. That's serious jail time — max of twenty years in federal prison. But we don't want your son. We want Rosemary McDevitt. We can cut a deal."

"I'm waiting for my lawyer," Mike said.

"Perfect," LeCrue said. "Because your charming attorney has just arrived."

29

Raped.

There wasn't so much silence after Susan Loriman said that word as there was a rushing sound, a feeling like they were losing cabin pressure, as if the whole diner were descending too fast and their ears were taking the brunt of it.

Raped.

Ilene Goldfarb did not know what to say. She had certainly heard her share of bad news and delivered much of it herself, but this had been so unexpected. She finally settled on the all-purpose, quasi-stall platitude.

"I'm sorry."

Susan Loriman's eyes weren't just closed but squeezed shut like a child. Her hands were still on the teacup, protecting it. Ilene considered reaching out but decided against it. The waitress started toward them, but Ilene shook her head. Susan still had her eyes shut.

"I never told Dante."

A waiter walked by with a tray teetering with plates. Someone called out for water. A woman at the neighboring table tried eavesdropping, but Ilene shot her a glare that made her turn away.

"I never told anyone. When I got pregnant, I figured it was probably Dante's. That's what I hoped anyway. And then Lucas came out and I guess I knew. But I blocked it. I moved on. It was a long time ago."

"You didn't report the rape?"

She shook her head. "You can't tell anyone. Please."

"Okay."

They sat there in silence.

"Susan?"

She looked up.

"I know it was a long time ago —" Ilene began.

"Eleven years," Susan said.

"Right. But you might want to think about reporting it."

"What?"

"If he's caught, we can test him. He might even be in the system already. Rapists normally don't stop at one."

Susan shook her head. "We're setting up this donor drive at the school."

"Do you know what the odds of that getting us what we need are?"

"It has to work."

"Susan, you need to go to the police."

"Please let this go."

And then a curious thought crossed Ilene's mind. "Do you know your rapist?"

"What? No."

"You should really think about what I'm saying."

"He won't be caught, okay? I have to go." Susan slid out of the booth and stood over Ilene. "If I thought there was a chance to help my son, I would. But there's not. Please, Dr. Goldfarb. Help with the donor drive. Help me find another way. Please, you know the truth now. You have to let this be."

In his classroom, Joe Lewiston cleaned the chalkboard with a sponge. Many things about being a teacher had changed over the years, including the replacement of green chalkboards with those new erasable white ones, but Joe had insisted on keeping this holdover from the previous generations. There was something about the dust, the clack of the chalk when you wrote, and cleaning it with a sponge that somehow linked him to the past and reminded him of who he was and what he did.

Joe used the giant sponge and right now it was a bit too wet. Water flowed down the board. He chased the cascades with the sponge, going in straight lines up and down, and he tried to lose himself in this simple task.

It almost worked.

He called this room "Lewiston Land." The kids loved it, but in truth not as much as he did. He wanted so very badly to be different, to not stand up here and do rote lectures and teach the required material and be totally forgettable. He let this be their place. The students had writing journals — so did he. He read the kids', and they were allowed to read his. He never yelled. When a kid did something good or noteworthy, he put a check next to his name. When he or she misbehaved, he erased a check. It was that simple. He didn't believe in singling kids out or embarrassing them.

He watched the other teachers grow old before his eyes, their enthusiasm bleeding out with each passing class. Not his. He dressed up in character when he did history. He had unusual scavenger hunts where you had to do math problems to find the next goodie. The class got to make its own movie. There was so much good that went on in this room, in Lewiston Land, and then there had been that one day when he should have stayed home because the stomach flu was still making his belly ache and then the air conditioner had conked out and he felt so horrible and was breaking out with a fever and . . .

Why did he say that? God, what a horrible thing to do to a child.

He turned on the computer. His hands shook. He typed in the address of his wife's school Web site. The password was JoeLovesDolly now.

There had been nothing wrong with her e-mail.

Dolly did not know much about computers or the Internet. So Joe had gone into it earlier and changed her password. That was why her e-mail hadn't "worked" properly. She had the wrong password, so when she tried to log in, it wouldn't let her.

Now, in the safety of this room he so dearly loved, Joe Lewiston checked what e-mails had come in for her. He hoped that he wouldn't see that same sender e-mail address again.

But he did.

He bit down so he didn't scream out loud. There was only so long he could stall before Dolly would want to know what was wrong with her e-mail. He had a day maybe, no more. And he did not think a day would be enough.

Tia dropped Jill back at Yasmin's. If Guy Novak minded or was surprised he didn't show it. Tia didn't have time to question it anyway. She sped to the FBI's field office at 26 Federal Plaza. Hester Crimstein arrived at almost exactly the same time. They met up in the waiting room.

"Check the playbill," Hester said. "You are to play the role of beloved wife. I'm the darling screen veteran who will cameo as his attorney."

"I know."

"Don't say a word in there. Let me handle this."

"It's why I called you."

Hester Crimstein started for the door. Tia followed. Hester opened it and burst through. Mike was sitting at a table. There were two other men in the room. One sat in the corner. The other hovered over Mike. The one doing the hovering stood upright when they entered and said, "Hello. My name is Special Agent Darryl LeCrue."

"I don't care," Hester said.

"Excuse me?"

"No, I don't think I will. Is my client under arrest?"

"We have reason to believe —"

"Don't care. It is a yes or no question. Is my client under arrest?"

"We are hoping that it won't —"

"Again, don't care." Hester looked over at Mike. "Dr. Baye, please get up and leave this room immediately. Your wife will escort you into the lobby, where you both can wait for me."

LeCrue said, "Wait a second, Ms. Crimstein."

"You know my name?"

He shrugged. "Yeah."

"How?"

"I've seen you on TV."

"You want my autograph?"

"No."

"Why not? Doesn't matter — you can't have it. My client is done for now. If you wanted to arrest him, you would have. So he's going to leave the room and you and I will have a nice chat. If I think it is necessary, I will bring him back in to speak to you. Are we clear?"

LeCrue looked at his partner in the corner.

Hester said, "The correct answer is, 'Crystal, Ms. Crimstein.' " Then, glancing back at Mike, she said, "Go."

Mike rose. He and Tia walked outside.

The door closed behind them. The first thing Mike asked was, "Where is Jill?"

"She's at the Novaks'."

He nodded.

"Do you want to fill me in?" Tia said.

He did. He told her everything — about his visit to Club Jaguar, about his meeting with Rosemary McDevitt, about nearly getting in the fight, about the feds jumping in, about the interrogation and the pharm parties.

"Club Jaguar," Mike said when he finished. "Think about those instant messages."

"From CeeJay8115," she said.

"Right. It's not a person's initials. It stands for Club Jaguar."

"And the 8115?"

"I don't know. Maybe there are a lot of people with those initials."

"So you think it's her — this Rosemary whatever?"

"Yes."

She tried to soak it in. "In some ways it makes sense. Spencer Hill stole drugs from his father's medicine chest. That's how he killed himself. Maybe he did it at one of these pharm parties. Maybe they were having one on the roof."

"So you think Adam was there?"

"It adds up. They were having a pharm

party. You mix these drugs, you think they're safe . . ."

They both stopped.

"So did Spencer commit suicide?" Mike asked.

"He sent out those texts."

Silence fell upon them. They didn't want to think that through to the other conclusion.

"We just need to find Adam," Mike said. "Let's just concentrate on that, okay?"

Tia nodded. The door to the interrogation room opened, and Hester came out. She walked over to them and said, "Not in here. Let's go outside and talk."

She kept walking. Mike and Tia quickly rose to follow. They got in the elevator, but Hester still would not speak. When the doors opened, Hester strode through the revolving door and outside. Again Mike and Tia followed.

"In my car," Hester said.

It was a stretch limo with a TV set and crystal glasses and an empty decanter. Hester gave them the good seats, facing the driver. She sat across from them.

"I don't trust federal buildings anymore, what with the monitoring," she said. Hester turned to Mike. "I assume you filled in your wife?"

"I did."

"So you can probably guess the deal. They have dozens of what appear to be fake prescriptions written by you. This Club Jaguar was wise enough to use a variety of pharmacies. They got them filled in state, out of state, through the Internet, wherever. Refills too. The fed's theory is fairly obvious."

"They think Adam stole them," Mike said.

"Yep. And they have a fair amount of evidence."

"Like?"

"Like they know your son attended pharm parties. At least, that's what they claim. They were also on the street outside this Club Jaguar last night. They saw Adam go in and a little later they spotted you too."

"They saw me get attacked?"

"They claim you ducked into an alley and they didn't know until later what went on in there. They were watching the club."

"And Adam was there?"

"That's what they claim. But they won't tell me anything else. Like if they saw him leave. But make no mistake about it. They want to find your son. They want him to turn state's evidence against Club Jaguar or whoever runs it. He's a kid, they say. He'll get a slap on the wrist if he cooperates."

"What did you say?" Tia asked.

"First I did the dance. I denied that your son knows anything about these parties or your prescription pads. Then I asked what their offer meant in terms of sentencing and charges. They aren't ready to be specific."

Tia said, "Adam wouldn't steal Mike's prescription pads. He knows better."

Hester just gave her flat eyes. Tia realized how naïve her protestations sounded.

"You know the score," Hester said. "It doesn't matter what you think or what I think. I'm telling you their theory. And they have a lever. You, Dr. Baye."

"How so?"

"They're pretending that they're not totally convinced you weren't in on this. They point out, for example, that last night you were on your way to Club Jaguar when you had a violent run-in with several men who hang out there. How would you know about the place, unless you were involved? Why were you in the neighborhood?"

"I was looking for my son."

"And how did you know your son was there? Don't answer that, we all know. But you see my point. They can make a case that you're in cahoots with this Rosemary McDevitt. You're an adult and a physician. You'd give the task force nice headlines and serve serious prison time. And if you're dumb enough to think you should take the bullet for this instead of your son, well, they can then say you and Adam were both in on it. Adam started it off. He went to pharm parties. He and the Club Jaguar lady saw a way of making extra money via a legit doctor. They approached you."

"That's insane."

"No, it's not. They have your prescriptions. That's solid evidence, in their view. Do you know how much money this involves? OxyContin is worth a fortune. It's becoming an epidemic problem. And you, Dr. Baye, would make for a wonderful example. You, Dr. Baye, would be the poster boy for being very careful with how you dispense your prescriptions. I might get you off, sure. I probably will. But at what cost?"

"So what do you advise?"

"While I abhor cooperating, I think that may end up being our best bet. But that's premature. Right now we need to find Adam. We sit him down and find out exactly what happened here. Then we make the informed decision."

Loren Muse handed the photograph to Neil Cordova.

"That's Reba," he said.

"Yes, I know," Muse said. "This is a picture from a security camera at the Target where she shopped yesterday."

He looked up. "So how does this help us?"

"Do you see this woman over here?"

Muse pointed with her index finger.

"Yes."

"Do you know her?"

"No, I don't think so. Do you have a different angle?"

Muse handed him the second photograph. Neil Cordova concentrated on the image, wishing that he'd find something tangible to help out here. But he just shook his head. "Who is she?"

"There was a witness who saw your wife get in a van and saw another woman drive off in Reba's Acura. We had that witness watch the surveillance tapes. He says that's the woman."

He looked again. "I don't know her."

"Okay, Mr. Cordova, thank you. I'll be right back."

"Can I keep the picture? In case something comes to me?"

"Sure."

He stared, still stunned from identifying the body. Muse stepped out. She headed down the hallway. The receptionist waved her by.

She knocked on Paul Copeland's door. He shouted for her to come in.

Cope sat at a table with a video monitor on it. The county office doesn't use one-way mirrors in the interrogation rooms. They use a TV camera. Cope had been watching. His eyes were still on the screen, watching Neil Cordova.

"Something else just came in," Cope said to her.

"Oh?"

"Marianne Gillespie was staying at the Travelodge in Livingston. She was supposed to check out this morning. We also have a hotel staff member who saw Marianne take a man back to her room."

"When?"

"He wasn't sure, but he thought it was four, five days ago, around the time she first checked in."

Muse nodded. "This is huge."

Cope kept his eyes on the monitor. "Maybe we should hold a news conference. Blow up the image of that woman in the surveillance photo. See if anyone can identify her."

"Maybe. I hate to open it up to the public if we don't have to."

Cope kept studying the husband on the TV monitor. Muse wondered what he was thinking. Cope had known so much damn tragedy, including the death of his first wife. Muse glanced about the office. There were five new iPods, still in the boxes, sitting on the table. "What's this?" she asked.

"iPods."

"I know that. I mean, what are they for?"

Cope's gaze never left Cordova's. "I'm almost hoping he did it."

"Cordova? He didn't."

"I know. You can almost feel the hurt coming off him."

Silence.

"The iPods are for the bridesmaids," Cope said.

"Sweet."

"Maybe I should talk to him."

"Cordova?"

Cope nodded.

"That might help," she said.

"Lucy loves sad songs," he said. "You know that, right?"

Though a bridesmaid, Muse hadn't known Lucy all that long or, in many ways, all that well. She nodded anyway, but Cope was still staring at the monitor.

"Every month I make her a new CD. It's corny, I know. But she loves it. So every month I scour for the absolute saddest songs I can find. Total heartbreakers. Like this month — I have 'Congratulations' by Blue

October, and 'Seed' by Angie Aparo."

"I never heard of either of those."

He smiled. "Oh, you will. That's the gift. You're getting all those playlists preloaded into the iPod."

"Great idea," she said. Muse felt the stab. Cope made CDs for the woman he loved. How lucky was she?

"I used to wonder why Lucy liked those songs so much. You know what I mean? She sits in the dark and listens and cries. Music does that to her. I didn't get it. And like last month? I had this song from Missy Higgins. Do you know her?"

"No."

"She's great. Her music is a total killer. This one song she talks about an ex-love and how she can't stand the thought of another hand upon him, even though she knows she should."

"Sad."

"Exactly. And Lucy is happy now, right? I mean, we are so good. We finally found each other, and we're getting married. So why does she still listen to the heartbreakers?"

"You're asking me?"

"No, Muse, I'm explaining something to you. I didn't understand for a long time. But I do now. The sad songs are a safe hurt. It's a diversion. It's controlled. And maybe it helps you imagine that real pain will be like that. But it's not. Lucy knows that, of course. You can't prepare for real pain. You just have to let it rip you apart."

His phone buzzed. Cope finally pulled away his gaze and answered the phone. "Copeland," he said. Then he looked up at Muse. "They found Marianne Gillespie's next of kin. You better go."

30

As soon as the two girls were alone in the bedroom, Yasmin started crying.

"What's wrong?" Jill asked.

Yasmin pointed at her computer and sat. "People are so horrible."

"What happened?'

"I'll show you. It's so mean."

Jill pulled the chair and sat next to her friend. She bit down on a fingernail.

"Yasmin?"

"What?"

"I'm worried about my brother. And something happened to my dad too. That's why Mom dropped me back off here."

"Did you ask your mom about it?"

"She won't tell me."

Yasmin wiped her tears, still typing. "They always want to protect us, don't they?"

Jill wondered if Yasmin was being sarcastic or serious or maybe a little of both. Yasmin's eyes were back on the monitor.

She pointed.

"Wait, here it is. Take a look."

It was a MySpace page entitled *"Male or Female? — The Story of XY."* The wallpaper had a plethora of gorillas and monkeys. Under favorite movies, the two listed were *Planet of the Apes* and *Hair.* The default song was Peter Gabriel's "Shock the Monkey." There were National Geographic videos, all involving primates. One was a YouTube short called "Dancing Gorilla."

But the worst part was the default picture — a school photograph of Yasmin with a beard drawn over the face.

Jill whispered, "I can't believe it."

Yasmin started crying again.

"How did you find this?"

"Marie Alexandra, that bitch, sent me the link. She copied in half the class."

"Who made it up?"

"I don't know. I bet she did. She sent it like she was all concerned but I could almost hear her giggling, you know?"

"And she copied other people in?"

"Yes. Heidi and Annie and . . ."

Jill shook her head. "I'm sorry."

"Sorry?"

Jill said nothing.

Yasmin's face turned red. "Someone has to pay for this."

Jill looked at her friend. Yasmin used to be so gentle. She used to love to play the piano and dance and laugh at dumb movies. Now all Jill could see was the rage. It scared her. So much had gone wrong in the past few days. Her brother had run away, her father was in some kind of trouble, and now Yasmin was angrier than ever.

"Girls?"

It was Mr. Novak calling from downstairs. Yasmin wiped the tears off her face. She opened the door and called out, "Yes, Daddy?"

"I made some popcorn."

"We'll be down in a minute."

"Beth and I were thinking about taking you guys to the mall. We can see a movie or maybe you two can play at the arcade. What do you think?"

"We'll be down in a second."

Yasmin closed the door again.

"My dad needs to get out of the house. He's been freaking."

"Why?"

"The weirdest thing happened. Mr. Lewiston's wife showed up."

"At your house? No way."

Yasmin nodded, her eyes widened. "I mean, I guess it was her. I've never seen her, but she was driving his crappy car."

"So what happened?"

"They started arguing."

"Oh my God."

"I couldn't hear. But she looked really pissed."

From downstairs: "Popcorn's ready!"

The two girls came downstairs. Guy Novak was waiting for them. His smile was strained. "IMAX has the new Spider-Man movie," he said.

The doorbell rang.

Guy Novak turned to it. His body tensed.

"Dad?"

"I'll get it," he said.

He started for the front door. The two girls followed, keeping a little distance. Beth was there. Mr. Novak looked out the little window, frowned, opened the door. A woman stood in the doorway. Jill looked at Yasmin. Yasmin shook her head. This woman was not Mr. Lewiston's wife.

Mr. Novak said, "Can I help you?"

The woman peeked behind him, saw the girls, then looked back up at Yasmin's dad.

"Are you Guy Novak?" the woman asked.

"Yes."

"My name is Loren Muse. Can we talk a moment in private?"

Loren Muse stood in the doorway.

She spotted the two little girls behind Guy Novak. One was probably his daughter, the other, well, maybe she belonged to the woman standing behind them both. The woman, she quickly noted, was not Reba Cordova. The woman looked fine and fairly relaxed, but you never know. Muse kept her eyes on her, looking for some sort of signal to show that she was under duress.

There were no signs of blood or trauma in the foyer. The girls looked a little timid but otherwise okay. Before she rang the bell, Muse had pressed her ear against the door. She'd heard nothing unusual, just Guy Novak calling upstairs about popcorn and a movie.

"What's this about?" Guy Novak asked.

"I think it would be better if we talked alone."

She stressed the word "alone," hoping he would get the hint. He didn't.

"Who are you?" he asked.

Muse did not want to identify herself as a law enforcement officer with the girls still in the room, so she leaned in, glanced at the girls, and then looked him hard in the eye. "I think it would be better in private, Mr. Novak."

He finally got the message. He turned back to the woman and said, "Beth, would you take the girls into the kitchen and give them popcorn?"

"Of course."

Muse watched them slip out of the room. She was trying to read Guy Novak. He seemed a little on edge, but something about his manner suggested that he was more irritated with her surprise arrival than truly scared.

Clarence Morrow and Frank Tremont, along with a few local cops, were nearby. They were surreptitiously checking around. There was still faint hope that maybe Guy Novak had kidnapped Reba Cordova and was holding her here, but as the seconds passed, that seemed less and less likely.

Guy Novak did not invite her in. "Well?"

Muse flashed her badge.

"You're kidding me," he said. "Did the Lewistons call you?"

Muse had no idea who the Lewistons were, but she decided to go with it. She made a yes-no gesture with a head tilt.

"I can't believe this. All I did was drive by their house. That's all. Since when is that against the law?"

"Depends," Muse said.

"On what?"

"On your intentions."

Guy Novak pushed his glasses up the

bridge of his nose. "Do you know what that man did to my daughter?"

She had no idea, but whatever it was, it had clearly agitated Guy Novak. That pleased her — she could work with that.

"I'll listen to your side," she said.

He started railing then about something a teacher had said about his daughter. Muse watched his face. Again, like with Neil Cordova, she got no sense that this was an act for her benefit. He ranted about the injustice of what had been done to his little girl, Yasmin, and how this teacher didn't even get a slap on the wrist.

When he took a breath, Muse asked, "How does your wife feel about this?"

"I'm not married."

Muse knew that already. "Oh, I thought the woman who was with the girls . . ."

"Beth. She's just a friend."

Again she waited him out, seeing what else he would tell her.

He took a few deep breaths and said, "Okay, I got the message."

"The message?"

"I assume the Lewistons called to complain. Message received. I will review my options with my lawyer."

This track was leading nowhere, Muse thought. Time to shift gears. "Can I ask you something else?"

"I guess."

"How did Yasmin's mother react to all this?"

His eyes narrowed. "Why would you ask that?"

"It's not an unreasonable question."

"Yasmin's mother isn't very involved in her life."

"Still. A big event like this."

"Marianne ran out on us when Yasmin was little. She lives in Florida and sees her daughter maybe four or five times a year."

"When was the last time she was up?"

He frowned. "What does that have to do with . . . wait a minute, can I see your badge again?"

Muse took it out. This time he studied it. "You're county?"

"Yes."

"Do you mind if I call your office and verify that this is legitimate?"

"Suit yourself." Muse reached into her pocket and pulled out a card. "Here."

He read it out loud. "Loren Muse, Chief Investigator."

"Yep."

"Chief," he repeated. "What are you, a personal friend of the Lewistons?"

Again Muse wondered if this was a clever act or if Guy Novak was for real.

"Tell me when you last saw your ex-wife."

He rubbed his chin. "I thought you said this was about the Lewistons."

"Please just answer my question. When was the last time you saw your ex-wife?"

"Three weeks ago."

"Why was she here?"

"She came up to visit Yasmin."

"Did you talk to her?"

"Not really. She picked up Yasmin. She promised that she'd have her back by a certain time. Marianne usually keeps to that. She doesn't like to spend a lot of time with her daughter."

"Have you spoken to her since?"

"No."

"Uh-huh. Do you know where she usually stayed when she visited?"

"At the Travelodge near the mall."

"Are you aware she's been staying there for the past four nights?"

He looked surprised. "She said she was heading to Los Angeles."

"When did she tell you that?"

"I got an e-mail from her, uh, I don't know. Yesterday I think."

"May I see it?"

"The e-mail? I deleted it."

"Do you know if your ex-wife had a boyfriend?"

Something approaching a sneer crossed his face. "I'm sure she had several but I wouldn't know about it."

"Any men in this area?"

"There were men in every area."

"Any names?"

Guy Novak shook his head. "I wouldn't know or care."

"Why so bitter, Mr. Novak?"

"I don't know if 'bitter' is the right word anymore." He took off his glasses, frowned at some speck of dirt, tried to clean them with his shirt. "I loved Marianne, but she really didn't earn it. If you're being kind, you would call her self-destructive. This town bored her. I bored her. Life bored her. She was a serial cheater. She abandoned her own daughter and then became nothing but a source of disappointment. Two years ago Marianne promised Yasmin she'd take her to Disney World. She called me the day before the trip and canceled. No reason."

"Do you pay alimony or child support?"

"Neither. I have sole custody."

"Does your ex-wife still have friends in the area?"

"I wouldn't really know, but I doubt it."

"How about Reba Cordova?"

Guy Novak thought about that. "They were good friends when Marianne lived here. Very close. I never knew why. The two women couldn't be more different. But yeah, I mean, if Marianne still kept in touch with anyone in the area, it would probably be Reba."

"When was the last time you saw Reba Cordova?"

He looked up and to his right. "It's been a while. I don't know, maybe a back-to-school night or something."

If he knew that his ex had been murdered, Muse thought, he was a pretty cool customer.

"Reba Cordova is missing."

Guy Novak opened his mouth, closed it. "And you think Marianne has something to do with it?"

"Do you?"

"She's self-destructive. But the key word is 'self.' I don't think she'd hurt anyone else, except maybe her own family."

"Mr. Novak, I would very much like to talk to your daughter."

"Why?"

"Because we think that your ex-wife was murdered."

She said it just like that and waited for the reaction. It was slow in coming. It was as if the words were floating toward him one at a time, and it was taking him a long time to hear and process them. For a few seconds he did nothing. He just stood and stared. Then he made a face like maybe he'd heard wrong.

"I don't . . . you *think* she's been murdered?"

Muse looked back and nodded. Clarence started toward the door.

"We found a body in an alley dressed like a prostitute. Neil Cordova believes that it's your ex-wife, Marianne Gillespie. What we need you to do, Mr. Novak, is to accompany my colleague Investigator Morrow to the medical examiner's office so that you can see the body for yourself. Do you understand?"

His tone was numb. "Marianne is dead?"

"We believe so, yes, but that's why we need your help. Investigator Morrow will take you to the body and ask you a few questions. Your friend Beth can stay with the children. I will be here too. I want to ask your daughter about her mother, if that's okay?"

"Fine," he said. And that took a lot of the pressure off him. If he had started hemming and hawing, well, the ex-husband is always a good candidate. Not that she was totally sure that he wasn't involved. She could have run into another great actor in the league of De

Niro or Cordova. But again she doubted it. Either way, Clarence would question him.

Clarence said, "Mr. Novak, you ready?"

"I need to tell my daughter."

"I would rather you didn't," Muse said.

"Excuse me?"

"Like I said, we don't know for sure. I will ask her questions, but I won't tell her. I will leave that to you, if it is necessary at all."

Guy Novak nodded through his daze. "Okay."

Clarence took his arm and said in the gentlest voice, "Let's go, Mr. Novak. This way."

Muse did not bother watching Clarence escort him down the path. She entered and headed into the kitchen. The two little girls sat wide-eyed, pretending to eat popcorn.

One of them asked, "Who are you?"

Muse managed a tight smile. "My name is Loren Muse. I work for the county."

"Where's my father?"

"Are you Yasmin?"

"Yes."

"Your dad is helping one of my officers. He'll be back. But right now I need to ask you a few questions, okay?"

31

Betsy Hill sat on the floor of her son's room. She had Spencer's old cell phone in her hand. The battery was long dead. She just held it and stared at it and wasn't sure what to do.

The day after her son was found dead, she had found Ron starting to pack away this room — the same way he had packed away Spencer's kitchen chair. Betsy stopped him in no uncertain terms. There was bend, and there was break; even Ron could see the difference.

For days after the suicide, she would lie on this floor in a fetal position and sob. Her stomach hurt so much. She just wanted to die, that's all, just let the agony conquer and devour her. But it didn't. She put her hands on his bed, smoothing the sheets. She stuck her face in his pillow, but the scent was gone.

How could it have happened?

She thought about her conversation with Tia Baye, what it meant, what it ultimately could mean. Nothing really. In the end Spencer was dead. Ron was right on that count. Knowing the truth wouldn't change that or even help her heal. Knowing the truth wouldn't give her that damn word "closure," because, in truth, she didn't want it. What kind of mother — a mother who had already failed her child in so much — would want to move on, to stop hurting, to be given some kind of pass?

"Hey."

She looked up. Ron stood in the doorway. He tried to smile at her. She slipped the phone into her back pocket.

"You okay?" he asked.

"Ron?"

He waited.

"I need to find out what really happened that night."

Ron said, "I know you do."

"It won't bring him back," she said. "I know that. It won't even make us feel better. But I think we need to do it anyway."

"Why?" he asked.

"I don't know."

Ron nodded. He stepped into the room and started to bend toward her. For a moment she thought that he was going to wrap his arms around her, and her body stiffened at the thought. He stopped when he saw it, blinked, stood upright again.

"I better go," he said.

He turned and left. Betsy took the phone out of her pocket. She plugged in the charger and turned it on. Still clutching the phone, Betsy curled into the fetal position and cried again. She thought about her son in that same fetal position — was that hereditary too? — up on that cold hard roof.

She checked the phone log on Spencer's phone. There were no surprises. She had done this before, but not in several weeks. Spencer had called Adam Baye three times that night. He had last spoken to him an hour before the suicide text. That call had lasted only a minute. Adam had said that Spencer left him a garbled message. Now she wondered if that was a lie.

The police had found this phone on the roof next to Spencer's body.

She held it now and closed her eyes. She was half-asleep, lulling in that cusp between consciousness and awake, when she heard the phone ring. For a moment she thought that maybe it was Spencer's cell, but no, it was the house phone.

Betsy wanted to let it go into voice mail, but it might be Tia Baye. She managed to peel herself from the floor. There was a phone in Spencer's room. She checked the caller ID and saw an unfamiliar number.

"Hello?"

There was silence.

"Hello?"

Then a boy's voice choked with tears said, "I saw you and my mom on the roof."

Betsy sat up. "Adam?"

"I'm so sorry, Mrs. Hill."

"Where are you calling from?" she asked.

"A pay phone."

"Where?"

She heard more crying.

"Adam?"

"Spencer and I used to meet in your backyard. In those woods where you used to have the swing set. Do you know it?"

"Yes."

"I can meet you there."

"Okay, when?"

"Spencer and I liked it there because you can see anyone coming or going. If you tell someone, I'll spot them. Promise me you won't."

"I promise. When?"

"One hour."

"Okay."

"Mrs. Hill?"

"Yes?"

"What happened to Spencer," Adam said. "It was my fault."

As soon as Mike and Tia turned onto their block, they could see the man with the long hair and those dirty fingernails pacing on their front lawn.

Mike said, "Isn't that Brett from your office?"

Tia nodded. "He was checking that e-mail for me. The one about the Huff party."

They pulled into the driveway. Susan and Dante Loriman were outside too. Dante waved. Mike waved back. He looked over at Susan. She forced up her hand and then moved toward her front door. Mike waved again and turned away. He had no time for this now.

His phone went off. Mike looked down at the number and frowned.

"Who is it?" Tia asked.

"Ilene," he said. "The feds questioned her too. I should take this."

She nodded. "I'll talk to Brett."

Tia got out of the car. Brett was still going back and forth, animated, talking to himself. She called out to him and he stopped.

"Someone is messing with your head, Tia," Brett said.

"How?"

"I need to go in and check Adam's computer to be sure."

Tia wanted to ask more, but that would just waste time. She opened the door and let Brett inside. He knew the way.

"Did you tell anyone about what I put on his computer?" he asked.

"About the spying program? No. Well, I mean, we did last night. With the police and everything."

"How about before that? Did you tell anyone?"

"No. It wasn't something Mike and I were very proud of. Oh, wait, our friend Mo."

"Who?"

"He's almost Adam's godfather. Mo would never hurt our son."

Brett shrugged. They were in Adam's room. The computer was on. Brett sat and started typing. He brought up Adam's e-mail and started running some kind of program. Symbols scrolled by. Tia watched without a clue.

"What are you trying to find?"

He tucked his stringy hair behind both ears and studied the screen. "Hold on. That e-mail you asked about was deleted, remember? I just want to see if he had some kind of timer send function, nope and then . . ." He stopped. "Wait . . . okay, yep."

"Yep what?"

"It's weird, that's all. You say Adam was out when he got the e-mail. But we know the e-mail was read at his computer, right?"

"Right."

"You have any candidates?"

"Not really. None of us were home."

"Because here's the interesting thing. Not only was the message read on Adam's computer, it was also sent from it."

Tia made a face. "So someone broke in, turned on his computer, sent him an e-mail from this computer about a party at the Huffs, opened it, and then deleted it?"

"That's pretty much what I'm saying."

"Why would someone do that?"

Brett shrugged. "Only reason I can come up with? To mess with your head."

"But no one knew about the E-SpyRight. Except Mike and me and Mo and" — her eyes tried to meet his, but his danced away — "you."

"Hey, don't look at me."

"You told Hester Crimstein."

"I'm sorry about that. But that's the only person who knows."

Tia wondered. And then she looked at Brett with his dirty fingernails and the unshaven stubble and the hip albeit flimsy T-shirt and thought about how she had trusted this man she really didn't know all that well with this task — and how foolish that really was.

How did she know anything he was telling her was accurate?

He had shown her that she could sign in and get reports from as far away as Boston. How much of a stretch was it to assume that he had set up a password too, one so that he could get into the software and read the reports? How would she know? How would anyone know what was actually on the computer? Companies put on spyware so that they knew where you surfed. Stores give out those discount cards so they can keep track of what you buy. Lord knows what computer companies must have preloaded into your computer's hard drive. Search engines kept track of what you looked up and, with the simple cost of storage these days, never had to delete it.

Was it such a stretch to think Brett might know more than he said?

"Hello?"

Ilene Goldfarb said, "Mike?"

Mike watched Tia and Brett enter the house. He pressed the phone up against his ear. "What's up?" he asked his partner.

"I talked to Susan Loriman about Lucas's biological father."

That surprised Mike. "When?"

"Today. She called me. We met at the diner."

"And?"

"And it's a dead end."

"The real father?"

"Yes."

"How so?"

"She wants it to be confidential."

"The name of the father? Too bad."

"Not the name of the father."

"What then?"

"She told me the reason why that particular avenue is not going to be helpful to us."

Mike said, "I'm not following."

"Just trust me here. She explained the situation to me. It's a dead end."

"I can't see how."

"Neither could I before Susan explained it to me."

"And she wants the reason kept confidential?"

"Correct."

"So I assume it is something embarrassing. That's why she spoke to you, not me."

"I wouldn't call it embarrassing."

"What would you call it?"

"You sound like you don't trust my judgment on this."

Mike switched ears. "Normally, Ilene, I

would trust you with my life."

"But?"

"But I just got through being grilled by a joint task force of the DEA and U.S. Attorney's Office."

There was silence.

"They also spoke to you, didn't they?" Mike asked.

"They did."

"Why didn't you tell me?"

"They were very specific. They said my talking to you would compromise an important federal investigation. They threatened me with hindering prosecution and losing my practice, if I said anything to you."

Mike said nothing.

"Keep in mind," Ilene went on, an edge in her voice now, "that my name is on those prescription pads too."

"I know."

"What the hell is going on, Mike?"

"It's a long story."

"Did you do what they said?"

"Please tell me you're not seriously asking me that."

"They showed me our prescription pads. They gave me a list of what was prescribed. None of those people are our patients. Hell, half that stuff prescribed we never use."

"I know."

"This is my career too," she said. "I started this practice. You know what this means to me."

There was something in her voice, something wounded beyond the obvious. "I'm sorry, Ilene. I'm trying to sort through it all too."

"I think I'm owed a little more than 'it's a long story.' "

"The truth is, I don't really know what's up. Adam is missing. I need to find him."

"What do you mean, missing?"

He quickly filled her in. When he finished, Ilene said, "I hate to ask the obvious question."

"Then don't."

"I don't want lose my practice, Mike."

"It's our practice, Ilene."

"True. So if there is anything I can do to help find Adam . . . ," she began.

"I'll let you know."

Nash stopped the van in front of Pietra's apartment in Hawthorne.

They needed time apart. He could see that. The cracks were starting to show. They would always be somehow connected — not in the way he had been with Cassandra, not even close. But there was something there, some draw that brought them back time and time again. It probably started out as some sort of payback, gratitude for rescuing her in that awful place, but in the end, maybe she hadn't wanted to be saved. Maybe his rescuing her had been a curse and now he was her obligation rather than vice versa.

Pietra looked out the window. "Nash?"

"Yes?"

She put her hand up to her neck. "Those soldiers who slaughtered my family. All of those unspeakable things they did to them. To me . . ."

She stopped.

"I'm listening," he said.

"Do you think those soldiers were all killers and rapists and torturers — and even if there was no war, they would have done things like that?"

Nash said nothing.

"The one we found was a baker," she said. "We used to go to his store. My whole family. He smiled. He gave out lollipops."

"What's your point?"

"If there was no war," Pietra said, "they would have just lived their lives. They would have been bakers or blacksmiths or carpenters. They would not have been killers."

"And do you think that's true of you too?" he asked. "That you would have just gone on being an actress?"

"I'm not asking about me," Pietra said. "I'm asking about those soldiers."

"Okay, fine. If I follow your logic, you think the pressures of war explain their behavior."

"You don't?"

"I don't."

Her head slowly swiveled in his direction. "Why not?"

"Your argument is that the war forced them to act in a way that was not in their nature."

"Yes."

"But maybe it is just the opposite," he said. "Maybe the war freed them to be their true selves. Maybe it is society, not war, that forces man to act in a way that's not in his true nature."

Pietra opened the door and got out. He watched her disappear into the building. He put the car in drive and started for his next destination. Thirty minutes later, he parked on a side street between two houses that appeared empty. He didn't want the van to be seen in the parking lot.

Nash put on the fake mustache and a baseball cap. He walked three blocks to the large brick building. It appeared abandoned. The front door, Nash was sure, would be locked. But one side door had a matchbook jammed into the opening. He pulled it open and started down the stairs.

The corridor was covered with children's artwork, paintings mostly. A bulletin board had essays hung up. Nash stopped and read a few. They were by third graders, and all the stories were about them. That was how kids were taught nowadays. Think only "me." You are fascinating. You are unique and special and no one but no one is ordinary, which, when you think about it, makes everyone ordinary.

He turned into the classroom on the lower level. Joe Lewiston sat cross-legged on the floor. He had papers in his hands and tears in his eyes. He looked up when Nash entered.

"It's not working," Joe Lewiston said. "She's still sending the e-mails."

32

Muse questioned Marianne Gillespie's daughter carefully, but Yasmin knew nothing.

Yasmin hadn't seen her mother. She hadn't even known she was back in town.

"I thought she was in L.A.," Yasmin said.

"Did she tell you that?" Muse asked.

"Yes." Then: "Well, she sent me an e-mail."

Muse remembered Guy Novak saying the same thing. "Do you still have it?"

"I can look. Is Marianne okay?"

"You call your mother by her first name?"

Yasmin shrugged. "She really didn't want to be a mother. I figure, why remind her? So I call her Marianne."

They grow up fast, Muse thought. She asked again, "Do you still have the e-mail?"

"I guess so. It's probably on my computer."

"I would like you to print out a copy for me."

Yasmin frowned. "But you won't tell me what this is about." It wasn't a question.

"Nothing to worry about yet."

"I see. You don't want to worry the little kid. If it was your mother and you were my age, would you want to know?"

"Fair point. But again we don't know anything yet. Your dad will be back soon. I would really like to see that e-mail."

Yasmin headed up the stairs. Her friend stayed in the room. Normally Muse would have wanted to question Yasmin alone, but the friend seemed to calm her.

"What's your name again?" Muse asked.

"Jill Baye."

"Jill, have you ever met Yasmin's mom?"

"A couple of times, yeah."

"You look worried."

Jill made a face. "You're a policewoman asking about my friend's mother. Shouldn't I be?"

Kids.

Yasmin trotted back down the stairs with a piece of paper in her hand. "Here it is."

Muse read:

Hi! I'm going to Los Angeles for a few weeks. I will be in touch when I get back.

This explained so much. Muse had wondered why no one had reported Jane Doe missing. Simple. She lived alone in Florida. Between her lifestyle and this e-mail, well, it could have been months, if not longer, before anyone figured out that she'd met up with foul play.

"Does that help?" Yasmin asked.

"Yes, thank you."

Tears filled Yasmin's eyes. "She's still my mom, you know."

"I know."

"She loves me." Yasmin started to cry. Muse stepped toward her, but the girl put her hand up to stop her. "She just doesn't know how to be a mom. She tries. She just doesn't get it."

"It's okay. I'm not judging her or anything."

"Then tell me what's wrong. Please?"

Muse said, "I can't."

"But it's bad, right? You can tell me that much. Is it bad?"

Muse wanted to be honest with the girl, but this was not the time or place.

"Your father will be here soon. I need to get back to work."

Nash said, "Calm down."

Joe Lewiston stood from his cross-legged position in one fluid movement. Teachers,

Nash figured, must get used to that movement. "I'm sorry. I shouldn't have gotten you involved."

"You did the right thing, calling me."

Nash looked at his former brother-in-law. You say "former" because "ex" implies divorce. Cassandra Lewiston, his beloved wife, had five brothers. Joe Lewiston was both the youngest and her favorite. When their oldest brother, Curtis, was murdered a little more than a decade ago, Cassandra had taken it so hard. She had cried for days and wouldn't get out of bed and sometimes, even though he knew that it was irrational to think such thoughts, Nash wondered if that anguish had made her sick. She grieved so hard over her brother that maybe her immune system had weakened. Maybe cancer is in all of us, those life-draining cells, and maybe they bide their time until our defenses are down and then they make their move.

"I promise I will find out who killed Curtis," Nash had told his beloved.

But he hadn't kept that promise, though that really hadn't mattered to Cassandra. She was not one for vengeance. She just missed her big brother. So he had sworn to her right then and there. He had sworn that he would never let her know this pain again. He would protect those she loved.

He would protect them always.

He had promised her that again on her deathbed.

It seemed to bring her comfort.

"You'll be there for them?" Cassandra had asked.

"Yes."

"And they will be there for you too."

He had not replied to that.

Joe came toward him. Nash took in the classroom. In so many ways they had not changed at all from the days he'd been a student. There were still the handwritten rules and the cursive alphabet in both capitals and small letters. There were splashes of color everywhere. Recent artwork was drying on a clothesline.

"Something else happened," Joe said.

"Tell me."

"Guy Novak keeps driving by my house. He slows down and glares. I think he's scaring Dolly and Allie."

"Since when?"

"He's been doing it for about a week now."

"Why didn't you tell me this before?"

"I didn't think it was important. I figured he'd stop."

Nash closed his eyes. "And why do you think it's important now?"

"Because Dolly got really upset when he did it this morning."

"Guy Novak drove by your house today?"

"Yes."

"And you think it's an attempt to harass you?"

"What else would it be?"

Nash shook his head. "We had it wrong from the get-go."

"What do you mean?"

But there was no reason to explain. Dolly Lewiston was still getting the e-mails. That meant one thing. Marianne hadn't sent them out, even though, after suffering so much, she had said that she had.

Guy Novak had.

He thought about Cassandra and his promise. He knew now what he would have to do to take care of this situation.

Joe Lewiston said, "I'm such a fool."

"Listen to me, Joe."

He looked so scared. Nash was glad that Cassandra would never see her baby brother like this. He thought about how Cassandra had been toward the end. She had lost her hair. Her skin was jaundiced. There were open wounds on her scalp and face. She lost control of her bowels. There were times the pain seemed unbearable, but she had made him promise not to interfere. Her lips would purse and her eyes would bulge and it was like steel talons were shredding her from inside. Sores covered the inside of her mouth toward the end so that she couldn't even speak. Nash would sit there and watch and feel the rage.

"It's going to be okay, Joe."

"What are you doing to do?"

"Don't worry about it, okay? It will be fine. I promise."

Betsy Hill waited for Adam in the small patch of woods behind her house.

This overgrown area was on their property, but they'd never bothered to clean it out. She and Ron had talked a few years back about razing it and putting in a pool, but the expense would cause a strain and the twins were still too young. So they never got around to it. Ron had built a fort back here when Spencer was nine. The kids would play on it. There had been an old swing set too, something they bought from Sears. Both had been abandoned years ago, but if she looked close enough, Betsy could still find the scattered nail or rusted piping.

The years passed and then Spencer started hanging back here with some of his friends. Betsy had found beer bottles once. She debated raising this with Spencer, but whenever she tried to broach the subject, he withdrew even more. He was a teen having a beer. What was the big deal?

"Mrs. Hill?"

She turned and saw Adam standing behind her. He had come in through the other side, from the Kadisons' backyard.

"My God," she said, "what happened to you?"

There was swelling on his dirty face. His arm had a huge bandage wrapped around it. His shirt was torn.

"I'm fine."

Betsy had heeded his warning and had not called his parents. She feared blowing this opportunity. Maybe that was wrong, but she had made so many wrong decisions over the past few months, one more barely seemed relevant.

Still, her next words to him were "Your parents are so worried."

"I know."

"What happened, Adam? Where have you been?"

He shook his head. Something about the way he did that reminded Betsy of his father. As kids get older, you see that more — not just looking like their parents but locked into the same mannerisms. Adam was big now, taller than his dad, almost a man.

"I guess that picture has been on the memorial page for a long time," Adam said. "I never go there."

"You don't?"

"No."

"Can I ask why?"

"It isn't Spencer to me. You know? I mean, I don't even know those girls who set it up. I got enough reminders. So I don't look at it."

"Do you know who took the picture?"

"DJ Huff, I think. I mean, I can't be sure because I'm just in the background. I'm looking away. But DJ uploaded a lot of pictures to that site. Probably just uploaded them all and didn't even realize it was from that night."

"What happened, Adam?"

Adam started to cry. She had been thinking just a few seconds ago that he seemed so close to manhood. Now the man vanished, and the boy was back.

"We had a fight."

Betsy just stood there. Maybe six feet separated them, but she could feel the hum of his blood.

"That was how he got that bruise on his face," Adam said.

"You punched him?"

Adam nodded.

"You were his friend," Betsy said. "Why would you fight?"

"We were drinking and getting high. It was over a girl. Things got out of hand. We pushed and then he threw a punch. I ducked it and then I hit him in the face."

"Over a girl?"

Adam lowered his eyes.

"Who else was there?" she asked.

Adam shook his head. "It doesn't matter."

"It matters to me."

"It shouldn't. I'm the one he had the fight with."

Betsy tried to imagine it. Her son. Her beautiful son and his last day on earth and his best friend in the world had struck him in the face. She tried to keep her tone even, but that wasn't happening. "I don't understand any of this. Where were you?"

"We were supposed to go to the Bronx. There's this place there. They let kids our age party."

"The Bronx?"

"But before we went, Spencer and I had the fight. I hit him and called him horrible names. I was so mad. And then he ran away. I should have gone after him. I didn't. I let him go. I should have known what he would do."

Betsy Hill just stood there, numb. She remembered what Ron had said, about how no one forced their son to steal vodka and pills from the house.

"Who killed my boy?" she asked.

But she knew.

She had known from the beginning. She had sought explanations for the unexplainable and maybe she would get one, but human behavior was usually much more complex. You find two siblings who were raised in the exact same manner and one will end up sweet and one will be a killer. Some people will chalk that up to "hardwiring," to nature over nurture, but then sometimes it isn't even that — it is just some random event that alters lives, something in the wind that mixes with your particular brain chemistry, anything really, and then after the tragedy, we look for explanations and maybe we find some, but it is just theorizing after the fact.

"Tell me what happened, Adam."

"He tried to call me later," Adam said. "Those were those calls. I saw it was him. And I didn't answer. I just let it go into voice mail. He was already so stoned. He was depressed and down and I should have seen it. I should have forgiven him. But I didn't. That was his last message to me. He said he was sorry and he knew the way out. He had thought about suicide before. We all talk about that. But with him it was different. It was more serious. And I fought with him. I called him names and said I'd never forgive him."

Betsy Hill shook her head.

"He was a good kid, Mrs. Hill."

"He was the one who took the drugs from our house, from our medicine cabinet . . . ," she said, more to herself than to him.

"I know. We all did."

His words rattled her, made it impossible to think. "A girl? You fought over a girl?"

"It was my fault," Adam said. "I lost control. I didn't look out for him. I listened to the messages too late. I got to the roof as soon as I could. But he was dead."

"You found him?"

He nodded.

"And you never said anything?"

"I was gutless. But not anymore. It ends now."

"What ends?"

"I'm so sorry, Mrs. Hill. I couldn't save him."

Then Betsy said, "Neither could I, Adam."

She took a step toward him, but Adam shook his head.

"It ends now," he said again.

Then he took two steps backward, turned, and ran away.

33

Paul Copeland stood in front of a plethora of network microphones and said, "We need your help in finding a missing woman named Reba Cordova."

Muse watched from the side of the stage. The monitors flashed an achingly sweet photograph of Reba on the screen. Her smile was the kind that made you smile too, or conversely, in a situation like this, ripped your heart right down the middle. There was a phone number on the bottom of the screen.

"We also need help in locating this woman."

Now they flashed the photograph from the Target store surveillance video.

"This woman is a person of interest. If you have any information, please call the number below."

The nut jobs would start in now, but in this situation, the potential pros outweighed, in Muse's view, the cons. She doubted anyone would have seen Reba Cordova, but there was a real chance that someone might recognize the woman in the surveillance photo. That was what Muse was hoping anyway.

Neil Cordova stood next to Cope. In front of him were his and Reba's two little girls. Cordova kept his chin high, but you could still see the tremble. The Cordova girls were beautiful and haunting and all eyes, like something you'd see staggering away from a burned-out building in a war newsreel. The networks, of course, loved this — the photogenic grieving family. Cope had told Cordova that he didn't have to attend or he could attend by himself without the kids. Neil Cordova had shaken that off.

"We need to do all we can to save her," Cordova had told Cope, "or those girls will look back and wonder."

"It's going to be traumatic," Cope replied.

"If their mother is dead, they'll go through hell no matter. At least I want them to know that we did all we could."

Muse felt her phone vibrate. She checked and saw it was Clarence Morrow calling from the morgue. About damn time.

"The body belongs to Marianne Gillespie,"

Clarence said. "The ex-husband is positive."

Muse stepped up a little, just so that Cope could see her. When he glanced toward her, she gave a small nod. Cope turned back to the microphone and said, "We have also identified a body that may be connected to Ms. Cordova's disappearance. A woman named Marianne Gillespie . . ."

Muse turned back to her call. "You questioned Novak?"

"We did. I don't think he's involved, do you?"

"No."

"He had no motive. His girlfriend isn't the woman in the surveillance tape, and he doesn't match the description of the guy in the van."

"Take him home. Let him tell his daughter in peace."

"On our way. Novak already called the girlfriend to make sure she kept the girls away from the news until he gets back."

Back on the monitor a photograph of Marianne Gillespie appeared. Weirdly enough, Novak did not have any old photos of his ex, but Reba Cordova had visited Marianne in Florida last spring and taken some snapshots. The picture was taken by the pool, Marianne working a bikini, but they'd cropped it into a headshot for the cameras. Marianne had been something of a bombshell, Muse noted, albeit one who had probably seen better days before the hard living. Things weren't as tight as they might have once been, but you could still see she had it.

Neil Cordova finally stepped up to speak. The camera flashes created the strobe that always shocked the uninitiated. Cordova blinked through it. He seemed calmer now, putting on a game face. He told everyone that he loved his wife and that she was a wonderful mother and if anyone had information, could they please call the number on the screen?

"Psst."

Muse turned. It was Frank Tremont. He waved her to come toward him.

"We got something," he said.

"Already?"

"A widow who used to be married to a Hawthorne cop called. She says the woman in the surveillance photo lives alone downstairs. Says the woman is from someplace overseas and that her name is Pietra."

On his way out of the school, Joe Lewiston checked his mailbox at the main office.

There was yet another flyer and personal note from the Loriman family to help find a donor for their son, Lucas. Joe had never had any of the Loriman kids, but he'd seen the mother around. Male teachers might pretend that they are above it, but they noticed the hot moms. Susan Loriman was one of them.

The flyer — the third he'd seen — said that next Friday they would have a "medical professional" coming through the school to take blood tests.

Please find it in your heart to help save Lucas's life. . . .

Joe felt terrible. The Lorimans were working feverishly to save their child's life. Mrs. Loriman had e-mailed and called him, urging him to help: "I know you've never taught any of my kids, but everyone in the school looks up to you as a leader," and Joe had thought, selfishly because all humans are selfish, that maybe it would help his standing since the XY-Yasmin controversy or at the very least assuage his own guilt. He thought about his own child, imagined little Allie in a hospital with tubes running out of her, sick and in pain. That thought should have put his problems into perspective, but it didn't. Someone is always worse off than you. That never seemed like much comfort.

He drove and thought about Nash. Joe still had three older brothers alive, but he relied on Nash more than any of them. Nash and Cassie had seemed like an unlikely mix, but when they were together, it was as though they were one entity. He heard that was how it sometimes worked, but he had never really seen it before or since. Lord knows he and Dolly didn't have it.

Corny as it sounded, Cassie and Nash had truly been two becoming one.

When Cassie died, it was beyond devastating. You just never thought it would happen. Even after the diagnosis. Even after watching the early horrifying effects of the illness. You somehow thought that Cassie would pull through. It shouldn't have been a shock by the time she succumbed. But it was.

Joe saw Nash change more than any of them — or maybe, when two are forced to become one again, something has to give. There was a coldness to Nash that Joe now found oddly comforting because there were so few Nash cared about. Outwardly warm people pretend that they are there for everyone, but when it really counted, like now, a man wants to call on a strong friend who only has his interest at heart, who could give a damn about right or wrong, who just wanted to make sure the one he cared about was safe.

That was Nash.

"I promised Cassandra," Nash had explained to him after the funeral. "I will protect you."

With anyone else that would have sounded bizarre or discomforting, but with Nash, you knew that he meant it and that he would do whatever was in his almost supernatural power to keep his word. It was scary and exhilarating and for someone like Joe, the unathletic son ignored by his demanding father, it meant a lot.

When Joe walked in the door, he saw that Dolly was on the computer. She had a funny expression on her face and Joe felt his stomach drop.

"Where were you?" Dolly asked.

"At school."

"Why?"

"Just some work I wanted to catch up on."

"My e-mail still isn't working."

"I'll take another look at it."

Dolly stood up. "Do you want some tea?"

"That would be nice, thanks."

She kissed his cheek. Joe sat at the computer. He waited until she was out of the room, then he signed into his account. He was about to check his e-mails when something on his home page caught his eye.

"Lead photos" from the news circulated

on his front page. There was international news, followed by local news, sports and then entertainment. It was the local news picture that had caught his eye. The picture was gone now, replaced with something about the New York Knicks.

Joe hit the back arrow and found the picture again.

It was a photograph of a man with his two little girls. He recognized one of them. She wasn't one of his students, but she went to his school. Or at least she looked like a girl who did. He clicked on the story. The headline read:

LOCAL WOMAN MISSING

He saw the name Reba Cordova. He knew her. She had been on the school library committee where Joe had been faculty liaison. She was vice president of the HSA and he remembered her smiling face at the back door when the children were let out.

She was missing?

Then he read the part beneath that, about the possible connection to a corpse recently found in Newark. He read the name of the murder victim and felt the breath squeeze out of him.

Oh dear Lord, what had he done?

Joe Lewiston ran to the bathroom and threw up. Then he grabbed his phone and dialed Nash's number.

34

First Ron Hill made sure that neither Betsy nor the twins were home. Then he headed up to his dead boy's bedroom.

He didn't want anyone to know.

Ron leaned against the doorway. He stared at the bed as though that might conjure up the image of his son — that he could look so hard that a figure would eventually materialize and it would be Spencer and he'd be lying on his back and he'd be staring at the ceiling the way he did, silent and with small tears in his eyes.

Why hadn't they seen it?

You look back and you know the kid was always a little morose, always a little too sad, too even. You don't want him labeled with words like manic depression. He's just a kid after all, and you figure that he will outgrow it. But now, with the wonder of hindsight, how often had he walked past this room and the door was closed and Ron would open it without knocking — this was his house, damnit, he didn't have to knock — and Spencer would just be lying on that bed with tears in his eyes and he'd look straight up and Ron would ask, "Is everything okay?" and he'd say, "Sure, Dad," and Ron would close the door and that would be the end?

Some father.

He blamed himself. He blamed himself for what he missed in his son's behavior. He blamed himself for leaving the pills and vodka where his son could so easily grab them. But mostly he blamed himself for what he'd been thinking.

Maybe it had been a midlife crisis. Ron didn't think so. He thought that was too convenient, too easy an out. The truth was, Ron hated this life. He hated his job. He hated coming home to this house and the kids not listening to him and the constant noise and running to Home Depot to get more lightbulbs and worrying about the gas bill and saving for the college fund and, God, he so wanted to escape. How had he gotten trapped in this life anyhow? How do so many men? He wanted a cabin in the woods and he loved being alone and just that, just being deep in the forest where no cell phone could reach him, just the way he could find an opening in the trees and raise his face up to the sun and feel it.

So he wished this life away and longed to escape, and pow, God answered his prayers by killing his son.

He dreaded being here, in this house, this coffin. Betsy would never move on. There was a disconnect between him and the twins. A man stays out of obligation, but why? What's the point? You sacrifice your happiness in the thin hope that it will make the next generation happier. But does that come with a guarantee — I remain unhappy but my kids will be more fulfilled? What a load of crap. Had it worked for Spencer?

He flashed back to the days after Spencer's death. He had come in here not so much to pack things away but to go through them. It helped. He didn't know why. He was drawn to sifting through his son's stuff, as if getting to know him now would make a difference. Betsy had walked in and threw a fit. So he stopped and never said a word about what he found — and though he would continue to try to reach Betsy, though he'd hunt and search and beckon, the woman he fell in love with was gone. She might have left a long time ago — he wasn't sure anymore — but whatever had remained had been buried in that damn box with Spencer.

The sound of the back door startled him.

He hadn't heard the car pull up. He hurried toward the stairs and saw Betsy. He saw the look on her face and said, "What happened?"

"Spencer killed himself," she said.

Ron just stood there, not sure how to reply to that one.

"I wanted there to be more," she said.

He nodded. "I know."

"We'll always wonder about what we could have done to save him. But maybe, I don't know, maybe there was nothing. Maybe we missed stuff, but maybe it wouldn't have mattered. And I hate thinking that because I don't want to let us off the hook — and then I think, well, I don't even care about hooks or blame or any of that. I just want to go back to another day. You know? Just another chance and maybe if we could change just one thing, the smallest thing, like if we took a left out of the driveway instead of a right or if we painted the house yellow instead of blue, anything, it would have all been different."

He waited for her to say more. When she didn't, he asked, "What happened, Betsy?"

"I just saw Adam Baye."

"Where?"

"In the backyard. Where they used to play."

"What did he say?"

She told him about the fight, about the calls, about how Adam blamed himself. Ron tried to process it.

"Over a girl?"

"Yes," she said.

But Ron knew that it was far more complicated than that.

Betsy turned away.

"Where are you going?" he asked.

"I have to tell Tia."

Tia and Mike decided to split the load.

Mo met them at the house. He and Mike drove back toward the Bronx while Tia took to the computer. Mike filled Mo in on what had happened. Mo drove without asking for elaboration. When Mike was done, Mo simply asked, "That instant message. From CeeJay8115."

"What about it?"

Mo kept driving.

"Mo?"

"I don't know. But there is no way that there's eight thousand one hundred and fourteen other CeeJays out there."

"So?"

"So numbers are never random," Mo said. "They always mean something. It is just a matter of figuring out what."

Mike should have known. Mo was something of an idiot savant when it came to numbers. That had been his ticket to Dartmouth — perfect math SAT scores and off-the-charts arithmetical testing.

"Any thoughts on what it could mean?"

Mo shook his head. "Not yet." Then: "So what next?"

"I need to make a call."

Mike dialed the number for Club Jaguar. He was surprised when Rosemary McDevitt herself answered the phone.

"It's Mike Baye."

"Yeah, I figured. We're closed today, but I was expecting your call."

"We need to talk."

"Indeed we do," Rosemary said. "You know where I'm at. Get here as fast as you can."

Tia checked Adam's e-mail, but again there was nothing relevant coming in. His friends Clark and Olivia were still sending messages, each somewhat more urgent, but still nothing from DJ Huff. That worried Tia.

She got up and headed outside. She checked the hidden key. It was where it was supposed to be. Mo had used it recently and said he put it back. Mo knew where it was and in some ways, she guessed, that would make him suspect. But while Tia had her issues with Mo, trust was not one of them. He would never harm this family. There were few people you knew would take a bullet for you. He might not for Tia, but Mo would for Mike and Adam and Jill.

She was still outside when she heard the phone. She sprinted back in and picked it up on the third ring. No time to check the caller ID.

"Hello?"

"Tia? It's Guy Novak."

His tone was like something dropping from a high building with no place safe to land.

"What's wrong?"

"The girls are fine, don't worry. Have you seen the news at all?"

"No, why?"

He stifled a sob. "My ex-wife was murdered. I just identified the body."

Whatever Tia had been expecting to hear, this was not it. "Oh God, I'm so sorry, Guy."

"I don't want you to worry about the girls. My friend Beth is watching them. I just called the house. They're fine."

"What happened to Marianne?" Tia asked.

"She was beaten to death."

"Oh, no . . ."

Tia had only met her a few times. Marianne had run off right about the time Yasmin and Jill had started school. It had been juicy town scandal — a mother not able to hack the pressures of motherhood, cracking, running off and leading some rumored wild life in warm weather, no responsibilities. Most of the mothers talked about it with such disgust that Tia couldn't help but wonder if there wasn't a little envy, a little admiration for shedding the chains, albeit in a destructive and selfish way.

"Did they catch the killer?"

"No. They didn't even know who she was until today."

"I'm so sorry, Guy."

"I'm on my way back to the house. Yasmin doesn't know yet. I need to tell her."

"Of course."

"I don't think Jill should be there when I do."

"Definitely not," Tia agreed. "I'll come pick her up right away. Is there anything else we can do?"

"No, we'll be fine. I mean, it might be good if Jill could come over later. I know that's asking a lot, but Yasmin might need a friend."

"Of course. Whatever you and Yasmin need."

"Thank you, Tia."

He hung up. Tia sat there stunned. Beaten to death. She couldn't wrap her brain around that. Too much. She had never been much of a multitasker, and the last few days were playing havoc with her inner control freak.

She grabbed her keys, wondered if she should call Mike, decided against it. He was laser-focused on finding Adam. She did not want to interrupt that. When she stepped outside, the sky was the blue of a robin's egg. She looked down the road, at the quiet homes, at the well-tended lawns. The Grahams were both outside. He was teaching his six-year-old how to ride a two-wheeler, holding on to the seat as the boy pedaled, one of those rites of passage, a question of trust too, like those exercises when you let yourself fall back because you know the person will catch you. He looked hopelessly out of shape. His wife watched from the yard. Her hand was cupped over her eyes to block the sun. She smiled. Dante Loriman pulled into the driveway in his BMW 550i.

"Hey, Tia."

"Hi, Dante."

"How are you?"

"Good, you?"

"Good."

Both lying, of course. She looked up and

down at the block. The houses were all so alike. She thought again about the sturdy structures trying to protect lives that were much too fragile. The Lorimans had a sick son. Hers was missing and probably involved in something illegal.

She was slipping behind the wheel when her cell phone buzzed. She checked the caller ID. It was from Betsy Hill. Might be best not to answer it. They were after different things here, she and Betsy. She wouldn't tell her about the pharm parties or what the police suspected. Not yet.

The phone rang again.

Her finger hovered near the SEND button. The important thing here was finding Adam. Everything else had to take a backseat to that. There was a chance that maybe Betsy had found something that could give her a clue about what was going on here.

She pressed down.

"Hello?"

Betsy said, "I just saw Adam."

Carson's broken nose was starting to ache. He watched Rosemary McDevitt put down the phone.

Club Jaguar was so quiet now. Rosemary had closed it down, sending everyone home after the near-fight with Baye and his crewcut buddy. They were the only two still here.

She was gorgeous, no question, a total hottie, but right now her usual tough exterior looked like it might crumble. She wrapped her arms around herself.

Carson sat across from her. He tried to sneer, but it made his nose hurt.

"That was Adam's old man?"

"Yes."

"We need to get rid of both of them."

She shook her head.

"What?"

"What you need to do," she said, "is let me handle it."

"You don't get it, do you?"

Rosemary said nothing.

"The people we work for —"

"We don't work for anybody," she interrupted.

"Fine, put it however you want. Our partners. Our distributors. Whatever."

She closed her eyes.

"These are bad people."

"Nobody can prove anything."

"Like hell they can't."

"Just let me handle it, okay?"

"He's coming here?"

"Yes. I'm going to talk to him. I know what I'm doing. You should just leave."

"So you can be alone with him?"

Rosemary shook her head. "Not like that."

"Then like what?"

"I can work this out. I can get him to see reason. Just let me take care of it."

Alone on this hill, Adam could still hear Spencer's voice:

"I'm so sorry. . . ."

Adam closed his eyes. Those voice messages. He had kept them on his phone, had listened to them every day, felt the pain rip through him anew.

"Adam, please pick up. . . ."

"Forgive me, okay? Just say you forgive me. . . ."

They still came to him every night, especially the last one, Spencer's voice already slurred, already hurtling toward death:

"This isn't on you, Adam. Okay, man. Just try to understand. It's not on anyone. It's just too hard. It's always been too hard. . . ."

Adam waited on the old hill by the middle school for DJ Huff. DJ's father, a police captain who grew up in this town, said that kids used to get high up here after school. The tough kids hung out here. The others would rather walk the extra half mile to avoid it.

He looked out. In the distance he could see the soccer field. Adam had played there in some league when he was eight, but soccer was never for him. He liked the ice. He liked the cold and the glide of the skate. He liked putting on all those pads and that mask and the focus it took to guard the goal. You were the man then. If you were good enough, if you were perfect, your team could not lose. Most kids hated that pressure. Adam thrived on it.

"Forgive me, okay? . . ."

No, Adam thought now, *you* have to forgive *me*.

Spencer had always been volatile, with swooping highs and earth-crushing lows. He talked about running away, about starting a business, and mostly about dying and ending the pain. All kids do, to some degree. Adam had even started making a suicide pact with Spencer last year. But for him it was talk.

He should have seen that Spencer would do it.

"Forgive me. . . ."

Would it have made a difference? That night, yeah, it would have. His friend would have lived another day. And then another. And then who knows?

"Adam?"

He turned to the voice. It was DJ Huff.

DJ said, "You okay?"

"No thanks to you."

"I didn't know that would happen. I just saw your dad following me and called Carson."

"And ran."

"I didn't know they'd go after him."

"What did you think would happen, DJ?"

He shrugged, and Adam could see it. The red in his eyes. The thin coat of sweat. The way DJ's body teetered.

"You're high," Adam said.

"So? I don't get you, man. How could you tell your father?"

"I didn't."

Adam had planned it all out for that night. He had even gone to the spy store in the city. He thought that he'd need a wire like you saw on TV, but they gave him what looked like an ordinary pen that would record audio and a belt buckle that worked as a video camera. He would get it all there and then bring it to the police — not the local police because DJ's dad worked there — and let the pieces fall where they would. He was taking the risk, but he had no choice.

He was drowning.

He was sinking and he could feel it and he knew that if he didn't rescue himself, he would end up like Spencer. So he planned and was ready for last night.

And then his father insisted that he had to go to that Rangers game.

He knew that he couldn't do that. Maybe he could postpone his plan a bit, but if he didn't show up that night, Rosemary and Carson and the rest of them would wonder. They already knew that he was on the fence. They'd already forced him with the blackmail threat. So he had sneaked out and gone to Club Jaguar.

When his father showed up, his plan all went to hell.

The knife wound on his arm stung. It would probably require stitches, might even get infected. He had tried to clean it out. The pain had nearly made him pass out. But it would do for now. Until he could put this right again.

"Carson and the guys think you were setting us up," DJ said.

"I wasn't," Adam lied.

"Your dad showed up at my house too."

"When?"

"I don't know. An hour before he got to the Bronx maybe. My dad saw him sitting in a car across the street."

Adam wanted to think about that, but there was no time.

"We need to put an end to this, DJ."

"Look, I talked to my old man. He's working on it for us. He's a cop. He gets this stuff."

"Spencer is dead."

"That's not on us."

"Yeah, DJ, it is."

"Spencer was messed up. He did it himself."

"We let him die." Adam looked at his right hand. He made a fist. That had been Spencer's final touch from another human being. His best friend's fist. "I hit him."

"Whatever, man. You want to feel guilty about it, that's on you. You can't take the rest of us down for that."

"It isn't about guilt. They tried to kill my father. Hell, they tried to kill me."

DJ shook his head. "You don't get it."

"What?"

"We turn ourselves in, we're done. We'll probably end up in jail. We can forget college. And who do you think Carson and Rosemary sold those drugs to — the Salvation Army? There are mob people involved in this, don't you get that? Carson is scared out of his mind."

Adam said nothing.

"My old man says if we just keep quiet, it will be fine."

"You really believe that?"

"I introduced you to that place, but that's

all they got on me. It's your father's prescription pads. We can just say we want out."

"And if they don't let us out?"

"My dad can apply pressure. He said it'll be okay. Worse come to worst, we just lawyer up and not say a word."

Adam looked at him, waiting.

"This decision affects us all," DJ said. "It's not just your future you're screwing with. It's mine. And Clark is involved. Olivia too."

"I'm not going to listen to that argument again."

"It's still true, Adam. Maybe they're not as directly involved as you and me, but they'll go down too."

"No."

"No what?"

He looked back at his friend. "This is how it's worked your whole life, DJ."

"What are you talking about?"

"You get into trouble and your father pulls you out."

"Who the hell do you think you're talking to?"

"We can't just walk away from this."

"Spencer killed himself. We didn't do anything to him."

Adam looked down through the trees. The soccer field was empty, but people were still jogging around the circle. He turned his head a little to the left. He tried to find that patch of roof, the one where Spencer had been found, but it was blocked off by the front tower. DJ moved and stood next to him.

"My dad used to hang up here," DJ said. "When he was in high school. He was one of those bad kids, you know? He smoked dope and drank beer. He got into fights."

"What's your point?"

"My point is this. In those days you could survive a mistake. People looked the other way. You were a kid — you were supposed to blow off steam. My father stole a car when he was our age. Got caught too, but they worked out a side deal. Now my old man is one of the most law-abiding citizens around. But if he had grown up today, he'd be screwed. It's ridiculous. If you whistle at a girl at school, you can go to jail. If you bump into someone's chest in the hallway, you can be brought up on some kind of charges. One mistake and you're out. My dad says that's nonsense. How are we supposed to find our way?"

"That doesn't give us a free pass."

"Adam, in another couple of years we'll be in college. This will all be behind us. We aren't criminals. We can't let this moment ruin our lives."

"It ruined Spencer's."

"That's not our fault."

"Those guys almost killed my father. He ended up in the hospital."

"I know. And I know how I would feel if it was my father. But you can't go off half-cocked because of that. You need to calm down and think it through. I spoke to Carson. He wants us to go in and talk to him."

Adam frowned. "Right."

"No, I mean it."

"He's crazy, DJ. You know that. You just said it yourself — he thinks I tried to set him up."

Adam tried to sort it through, but he was so damn tired. He had been up all night. He was in pain and exhausted and confused. He had spent the night thinking and really had no idea what to do.

He should have told his parents the truth.

But he couldn't. He had messed up and gotten high too often and you start to buy that belief that the only people in the world who love you unconditionally, the only people who will love you forever no matter how you screw up, that somehow they were the enemy.

But they'd spied on him.

That much he now knew. They hadn't trusted him. That had gotten him furious, but really, when he thought about, had he earned their trust?

So after last night, he panicked. He ran and stayed hidden. He just needed time to think.

"I need to talk to my parents," he said.

"I don't think that's a good idea."

Adam looked at him. "Let me use your phone."

DJ shook his head. Adam took a step toward him and made a fist.

"Don't make me take it from you."

DJ's eyes were wet. He held up a hand, took out his cell, and handed it to Adam. Adam dialed home. No answer. He dialed his father's cell. No answer. He tried his mom's. Same thing.

DJ said, "Adam?"

He thought about making the call. He had already called her once, staying on long enough to let her know that he was okay and making her swear not to tell his parents.

He dialed Jill's phone.

"Hello?"

"It's me."

"Adam? Please come home. I'm so scared."

"Do you know where Mom and Dad are?"

"Mom is picking me up at Yasmin's. Dad

went to look for you."

"Do you know where?"

"I think he went to the Bronx or something. I heard Mom say something about that. Something about Club Jaguar."

Adam closed his eyes. Damn. They knew.

"Listen, I have to go."

"Where?"

"It'll be okay. Don't worry. When you see Mom, tell her you heard from me. Tell her I'm fine and I'll be home soon. Tell her to reach Dad and get him to come home, okay?"

"Adam?"

"Just tell her."

"I'm really scared."

"Don't worry, Jill, okay? Just keep doing what I say. It's almost over."

He hung up and looked at DJ. "You have your car?"

"Yeah."

"We gotta hurry."

Nash saw the unmarked police car pull up to the house.

Guy Novak got out. A plainclothes cop started getting out of the car, but Novak waved him off. He reached back into the car, shook the cop's hand and stumbled in a daze toward the front door.

Nash felt his phone vibrate. He didn't need to check the incoming number anymore. He knew it would be Joe Lewiston again. He had listened to the first desperate message a few minutes ago:

"Oh God, Nash, what's going on? I didn't want that. Please don't hurt anyone else, okay? Just . . . I just thought you could talk to her or get the video or something. And if you know something about the other woman, please don't hurt her. Oh God, oh God . . ."

Like that.

Guy Novak entered his house. Nash moved closer. Three minutes later, the front door opened again. A woman came out. Guy Novak's girlfriend. He kissed her on the cheek. The door closed behind her. The date walked down the path. When she reached the curb, she looked back and shook her head. She might have been crying, but it was hard to tell from here.

Thirty seconds later, she too was gone.

Time was limited now. Somehow Nash had messed up. They had figured out who Marianne was. It was on the news. The husband had been questioned by the police. People think that law enforcement officers are stupid. They are not. They have every advantage. Nash respected that. It was one of the reasons he'd gone through such great lengths to hide Marianne's identity.

Self-preservation told him to run away, hide, sneak out of the country. But that wouldn't do. He could still help Joe Lewiston, even if Joe wouldn't help himself. He would call him later and persuade him to keep quiet. Or maybe Joe would see the light on his own. Joe was panicked right now, but he had, after all, contacted Nash to help in the first place. Maybe he would end up making the smart move.

The itch was there. The crazy, as Nash liked to call it. He knew that there were children in the home. He had no interest in hurting them — or was that a lie? Hard to know sometimes. Humans are all about self-delusion, and Nash wasn't above wallowing in that overindulgence on occasion.

But on a purely practical level, there was no time to wait. He had to act now. That meant — with the crazy or without it — the children could very well end up collateral damage.

There was a knife in his pocket. He took it out now and held it in his hand.

Nash moved toward Novak's back door and worked on the lock.

35

Rosemary McDevitt sat in her Club Jaguar office, her vest and tattoos now covered by a too-large gray sweatshirt. She swam in it, her hands disappearing into the long sleeves. It made her look smaller, less threatening and powerful, and Mike wondered if that was the point. She had coffee in front of her. Mike had one too.

"The cops put a wire on you?" she asked.

"No."

"You mind giving me your cell phone, just to be sure?"

Mike shrugged and tossed it to her. She turned it off and left it on the desk between them.

Her knees were up on the chair, again disappearing into the sweatshirt. Mo was outside, waiting in the car. He hadn't wanted Mike to do this, fearing a trap, but he also knew that they had no choice. This was the best lead they had on Adam.

Mike said, "I don't really care about what you're doing in there, except in how it relates to my son. Do you know where he is?"

"No."

"When did you last see him?"

She looked up at him with doe-brown eyes. He wasn't sure if he was being worked here or not, but it didn't much matter. He wanted answers. He could play the game back if that helped.

"Last night."

"Where exactly?"

"Downstairs at the club."

"He came here to party?"

Rosemary smiled. "I don't think so."

He let that go. "You talked to him by instant message, didn't you? You're Cee-Jay8115."

She did not reply.

"You told Adam to stay quiet and it'd be safe. He messaged you that he'd been approached by Spencer Hill's mother, right?"

Her knees were still up on the chair. She wrapped her arms around them. "How would you know so much about his private messages, Dr. Baye?"

"That's not your concern."

"How did you follow him to Club Jaguar last night?"

Mike said nothing.

"Are you sure you want to travel down this road?" she asked.

"I don't think I have a choice."

She glanced over his shoulder. Mike turned around. Carson with the broken nose was glaring through the glass. Mike met his eyes and calmly waited. A few seconds later, Carson broke eye contact and hurried away.

"They're just boys," Mike said.

"No, they're not."

He let it drop. "Talk to me."

Rosemary settled back. "Let's speak in hypotheticals, okay?"

"If that's what you want."

"That's what I want. Let's say you're a girl from a small town. Your brother dies of a drug overdose."

"Not according to the police. They say there is no evidence any of that happened."

She smirked. "The feds told you that?"

"They said they can't find anything to back up the claim."

"I changed some of the facts, that's why."

"Which facts?"

"Name of the town, name of the state."

"Why?"

"Major reason? On the night my brother died, I was arrested for possession with intent to sell." She met his eye. "That's right. I gave my brother the drugs. I was his supplier. I leave that part out of the story. People tend to judge."

"Go on."

"So I formed Club Jaguar. I already told you my philosophy. I wanted to create a safe haven where kids could party and let loose. I wanted to channel their natural inclination to rebel in a protected way."

"Right."

"So it started that way. I busted my butt and raised enough money to get it off the ground. We opened this place in a year. You can't imagine how difficult that was."

"I can, but I really don't need to hear about it. How about fast-forwarding to the part where you started holding pharm parties and stealing prescription pads?"

She smiled and shook her head. "It's not like that."

"Uh-huh."

"I read in the paper today about a widow who did volunteer work for her local parish. Over the last five years she's skimmed twenty-eight thousand dollars from the tithing basket. Did you see that?"

"No."

"But you've heard of others, right? Dozen of cases like that. The guy who works for the charity and siphons off money to buy himself a Lexus — do you think one day he just woke up and decided to do that?"

"I don't really know."

"That church lady. You know what I bet happened? One day she's counting out the money in the tithing basket and she stays late and maybe her car is broken down and she can't get home. It's getting dark. So maybe she calls the taxi company and figures, well, she volunteers all this time and the church should pay for it. She doesn't ask. She grabs five bucks out of the basket. That's all. She's more than owed it. That's how this stuff starts, I think. It's an incremental thing. You see all these decent people getting arrested for embezzling from schools or churches or charities. They start small and move so slow it's like watching clocks — they don't even see. They don't think they're doing anything wrong."

"And that's what happened with Club Jaguar?"

"I thought that teens wanted to party in a social way. But it was like the midnight basketball program. They wanted to party, yes, but with booze and drugs. You can't create a place to rebel. You can't make it safe and drug-free because that's the whole purpose — they don't want it safe."

"Your concept failed," Mike said.

"No one showed — or if they did, they

didn't stay. We were labeled as lame. We were viewed like one of those evangelical groups that make you take a virginity pledge."

"So I don't get what happened next," Mike said. "You just started letting them bring in their own drugs?"

"It wasn't like that. They just did. I didn't even know about it at first, but in a way it made sense. Incremental, remember? One or two kids brought some prescription drugs from home. Nothing too heavy-duty. And we aren't talking cocaine or heroin here. These were FDA-approved medicines."

"Bull," Mike said.

"What?"

"These are drugs. Hard-core drugs, in many cases. There's a reason you need a prescription to get them."

She made a scoffing noise. "Well, sure, a doctor would say that, wouldn't he? Without you being the arbiter of who gets what medicine, your business is dead — and you've already lost a lot of money to Medicare and Medicaid and all the squeezing from insurance companies."

"That's crap."

"Maybe it is in your case. But not every doctor is as caring as you are."

"You're justifying a crime."

Rosemary shrugged. "You could be right.

But that was how it started — a few teens bringing in some pills from home. Medicine, when you think about. Prescribed and legal. When I first heard about it, I was upset and then I saw how many kids we were attracting. They were going to do it anyway and I was giving them a safe place. I even hired a medical practitioner. She worked at the club just in case something went wrong. Don't you see? I was getting them in the doors. They were better off here than somewhere else. I had programs too — so they could talk out their problems. You saw the flyers about counseling. Some of the kids signed up for those. We were doing more good than harm."

Mike said, "Incremental."

"Exactly."

"So naturally you still need to make money," he said. "You find out how much these drugs are worth on the street. So you start asking for a cut."

"For the house. For expenses. I hired the medical professional, for example."

"Like the church lady needing taxi money."

Rosemary smiled, though there was no joy in it. "Yes."

"And then Adam walked in the door. The son of a doctor."

It was like the cops told him. Entrepreneurial. He didn't care about her reasons really. She may be handing him a line or maybe not. It didn't much matter. She had a point about how people slip-slide into trouble. That church lady probably didn't volunteer her time in order to start skimming money. It just starts to happen. It happened in their town Little League a couple of years ago. It happened with school boards and the local mayor's office, and every time you hear it you can't believe it. You know these people. They aren't evil. Or are they? Is it circumstances that make them do it — or is it more this self-denial that Rosemary was describing?

"What happened to Spencer Hill?" Mike asked.

"He committed suicide."

Mike shook his head.

"I'm telling you what I know," she said.

"Then why should Adam — as you put in your IM — need to keep quiet about that?"

"Spencer Hill killed himself."

Mike shook his head again. "He overdosed here, didn't he?"

"No."

"It's the only thing that makes sense. It is why Adam and his friends needed to keep quiet. They were afraid. I don't know what sort of pressure you applied. Maybe you reminded them that they'd be arrested too. This is why they all feel guilty. This is why Adam can't stand himself anymore. He was with Spencer that night. Not only was he with him, but he helped move the body to that rooftop."

A small smile curled her lips. "You really don't have a clue, do you, Dr. Baye?"

He didn't like the way she said that. "So tell me then."

Rosemary still had her legs up and under her sweatshirt. It was such a teenage move; it gave her an air of youth and innocence that he knew was undeserved. "You don't know your son at all, do you?"

"I used to."

"No, you didn't. You think you did. But you're his dad. You're not supposed to know all. They're supposed to break away. When I said you don't know him, I actually meant it as a good thing."

"I'm not following."

"You put a GPS in his phone. That was how you found out where he was. You clearly monitor his computer and read his communications. You probably think it helps, but actually it stifles. A parent isn't supposed to know what their kid is up to all the time."

"Give them room to rebel, is that it?"

"In part, yes."

Mike sat up. "If I had known about you earlier, maybe I could have stopped him."

"Do you really think that?" Rosemary tilted her head as though genuinely interested in his response. When he said nothing, she continued, "Is that your plan for the future? Monitoring your children's every move?"

"Do me a favor, Rosemary. Don't worry about my child-rearing plans, okay?"

She looked at him carefully. She pointed to the bruise on his forehead. "I'm sorry about that."

"Did you sic those goths on me?"

"No. I didn't know about that until this morning."

"Who told you?"

"It's not important. Last night, your son was here and it was a sensitive situation. And then, wham, you showed up. DJ Huff saw you following him. He called and Carson answered."

"He and his buddies tried to kill me."

"And they probably would have. Still think they're just boys?"

"A bouncer saved me."

"No. A bouncer found you."

"What do you mean by that?"

She shook her head. "When I learned they

attacked you and the police came by . . . it was something of a wake-up call. Now I just want to find a way to end this."

"How?"

"I'm not sure, but that's why I wanted us to meet. To come up with a plan."

He saw it now — why she was so willing to share all this with him. She knew that the feds were closing in, that now was the time to cash in her chips and leave the table. She wanted help and figured a scared father would fall into line.

"I got a plan," he said. "We go to the feds and tell them the truth."

She shook her head. "That might not be best for your son."

"He's a minor."

"Still. We are all in this mess together. We need to find a way to make it go away."

"You were providing illegal drugs to minors."

"Not true, as I just explained. They may have used my facility for the purposes of exchanging prescribed medicines. That's all you can maybe prove. You can't prove I knew about it."

"And the stolen prescription scripts?"

She arched an eyebrow. "You think I stole them?"

Silence.

She met his eye. "Do I have access to your home or office, Dr. Baye?"

"The feds have been watching you. They've been building a case. Do you think those little goths will stand up to the threat of jail time?"

"They love this place. They almost killed you to protect it."

"Please. Once they get into an interrogation room, they'll fold."

"There are other considerations too."

"Like what?"

"Like who do you think distributed the medications out on the streets? Do you really want your son testifying against those kinds of people?"

Mike wanted to reach across the table and wring her neck. "What did you get my son into, Rosemary?"

"It's what we have to get him out of. That's what you need to concentrate on. We need to make this go away — for my sake, yes, but for your son's even more."

Mike reached for his cell phone. "I don't know what else there is to say."

"You have a lawyer, right?"

"Yes."

"Don't do anything until you let me talk to him, okay? There is so much at stake. You have other kids to worry about — your son's friends."

"I don't care about other kids. Only mine."

He flipped on the phone and it immediately rang. Mike checked the caller ID. It read a number he didn't recognize. He put the phone to his ear.

"Dad?"

His heart stopped.

"Adam? Are you okay? Where are you?"

"Are you in Club Jaguar?"

"Yes."

"Get out. I'm on the street heading toward you. Please get out of there right now."

36

Anthony worked as a bouncer three days a week at a skeezy gentlemen's club called Upscale Pleasure. The name was a joke. The place was a dank pit. Before this, Anthony had worked at a strip joint called Home-wreckers. He liked that better, the more honest moniker giving the place a real identity.

For the most part, Anthony worked the lunch crowd. One would think that this would be a slow time for business, that places like this would not draw much of a crowd until late night. One would be wrong.

The daytime crowd at a strip club is a United Nations event. Every race, creed, color and socioeconomic group was well represented. There were men in business suits, in those red flannel tops Anthony always associated with hunting, with Gucci loafers and off-brand Timberland boots. There were pretty boys and smooth talkers and suburbanites and inbreds. You got them all in a place like this.

Sleazy sex — the great unifier.

"You're on break, Anthony. Take ten."

Anthony headed toward the door. The sun was fading, but it still made him blink. That was always true with these joints, even at night. It is a different dark in strip clubs. You go outside and you have to blink that dark away like Dracula on a bender.

He reached for a cigarette and then remembered that he was quitting. He didn't want to, but his wife was pregnant and that was the promise he always made — no secondhand smoke around the baby. He thought about Mike Baye, his problems with his kids. Anthony liked Mike. Tough dude, even if he had gone to Dartmouth. Didn't back down. Some guys get brave from alcohol or to impress a girl or a friend. Some guys are just plain stupid. But Mike wasn't like that. He just didn't have a backup switch. He was a solid guy. Weird as this sounded, he made Anthony want to be more solid too.

Anthony checked his watch. Two more minutes for his break. Man, he wanted to light up. This job didn't pay as well as his night gig, but it was total cake. He didn't believe much in superstitious nonsense, but the moon definitely had an effect. Nights were for fighting, and if the moon was full, he knew that he'd have his hands full. Guys were more mellow at lunchtime. They sat quietly and watched and ate the most wretched "buffet" known to mankind, stuff Michael Vick wouldn't let a dog eat.

"Anthony? Time's up."

He nodded and started turning for the door, when he saw a kid hurry past him with a phone pressed against his ear. He only saw the kid for a second, maybe less, and he never really saw his face clearly. There was another kid with him, trailing a little. The kid had on a jacket.

A varsity jacket.

"Anthony?"

"I'll be right back," he said. "Something I gotta check out."

At the front door of his home, Guy Novak had kissed Beth good-bye.

"Thank you so much for watching the girls."

"It was no trouble. I'm glad I could help. I'm really sorry to hear about your ex."

Some date, Guy thought.

He idly wondered if Beth would ever be back or if this day would understandably chase her away. He didn't dwell on it much.

"Thank you," he said again.

Guy closed the door and moved to the liquor cabinet. He wasn't much of a drinker, but he needed one now. The girls were upstairs watching a movie on DVD. He had yelled up for them to relax and finish the movie. This would give Tia time to pick up Jill — and Guy time to figure out how to break the news to Yasmin.

He poured himself whiskey from a bottle that probably hadn't been touched in three years. He downed it, let it burn his throat, and poured another.

Marianne.

He remembered how it started all those years ago — a summer romance down the shore, both of them working in a restaurant that catered to the tourist crowd. They would finish cleaning up at midnight and bring a blanket to the beach and stare at the stars. The waves would crash and the wonderful scent of saltwater would soothe their naked bodies. When they went back to college — he at Syracuse, she at Delaware — they talked on the phone every day. They wrote letters. He bought a very used Oldsmobile Ciera so he could drive the four-plus hours to see Marianne every weekend. The drive seemed interminable. He couldn't wait to sprint out of the car and into her arms.

Sitting in this house now, time zoomed in and out, toying the way it does, making something far away suddenly appear right over your shoulder.

Guy took another deep swig of whiskey. It warmed him.

God, he had loved Marianne — and she had pissed it all away. For what? This ending? Horribly murdered, that face he had so tenderly kissed at the beach crushed like eggshells, her wonderful body dumped in an alley like so much refuse.

How do you lose that? When you fall so hard, when you want to spend every moment with a person and find everything they do wonderful and fascinating, how the hell does that just go away?

Guy had stopped blaming himself. He finished the whiskey, stumbled up, and poured himself another. Marianne had made her bed — and died in it.

You dumb bitch.

What were you looking for out there, Marianne? We had something here. Those blurry nights in bars and all that bed-hopping — where did it lead you, my one true love? Did it give you fulfillment? Joy? Anything besides the empty? You had a beautiful daughter, a husband who worshipped you, a home, friends, a community, a life

— why wasn't that enough?

You dumb crazy bitch.

He let his head loll back. The pulp of what was left of her beautiful face . . . he would never lose that image. It would stay with him always. He might put it away, force it into some closet in the corner of his mind, but it would come out at night and haunt him. That wasn't fair. He had been the good guy. Marianne had been the one who decided to make her life a destructive search — not just *self*-destructive, because in the end she'd taken plenty of victims — for some unreachable nirvana.

He sat in the dark and rehearsed the words he would say to Yasmin. Keep it simple, he thought. Her mother was dead. Don't tell the how. But Yasmin was curious. She would want details. She would go online and find them or hear them from friends at school. Another parental dilemma: Tell the truth or try to protect? Protection wouldn't work here. The Internet would make sure that there would be no secrets. So he would have to tell it all to her.

But slowly. Not all at once. Start simple.

Guy closed his eyes. There was no sound, no warning, until the hand cupped his mouth and the blade pressed up against his neck, breaking through the skin.

"Shh," a voice whispered in his ear. "Don't make me kill the girls."

Susan Loriman sat by herself in her backyard.

The garden was having a good year. She and Dante worked hard on it, but they rarely enjoyed the fruits of their labor. She would try to sit here and relax amongst the fauna and green, but she couldn't shut off her critical eye. One plant might be dying, another might need trimming back, another wasn't blooming as wonderfully as last year. Today she turned off the voices and tried to fade into the landscape.

"Hon?"

She kept her eyes on the garden. Dante came up behind her and put his hands on her shoulders.

"You okay?" he asked.

"Yes."

"We'll find a donor."

"I know."

"We don't give up. We get everyone we know to give blood. We beg, if we have to. I know you don't have much family, but I do. They'll all get tested, I promise."

She nodded.

Blood, she thought. Blood doesn't matter because Dante was Lucas's true father.

She fiddled with the gold cross around her neck. She should tell him the truth. But the lie had been there for so long. After the rape she had quickly slept with Dante as often as possible. Why? Did she know? When Lucas was born, she was certain it was Dante's. Those were the odds. The rape had been once. She had made love to her husband many times that month. Looks-wise, Lucas had favored her, not either man, so she made herself forget.

But of course she hadn't forgotten. She had never moved past it, despite what her mother had promised her.

"This is best. You'll go forward. You protect your family. . . ."

She hoped Ilene Goldfarb would keep her secret. Nobody else knew the truth anymore. Her parents had, but they were both dead now — Dad from heart disease, Mom from cancer. While they were alive, they never spoke of what happened. Not once. They never pulled her aside and gave her a hug, never called to ask how she was doing or if she was coping. There was not even an eye twitch when, three months after the rape, she and Dante told them that they were going to be grandparents.

Ilene Goldfarb wanted to find the rapist and see if he would help.

But that wasn't possible.

Dante had been away on a trip to Las Vegas with some friends. She hadn't been happy about that. Their relationship was going through an awkward stage, and just as Susan was questioning if she'd gotten married too young, her husband decides to run off with the boys and gamble and probably hit some strip clubs.

Before that night, Susan Loriman had not been a religious person. Growing up, her parents had taken her to church every Sunday, but it never stuck. When she began to blossom into what many considered a beauty, her parents kept a stern eye. Eventually Susan rebelled, of course, but that horrible night sent her back to the fold.

She had gone with three girlfriends to a bar in West Orange. The other girls were single and for one night, with her husband running off to Vegas, she wanted to be too. Not all the way single, of course. She was married, mostly happily, but a little flirting couldn't hurt. So she drank and acted like the other girls. But she drank way too much. The bar seemed to grow darker, the music louder. She danced. Her head spun.

As the night wore on, her girlfriends hooked up with different guys, disappearing one by one, thinning the herd.

Later she would read about roofies or date-rape drugs and she wondered if that was part of it. She remembered very little. Suddenly she was in a man's car. She was crying and wanted to get out and he wouldn't let her. At some point he took out a knife and dragged her to a motel room. He called her horrible names and raped her. When she struggled, he hit her.

The horror seemed to go on for a very long time. She remembered hoping that he would kill her when this was over. That was how bad it was. She didn't think about survival. She longed for death.

The next part was a blur too. She remembered reading somewhere that you should relax and not fight — get your rapist to think he's won or something like that. So Susan did that. When his guard was down, she got a hand free and grabbed his testicles as hard as she could. She held on and twisted and he screamed and pulled away.

Susan rolled off the bed and found the knife.

Her rapist was down and rolling on the ground. There was no more fight in him. She could have opened the door and run out of the room and screamed for help. That would have been the smart move. But she didn't do that.

Instead Susan plunged the knife deep into his chest.

His body went rigid. There was this horrible convulsion as the blade pierced the heart.

And then her rapist was dead.

"You feel tense, hon," Dante said to her now, eleven years later.

Dante began to knead her shoulders. She let him, though it offered no comfort.

With the knife still in the rapist's chest, Susan ran from that motel room.

She ran for a very long time. Her head began to clear. She found a pay phone and called her parents. Her father picked her up. They talked. Her father drove past the motel. There were red lights flashing. The cops were already there. So her father took her to her childhood home.

"Who will believe you now?" her mother said to her.

She wondered.

"What will Dante think?"

Another good question.

"A mother needs to protect her family. This is what a woman does. We are stronger than the men this way. We can take this blow and go on. If you tell him, your husband will never look at you the same. No man will. You like the way he looks at you, yes? He will always wonder why you went out. He will wonder how you ended up in that man's room. He may believe you, but it will never be right. Do you understand?"

So she waited for the police to come to her. But they never did. She read about the dead man in the papers — saw his name even — but those stories only lasted a day or two. The police suspected that her rapist died in a robbery or drug deal gone wrong. The man had a record.

So Susan went on, just like her mother said. Dante came home. She made love to him. She did not like it. She still did not like it. But she loved him and wanted him happy. Dante wondered why his beautiful bride was more sullen, but he somehow knew better than to ask.

Susan started going to church again. Her mother had been right. The truth would have destroyed her family. So she carried the secret and protected Dante and their children. Time did indeed make it better. Sometimes she went whole days without thinking about that night. If Dante realized that she no longer liked sex, he didn't show it. Where Susan used to like the admiring looks from men, now they made her stomach hurt.

That was what she couldn't tell Ilene

Goldfarb. There was no point in asking the rapist for help.

He was dead.

"You're skin is so cold," Dante said.

"I'm fine."

"Let me get you a blanket."

"No, I'm okay."

He could see that she just wanted to be alone. Those moments never happened before that night. But they happened now. He never asked either, never pushed it, always giving her exactly the space she needed.

"We will save him," he said.

He walked back into the house. She stayed out there and sipped her drink. Her finger still toyed with the gold cross. It had been her mother's. She had given it to her only child on her deathbed.

"You pay for your sins," her mother had told her.

That she could accept. Susan would pay gladly for her sins. But God should leave her son the hell alone.

37

Pietra heard the cars pull up. She looked out the window and saw a small woman with a purposeful stride moving toward the front door. Pietra looked out the window to her right and saw four squad cars, and she knew.

There was no hesitation. She picked up her cell phone. There was only one number in the speed dial. She pressed down and heard it ring twice.

Nash said, "What's wrong?"

"The police are here."

When Joe Lewiston came back down the stairs, Dolly took one look and said, "What happened?"

"Nothing," he said, his lips feeling numb.

"You look flushed."

"I'm fine."

But Dolly knew her husband. She wasn't buying. She got up and moved toward him.

He almost backpedaled and started running away.

"What is it?"

"Nothing, I swear."

She was now standing directly in front of him.

"Was it Guy Novak?" she asked. "Did he do something else? Because if he did . . ."

Joe put his hands on his wife's shoulders. Her eyes moved over her face. She could always read him. That was the problem. She knew him so well. They had so very few secrets. But this was one of them.

Marianne Gillespie.

She had called for a parent–teacher conference, playing the role of a concerned parent. Marianne had heard about the terrible thing Joe had said to her daughter, Yasmin, but she sounded understanding. People blurt things out, she told him on the phone. People make mistakes. Her ex-husband was crazed with anger, yes, but Marianne said that she was not. She wanted to sit and talk and hear Joe's side of the story.

Maybe, Marianne had suggested, there was a way to make this better.

Joe had been so relieved.

They sat and they talked. Marianne sympathized. She touched his arm. She loved his teaching philosophy. She looked at him with longing and she wore something low-cut and clingy. When they embraced at the end of the conference, it lasted a few seconds too long. She kept her lips near his neck. Her breathing grew funny. So did his.

How could he have been so stupid?

"Joe?" Dolly took a step back. "What is it?"

Marianne had planned the seduction revenge from the beginning. How could he have not seen that? And once Marianne got her way, within hours of leaving her hotel room, the calls started:

"I have it on tape, you bastard. . . ."

Marianne had hidden a camera in the hotel room and threatened to send the tape first to Dolly, then the school board, then every e-mail she could dig out of the school directory. For three days she made the threats. Joe couldn't sleep, couldn't eat. He lost weight. He begged her not to do it. At some point Marianne seemed to lose her drive, as though the whole enterprise of vengeance suddenly wore her out. She called and told him that she wasn't sure if she would send it or not.

She had wanted him to suffer — and he had — and maybe that would be enough for her.

The next day, Marianne sent an e-mail to

his wife's work address.

The lying bitch.

Fortunately Dolly was not big on e-mail. Joe had her access code. When he saw the e-mail with the video attached, he totally freaked. He deleted it and changed Dolly's password, so that she couldn't see her own e-mail.

But how long would he be able to pull that off?

He didn't know what to do. There was no one he could talk to about it, no one who would understand and be unconditionally on his side.

And then he thought of Nash.

"Oh God, Dolly . . ."

"What?"

He had to put an end to this. Nash had killed someone. He had actually murdered Marianne Gillespie. And the Cordova woman was missing. Joe tried to put it together. Maybe Marianne had given a copy to Reba Cordova. That would make sense.

"Joe, talk to me."

What Joe had done was bad, but bringing in Nash had compounded his crime a thousandfold. He wanted to tell Dolly everything. He knew that it was the only way.

Dolly looked him in the eyes and nodded. "It's okay," she said. "Just tell me."

But then a funny thing happened to Joe Lewiston. The survival instinct kicked in. Yes, what Nash had done was horrible, but why amplify it by committing marital suicide? Why make it worse by destroying Dolly and maybe his family? This was, after all, on Nash. Joe hadn't asked him to go this far — certainly not to kill anyone! He had assumed that maybe Nash would offer to buy the tape from Marianne or make a deal with her or, at worst, scare her. Nash always hit Joe as playing near the edge, but he never in a million years dreamed that he'd do something like this.

What good would it do now to report it?

Nash, who'd been trying to help, would end up in prison. Moreover, who had been the one to recruit Nash in the first place?

Joe.

Would the police believe that Joe didn't know what Nash was up to? When you thought about it, Nash could be viewed as the hitman, but didn't the police always want the guy who'd hired out the hit more?

Again that would be Joe.

There was still a chance, albeit slight, that this could all end somewhat okay. Nash doesn't get caught. The tape never gets shown. Marianne ends up dead, yes, but there was nothing to be done about that —

and hadn't she pretty much asked for that? Hadn't she taken it too far with her blackmail scheme? Joe had made an inadvertent blunder — but hadn't Marianne gone out of her way to seek out and destroy his family?

Except for one thing.

An e-mail had come today. Marianne was dead. Which meant that whatever damage Nash had done, he hadn't plugged all the leaks.

Guy Novak.

He was the last hole to plug. That was where Nash would go. Nash hadn't answered his phone or responded to Joe's messages because he was on a mission to finish the job.

So now Joe knew.

He could sit here and hope it turned out for the best for him. But that would mean that Guy Novak could end up dead.

Which might mean the end of his problems.

"Joe?" Dolly said. "Joe, tell me."

He didn't know what to do. But he wouldn't tell Dolly. They had a young daughter, a budding family. You don't mess around with that.

But you don't just let a man die either.

"I have to go," he said, and he ran for the door.

■ ■ ■ ■

Nash whispered into Guy Novak's ear: "Yell up to the girls that you're going into the basement and you don't want to be disturbed. Do you understand?"

Guy nodded. He walked to the foot of the stairs. Nash pressed the knife against the back, right near the kidney. The best technique, Nash had learned, was to go a little too far with the pressure. Let them feel enough pain to know that you mean what you're saying.

"Girls! I'm going to the basement for a few minutes. You stay up there, okay? I don't want to be bothered."

A faint voice shouted down, "Okay."

Guy turned toward Nash. Nash let the knife slide across his back and come to rest at his belly. Guy did not flinch or step back. "Did you kill my wife?"

Nash smiled. "I thought she was your ex."

"What do you want?"

"Where are your computers?"

"My laptop is in my bag next to the chair. My desktop is in the kitchen."

"Any others?"

"No. Just take them and get out."

"We need to talk first, Guy."

"I'll tell you whatever you want to know. I have money too. It's yours. Just don't hurt the girls."

Nash looked at this man. He had to know that there was a good chance he would die today. Nothing in his life had ever suggested heroism, yet now it was as though he had enough and was making some sort of final stand.

"I won't touch them if you cooperate," Nash said.

Guy checked Nash's eyes as though searching for the lie. Nash opened the basement door. They both headed down. Nash closed it behind him and flipped on the light. The basement was unfinished. The floor was cold concrete. Water gurgled through pipes. A watercolor canvas leaned against a storage chest. There were old hats and posters and cardboard boxes scattered everywhere.

Nash had everything he needed in a gym bag he'd kept over his shoulder. He reached for the duct tape, and Guy Novak made a big mistake.

He threw a punch and shouted, "Run, girls!"

Nash threw a hard elbow to Guy's throat, choking off his words. He followed up with a palm strike to the forehead. Guy crashed to the floor, grabbing his throat.

"If you so much as breathe," Nash said, "I will bring your daughter down here and make you watch. Do you understand?"

Guy froze. Fatherhood could even make a gutless worm like Guy Novak turn valiant. Nash wondered if he and Cassandra would have had children by now. Almost definitely. Cassandra had come from a big family. She had wanted a lot of kids. He wasn't so sure — his outlook on the world was considerably dimmer than hers — but he would never deny her.

Nash looked down. He considered stabbing Novak in the leg or maybe slicing off a finger, but there was no need. Guy had made his move and learned from it. There would be no more.

"Roll onto your stomach and put your hands behind your back."

Guy cooperated. Nash wrapped the duct tape around his wrists and forearms. Then he did the same with the legs. He attached the wrists to the ankles, pulling the arms back and making the legs bend at the knee. Classic hog-tie. The last thing he did was cover Guy's mouth by wrapping tape around his head five times.

Once that was done Nash made his way to the basement door.

Guy started bucking, but there was no need. Nash just wanted to make sure that the girls hadn't heard Guy's stupid scream. He opened the door. In the distance he could still hear the TV. The girls were nowhere in sight. He closed the door and moved back down.

"Your ex-wife made a video. I want you to tell me where it is."

The duct tape was still wrapped around Guy's mouth. The confusion on his face was obvious — how was he supposed to answer the question when his mouth was taped? Nash smiled down at him and showed him the blade.

"You'll tell me in a few minutes, okay?"

Nash's phone vibrated again. Lewiston, he figured, but when he checked the caller ID, he knew the news was not good.

"What's wrong?" he asked.

"The police are here," Pietra said.

Nash was barely surprised. One prop goes, it all starts to cave in on itself. Time was tight now. He couldn't stand here and hurt Guy at leisure. He needed to move fast.

So what would make Guy talk fast?

Nash shook his head. That which makes us brave — that which is worth dying for — also makes us weak.

"I'm going to pay your daughter a little

visit," he told Guy. "And then you'll talk, right?"

Guy's eyes bulged. Still hog-tied he squirmed and tried to signal what Nash already knew. He would talk. He would tell him everything that he wanted to know if only he'd leave his daughter alone. But Nash knew it would be easier to get the information with his daughter in front of him. Some would say that the threat was enough. They might be right.

But Nash wanted the daughter down here for other reasons.

He took a deep breath. The end was coming now. He could see that. Yes, he wanted to survive and get out of here, but the crazy had not only seeped in but taken over. The crazy lit up his veins, made him feel tingly and alive.

He started up the basement stairs. Behind him, he could hear Guy going nuts in his bindings. For a moment the crazy let up and Nash considered going back. Guy would say anything now. But then again, maybe not. Maybe then it would look like just a threat.

No, he needed to carry through.

He opened the basement door and stepped into the front foyer. He looked at the stairs. The TV was still on. He took one more step.

He stopped when he heard the doorbell ring.

Tia pulled into the Novak driveway. She left her phone and purse in the car and hurried to the front door. She tried to process what Betsy Hill had told her. Her son was okay. That was what was most important. He might have some minor injuries, but he was alive and could stand upright and even dash away. There were other things Adam had told Betsy — about feeling guilty over Spencer, stuff like that. But that could all be handled. You need to survive first. Get him home. After that, you can worry about the other things.

Still lost in these thoughts, Tia rang the Novaks' doorbell.

She swallowed and remembered that this family had just suffered a devastating loss. It was important to reach out, she guessed, but all she really wanted to do was grab her daughter, find her son and husband, get them all back in the house and lock the doors forever.

No one answered the door.

Tia tried to peek through the little window, but there was too much reflection. She cupped her hands around her eyes and peered into the foyer. A figure seemed to jump back. Might have just been a shadow. She pressed the doorbell again. This time there was plenty of noise. The girls made a ruckus stampeding down the stairs.

They charged the door. Yasmin opened it. Jill stood a few feet behind her.

"Hi, Mrs. Baye."

"Hi, Yasmin."

She could see from the girl's face that Guy hadn't told her yet, but that wasn't a surprise. He was waiting for Jill to leave so he could be alone with Yasmin.

"Where's your father?"

Yasmin shrugged. "I think he said something about going in the basement."

For a moment the three just stood there. The house was tomb still. They waited another second or two, waiting for some kind of sound or sign. But there was nothing.

Guy was probably dealing with his grief, Tia figured. She should just take Jill and go home. None of them moved. This suddenly felt wrong. The normal pattern was to act this way when you dropped your child off — walking your child to the door to make sure a parent or babysitter was inside.

Now it felt as though they were leaving Yasmin alone.

Tia called out, "Guy?"

"It's okay, Mrs. Baye. I'm old enough to be by myself now."

That was questionable. They were at that uncertain age. They were probably okay on their own, what with cell phones and all. Jill had started wanting more independence. She had proved herself, she said, to be responsible. Adam had been left on his own when he was her age, which in the end was not such a ringing endorsement.

But that wasn't what was troubling Tia right now. It wasn't a question of leaving Yasmin alone. Her father's car was in the driveway. He was supposed to be here. He was supposed to tell Yasmin what had happened to her mother.

"Guy?"

Still no answer.

The girls looked at each other. Something crossed their faces.

"Where did you say you thought he was?" Tia asked.

"In the basement."

"What's down there?"

"Nothing really. Just some old boxes and stuff. It's kinda gross."

So why would Guy Novak have suddenly decided to go down there?

The obvious answer was to be alone. Yasmin had said there were old boxes down there. Maybe Guy had packed away some memories of Marianne and he was right now sitting on the floor and sorting through old pictures. Something like that. And maybe with the basement door closed he hadn't heard her.

That made the most sense.

Tia remembered that darting shadow, the one she saw when she peered through the window. Could that have been Guy? Could he be hiding from her? That too made some sense. Maybe he simply didn't have the strength to face her right now. Maybe he didn't want company of any kind. That could be it.

Fine and good, Tia thought, but she still did not like the idea of leaving Yasmin like this.

"Guy?"

Her voice was louder now.

Still nothing.

She moved toward the basement door. Too bad if he wanted his privacy. A quick yell of "I'm right here" would have done the trick. She knocked. No answer. Her hand gripped the knob and turned. She pushed it open a little.

The light was off.

She turned back to the girls. "Honey, are

you sure he was going down here?"

"That's what he said."

Tia glanced at Jill. She nodded in agreement. Fear started to play around the fringes now. Guy had sounded so down on the phone and then he'd gone to be alone in a dark basement. . . .

No, he wouldn't. He wouldn't do that to Yasmin. . . .

Then Tia heard a noise. Something muffled maybe. Something scraping or struggling. A rat or something.

She heard it again. Not a rat. It sounded like something bigger.

What the . . . ?

She looked at the two girls hard. "I want you to stay up here. Do you hear me? Don't come down unless I call you."

Tia's hand fumbled for the switch on the wall. She found it, turned it on. Her legs were already taking her all the way down. And when she got there, when she looked across the room and saw Guy Novak gagged and tied, she pulled up short and didn't think twice.

She turned and started back up.

"Girls, run! Get out of the . . ."

The words died in her throat. The basement door in front of her was already closing.

A man stepped into the room. He held a wincing Yasmin by the neck with his right hand. With his left, he held Jill.

38

Carson fumed. Dismissed. After all he had done for her, Rosemary simply sent him out of the room like a child. She was in there now, talking to that old man who'd made him look bad in front of his friends.

She just didn't get it.

He knew her. She was always using her beauty and her mouth to get out of trouble. But that wouldn't work here. She would look for a way to save her own butt, that was all. The more Carson looked at it, the worse it got for him. If the cops moved in and they were going to offer someone up as the sacrificial lamb, Carson had to be their leading candidate.

Maybe that was what they were discussing right now.

Made sense. Carson was twenty-two now — more than old enough to be tried and convicted as an adult. He was the one the teens mostly dealt with — Rosemary had been smart enough to keep her hands clean in that respect. He, Carson, was also the go-between with the distributor.

Damn, he should have known this would happen. As soon as the Spencer kid bit the dust, they should have gone quiet for a while. But the money had been huge and his distributors were pressing them. Carson's contact was a man named Barry Watkins who always wore Armani suits. He took him to classy gentlemen's clubs. He tossed cash around. He got him girls and respect. He treated him right.

But last night, when Carson didn't deliver, Watkins's voice changed. He didn't shout. It just went cold and it felt like an ice pick between the ribs.

"We need to get this done," he had told Carson.

"I think we got a problem."

"What do you mean?"

"The doctor's kid freaked out. His father showed up tonight."

Silence.

"Hello?"

"Carson?"

"What?"

"My employers won't let it be tracked back to me. Do you understand? They'll make sure it doesn't reach that level."

He hung up. The message had been sent and received.

So Carson waited with the gun.

He heard a noise at the front door. Someone was trying to get in. The door was locked from both sides. You needed to know the alarm code to get in or out. Whoever it was started pounding on the door. Carson looked out the window.

It was Adam Baye. He was with the Huff kid.

"Open up!" Adam shouted. He slapped the door some more. "Come on, open up!"

Carson smothered his smile. Father and son in one place. This would be the perfect way to end it.

"Hold on," Carson said.

Jamming the gun into his waist in the back, Carson pushed four digits and saw the red light turn green. The door unlocked.

Adam burst in, DJ followed.

"Is my father here?" Adam asked.

Carson nodded. "He's in Rosemary's office."

Adam started that way. DJ Huff followed.

Carson let the door close, locking them in. He reached behind him and pulled out his gun.

Anthony was following Adam Baye.

He kept a little distance, not much, but he wasn't sure how to play it. The kid didn't know him, so Anthony couldn't simply call out to him — plus who knew what his mind frame was? If Anthony identified himself as a friend of his father's, he might just run and disappear again.

Play it cool, Anthony thought.

Up ahead, Adam was shouting into his cell phone. Not a bad idea. Anthony took out his mobile in midstride. He dialed Mike's number.

No answer.

When the voice mail came on, Anthony said, "Mike, I see your kid. He's heading back to that club I was telling you about. I'll follow him."

He snapped the phone closed and jammed it back in his pocket. Adam had already put away his phone, and now he hurried his step. Anthony kept pace. When Adam reached the club, he took the steps two at a time and tried the door.

Locked.

Anthony saw him look at the alarm pad. He turned to his friend, who shrugged. Adam started pounding on the door.

"Open up!"

The tone, Anthony thought. There was more than impatience in that tone — there was pure desperation. Fear even. Anthony moved closer.

"Come on, open up!"

He kept pounding harder and harder. A few seconds later, the door opened. One of those goths stood there. Anthony had seen him around. He was a little older than the others and the quasi-leader for that band of full-fledged losers. He had a strip across his nose, like it'd been broken. Anthony wondered if he was one of the kids who jumped Mike and decided that, yeah, he probably was.

So what should he do?

Should he stop Adam from going in? That might work, but then again it might backfire in a big way. The kid would probably run. Anthony could grab him and hold him, but if they all made enough of a fuss, what good would that do?

Anthony slid closer to the door.

Adam hurried inside, disappearing entirely, and it seemed to Anthony as if the building had swallowed him whole. Adam's friend with the varsity jacket entered behind him, slower. From where he stood, Anthony could see the goth let the door close. As he did, as the door began to slowly swing shut, the goth turned his back.

And Anthony saw it.

There was a gun sticking out of the back waist of his pants.

And right before the door closed entirely, it looked like maybe the goth was reaching for it.

Mo sat in the car and worked those damn numbers.

CeeJay8115.

He started with the obvious. Turn Cee into C or the third letter. Three. He took the Jay or J, the tenth number. So what did he have? 3108115. He added the numbers together, tried dividing them, searched for patterns. He looked at Adam's IM handle — HockeyAdam1117. Mike had told him that 11 was Messier's number, 17 was Mike's old Dartmouth number. Still he added them to 8115 and then 3108115. He turned Hockey-Adam into numbers, did more equations, tried to solve the problem.

Nothing.

The numbers were not random. He knew that. Even Adam's numbers, while not telling, were not random. There was a pattern here. Mo just had to find it.

Mo had been doing the math in his head, but now he opened the glove compartment and grabbed a sheet of paper. He started jotting down number possibilities when he heard a familiar voice shout, "Open up!"

Mo looked through the windshield.

Adam was banging on the front door of Club Jaguar.

"Come on, open up!"

Mo reached for the handle as the front door of the club opened. Adam vanished inside. Mo wondered what to do here, what move to make, when he saw something else weird.

It was Anthony, the black bouncer Mike had visited earlier in the day. He was sprinting toward the Club Jaguar door. Mo rolled out of the car and started toward him. Anthony got to the door first and twisted the knob. It wouldn't budge.

"What's going on?" Mo asked.

"We gotta get in," Anthony said.

Mo put his hand on the door. "It's steel enforced. No way we can kick it down."

"Well, we better try."

"Why, what's up?"

"The guy who let Adam in," Anthony said. "He was pulling a gun."

Carson kept the gun hidden behind his back.

"Is my father here?" Adam asked.

"He's in Rosemary's office."

Adam started past him. There was a sudden commotion from down the hall.

"Adam?"

The voice belonged to Mike Baye.

"Dad?"

Baye turned the corner right as Adam was arriving. Father and son met up near the corridor and embraced.

Aw, Carson thought, isn't that sweet.

Carson gripped the gun and raised it in front of him.

He did not call out. He did not warn them. There was no reason to. He had no choice here. There was no time to negotiate or make requests. He needed to end this.

He needed to kill them.

Rosemary shouted, "Carson, don't!"

But there was no way he was listening to that bitch. Carson aimed the gun toward Adam, got him in his sights, and prepared to fire.

Even as Mike hugged his son — even as he felt the wonderful substance of his boy and nearly collapsed in relief that he was okay — Mike saw it out of the corner of his eye.

Carson had a gun.

There weren't seconds to consider his next move. There was no conscious thought in what he did next — just a primitive, base response. He saw Carson aiming the gun at

Adam and he reacted.

Mike pushed his son.

He pushed him very hard. Adam's feet actually left the ground. He flew through the air, his eyes widening in surprise. The gun exploded, the bullet shattering the glass behind him, right where Adam had been standing less than a second earlier. Mike felt the shards rain down on him.

But the push had not only surprised Adam — it had surprised Carson. He had clearly figured that they would either not see him or react as most people do when faced with a gun — freeze or put their hands up.

Carson recovered quickly. He was already swinging his gun to the right, toward where Adam had landed. But that was why the push had been so hard. Even in that reactionary state, there had been a method to Mike's madness. He needed not only to get his son out of the way of the incoming bullet, but he needed to give him distance. And he got it.

Adam landed down the corridor, behind a wall.

Carson aimed but he had no angle to shoot Adam. That left him with one other alternative — shooting the father first.

Mike felt a strange sense of peace then.

He knew what had to be done here. There was no choice. He needed to protect his son. As Carson began to swing the gun back in the father's direction, Mike knew what that meant.

He would need to make a sacrifice.

He didn't think this out. It just was. A father saves his son. That was the way it should be. Carson was going to be able to shoot one of them. There seemed no way around that. So Mike did the only thing he could.

He made sure that it was him.

Working on instinct, Mike charged Carson.

He flashed back to hockey games, to going for the puck, and realized that even if Carson shot him, he might still have enough. He might still have enough to reach Carson and stop him from doing more harm.

He would save his son.

But as he got closer, Mike realized that the heart was one thing, reality another. The distance was too great. Carson already had the gun raised. Mike wouldn't be able to make it before taking at least one bullet, maybe two. There was very little chance of survival or even doing much good.

Still there was no choice. So Mike closed his eyes and lowered his head and churned his legs.

They were still a good fifteen feet away, but if Carson let him get just a little closer, he couldn't miss.

He lowered his aim a little, pointed the gun at Mike's head and watched the target grow bigger and bigger.

Anthony pushed his shoulder against the door, but it wouldn't budge.

Mo said, "All those complicated calculations — and that's it?"

"What are you mumbling about?"

"Eight-one-one-five."

"Come again?"

There was no time to explain. Mo pressed 8115 into the alarm pad. The red light turned green, signaling that the door was now unlocked.

Anthony pulled open the door and both men dived inside.

Carson had him in his sights now.

The gun was aimed at the top of Mike's charging head. Carson was surprised by how calm he felt. He thought that he might panic, but his hand was steady. Firing the first time had felt good. This would feel even better. He was in the zone now. He wouldn't miss. No way.

Carson started to pull the trigger.

And then the gun was gone.

A giant hand came from behind him and snatched the gun away. Just like that. One second it was there, the next gone. Carson turned and saw the big black bouncer from down the street. The bouncer was holding the gun and smiling.

But there was no time to even register much surprise. Something powerful — another guy — hit Carson low and hard in the back. Carson felt pain in his entire body. He cried out and jerked forward where he ran into Mike Baye's shoulder coming in the other direction. Carson's body nearly snapped in half from the impact. He landed as if someone had dropped him from a great height. His wind was gone. His ribs felt like they'd caved in.

Standing over him, Mike said, "It's over." Then turning back to where Rosemary now stood, he added, "No deals."

39

Nash kept his hold on either side of the girls' necks.

His grip was light, but these were pressure-point-sensitive areas. He could see Yasmin, the one who had started all the trouble by being rude in Joe's class, grimacing. The other girl — the daughter of the lady who had stumbled in on all this — quaked like a leaf.

The woman said, "Let them go."

Nash shook his head. He felt giddy now. The crazy was running through him like a live wire. Every neuron had been switched into high gear. One of the girls started crying. He knew that should have an effect on him, that as a human being their tears should move him in some way.

But they just heightened the sensation.

Is it still crazy when you know it's crazy?

"Please," the woman said. "They're just children."

She stopped talking then. So maybe she

saw it. Her words were not reaching him. Worse, they seemed to give him pleasure. He admired the woman. He wondered again if she was always this way, brave and feisty, or had she turned into the mother bear protecting her cub?

He would have to kill the mother first.

She would be the most trouble. He was sure of it. There was no way she would stand idly by while he hurt the girls.

But then a new thought aroused him. If this was going to be it, if this was going to be his final stand, would there be any greater high than making the parents watch?

Oh, he knew that was sick. But once the thought was voiced in his head, Nash couldn't let it go. You can't help who you are. Nash had met a few pedophiles in prison and they always tried so hard to convince themselves that what they did was not depraved. They talked about history and ancient civilizations and earlier eras where girls were married when they were twelve and all the while Nash wondered why they bothered. It was simpler. This was how you're hardwired. You have an itch. You have a need to do what others find reprehensible.

This was how God made you. So who was really to blame?

All those pious freaks should understand

that if you really thought about it, you were criticizing God's work when you condemned such men. Oh, sure they would counter about temptation, but this was more than that. They knew that too. Because everybody has some itch. It isn't discipline that keeps it in check. It is circumstances. That was what Pietra didn't understand about the soldiers. The circumstances didn't force them to relish in the brutality.

It gave them the opportunity to.

So now he knew. He would kill them all. He would grab the computers and be gone. When the police arrived, the bloodbath would occupy them. They would assume a serial killer. Nobody would wonder about some video made by a blackmailing woman to destroy a kind man and good teacher. Joe could very well be off the hook.

First things first. Tie up the mother.

"Girls?" Nash said.

He turned them so that they could look at him.

"If you run away, I will kill Mommy and Daddy. Do you understand?"

They both nodded. He moved them away from the basement door anyway. He let go of their necks — and that was when Yasmin let out the most piercing scream he had ever heard. She darted toward her father.

Nash leaned that way.

That would prove to be a mistake.

The other girl sprinted straight for the steps.

Nash quickly spun to follow, but she was fast.

The woman yelled, "Run, Jill!"

Nash leaped toward the stairs, his hand outstretched to grab her ankle. He touched the skin, but she pulled away. Nash tried to get up but he felt a sudden weight on him.

It was the mother.

She had jumped on his back. She bit down hard into his leg. Nash howled and kicked her away.

"Jill!" Nash called out. "Your mommy will be dead if you don't come down here right now!"

The woman rolled away from him. "Run! Don't listen to him!"

Nash rose and took out the knife. For the first time he was not sure what to do. The telephone box was across the room. He could knock it out, but the girl probably had a cell phone.

Time was running out.

He needed the computers. That was the key thing. So he would kill them, grab the computers, and get out. He would make sure that the hard drives were destroyed.

Nash looked toward Yasmin. She jumped behind her father. Guy tried to roll, tried to sit up, tried to do anything to make himself something of a protective wall for his daughter. The effort, what with him hog-tied with duct tape, was almost comical.

The woman got up too. She moved toward the little girl. Not even hers this time. Brave. But now all three were in one spot. Good. He could take care of them quickly. It would take very little time.

"Jill!" Nash called out again. "Last chance!"

Yasmin screamed again. Nash moved toward them, knife raised, but a voice made him pull up.

"Please don't hurt my mommy."

The voice came from behind him. He could hear her sobs.

Jill had come back.

Nash looked at the mother and smiled. The mother's face collapsed in anguish.

"No!" screamed her mother. "Jill, no! Run!"

"Mommy?"

"Run! God, honey, please run!"

But Jill didn't listen. She came down the stairs. Nash turned toward her and that was when he realized his mistake. He wondered for a second if he had intentionally let Jill make it to the stairway in the first place. He had let go of their necks, hadn't he? Had he been careless or was there something more? He wondered if somehow he had been directed by someone, someone who had seen enough and wanted him at peace.

He thought that he saw her standing next to the girl.

"Cassandra," he said out loud.

A minute or two earlier, Jill had felt the man's hand press down on her neck.

The man was strong. He didn't seem to be trying at all. His fingers found a spot and it really hurt. Then she saw her mom and the way Mr. Novak was tied up on the floor. Jill was so scared.

Her mom said, "Let them go."

The way she said it calmed Jill a little. It was horrible and scary, but her mother was here. She would do anything to save Jill. And Jill knew that it was time to show that she would do anything for her.

The man's grip tightened. Jill gasped a little and glanced up at his face. The man looked happy. Her eyes moved toward Yasmin. Yasmin was looking directly at Jill. She managed to tilt her head a little. That was what Yasmin did in class when the teacher was looking but she wanted to get Jill a message.

Jill didn't get it. Yasmin started looking

down at her own hand.

Puzzled, Jill followed her eyes and saw what Yasmin was doing.

She was making a gun with her forefinger and thumb.

"Girls?"

The man holding them by the neck squeezed and turned a little so that they would have to look at him.

"If you run away, I will kill Mommy and Daddy. Do you understand?"

They both nodded. Their eyes met again. Yasmin opened her mouth. Jill got the idea. The man released them. Jill waited for the diversion. It didn't take long.

Yasmin screamed and Jill ran for her life. Not her life, actually. All their lives.

She felt the man's fingertips on her ankle but she pulled away. She heard him howl, but she didn't look back.

"Jill! Your mommy will be dead if you don't come down here right now!"

No choice. Jill ran up the stairs. She thought about the anonymous e-mail she'd sent to Mr. Novak just earlier today:

Please listen to me. You need to hide your gun better.

She prayed that he hadn't read it or if he

had, that he hadn't had time to do anything about it. Jill dived into his bedroom and pulled the drawer all the way out. She dumped the contents on the floor.

The gun was gone.

Her heart fell. She heard screaming coming from downstairs. The man could be killing them all. She started tossing his things around when her hand hit something metallic.

The gun.

"Jill! Last chance!"

How did she get rid of the safety? Damn it. She didn't know. But then Jill remembered something.

Yasmin had never put it back on. The safety was probably still off.

Yasmin screamed.

Jill scrambled back to her feet. She wasn't even down the stairs when she called out in the littlest, baby-est voice she could muster: "Please don't hurt my mommy."

She hurried down to the basement level. She wondered if she would be able to apply enough pressure to make the gun fire. She figured that she'd hold the gun with both hands and use two fingers.

Turns out, that was pressure enough.

Nash heard the sirens.

He saw the gun and smiled. Part of him wanted to make a leap, but Cassandra shook her head. He didn't want that either. The girl hesitated. So he moved a little closer to her and raised the knife over her head.

When Nash was ten, he asked his father what happens to us when we die. His father said that Shakespeare probably said it best, that death was "the undiscovered country from whose bourn no traveler returns."

In sum, how can we know?

The first bullet hit him square in the chest.

He staggered closer to her, keeping the knife raised, waiting.

Nash didn't know where the second bullet would take him, but he hoped it would be to Cassandra.

40

Mike sat in the same interrogation room as before. This time he was with his son.

Special Agent Darryl LeCrue and U.S. Assistant Attorney Scott Duncan had been trying to put together the case. Mike knew that they were all here somewhere — Rosemary, Carson, DJ Huff and probably his father, the other goths. They separated them out, hoping to cut deals and file charges.

They'd been here for hours. Mike and Adam had yet to answer a single question. Hester Crimstein, their attorney, refused to let them speak. Right now Mike and Adam sat alone in the interrogation room.

Mike looked at his son, felt his heart break, and said, "It's going to be okay," for maybe the fifth or sixth time.

Adam had gone nonresponsive. Shock probably. Of course, there was a fine line between shock and teenage sullenness. Hester was in crazed mode and it was getting worse.

You could see it. She kept bouncing in and out and asking questions. Adam just shook his head when she demanded details.

Her last visit had been half an hour ago and ended with her saying two words to Mike: "Not good."

The door burst open again now. Hester walked in, grabbed a chair, pulled it close to Adam. She sat down and moved her face an inch away from his. He turned away. She took his face in her hands, turned it toward hers, and said, "Look at me, Adam."

He did so with great reluctance.

"Here is your problem. Rosemary and Carson are blaming you. They say it was your idea to steal your father's prescription pads and take this to the next level. They say you sought them out. Depending on their mood, they also claim that your father was behind it too. Daddy here was looking for a way to pick up extra cash. The DEA officers in this very building just got themselves wonderful ink for arresting a doctor in Bloomfield for doing the same thing — providing illegal prescriptions for the black market. So they like that angle, Adam. They want the doctor and his son in cahoots because it makes a media splash and gets them promotions. Do you get what I'm saying?"

Adam nodded.

"So why aren't you telling me the truth?"

"It doesn't matter," Adam said.

She spread her hands. "What does that mean?"

He just shook his head. "It's my word against theirs."

"Right, but see, there's two problems. First off, it's not just them. They got a couple of Carson's buddies to back up their story. Of course these buddies would back up the claim that you performed anal probes on a spaceship if Carson and Rosemary asked them to. So that's not our big problem."

Mike said, "So what is?"

"The firmest piece of evidence is those prescription pads. You can't tie them directly to Rosemary and Carson. It's not a nice neat package. But they can tie them directly to you, Dr. Baye. Obviously. They are yours. They can also pretty much tie how they got from point A — you, Dr. Baye — to point B — the illegal market. Via your son."

Adam closed his eyes and shook his head.

"What?" Hester said.

"You won't believe me."

"Sweetheart, listen to me. It's not my job to believe you. It's my job to defend you. You can worry about your mommy believing you, okay? I'm not your mommy. I'm your attorney and, right now, that's a whole lot better."

Adam looked at his father.

"I will believe you," Mike said.

"But you didn't trust me."

Mike was not sure how to reply to that.

"You put that thing on my computer. You eavesdropped on my private conversations."

"We were worried about you."

"You could have asked."

"I did, Adam. I asked a thousand times. You told me to leave you alone. You told me to get out of your room."

"Uh, fellas?" It was Hester. "I'm enjoying this touching father-son scene, really, it's beautiful, I want to weep, but I bill by the hour and I'm damn expensive, so can we get back to this case?"

There was a sharp knock on the door. It opened and Special Agent Darryl LeCrue and U.S. Assistant Attorney Scott Duncan entered.

Hester said, "Get out. This is a private conference."

"There is someone here who wants to see your clients," LeCrue said.

"I don't care if it's Jessica Alba in a tube top —"

"Hester?"

It was LeCrue.

"Trust me here. This is important."

They stepped to the side. Mike looked up. He wasn't sure what to expect, but certainly not this. Adam started to cry as soon as he saw them.

Betsy and Ron Hill stepped into the room.

"Who the hell are they?" Hester asked.

"Spencer's parents," Mike said.

"Whoa, what kind of emotional trick is this? I want them out. I want them out now."

LeCrue said, "Shh. Just listen. Don't talk. Just listen."

Hester turned to Adam. She put his hand on his forearm. "Don't say one word. Do you hear me? Not one word."

Adam just kept crying.

Betsy Hill took a seat across the table from him. There were tears in her eyes too. Ron stood behind her. He crossed his arms and looked at the ceiling. Mike could see the tremble in his lips. LeCrue stood back in one corner, Duncan the other.

LeCrue said, "Mrs. Hill, can you tell them what you just told us?"

Hester Crimstein still had her hand on Adam's forearm, readying to quiet him. Betsy Hill just looked at Adam. Adam finally lifted his head. He met her eyes.

"What's going on?" Mike asked.

Betsy Hill finally spoke. "You lied to me, Adam."

"Whoa, whoa," Hester said. "If she's going to start with accusations about deception, we're going to stop this right here and right now."

Betsy kept her eyes on Adam, ignoring the outburst. "You and Spencer didn't fight over a girl, did you?"

Adam said nothing.

"Did you?"

"Don't answer," Hester said, giving his forearm a little squeeze. "We are not commenting on any alleged fight —"

Adam pulled his arm away. "Mrs. Hill . . ."

"You're afraid they won't believe you," Betsy said. "And you're afraid you're going to hurt your friend. But you can't hurt Spencer. He's dead, Adam. And it's not your fault."

The tears kept coming down Adam's face.

"Do you hear me? It's not your fault. You had every reason to get angry with him. His father and I missed so much with Spencer. We'll have to deal with that for the rest of our lives. Maybe we could have stopped him if we had kept a closer eye — or maybe there was no way to save him. I don't know right now. But I know this: It is not your fault and you can't take the blame for this. He's dead, Adam. No one can hurt him anymore."

Hester opened her mouth, but no words came out. She stopped herself, pulled back, watched. Mike did not know what to make of this either.

"Tell them the truth," Betsy said.

Adam said, "Doesn't matter."

"Yes, it does, Adam."

"No one is going to believe me."

"We believe you," Betsy said.

"Rosemary and Carson will say it was me and my dad. They're already doing it. So why drag someone's name through the mud?"

LeCrue said, "That's why you tried to end it last night. With that wire you were telling us about. Rosemary and Carson blackmailed you, didn't they? They said if you told, they'd put it on you. They'd say you stole the prescription pads. Just like they're doing now. And then you had your friends to worry about. They could all get in trouble too. So what choice did you have? You let it go on."

"I wasn't worried about my friends," Adam said. "But they were going to put it on my dad. He'd lose his license, for sure."

Mike felt his breathing go funny. "Adam?"

He turned toward his father.

"Just tell the truth. Don't worry about me."

Adam shook his head.

Betsy reached out and touched Adam's hand. "We have proof."

Adam looked confused.

Ron Hill moved forward. "When Spencer died I went through his room. I found . . ." He stopped, swallowed, looked at the ceiling again. "I didn't want to tell Betsy. She was going through enough and I figured, what difference did it make? He was dead. Why put her through any more? You were thinking something like that too, weren't you, Adam?"

Adam said nothing.

"So I didn't say anything. But the night he died . . . I went through his room. Under his bed, I found eight thousand dollars in cash — and these."

Ron tossed a prescription pad onto the table. For a moment, everyone just stared at it.

"You didn't steal your father's prescription pads," Betsy said. "Spencer did. He stole them from your house, didn't he?"

Adam had his head down.

"And the night he killed himself, you found out. You confronted him. You were furious. You two fought. That's when you hit him. When he called you back, you didn't want to hear his apologies. He had gone too far this time. So you let his calls go into voice mail."

Adam squeezed his eyes shut. "I should have answered it. I hit him. I called him names and said I never wanted to speak to him again. Then I left him alone and when he called for help . . ."

The room pretty much exploded then. There were tears, of course. Hugs. Apologies. Wounds were ripped open and closed. Hester worked it. She grabbed LeCrue and Duncan. They all saw what happened here. No one wanted to prosecute the Bayes. Adam would cooperate and help send Rosemary and Carson to prison.

But that was for another day.

Later that night, after Adam had gotten home and had his cell phone back, Betsy Hill came over.

"I want to hear," she said to him.

And together they listened to Spencer's very last message before ending his own life:

"This isn't on you, Adam. Okay, man. Just try to understand. It's not on anyone. It's just too

hard. It's always been too hard. . . ."

One week later, Susan Loriman knocked on the door of Joe Lewiston's house.

"Who is it?"

"Mr. Lewiston? It's Susan Loriman."

"I'm pretty busy."

"Please open up. It's very important."

There were a few seconds of silence before Joe Lewiston did as she asked. He was unshaven and in a gray T-shirt. His hair jutted up in different directions and there was still sleep in his eyes.

"Mrs. Loriman, this isn't really a good time."

"It's not a good time for me either."

"I've been dismissed from my teaching post."

"I know. I'm sorry to hear that."

"So if this is about your son's donor drive . . ."

"It is."

"You can't possibly think I'm the one to lead this anymore."

"That's where you're wrong. I do."

"Mrs. Loriman . . ."

"Has anyone close to you ever died?"

"Yes."

"Do you mind telling me who?"

The question was an odd one. Lewiston

sighed and looked into Susan Loriman's eyes. Her son was dying and for some reason this question seemed very important to her. "There was my sister, Cassie. She was an angel. You never believed anything could happen to her."

Susan knew all about it, of course. The news had been full of stories on Cassandra Lewiston's widowed husband and the murders.

"Anyone else?"

"My brother Curtis."

"Was he an angel too?"

"No. Just the opposite. I look like him. They say we're the spitting image. But he was troubled his whole life."

"How did he die?"

"Murdered. Probably in a robbery."

"I have the donor nurse right here." Susan looked behind her. A woman came out of the car and moved toward them. "She can take your blood right now."

"I don't see the point."

"You really didn't do anything that terrible, Mr. Lewiston. You even called the police when you realized what your former brother-in-law was doing. You need to start thinking about rebuilding. And this step, your willingness to help here, to try to save my child even when you have all of this going on in your real life, I think that will matter to people. Please, Mr. Lewiston. Won't you try to help my son?"

He looked as though he was about to protest. Susan hoped that he wouldn't. But she was ready if he did. She was ready to tell him that her son, Lucas, was ten years old. She was ready to remind him that his brother Curtis had died eleven years ago — or nine months before Lucas's birth. She would tell Joe Lewiston that the best odds now of finding a good donor was via a genetic uncle. Susan hoped that it wouldn't come to that. But she was willing to go that far now. She had to be.

"Please," she said again.

The nurse kept approaching. Joe Lewiston looked at Susan's face again and must have seen the desperation.

"Sure, okay," he said. "Why don't you come inside so we can do this?"

It amazed Tia how quickly life went back to normal.

Hester had been good to her word. No second chances, professionally speaking. So Tia handed in her resignation and was currently looking for another job. Mike and Ilene Goldfarb were off the hook for any crimes involving their prescriptions. The medical board was doing a for-show investigation, but in the meantime, their practice continued on as before. There were rumors that they had found a good match for Lucas Loriman, but Mike didn't want to talk about it and so she didn't push.

During those first few emotional days, Tia figured that Adam would turn his life around and be the sweet, kind boy . . . well, that he never really was. But a boy doesn't work like a light switch. Adam was better, no question about it. Right now he was outside in the driveway playing goalie while his father took shots on him. When Mike got one past him, he would yell, "Score!" and start singing the Rangers goal-scoring music. The sound was comforting and familiar, but in the old days, she would hear Adam too. Now, today, not a sound came from him. He played in silence, while there was something strange in Mike's voice, a blend of joy and desperation.

Mike still wanted that kid back. But that kid was probably gone. Maybe that was okay.

Mo pulled into the driveway. He was taking them to the Rangers versus Devils game down in Newark. Anthony, who along with Mo had saved their lives, was going too. Mike had thought Anthony saved his life the first time, in that alley, but it had been

Adam who'd delayed them long enough — and had the knife scar to prove it. It was a heady thing for a parent to realize — the son saving the father. Mike would get teary and want to say something, but Adam wouldn't hear it. He was silent brave, that kid.

Like his father.

Tia looked out the window. Her two men-boys started toward the door to say good-bye. She waved at them and blew them a kiss. They waved back. She watched them get into Mo's car. She kept her eyes on them until the car faded away at the turn down the road.

She called out. "Jill?"

"I'm upstairs, Mom!"

They had taken the spy software off Adam's computer. You could argue it a dozen different ways. Maybe if Ron and Betsy had been watching Spencer more closely, they could have saved him. But maybe not. There is a certain fate to the universe and a certain randomness. Here Mike and Tia had been so worried about their son — and in the end, it was Jill who came closer to dying. It was Jill who suffered the trauma of having to shoot and kill another human being. Why?

Randomness. She happened to be at the wrong place at the wrong time.

You can spy, but you can't predict. Adam

might have found a way out of this on his own. He could have made that tape and Mike wouldn't have been assaulted and nearly killed. That crazy kid Carson wouldn't have pulled a gun on them. Adam wouldn't still be wondering if his parents truly trusted him.

Trust is like that. You can break it for a good reason. But it still remains broken.

So what had Tia the mother learned from all this? You do your best. That's all. You go in with the best intentions. You let them know that they are loved, but life is too random to do much more. You can't really control it. Mike had this friend, a former basketball star, who liked to quote Yiddish expressions. His favorite was "Man plans, God laughs." Tia had never really gotten that. She thought that it gave you an excuse to not try your hardest because, hey, God is going to mess with you anyway. But that wasn't it. It was more about understanding that you could give it your all, give yourself the best chances, but control is an illusion.

Or was it still more complex than even that?

One could argue just the opposite — snooping had saved them all. For one thing, snooping had helped them realize that Adam was in over his head.

But more than that, the fact that Jill and Yasmin snooped and knew about Guy Novak's gun — without that, they would all be dead.

So ironic. Guy Novak keeps a loaded gun in his house and rather than it leading to disaster, it saves them all.

She shook her head at the thought and opened the fridge door. They were low on groceries.

"Jill?"

"What?"

Tia grabbed her keys and wallet. She looked for her cell phone.

Her daughter had recovered from the shooting with surprising ease. The doctors warned her that it could be a delayed reaction or maybe she realized that what she did was proper and necessary and even heroic. Jill wasn't a baby anymore.

Where had Tia put her cell phone?

She had been sure that she had left it on the counter. Right here. Not more than ten minutes ago.

And it was that simple thought that turned everything around.

Tia felt her body go rigid. In the relief of survival, they had let a lot of things go. But suddenly, as she stared down at the spot where she was sure she had left her cell phone, she thought about those unanswered questions.

That first e-mail, the one that started it all, about going to DJ Huff's house for a party. There had been no party. Adam had never even read it.

So who had sent it?

No . . .

Still searching for her cell, Tia lifted the house phone, picked it up, and dialed. Guy Novak answered on the third ring.

"Hey, Tia, how are you?"

"You told the police that you sent out that video."

"What?"

"The one with Marianne having sex with Mr. Lewiston. You said you sent it out. To get revenge."

"So?"

"You didn't know about it at all, did you, Guy?"

Silence.

"Guy?"

"Let it go, Tia."

He hung up.

She crept up the stairs quietly. Jill was in her own room. Tia didn't want her to hear. It was all coming together. Tia had wondered about that, about these two horrible things — Nash going on his rampage, Adam vanishing — happening at the same time. Someone had joked that bad things come in threes and you better watch out. But Tia had never quite bought that.

The e-mail about the Huff party.

The gun in Guy Novak's drawer.

The explicit video that was sent to Dolly Lewiston's address.

What tied them all together?

Tia turned the corner and said, "What are you doing?"

Jill jumped at the sound of her mother's voice. "Oh, hi. Just playing Brickbreaker."

"No."

"What?"

They joked about it, she and Mike. Jill was nosy. Jill was their Harriet the Spy.

"I'm just playing."

But she wasn't. Tia knew that now. Jill didn't take her phone all the time to play video games. She did it to check Tia's messages. Jill didn't use the computer in their room because it was newer and worked better. She did it to see what was going on. Jill hated to be treated like a little kid. So she snooped. She and her friend Yasmin.

Innocent kid stuff, right?

"You knew we were watching Adam's computer, didn't you?"

"What?"

"Brett said that whoever sent that e-mail had done it from inside the house. They sent it, they went on Adam's e-mail because he wasn't home, they deleted it. I couldn't figure out who would or could do that. But it was you, Jill. Why?"

Jill shook her head. But at the end of the day, a mother knows.

"Jill?"

"I didn't mean for this to happen."

"I know. Tell me."

"You guys shredded the reports, but I mean, why did you suddenly have a shredder in your bedroom? I could hear you whispering about it at night. And you even bookmarked the site for E-SpyRight on your computer."

"So you knew we were spying?"

"Of course."

"So why did you send that e-mail?"

"Because I knew you'd see it."

"I don't understand. Why would you want us to see something about a party that wasn't really happening?"

"I knew what Adam was going to do. I thought it was too dangerous. I wanted to stop him, but I couldn't tell you the truth about Club Jaguar and all that. I didn't want to get him in trouble."

Tia nodded now. "So you made up a party."

"Yes. I said there would be drinking and drugs."

"You figured that we'd make him stay home."

"Right. So he'd be safe. But Adam ran away. I didn't think he'd do that. I messed up. Don't you see? It's all my fault."

"It's not your fault."

Jill started to sob. "Yasmin and me. Everyone treats us like babies, you know? So we spy. It's like a game. The adults hide stuff, and then we find out about it. And then Mr. Lewiston said that horrible thing about Yasmin. It changed everything. The other kids were so mean. At first Yasmin got really sad, but then it was like, I don't know, like she went crazy mad. Her mom had always been so useless, you know, and I think she saw this as a chance to help Yasmin."

"So she . . . she set up Mr. Lewiston. Did Marianne tell you about it?"

"No. But see, Yasmin spied on her too. We saw the video on her camera phone. Yasmin asked Marianne about it, but she said it was over and that Mr. Lewiston was suffering too."

"So you and Yasmin . . . ?"

"We didn't mean any harm. But Yasmin

had had enough. All the adults telling us what was best. All the kids in school picking on her. On us, really. So we did it on the same day. We didn't go to her house after school. We came here first. I sent out the e-mail about that party to get you to act — and then Yasmin sent out the video to make Mr. Lewiston pay for what he'd done."

Tia stood there and waited for something to come to her. Kids don't do what their parents say — they do what they see their parents do. So who was to blame here? Tia was not sure.

"That's all we did," Jill said. "We just sent out a couple of e-mails. That's all."

And that was true.

"It's going to be okay," Tia said, echoing the words her husband had repeated to her son in that interrogation room.

She kneeled down and took her daughter in her arms. Whatever had been holding back Jill's tears gave way. She leaned against her mother and cried. Tia stroked her hair and made comforting sounds and let the sobs come.

You do what you can, Tia reminded herself. You love them the best you can.

"It's going to be okay," she said once more.

This time, she almost believed it.

■ ■ ■ ■

On a cold Saturday morning — the very day that Essex County Prosecutor Paul Copeland was to be married for the second time — Cope found himself standing in front of a U-Store-It unit on Route 15.

Loren Muse stood next to him. "You don't have to be here."

"The wedding isn't for six hours," Cope said.

"But Lucy —"

"Lucy understands."

Cope glanced over his shoulder where Neil Cordova waited in the car. Pietra had broken her silence a few hours ago. After all her stonewalling, Cope had come up with the simple idea of letting Neil Cordova talk to her. Two minutes in, with her boyfriend dead and a deal firmly in place with her lawyer, Pietra broke down and told them where they would find the body of Reba Cordova.

"I want to be here," Cope said.

Muse followed his gaze. "You shouldn't have let him come either."

"I promised."

Cope and Neil Cordova had talked a lot since Reba had vanished. In a few minutes, if Pietra was telling the truth, they would now have something horrible in common

— dead wives. Weirdly enough, when they looked into the background of the killer, he too shared this horrific attribute.

As if reading his thoughts, Muse asked, "Do you leave any room for the chance that Pietra is lying?"

"Very little. You?"

"Same," Muse said. "So Nash killed these two women to help his brother-in-law. To find and destroy this tape of Lewiston's infidelity."

"So it seems. But Nash had priors. I bet if we go back, we'll find a lot of bad in his past. I think this was probably an excuse for him to wreak damage more than anything else. But I don't know or care about the psychology. You can't prosecute psychology."

"He tortured them."

"Yes. In theory to see who else knew about the tape."

"Like Reba Cordova."

"Right."

Muse shook her head. "What about the brother-in-law, the schoolteacher?"

"Lewiston? What about him?"

"Are you going to prosecute him?"

Cope shrugged. "He claims that he told Nash as a confidante and that he didn't know that he'd go so crazy."

"Do you buy that?"

"Pietra backs it, but I don't have enough evidence one way or the other yet." He looked at her. "That's where my detectives come in."

The storage unit supervisor found the key and put it in the lock. The door was opened and the detectives poured in.

"All that," Muse said, "and Marianne Gillespie never sent the tape."

"Seems not. She just threatened to. We checked it out. Guy Novak claims that Marianne told him about the tape. She wanted to let it slide — thought just the threat was punishment enough. Guy didn't. So he sent the tape to Lewiston's wife."

Muse frowned.

"What?" Cope asked.

"Nothing. You going to prosecute Guy?"

"For what? He sent out an e-mail. That's not against the law."

Two of the officers walked out of the storage unit slowly. Too slowly. Cope knew what it meant. One of the officers met Cope's eyes and nodded.

Muse said, "Damn."

Cope turned and walked toward Neil Cordova. Cordova watched him. Cope kept his eyes up and tried not to teeter. Neil started shaking his head as he saw Cope move closer. He shook his head harder now, as if the very act could deny the reality. Cope kept his pace steady. Neil had braced for this, knew it was coming, but that never cushioned blows like these. You have no choice. You can no longer divert or fight it. You simply have to let it crush you.

So when Cope got to him, Neil Cordova stopped shaking his head and collapsed against Cope's chest. He started sobbing Reba's name over and over, saying it wasn't true, couldn't be true, begging some higher power to return his beloved to him. Cope held him up. Minutes passed. Hard to say how many. Cope stood there and held the man and said nothing.

An hour later Cope drove himself home. He took a shower and put on his tuxedo and stood with his groomsmen. Cara, his seven-year-old daughter, got "awws" as she walked down the aisle. The governor himself presided over the nuptials. They had a big party with a band and all the trimmings. Muse was there as a bridesmaid, all dressed up and looking elegant and beautiful. She congratulated him with a kiss on the cheek. Cope thanked her. That was the extent of their wedding conversation.

The evening was a colorful whirlwind, but at some point, Cope got two minutes to sit alone. He loosened his bow tie and undid the top button of his tux shirt. He had gone through the cycle today, starting with death and ending with something as joyous as the joining of two. Most people could probably find something profound in that. Cope didn't. He sat there and listened to the band wreak havoc on some up-tempo number by Justin Timberlake and watched his guests try to dance to it. For a moment, he let himself drift into the dark. He thought about Neil Cordova, about the crushing blow, about what he and his little girls were going through right now.

"Daddy?"

He turned. It was Cara. His daughter grabbed his hand and looked at him, all seven years of her. And she knew.

"Will you dance with me?" Cara asked.

"I thought you hated to dance."

"I love this song. Please?"

He rose and walked to the dance floor. The song repeated its silly refrain about bringing sexy back. Cope started to move. Cara grabbed his new bride away from some well-wishers and dragged her onto the dance floor too. Lucy and Cara and Cope, the new family, danced. The music seemed to grow louder. Their friends and family started clapping encouragement. Cope danced hard and horribly. The two women in his life smothered laughs.

When he heard that sound, Paul Copeland danced even harder, flapping his arms, twisting his hips, sweating now, spinning himself until there was nothing left in the world but those two beautiful faces and the wondrous sound of their laughter.

ACKNOWLEDGMENTS

The idea for this one came to me when I was having dinner with my friends Beth and Dennis McConnell. Thanks for sharing and debating. See what it led to?

I would also like to thank the following for contributing in one way or another: Ben Sevier, Brian Tart, Lisa Johnson, Lisa Erbach Vance, Aaron Priest, Jon Wood, Eliane Benisti, Françoise Triffaux, Christopher J. Christie, David Gold, Anne Armstrong-Coben, and Charlotte Coben.

ABOUT THE AUTHOR

Winner of the Edgar Award, the Shamus Award and the Anthony Award, **Harlan Coben** is the #1 bestselling author of fourteen previous novels, including *The Woods, Promise Me, The Innocent, Just One Look, No Second Chance, Gone for Good* and *Tell No One,* as well as the popular Myron Bolitar novels. His books are published around the world in more than thirty-seven languages. He lives in New Jersey with his wife and four children.

We hope you have enjoyed this Large Print book. Other Thorndike, Wheeler, and Chivers Press Large Print books are available at your library or directly from the publishers.

For information about current and upcoming titles, please call or write, without obligaton, to:

Publisher
Thorndike Press
295 Kennedy Memorial Drive
Waterville, ME 04901
Tel. (800) 223-1244

or visit our Web site at:

http://gale.cengage.com/thorndike

OR

Chivers Large Print
published by BBC Audiobooks Ltd
St. James House, The Square
Lower Bristol Road
Bath BA2 3SB
England
Tel. +44(0) 800 136919
email: bbcaudiobooksbbc.co.uk
www.bbcaudiobooks.co.uk

All our Large Print titles are designed for easy reading, and all our books are made to last.